ISBN: 979-8-9994233-5-1

www.RyanOneillBooks.com

DARK TIDINGS

THE DARKBORN SAGA
BOOK 1

RYAN O'NEILL

SPECIAL THANKS

There are many people without this book would never have been written. Casey Patten, the person who first challenged me to put my money where my mouth was, and my first and most ardent test reader. Andrew Moulton, who encouraged me to chase a dream. The many people on F1 who read and encouraged my progress. And finally, my dad, who held my universe together while I was busy inventing new ones.

Thank you,

Ryan

FOR MOM

Glass Sea
The Kingdom of Fhael
Fhaerhals
Narrhash
Berbrehals
Church
Westhals
The Bridge of Cantel Pas
Shara
Sitfrael
Moulton's Landing
Serpent Sea
The Republics of Sharaad
Southern Wastes
Ahman
Kamaar
Bay of Kamaar
Razaam
Fhaeru
Eastern Peaks
Isle of Sharaadi Pirates
Sharrad Sea
Commissioned by Cornelius Y. Haerrun, First Prefect
Westfhael Chapter.
Fraternal Order of Celestial Light

The Continent of Man

Barrowlands

Fool's Rock

...erwood

Patcha's Bay

North Threschian Mountains

Threschia's Pass

Gray Mountains

Scholars Peninsula

Kingdom of Threschia

Illwick

Arseha

Thentia

Southport

Monk's End

The Step

Elvish Sea

Elven Continent

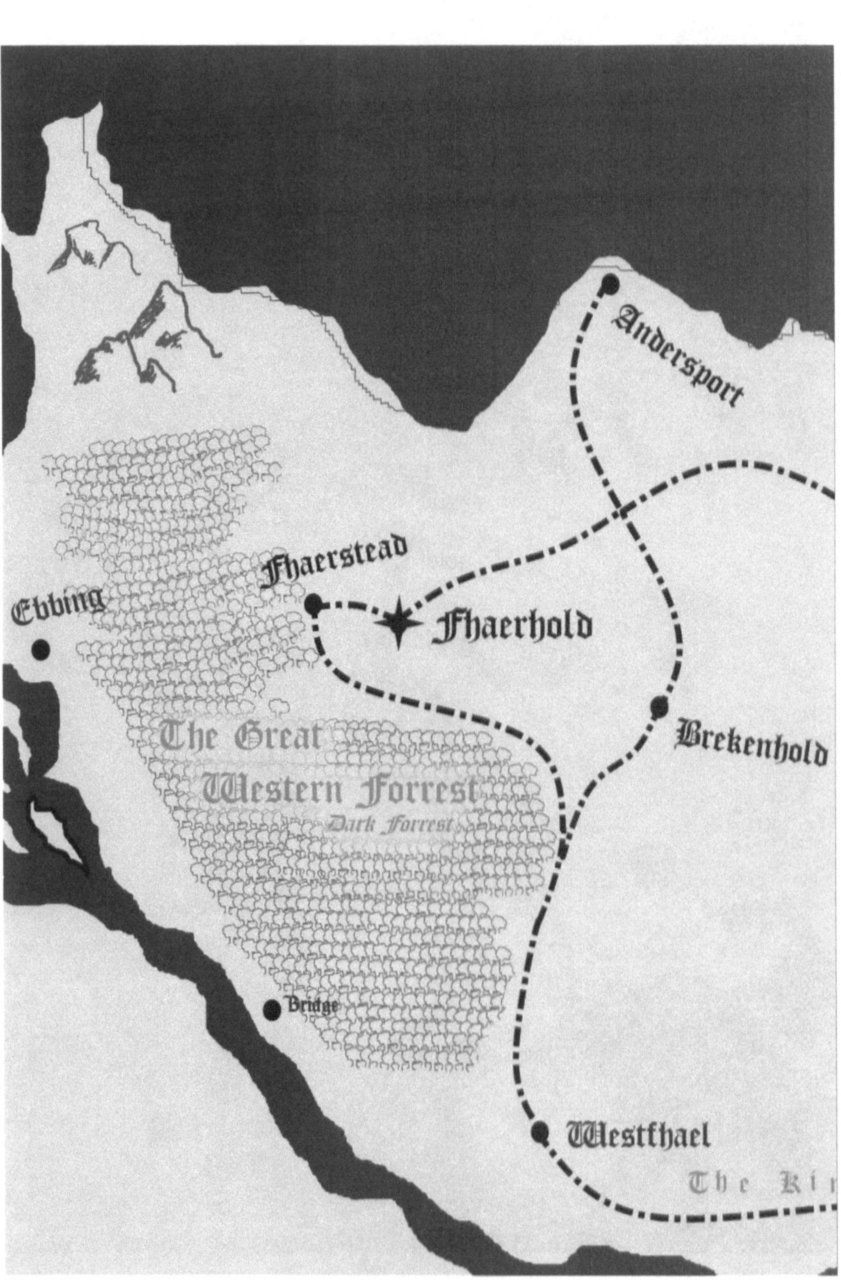

Andersport
Fhaerstead
Fhaerhold
Ebbing
Brekenhold
The Great
Western Forrest
Dark Forrest
Bridge
Westkhael
The Ri

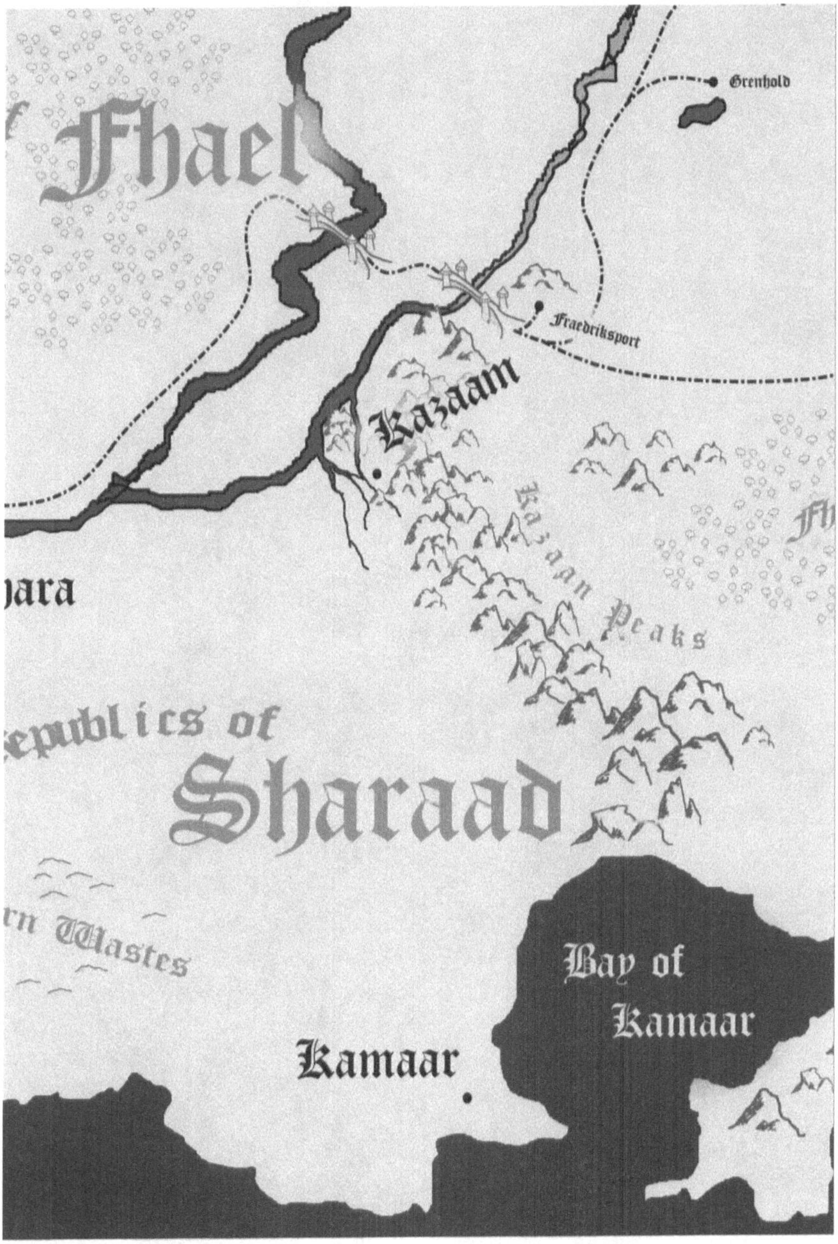

Grenhold
Fhael
Fraedriksport
Kazaam
Kazaan Peaks
Fh
para
epublics of
Sharaad
rn Wastes
Bay of
Kamaar
Kamaar

Prologue

He awoke. The chains holding him to the glacier still seared the long-dead flesh of his extremities. From the sea, icy winds buffeted the throne upon which he had been placed so many years ago. His throne, his prison, and his tomb. But today the cold winds carried something else to complement their icy bite. Life.

Here in the frozen fjords of the far North, well beyond the notice of the realms of man, life was not at all common. This was a land of cold and death; it was why he had been brought here.

Several leagues away, a small vessel reached the shore of the island that served as prison to the forgotten god. A woman was the first off the side of the boat. She was tall, raven-haired, with a few streaks of gray that did nothing to diminish the slender beauty of her face.

Pulling back the black hood that covered her, she commanded the others, "Hurry! We must set up camp before nightfall."

Two of her companions followed her off the boat. Both were men of some stature and wearing the same black cloaks and hoods as their mistress. Between them, they carried the fourth and final member of their party, a young man. He was bound with rope and had spent the majority of the trip north in a drug-induced state of unconsciousness. They hauled their prisoner up the beach and onto a frostbitten plateau of rock.

"Here is fine, now build a fire while I prepare," the woman commanded.

The hooded men dropped their prisoner onto the ice and headed back to the boat where they stowed the necessary commodities to survive for a short time in this desolate place. The prisoner stirred.

"Wh—where am I?" he stammered.

"You are on an island of the northern fjords, north of the barrowlands and the glass sea," the woman said. "It is just beyond midsummer if you wanted to know, but that hardly matters in this place."

Now fully awake, the bound man fought furiously against his restraints. The woman watched him struggle dispassionately.

There is no escape, she thought, *even if you could free yourself.* "You're only going to chafe your wrists doing that," she finally said.

"Why have you brought me here?" the man demanded.

"Why indeed?" The raven-haired woman replied. "You are here because you are precious my dear, Alric." The man blanched at the sound of his name. "Yes, I know your name. In fact, I know everything about you, my Starborn child." The two hooded men returned with firewood from the small boat and set to work building a small fire for their camp.

Alric watched them for a moment, peering intently, trying to see if he could recognize the men and perhaps divine their motives, though he knew he had never seen the woman before. They were both tall, although one was quite thicker than the other. And though it was difficult to see under their hoods, the thicker one had a large plunging scar that bisected his face from his right eye to the left side of his mouth. The slenderer of the two had white and blue tattoos covering his hands that snaked past his wrists and disappeared into his black sleeves. Alric shook his head; he did not know these people and couldn't possibly guess why they had taken him.

The woman noticed him staring at her subordinates and placed a slender finger on his chin, tilting his head back towards her. In her lurid yet strangely seductive tongue she said, "You are going to help me change the world, would you like that?"

"I don't know who you are! Please," the man begged. "I'm just a farmer's son. I can't help you!" He began thrashing violently against his restraints again.

The many weeks of travel and malnourishment had shrunk his once powerful arms. After several more minutes of struggling and twisting, he was finally able to slip his hand out of the rope that bound him. Now free, Alric took off, sprinting across the frozen rocks in the direction of the waiting boat, not fifty yards away.

His mind worked quickly. If he made it to the sloop, he could sail south back to the continent and join one of the trade caravans that brought salted fish down from the northern sea. He would make it home; he was sure of it. His friends would have a good laugh at his expense and his father would flay him for missing planting season, but he could…

The world went dark. Alric's unconscious form fell face first into the pebbled beach of the island, a few feet from the moored vessel. Drops of scarlet blood fell from the wound on Alric's scalp from where one of the woman's acolytes had hit him with a log. It painted the only bit of color onto the otherwise dull, white, and gray landscape.

"Fool!" the woman hissed at her underling. "You could have killed him! Now, bring him back here and tie him up properly."

Chastised, the hooded man dragged Alric's body back up to the camp. He glanced at his companion, who smirked back, clearly pleased at the other man's scolding.

Alric woke several hours later, lying near the fire. The woman was asleep next to him, breathing softly, her form silhouetted by the firelight. His arms were tied behind his back and then tied to the ropes binding his legs. It was not dissimilar to the way he would tie up livestock back on the farm, he thought. Despite their brutal treatment, they clearly wanted him alive—at least for now.

They had placed several furs over him and had stuffed him inside a bedroll. His head throbbed where the brute had struck him. The memory of his near escape and subsequent fall broke him from his silent reverie and caused a storm of furious energy within him. He fought his bonds once more, straining against the corded rope.

There is no escape, she thought, even if you could free yourself. "You're only going to chafe your wrists doing that," she finally said.even if you could free yourself. "You're only going to chafe your wrists doing that," she finally said.

Lying there immobile, he thought back to the last memory he had before this nightmare had taken him. He closed his eyes and tried to concentrate through the throbs of pain. He was vaguely aware of pieces of the journey here, but the memories were distant and hazy, as if remembered from a dream.

The first concrete memory he could hold on to was of the barn at his home. The image of a young woman materialized in his mind. She was in the beginning of her seventeenth year, like him. Blonde hair framed a porcelain face.

"Anne," he breathed aloud.

She had come to his father's farm that night, and they snuck off to the barn. He had already asked her father for permission to wed her twice and both times had been rebuffed; he was only a farmer's son, after all. They didn't even own the land, they leased it from Anne's father. That night, she suggested they simply run away and start a new life in one of the cities.

Alric was lean and muscled. She said he could get work as a guard, and she would mend clothes. They would be together. But Alric couldn't abandon his father. He would find a way to convince her father, he had assured her. Anne left the barn in tears.

The image in his mind shifted; Anne's perfect face distorted. The visage of his love twisted into a hateful mask. Her perfect ivory skin became blotchy and swollen with purple bruises. Blood ran down from her eyes, pooling in her mouth, staining her perfect teeth.

"You killed me!" she screamed. "You left and now all there is, is cold and dark and hunger!"

The creature that used to be Anne lunged at him, claws replacing slender fingers as she reached for his throat. Alric opened his eyes. Somehow, dawn had arrived, and the sun was rising over the glacial mountain that loomed over their camp.

The small group was marching up the mountain on a narrow icy path that wound its way up to the frozen peak. The woman led, her hands clutching a length of rope, dragging Alric along. Her two hooded companions brought up the rear.

It was well past midday when they finally stopped. Alric dropped to the snow, exhausted from the hasty climb. *At least they untied my feet,* he thought bitterly.

As he regained his breath, Alric took a moment to look around at his surroundings. They had reached a small, flat clearing near the peak of the mountain. Around him were walls of ice and rock that formed a small alcove in the mountain face before climbing upward to the summit.

Alric let out a gasp. At the far end of the clearing, on a raised dais, was a corpse.

The cold, dry air had mummified its weathered body. Gray paper skin stuck to a giant throne hewn from the ice and rock of the mountainside. On its wrists and feet were black iron manacles that plunged back into the frozen chair upon which it sat. Its mouth hung open, revealing rotten teeth and no tongue. The only other feature adorning the poor creature was an iron spike impaling the corpse through the heart and adhering it to the mountainside.

The two men hauled Alric to his feet. "It's time, my love," she cooed.

As the men held him fast, the woman to sing. Alric couldn't understand the words but, despite himself, he was soon lost in the melody. Alric closed his eyes and his mind drifted. He didn't know the language she was using, but it didn't matter. The intonations of her voice carried him on a journey of love, loss, and regret. Tears froze on his cheeks as his head swayed to the hypnotic melody of her voice.

She stopped.

Alric weakly opened his eyes, breaking the ice that had already frozen his lashes to his face. The woman was just inches from him now. He had known she was beautiful before, but this was the first time he had been able to study her face. She was flawless. Her bright green eyes bore into his soul.

She leaned in and kissed him, passionately, exploring his mouth with her tongue. The sensation was electric. His every muscle pulsed and contracted, and were it not for the strong hands still holding him up, he would have fallen again to the snow. He didn't notice the curved dagger on her hand, not until she plunged it into his chest.

The corpse watched the boat slip away from the island of his frozen prison. The body of the man they had brought still lay in the snow in front of Him, lifeless. He felt the power of the blood these strangers had spilled for Him. The red stain stood stark against the white snow that covered the floor of His tomb. He took hold of that power, channeling it into

Him, then staking it against the power of the chains that held His soul trapped in this frozen prison.

Cracks began to form in the ice around the chains. Tiny, barely visible imperfections broke the crystalline structure of His prison. The power of this man's blood faded. The cracking stopped.

Cold wind, once again, blew across the glacier, and He waited.

Chapter I

Present Day

Pale beams of light broke through the dense forest canopy, illuminating the frost on the fallen leaves below. The air was cool and thick with the smell of autumn morning. Chael crouched, hidden in the shadow of the leeward side of a particularly large oak tree. He had been pursuing his quarry through the night, having discovered the signs of its passing the day before.

Damn demons, Chael grumbled to himself.

The signs he had discovered were the fractured remains of his smokehouse and one truly unfortunate goat, the sight of which would haunt even Chael's dreams. He lived in a small, abandoned house he discovered just within the outer edge of the Great Western Forest, several leagues from the small town of Ehbing. The forest was totally uninhabited and seldom traversed due to the demons that mysteriously congregated here; for this, it was also commonly called the Dark Forest.

The beast's trail led from Chael's desecrated home straight toward the town. The good people of Ehbing didn't particularly like Chael, which suited him well because Chael didn't particularly like people. But, despite their mutual animosity, their arrangement held: the townsfolk provided

Chael with the supplies he required, and Chael killed all the monsters.

There is no escape, she thought, even if you could free yourself. "You're only going to chafe your wrists doing that," she finally said.even if you could free yourself. "You're only going to chafe your wrists doing that," she finally said.

Why had it come to his home? That was particularly strange. Creatures of the Dark had a sense about these things, and most knew to avoid the man who had taken residence in the wood.

Across the small patch of forest from Chael's hiding place, a shape emerged in the dim morning light. The muzzle of an enormous wolf, its upper lip curled back, revealing yellow-gray teeth, bared and menacing.

As more of the enormous canine emerged, matted gray fur gave way on its snout to where old battle wounds had completely torn away the flesh and sinew leaving behind bare bone. The wound went all the way past its right eye revealing a full quarter of the wolf's skull. Its eyes, glowing an unearthly azure, the precise shade of Chael's own, turned toward him. Their eyes met, and Chael couldn't help but smile at his oldest friend.

The wolf leapt away, pursuing the nearby demon in a wide arc. They both knew what to do, they had performed this ritual a thousand times before. Michik, Chael's wolf, would flush out their prey, pushing it to where Chael lay in wait. If they did it correctly, there wouldn't even be a fight.

Chael tensed, steadying himself to strike. His breath fogged in front of his face. *Do demons get cold?* he thought absently. He then shook his head, clearing his mind for the fight. Michik snarled and barked, but there were no sounds of the demon retreating from his mighty wolf.

Chael paused, considering for a moment. He could sense his companion's spirit about one hundred paces away. Chael burst from his cover and sprinted towards him. He flew past a copse of trees, turned and nearly ran into the gargantuan demon.

It was a lesser demon—lesser on account of its intelligence and not its size, for it stood several heads taller than Chael. The demon had cloven hooves attached to human shaped but furry legs. Its chest was that of a large, muscular man but scarred and mottled and its head resembled a giant hairless rat, complete with a set of jagged uncomplimentary teeth that would tear its own flesh as its jaw snapped.

In its giant clawed hands, the demon held the trunk of a small tree as if it were a stick and was swinging it wildly at Michik. To the wolf's credit, he was deftly ducking the blows, using the trees to negate the thing's lumbering size and diminish the arc of its swing.

Chael rolled forward, partly to duck the backswing of the enormous tree club, but mostly to avoid simply running headlong into the thing.

Stupid! Chael cursed himself. He had been reckless worrying about Michik; the wolf was not easy prey, even for a demon this large.

Chael finished the roll, coming to his feet in front and to the side of the creature, slashing out with his curved sword as he did. He scored a hit on the thing's chest, black blood oozing from the shallow wound. Bleeding wouldn't kill it; demons were not of this world. He had to banish it back to its home in the Dark. The easiest way to do that was to take its head. That is, if Chael could even reach it.

The demon roared in fury at the painful cut, swinging its club in a downward arc at Chael's head. Chael leaned back, dodging the blow while preparing his own downward strike across the demon's extended arm, hoping to sever it. Chael's sword sliced hard into its muscled flesh, emitting a shower of dark demonic gore and bit into the bone of its left forearm.

The demon yanked back its arm, pulling the sword from Chael's grip and throwing him off balance as it swung its right fist at Chael's head. The blow would probably have knocked him unconscious, but Michik had already leaped at the creature, jaws clamping around its arm. Michik's attack broke the momentum and slightly diverted the swing, but even so, Chael received a mighty blow to his shoulder, throwing him into a nearby tree.

Michik had saved his life, but had paid a steep price. Fresh wounds appeared on his flank where the demon had raked him with foul, black claws. The wolf now limped as it whined at his master. The limp would go away; the wounds would not.

"Fine!" Chael yelled aloud, wincing as he rose to his feet. He inhaled deeply, feeling the power of the life all around him. He could feel the sap running through the veins of the trees, the damp living grass, and prickly bushes. The life of the forest glade glowed with brilliant light to his senses, but in the center was a black void where the demon stood, alive but also not alive.

In a tree twenty feet behind him, Chael felt a family of squirrels. They had been hard at work preparing for the coming winter, but now they were just hiding. Chael could feel their fear of this preternatural being that had invaded their home. Chael exhaled, feeling all, taking in the power of the surrounding life, and then he felt nothing.

Chael's eyes were already the shade of Michik's, but now they took on his dog's supernatural glow as the power of death flowed through him. He could feel the wind on each individual jet-black hair of his head as his senses were heightened by the Dark magic. His hand twitched, itching with the supernatural strength that had poured down his arms and into his fingers. Chael darted back into the fight.

Rage joined the necromantic energy that surged in Chael's limbs. He reached the demon, ducked under another blow, and retrieved his sword in the same motion. It sliced through sinew and bone as Chael wrenched it free, leaving the demon's arm hanging loosely as its club fell to the forest floor.

Chael continued his momentum into a roll between the demon's legs and came up twisting, using the power of his magic and the momentum of his roll to slice horizontally through the demon's left leg. His powerful stroke cut straight through the leg, cleanly severing it from the demon as it fell, howling in pain.

With the creature disabled, Chael heaved a two-handed strike with all his might at its thick, muscled neck. The demon's head hit the ground with a satisfying, meaty thud.

Chael cleaned the black ichor from his sword and attempted to wipe it from his clothing. He knew it was no use. In addition to a new smokehouse and goat, he was going to need new clothes.

"Meeshee, come here, boy," he called.

Michik padded over, still limping slightly, but his tail was wagging, nonetheless. Chael was unconcerned with the limp; it wasn't due to anything physical. Michik's movements were not tied to the contraction of muscles or the beating of a heart. The limp, Chael suspected, was a vestige of how the dog reacted to injury when he was still alive.

What was concerning to Chael were the claw marks from the demon on his dog's flank. It had torn away fur and skin, and in some places, exposed his ribs. Michik couldn't die, he had already been dead for over three years, and his soul would stay as long Chael's soul remained in the mortal plane.

But Michik's body was another matter. It couldn't heal. There was no blood to carry nutrients or repair damage. And though the soul of his mighty wolf retained a substantial amount of vigor, it still needed a corporeal vessel. Chael sighed as he lovingly scratched Michik's ears.

Chael got up, surveying the small glade that had become their battleground. He grimaced as he surveyed the aftermath of the brief fight. The demon lay still. Its soul—*or whatever a demon had*—was departed, banished back to the Dark where its kind was from.

Below the demon, in a ring about thirty paces wide, was death. Gray, lifeless grass now clung limply to hard, inhospitable dirt. One of the trees that ringed the small clearing was dead. The rest of its leaves had fallen and its branches, dry and brittle, clung to a gray-dead trunk.

Sighing, Chael stalked further from the battleground and spied two plump squirrels on the ground. He winced. They were physically undamaged after falling from their home in the tree, but now lay cold and lifeless amidst the carnage.

Lifeless because of him.

Chapter 2

Present Day

"Ok, buddy you know the drill," Chael said to his dog. "Stay here, look menacing and don't eat any villagers unless you have to." Michik looked up at Chael and snorted. "Good boy," he told the wolf as he gave him a final scratch.

They were at the edge of the forest on the border of Ehbing. Chael had business in town and was forced to leave Michik behind. The people were fairly wary of him, but they were positively terrified of his four-legged companion.

Ehbing wasn't a particularly large town. The dense Western Forest nearly surrounded it and completely blocked off any easy land routes from Ehbing to the rest of the Kingdom of Fhael. This and suspiciously inarable land hampered its growth despite its advantageous geography.

What it did have, however, was a newly enlarged port situated at the southwestern shore of the continent and at the delta of the Amberwyne River. Swift river boats could take goods from the coast across the Kingdom and into the so-called Sharaad Republics and back in a matter of weeks. Other than the harbor, the town itself had little industry to speak of, save for the types of businesses that generally arose near ports.

Just south of the town square, situated on a small hill, was the home of Baron Janus Al-Fhaelan. He maintained a small keep and his house guard served as both his personal protection and the city watch. The Baron was the first of Chael's appointments for the day.

Chael skirted the edge of Ehbing and did his best to avoid any of the people on his way to the keep. He was dressed in simple brown trousers and boots, with a white linen shirt. On his shoulders, he wore a green cloak, as was his custom. He had managed to bathe and change most of his clothes after the encounter with the lesser demon that morning, though the cloak would need some professional repair in town.

He kept his curved falchion on his belt as well as various knives he stashed in his boots, belt, and even the shoulders of his cloak. In his hands, he carried a large weight sack, a special surprise for today's visit.

As he walked, the encounter with the demon was still playing through his mind. He had never before fought one that big and demons never strayed too close to his house. Like the easily frightened townspeople of Ehbing, the demons could sense what he was and were never too eager to pick a fight.

Before long, Chael reached the outer wooden palisade of the keep. The lone guard outside held out his hand, directing Chael to stop. He was shorter than Chael and quite a bit rounder, but he did admire the man's impressive mustache, the ends of which fell past the guard's face and dangled below his chin. "State your business, stranger," the guard stated haughtily.

"Must we do this," Chael said in exasperation. "You know who I am, you know what my business is. So Let me in, I have to talk to the Baron."

"Who ya are is different than what," the man spat. "And what ya are is a Darkborn menace. I canne seem to figure why the Baron allows ya to continue drawin' breath."

Chael sighed, smiled, and then heaved the contents of the sack at the obstinate guard. The head of the lesser demon hit the guard in the stomach and knocked him from his feet.

The guard yelped as he saw the hairless rat-like head roll along the cobblestones of the keep entrance like a giant melon, leaking more of its viscous black demon blood as it went.

Chael smiled as he bent over to pick it up. The guard was too busy retching all over his uniform to impede his progress any further. He moved on to the stone keep proper. There were few other guards about and none of the various courtiers of the Baron deigned to acknowledge him or dared to contest his presence.

After a short wait, he was granted an audience with the Baron and was to be received in his personal chambers, up on the highest floor of the squat castle. *Can't let them see you dealing with the town spook,* Chael thought as he was quickly conducted by a timid house servant to the third level of the keep and into the lord's apartments.

The servant kept her head down and refused to make eye contact as she led Chael past several sleeping rooms and into the Baron's study. Baron Janus Al-Fhaelan was ostentatious, Chael thought. Although, he was the only Fhaelan nobleman Chael could name offhand, so perhaps that was a normal affectation for such people.

The study was lavished with fine red and purple rugs and had several paintings of the Baron and his cousin, the King, adorning the walls. Janus himself sat behind a large, intricately carved wooden writing desk. He dismissed the servant girl, who gratefully exited, and stood up to greet Chael.

"Right," the Baron said with a false air of joviality. "What can I do for the great demon hunter of the Western Wood?"

"Well, for starters, you can order your guards to give up the charade of denying my entrance, every time I come to see you," Chael replied, and the Baron let out a short burst of genuine laughter.

"Lad, we both know there's nothing I can say that will make them like ya any better. And besides, I'm fairly certain that mocking my guards is fully half the reason you come here at all."

Damn, Chael thought. The Baron probably had a point there. Chael fought back the retort that had flown to his lips. He was annoyed that the Baron had figured him so well.

The truth was, Baron Janus Al-Fhaelan didn't like him any more than his guards or the rest of the town. They had some knowledge of his abilities, and they all knew about his undead wolf. He was different and powerful and so they feared him, and what men fear, they generally grow to hate. But, since he had taken up residence in their wood, he had almost completely eliminated the havoc the demons would wreak on the shipping that was so vital to Ehbing.

Because of Chael, the Baron had grown quite wealthy these last few years, and the town had grown greatly in importance now that goods from the sea could reliably make it inland past the marauding demons. If Chael stuck around Ehbing would probably grow to rival some of the great cities of the Kingdom, the Baron was well aware of this and so continued to feign his congeniality.

"I don't know why but the demons seem to be getting larger and more numerous lately," Chael stated after collecting his thoughts. He removed the head from the sack, careful this time to not spill any demon gore on the Baron's luxurious floor.

"Darkness!" Janus cursed quietly. Lesser demons like the one Chael had slain were generally about six feet tall, with heads roughly the size of a man's, albeit shaped like a tortured rodent. The head that Chael produced was that and half again as big. It required two hands and no small amount of Chael's strength to hold.

"This one was cleverer as well, or at least braver," Chael continued. "It attacked my homestead and avoided the ambush I set up in the woods."

The Baron stood transfixed, staring in disgust at the enormous demon head in his chambers. Chael spied a precarious droplet of dark ichor starting to fall from the demon's gnarled ear; he managed to catch it with his boot before it could stain the Baron's garish rug.

"I caught the creature a mere league from Ehbing. It was coming to the town, not the river." That gave Janus pause. The demons that sporadically came out of the Great Western Wood didn't normally attack settlements. They raided small groups of travelers and particularly liked to assault the vulnerable river boats heading east out of Ehbing. This indeed concerned. After a long moment, the Baron managed to speak.

"What do you suppose this means?" He asked Chael, still staring at the head.

"I don't know," he replied honestly. "But I may be unable to prevent an attack on the town if another one tries. You need to start posting guards and watchers near the forest."

The Baron scoffed, "I don't have enough men to garrison my own keep let alone guard the town. No, no, the demons have never come here before, I'm sure you're mistaken. They won't come here." He repeated that to himself for a moment, as if chanting the words would make it so.

After a moment, he looked back up at Chael, regaining his former forced cordiality. "I'm sure the legendary demon hunter Kee-el-" the Baron mispronounced his name. Chael had long suspected he did this on purpose to annoy him. It worked—"and his faithful companion will keep the monsters at bay. After all, it's what I pay ya for!"

Janus then winked at Chael and fetched a small sack of coins from his desk. He tossed the sack at Chael, apparently bringing the meeting to a close, and ushered him to the door. Chael began to protest but knew it was useless and so allowed himself to be shooed from the office and escorted from the keep.

On his way out from the keep, he passed the portly, mustachioed guard from earlier. Chunks of the guard's lunch still clung to the man's facial hair and his uniform was stained black in various places across his belly. He scowled at Chael as he passed and Chael brandished the sack, shaking it menacingly in the guard's direction. He laughed audibly as the guard doubled over, nearly vomiting for a second time. Chael had to admit the damned thing did smell quite awful. He waved at the poor guard over his shoulder as he continued down the hill into Ehbing.

"Son, this is why ya don' have any friends," the man said.

Chael had just finished relating the visit to Brod, one of the many new tradesmen in Ehbing, and one of the few people who would speak to him. Chael had given particular attention to the unfortunate gate guard in his tale. Brod was a smith by trade, and a damned good one as far as Chael was concerned, but the need in Ehbing had waned with the increase in shipped goods, both up the river and from the sea.

So, Brod smithed what he could and otherwise found work building and maintaining the various structures that supported the harbor. His wife, Maelon, worked as a seamstress and was busy mending his cloak.

"Still," Brod continued, "these are strange times. I've heard sailors talk of red sails along the coast." Chael shook his head. As a general rule, sailors were a superstitious bunch and were unreliable storytellers at the best of times, but Chael found reports of red sails concerning.

"Why would elves come here?" Chael asked, regaining some of his natural skepticism. "The republics are closer to their home and wealthier, if it's plunder they're after."

The elves—or "draug," as they called themselves—were an enigmatic people who lived on an island somewhat south and to the east of the continent. They were mostly notable for three things: the bright red sails they used on their ships, their dark almost purple blue skin, and their antipathy towards humans. Or at least any humans that ventured too close to their home. Many enterprising merchants and businessmen had tried to establish connections with the elves; the few survivors of all such missions spoke only of red sails and death.

Itching to change the subject, Chael asked, "So how are the kids?"

"The twins are fine," Brod responded. "Ya know, they ask me about that beast ya keep in the woods."

"Michik?" Chael chuckled. "He loves children, probably his favorite snack." Brod gave Chael a raised eyebrow, but otherwise didn't respond to the jest. "You're welcome to bring them out any time, he's shockingly gentle for his size."

Brod gave him a hard look. "That forest isn't right, lad. Ya shouldn't stay there, it's evil, I don't care how good ya are with that steel."

"Evil?" Chael mocked. "Just because demons who manage to crawl out of the Dark somehow end up there?"

This was a conversation the two had quite often. Brod didn't like the forest for good reason, but it was indeed Chael's home. He belonged there. There was something special about that forest that drew him, just as it did the Darkborn. Even if the people of Ehbing had been agreeable towards him, he knew it was his home. Besides, it was only recently that a demon had ever gone out of its way to bother him.

Their conversation was soon broken by Maelon, who had finished mending his increasingly tattered cloak. She liked his gold well enough, but like most, she was suspicious of him and rarely spoke. He paid her for the work, as well as for some new trousers, and gave Brod a quick nod as he departed.

On his way out of town, Chael stopped by one of the few farms that managed to survive around Ehbing. The soil was hard and stubborn, and few people could get much of anything useful to grow. This had been a fact for essentially the town's entire existence, but the fine folks of Ehbing had still managed to blame him for it.

He needed a new goat but didn't suspect that the owner of the farm would be interested in his business, so he left a gold piece from the wage he had earned from the Baron and simply took a goat from the farm. This was approximately seven times the value of the goat, as best Chael could figure. He wasn't precisely sure of the exchange rates between goats and gold, but he figured that between the substantial amount of money and the fact that he stopped a gigantic demon from pillaging the town, the exchange heavily favored the farmer, so he didn't trouble himself over the theft.

From the edge of the forest, he could see a pair of glowing azure eyes watching him, as well as a gray tail swaying with increasing urgency as he neared the tree line.

Chapter 3

17 years ago

Chael awoke, much the same as he had the previous week, to the sound of screams. The older boys liked to sneak into the barracks of the newcomers searching for any valuables they might still have after being sold to the school. Some of the more sadistic boys liked to sneak in and simply distribute pain as they saw fit. Chael had been no exception to this practice and still bore the bruises from his first night at the school.

He supposed it was how some boys reacted to being sold by their families. It was a common practice in the Sharaad Republics for indebted merchants or desperate gamblers to sell their younger offspring. The pain of being disposed of by family cheapened the value of all human connections. Chael understood that pain all too well. He had been abandoned on the streets of the Republic of Kazaam and simply scooped up by one of the many slaving enterprises in the city.

Chael had no valuables save the rags on his back, but those were hardly worth stealing, so the other boys had left him alone since that inaugural beating. The tradition wasn't explicitly forbidden by the schoolmasters, but permanently damaging new recruits was heavily frowned upon. Thus, for the past week of Chael's time at the school, he observed the more brutal recruits amongst the older boys delivered beatings in a stunningly well-organized schedule to not permanently injure anyone.

Breakfast at the school wasn't much better than the sleeping conditions. Though Chael liked the fare or as street urchin, at least appreciated consistency, here once again a certain hierarchy arose. The older and bigger boys would eat their fill and this pattern would filter down to the younger and smaller until there was little left but scraps and sometimes nothing at all.

After breakfast, one of the masters gathered the youngsters and newcomers and led them out onto the central lawn. Chael stretched his bruised neck and arms in anticipation of the highly physical nature of the training that was about to occur.

"Do you think they'll run us again today? I hate running." Chael turned to look at his sparring partner Darrik.

"I suppose so, they've done it every day so far haven't they?" responded Chael. The morning after his arrival at the school, he had been paired with Darrik. He supposed it was because they were roughly the same size, if not the same age.

Chael was small for a thirteen-year-old and though merely eleven, Darrik was large and already showed the beginnings of what might become a large muscular man. To Darrik's great dismay, there was running, lots of running.

Present Day

Michik let out a bark and a low growl, stirring Chael from his labors in his ransacked smokehouse. *A carpenter I am not,* he thought out loud, looking at his questionable work. He turned to look down the path that led from his home and into the forest towards Ehbing. After a moment, he was also able to hear the approach of at least several people and a horse which had set off the keen senses of his dog.

Chael glanced at Michik and gave a quick, high-pitched whistle. The wolf padded out into the forest and his dark gray fur became one with the shadows of the trees, ready to pounce out and ambush any unwelcome guests. Chael tensed, unsure of what to expect. This group certainly wasn't a band of demons. For starters, they clearly had at least one horse which, as a rule, the Darkborn didn't use.

At least they untied my feet, he thought bitterly. Damn demons, Chael grumbled to himself.

Chael waited until he heard cries of alarm go up amongst the approaching group, followed by a few short barks from Michik. "Darkness!" Chael cursed as he jogged toward the diplomatic disaster he was certain was playing out in front of his house. He charged down the rough worn path he had managed to carve since taking up residence near Ehbing and came upon an alarming sight.

Three armored men with spears held their weapons leveled at his dog. Behind them stood a pack horse whinnying nervously at the presence of the undead wolf. Michik was pacing out of reach of the spearmen, snapping his impressive jaws at any who ventured too close. On the other side of Michik, from the spearmen, were the twin children of Brod Smith, Alyce and Jehrom.

"Stop this idiocy!" Chael shouted at the group. He gave another whistle and Michik reluctantly came to his side, sparing a departing tail wag for the children and a ghoulish snarl at the guards. Brod then emerged from behind the nervous horse, pushing between the spearman, his arms held out plaintively in front of him.

"S'alright lad, nothin' but a misunderstandin', that's all. My boy strayed a bit too far inta the wood and so this one," he pointed accusingly at one of the spearmen, a frown forming on his face. "He decided ta frighten me boy, that's when your beast leapeded from the wood, and put the fear of Dark in 'im."

"That demon attacked me!" screamed the outraged spearman Brod had indicated. "The Baron will have your head Darkborn! An attack on his men is an attack on the Baron hisself."

Chael sighed, rubbing his temples. A headache was already forming there. *I hate people,* he thought, and then glanced down at his dog.

"And you!" he said accusingly at the wolf. "Twice in as many days, you drag me into some kind of trouble!"

Michik snorted defiantly, clearly displaying a different interpretation of the past day's events. The still enraged spearman, feeling that Chael was distracted while teasing his dog, took that moment to advance with his spear.

Chael was still looking down at his impertinent companion, failing to feign anger as he reached into his cloak, and deftly flicked a small dagger at the spearman's hands, slicing a shallow arc across the back of his palm. The guard jumped backward in both pain and surprise, dropping the spear and clutching his bleeding hand.

"First of all, Michik is not a demon, and attacking him is an attack on…" he paused, hiding a sinister smile, "an attack on misself," he added, mocking the injured spearman with a wagging, accusatory finger. "Secondly, if he had attacked you, he would have certainly killed you and would currently be chewing on your femur bone, trying to extract the marrow."

Michik stamped a paw as if to accentuate that point.

"You seem to be fairly alive and possess both lower limbs," Chael chided, his initial flash of anger giving way to amusement. He swept down his accusatory finger to point out the man's quite intact legs to further accentuate his point. "Where is the fat one with the mustache?"

Chael continued, "He found out firsthand what happens when I lose my head."

Chael took a breath as he struggled to appear menacing and hide the smile that was fighting to form on his lips. These three guards had certainly heard about their colleagues' experience with the demon's head. He glanced at Brod, who still held a frown, though whether it was from disapproval of Chael's words or of the guard's actions, he couldn't be sure.

I suppose that's sufficient mockery for the moment, he conceded to himself. "Now," he continued more earnestly, "why in Darkness have you come here?"

"I believe I can answer that." Baron Janus emerged from behind his guards, badly out of breath. With him was another armsman, though much better dressed than the spearmen, and a sister of the Fraternal Order of Celestial Light. They had apparently lagged behind the rest of the party and were just now catching up.

Curious, Chael thought.

"If you promise your hound will stay far away from my leg bones," Janus breathed, a wry grin on his face. Chael sighed. He simply knew he wasn't going to like this at all. "Now if you would please Chael," the Baron wheezed. "I need a place to sit and then we can discuss business."

At that moment, Michik got up and trotted over to where the children still stood frightened on the side of the rough forest path. Jehrom was hugging his crying sister, doing his best not to join in. The giant wolf was at least a handsbreadth taller at the shoulder than the six-year-old children. He stooped down, careful to present the side of his snout that still had fur, and nuzzled the frightened girl, who gave him a hesitant head pat.

"Traitor," Chael mumbled silently at his dog. He briefly considered leaving them here and returning home, but the group was already essentially at his doorstep. Besides, this was the Baron's first time visiting him or even entering the forest as far as Chael knew.

Chael sighed again. "Well, come along then, let's hear this business." With that, he turned and directed the party to his home.

Chapter 4

Present Day

Chael led the way back up the forest path to his small homestead. His house was a small single-story cottage, with a roof that was a somewhat haphazard mixture of rough thatch and tile. He had come across it when he first came to the forest several years earlier. It had been abandoned by the previous owner and didn't require much of Chael's limited carpentry skills to make livable.

He led most of them inside before turning to three spearmen, saying, "I need you brave young knights to stay out here and guard against demons, can't have something like that spooking the horse now, can we?" Before they could respond Chael turned around and shut his front door behind him.

Inside was a single room about forty feet wide. In the far corner from the door was a simple straw mattress on the floor for Chael and a small circular version of the same for Michik.

On the opposite side of the cottage was a fireplace, a pot, and a small table with a single chair. The red-faced baron unceremoniously plopped himself down onto it immediately upon entering. "Smith!" the Baron called, motioning for Brod. "Make the necessary introductions, would you? I need to catch my breath."

"Right," intoned Brod, "Jehrom take your sister over there and play with that giant beast." He glanced at Chael, who nodded curtly. Brod reciprocated the nod and began clearing his throat, clearly attempting to sound formal. "Chael, this is sister Aelisa from the Fraternal Order of Celestial Light and her escort Sir Andon Al-Fhaelan, nephew of King Inarus Al-Fhaelan, sworn knight of the realm," Brod recited carefully.

Chael gave a nod to the knight and a slight bow to the priestess. He then gave a quizzical glance over to the Baron, who was still recovering from what was apparently a strenuous walk. Sister Aelisa was somewhere in her sixth decade, Chael estimated. She was short and slender, and waves of curly blonde hair were giving way to gray, but her piercing blue eyes belied fierce intelligence. Something about her made Chael's skin itch.

"What is a stargazer doing all the way out here?" Chael asked the priestess.

Aelisa ignored the small jibe and responded, "I go where the stars summon me, and today they saw fit to bring me here, young wolf."

"Sister, the wolf is over there having what looks to be an amateur dental exam."

All except Sister Aelisa glanced over at the far corner of the room where the children were curiously poking at the exposed bone on Michik's snout and face. To his credit, the wolf simply laid on his bed and took the abuse. Sister Aelisa, however, never took her eyes from Chael's own. He wasn't sure what he saw there, but it unnerved him all the same.

"Stars in Heaven…" Sir Andon gasped, clearly seeing the ghoulish visage of the wolf for the first time. Chael, finally breaking eye contact with the sister, smiled at him and gave a quick wink.

"The King has summoned me for an emergency council in the capitol, Sir Andon and Sister Aelisa arrived with the summons this morning," the Baron called from his chair,

"His Majesty has asked that I make all haste and arrive in Fhaerhold no later than five days hence and also that we travel with some level of discretion. The river would take more than a week and passes too close to those cursed republics."

"He needs ya to lead 'im through the Dark Forest lad," Brod cut in. Chael looked from Brod to the Baron, scarcely believing what he was hearing.

Chael could feel his temper growing once again. "Am I now your errand boy?" He seethed at the Baron, "what makes you think I would take on such a blatantly idiotic task? The lot of you made so much noise coming here that I'm shocked that every demon in the darkened forest didn't arrive with you!"

Heat rose on the collar of Chael's shirt; these people openly despised him but now wanted him to risk his life leading him through the Dark-cursed forest.

"And you," Chael gestured at the Baron, "could barely manage the walk here from town. There's no paths out there Janus, it's nothing but trees and brambles and creeping things just as deadly as demons if you let your guard down."

"Now listen here, boy!" The enraged baron finally rose from his chair and stalked over to Chael. The Baron was only a little taller than average, but he still managed to loom, menacingly over Chael. "I am Baron Janus Al-Fhaelan of the western lands of Fhael and your liege lord!"

The Baron's face returned to the deep shade of red he exhibited on his hike to Chael's home. Chael merely stood facing him impassively, his hand unconsciously creeping over to the hilt of his sword. Sir Andon noticed the gesture and placed his hand over his hilt as well. Brod attempted to clear the tension of the moment, but Sister Aelisa beat him to it.

"Gentlemen," she cooed, eyeing Chael and Sir Andon with a raised eyebrow.

Chael only then realized the aggressive posture he had taken and slowly lowered his hands to his sides, but still glowered at the Baron. Across the room, Sir Andon likewise lowered his hands from his weapon.

With the tension momentarily settled, Sister Aelisa continued, "fifteen days ago a man appeared in Fhaerhold claiming to be a refugee of the court of High Minister Khalim of the Sharaad Republics. He governs Kazaam I believe. He had dire warnings, warnings that necessitated the immediate convening of the King's war council," she gestured toward the Baron. "It was also believed that he consorted with Dark worshippers, so I was called to continue his interrogation."

At the mention of Dark worshippers, her eyes took on a steely, resolute glow and her aged face soured. "He would not speak on those allegations no matter how vigorous our questioning, but physical examinations revealed certain," she paused, searching for the right word. "Anomalies," she continued. "However, he told us he would speak and reveal all his Dark secrets if we fetched for him a strange man. A man that lives in the Dark Forest and hunts demons. He said that we should pass on the name Darrik."

There is no escape, she thought, even if you could free yourself. "You're only going to chafe your wrists doing that," she finally said.even if you could free yourself. "You're only going to chafe your wrists doing that," she finally said.

"That's not possible," he responded after a significant pause. "Darrik is dead. I killed him years ago."

Chael's mind drifted back to that day. *It's not possible. It couldn't be.* But someone knew him, and knew to use that name; that was deeply concerning.

Sister Aelisa turned and looked at Michik still undergoing his impromptu examination at the hands of Brod's children. "It would seem," she said dryly, "that death isn't so grand an obstacle for those in your company."

She turned back to Chael, her eyes hard, boring intensely into his for several seconds before softening and added, "so, the light of the stars bid I travel here and seek you out so we can learn the Dark truth of this Darrik." She spat his name with what Chael thought to be an impressive level of disgust. "I don't suppose that the great demon hunter of the Western Forest would let a baron and an old woman wander around in that dark accursed place without a guide?"

She almost appeared sweet; Chael simply cursed.

"Are you sure you won't come with," Chael asked Brod. Though it was already past midday, the Baron had insisted they depart immediately, so Chael hastily packed for the several days it would take to traverse the wood and the spearmen unloaded Brod's horse. As Chael threw together a rough traveler's pack, Brod had attempted to make a stealthy exit.

"No, lad," Brod replied with a weak smile. "He only brought me here because I have the only horse that will venture even this far into the woods. And I suppose to convince ya if ya refused 'im. But the lass beat me to it seems." Brod became suddenly more serious. "Look out for yourself, Chael. Between the forest and the priestess somethin' ain't right."

Chael raised his eyebrows; it wasn't often that Brod used his actual name. Brod gave him a quick smile, clapped him on the shoulder and headed out, back to the forest trail with his two children and newly unladen horse in tow. That horse had helped Chael during his time here to bring larger supplies for his home. Of the horses in Ehbing, it was one of the bravest, but still not willing to venture deeper into the forest than Chael's home.

Chael watched them go until they disappeared into the dark, foreboding forest. He immediately felt a pang of worry for his friend, but it wasn't really a long walk and there was plenty of daylight left.

He glanced down and noticed that Michik had joined his vigil at the door. "Did someone make a friend today?" he asked his dog wryly. In response, Michik stared up at him for a moment, snorted, and then headed back inside.

When they were all prepped for the journey, Chael addressed the group, looking at them each in turn, trying his best to sound authoritative. "The crossing should take three or perhaps four days depending on how fast we can travel." He shot a glance at the Baron before continuing, "the terrain will be rough and there are no charts detailing the interior of the forest. If you get lost no one is going to find you. If we see a demon Michik and I will take care of it, the rest of you will just get in our way."

At the last comment, the knight squirmed a bit but did not comment. Chael smiled at him and continued, "Right, well I suppose we should get going."

Chael led the group out of his home and towards the eastern edge of his property. He sighed, looking at his companions. He didn't like the blatant attempt at manipulating him into joining their cause. But the notion that Darrik was alive, or that someone who knew that name also knew his whereabouts, raised far too many questions to ignore. And Chael begrudgingly admitted that the woman had a point.

He had no particular love for the Baron, and the priestess unnerved him, but allowing them to disappear into the forest and get mauled by demons would almost certainly cause him some headaches down the road. *I hate people,* he thought bitterly once again.

Chael took a deep steadying breath, feeling anew the life teeming in the surrounding wood. He didn't draw the power that the life proffered, but he suspected that before long a trail of death would be forever left to mark his party's passage. He slowly exhaled, adjusted his pack, and marched into the forest.

Chapter 5

12 Years Ago

"Begin!" shouted the arms master to the assembled boys.

Chael immediately launched into a flurry of motion, striking out with his wooden practice sword, hoping to get a quick kill before Darrik could get his guard up. His attack was rebuffed at the last second with a flick of Darrik's sword. At that point, the fight began in earnest.

Despite being two years Chael's junior, Darrik was significantly taller and stronger. The years of hard training and exercise of the school had forged him into an impressive figure at sixteen years old.

Darrik swung at Chael's shoulder with a heavy blow; Chael knew he couldn't block it outright; there was too much power in the swing, so he dodged and tried to redirect the blow. Darrik anticipated his moves and conserved the momentum of his swing, bent it, and swung on his backhand to where Chael had dodged, avoiding his parry.

This was the game they had learned to play. Darrik had quickly outpaced Chael in physical stature over their time training together. His strategy became to use his superior reach and size to bludgeon Chael into submission. Chael was smaller, in fact he was among the smaller boys at the school standing only a hair over five feet, but he was also much quicker. His strategy was to weave in and out of Darrik's heavy strikes until the larger boy tired and then strike quickly. Sometimes he was able to dodge and dive with a dancer's grace and score a dramatic, even poetic and beautiful kill. Other times Darrik would hit him so hard in the head he'd lose feeling in his toes.

Darrik and Chael settled into a comfortable, familiar rhythm. Chael would score minor hits here and there, and Darrik would only just barely miss breaking Chael's collarbone.

Why had it come to his home? That was particularly strange. Creatures of the Dark had a sense about these things, and most knew to avoid the man who had taken residence in the wood. Do demons get cold? he thought absently. He then shook his head, clearing his mind for the fight. Michik snarled and barked, but there were no sounds of the demon retreating from his mighty wolf.

Up to this point, the rules of their combative dance had dictated that Darrik led. They were evenly matched and the strategy of wearing down the larger, slower fighter had won him numerous victories.

Take initiative. Chael ground his teeth, trying to come up with a novel strategy to surprise his long-time sparring partner while also ducking bone shattering swings.

Slowly, an audacious plan formed in his head. He debated with himself for a moment before deciding, feeling as if some unseen force was guiding his mind.

He confidently avoided another blow, but instead of dodging back to the relative safety of the practice ring's edge, he dove forward, attempting to take Darrik's legs and force him to the ground.

As he lunged, Darrik's knee came up and met his face faster than he could blink. Chael could hear the sickening crunch as his nose was broken, and he spun to the ground in pain. Thick streams of blood poured from his nostrils, and for a moment he was blinded by the pain and surprise of his failed grapple. It took several seconds for him to gather the wherewithal to look down and notice the practice sword tip touching his chest, cementing Darrik's victory.

"Kill!" the arms master cried from somewhere behind him.

Sounds about right, Chael thought ruefully as his head slumped back down.

Like all the so-called Republics of Sharaad, Kazaam was essentially just a large city state that controlled most of the surrounding land. At one time, most of them had truly been republics, with elected ministers and a loose confederation between the cities. Now, however, the term "republic" was simply a jest the high houses told themselves for amusement. The high houses of the cities "elected" themselves with games of treachery, bribery, and assassination every three years until one house was able to cement a firm enough position to confirm themselves the winner of that year's "election." After which, the patriarch of the winning house would be sworn in as High Minister.

Between election seasons, some of the smaller houses would inevitably try to better their position in some way, but overt action was considered unseemly by the more powerful houses. The time between elections was a time to scheme and forge alliances and otherwise work in the shadows. Many of the wealthier houses funded small private armies or trained assassins, but bloodshed outside of an election was considered unfair and was harshly dealt with by those with the most power. Chael's eighteenth birthday coincided with the first anniversary of a particularly eventful election.

"You almost had me yesterday, you know that right?"

Darrik and Chael were slowly walking down a side alley in the market district of Kazaam. Chael snorted in derision and immediately regretted the action as a sharp needle of pain shot up his nose.

"I mean it," Darrik insisted. He leaned in conspiratorially before adding, "I hit you by accident. I thought you were preparing to dodge backwards, and I was trying to press my attack. I knew I couldn't keep it up much longer, so I tried to end it right there." He chuckled softly before adding, "you ran right into my knee as I lunged forward."

That his defeat and broken nose were the product of pure chance did not lighten Chael's dark mood. Darrik caught Chael glowering and quickly added, "but, if I hadn't gotten lucky you would have taken me to the ground for sure, I don't know what I would have done."

He smiled at Chael reassuringly and clapped him on the shoulder. Chael started the night determined to be in bad humor but couldn't help but crack a small smile as they walked.

Before long, they came to their destination, The Winged Stallion alehouse, named for a local legend regarding a suspiciously successful racehorse. *A bit on the nose,* Chael thought, considering the business alleged to be conducted out of the basement of the alehouse.

"Alright," Darrik whispered, turning to Chael. "I'll go in, you follow me in twenty minutes or so."

"Twenty minutes!" Chael huffed; he certainly didn't plan on waiting around in the shadows for that long.

"We can't be seen coming in together you dolt!" Darrik chided Chael. "Besides, I'm not the one who got his nose broken."

Chael was about to fire back a retort, reminding Darrik that his injury was simply bad luck, but Darrik was already heading inside the alehouse, snickering at his expense. Chael let out an exasperated breath and moved away from the entrance of the pub and into the shadows where he could hide.

After he had broken his nose, the master of the school had asked to see him and Darrik and had given them this mission. It was the first time Chael had met the man who technically owned him. Minister Khalim House Ourda was tall and slender and had an especially long hooked nose. He wore no special ornamentation to mark his station, just a plain white tunic and brown trousers. But the one thing that stood out about the man were his eyes, fiercely intelligent and eternally unforgiving orbs of dark brown.

As Chael stood crouched in the shadows, he remembered the intensity of those eyes as he was given his mission. He suppressed a shudder that he told himself was simply due to the cold night air.

After what he hoped was twenty minutes, Chael emerged from the shadows and stalked over to the door of the Winged Stallion. He collected his thoughts and attempted to steady his nerves and then pushed into the alehouse.

The interior was hazy from several smokers, and it took Chael a moment for his eyes to adjust to the greater light of the alehouse compared to the dark market outside. The walls were rough cut gray stone with several wooden pillars that braced the walls and arched up to the ceiling. By Chael's count, there were roughly a dozen tables scattered around the large common area of the alehouse, and on the opposite wall from the door was the bar.

In his quick scan of the room, he estimated that there were approximately fifteen patrons, the barman, and one woman making the rounds around the room distributing drinks. As Chael strode into the alehouse, he affected a whiny sneer and an uneasy, drunken gait.

"Hey, you!" Chael pointed an accusatory finger across the room to where Darrik sat drinking an ale. "You broke my nose, you lousy bastard!"

He took several more stumbling steps, intentionally spilling the drink of a patron to his right. Chael did his best attempt at slurring his speech before adding, "Come here so I can kick your ruddy ass!"

Chael stole the mug from the man he had bumped and elbowed him in the gut for good measure. He gave the room one last scan, picking the target that looked the most likely to take such a thing personally and hurled the mug at the man's shoulder. He wanted the man angry, not unconscious.

At that moment, the man he had elbowed shoved him into the table next to him. Chael allowed the momentum of the push to throw him into even more bystanders. Chael made a show of uneasily regaining his feet and stood shaking as no less than seven of the bar's patrons encircled him.

Not enough, Chael grimaced. He took a steadying breath, weighing his ever-decreasing options before the serious-looking men would reach him and he'd fight. He caught sight of the serving woman five paces behind and slightly to the left of the man he had hit with the ale mug.

Chael reached into his boot and pulled out on his daggers. *Forgive me,* he sighed, and threw the blade just past the man's ear as it spun and struck the woman in the arm.

For a moment, the approaching men stopped and stared dumbfounded at the blood seeping through the blouse of the injured serving woman. There were some things one simply didn't do, even in a seedy alehouse secretly run by one of Kazaam's most notorious gangs.

Chael heard the screeching of several chairs as the majority of the other patrons rose and planned on joining the beating they were about to inflict on the poor drunk. From the back, he heard a distinctly familiar voice call out.

"He's insane! Get him, lads! Before he bleeds anyone else!"

Subtle, Chael huffed as the first contender for the lady's honor emerged from the circling pack. He stretched his neck and prepared for the predictable opening attack.

As Chael predicted, the man launched a hard right fist at his temple. He deftly dodged the punch, allowing the man to overextend and used his momentum to heave the man into a table.

Chael immediately went on the offensive. These men were drunken brawlers at best, but if they managed to actually surround him, he was going to take a rather unpleasant beating.

He immediately sidestepped to put himself in front of the left-most member of the small mob, using him as a shield to stave off the others. He was a gangly red-haired man, and he eyed Chael uneasily.

The red-haired man punched at Chael with an unsteady arm, far too slow to make contact. Chael ducked underneath the feeble attempt and came up with an uppercut to the man's jaw, knocking him from his feet.

Chael continued sidestepping, avoiding their encirclement and selected his next victim. This time it was a shorter, pudgier man, a little too eager to step up to the challenge. He timed a kick just as the hefty bar patron planted his right foot, full weight coming down with the stride. Chael heard the awful crunch followed by a pitiful scream as the man's knee bent backward and the fat man fell to the floor.

Upon seeing this, three of the men fled out the front door of the alehouse. *Probably off to fetch the watch. Darkness!* Chael had to hurry this along.

"Ten minutes!" Chael shouted to Darrik, who was trying to hide out of sight from the fray.

Chael reached inside his cloak and pulled out two more daggers and threw them in quick succession at the drunken brawlers. One dagger sunk up to the hilt in the arm of an attacker and the other merely grazed a man's thigh. Both should be nonlethal; he had a mission to complete but didn't desire to kill any of these men.

The daggers successfully created an opening in the throng and Chael spied the man at whom he had thrown the mug. He was tall and lean and had several tattoos snaking up bare arms. From the way he held himself, Chael could tell that professionally the man engaged in some kind of soldiery. When Chael had first arrived in the alehouse, he had marked this man as the alpha in the room. The man, from whom the others would take the lead even if they didn't know him.

Chael charged, parrying a jab with his elbow and throwing a hook punch into the man's side, breaking several ribs. He dodged the retaliatory strike and followed with a straight punch to the man's temple, another shot at his side, and a front kick to the man's sternum, knocking him from his feet. The soldier, or whatever he was, laid on the ground moaning, making no attempt to stand.

The rest of Chael's would-be attackers took that as their sign to seek accommodations elsewhere and bolted from the alehouse. Now the real fight could begin.

As they predicted, a trapdoor burst open from behind the bar and several armed men came filing out. Hardened soldiers of the four fingers gang, so named for their territory at the convergence of the four tributary rivers that snaked through the lower quarter of the city. Though Chael could already see that at least two of them had taken their gang's namesake a bit literally.

The fight didn't last long. Just as the criminals converged on Chael, Darrik emerged from the shadows where he had managed to conceal himself in the cacophony of the bar brawl. He cut two of the men down before they could react and Chael was able to quickly fell a third, slicing his neck with a dagger in the momentary confusion.

This left Darrik and Chael with one man each. Darrik began with his customary powerful arcing blows and beat his opponent into submission before stabbing him in the chest. Chael's opponent roared a fierce battle cry and charged Chael with a broad-headed ax. Chael threw his remaining dagger, this time aiming true, and it sunk into his attacker's throat.

Chael watched as the man stumbled forward and then fell on his face, his neck intermittently spurting out gobs of viscous blood. Darrik spared him a glance, raising an eyebrow at the side; Chael merely shrugged.

They had precious few minutes to finish their mission until the city watch would arrive. Anonymity was paramount to the task they had been given. Khalim had discovered that one of his rival ministers was using the four fingers gang to amass wealth as well as strike out at other high house scions with the deniability of simple street violence. This act could not be traced back to their master or he would have their heads.

Chael entered the trapdoor first, sliding down the ladder and landing softly in the basement of The Winged Stallion. He entered a narrow hallway dimly lit by distant torches. Chael proceeded cautiously, wary of any more members of the gang that didn't respond to the commotion above. Behind him, he heard a thud as Darrik barreled in after him.

"Oaf!" Chael spat quietly, which earned him a nudge in the ribs. He smiled as he continued forward, scanning every shadow for threats.

The hall opened up into a large common room where they found another member of the gang. He was sitting on a large comfortable looking sofa underneath the torches that dimly lit the hall that led to the trapdoor. He stood, confused, as the pair emerged from the shadows, not sure at first if they were his comrades or strangers.

Chael rushed him, closing the distance before he could properly react, and plunged his dagger into the man's chest while covering his mouth with his left hand. Chael held the dying man in his arms, muffling the man's screams in a stiff, choking hug and watched as the life faded from his eyes. He set the man down gently and breathed a sigh of relief that the man hadn't called out an alarm.

Just then, he felt a small tingle in his arm as if he had slept on it. The feeling spread to his other limbs, but just as quickly as it had come, it faded with his following breath. He glanced at his hands; the ache and soreness of the fight above was replaced by new strength as he flexed his fingers. Chael caught a suspicious look from Darrik and immediately dropped his hands and looked around the room.

They found what they were looking for in an adjacent office. Several letters implicating a high house minister in the criminal affairs of the Four Fingers gang, as well as a strong box laden with valuables. They took as many valuables as they could carry, and Chael stashed the letters into one of the many pockets of his green cloak. Their mission complete, they used the torches from the common room to light the place ablaze and fled up the ladder, out of the alehouse, and into the night.

When they had made it a few leagues away from The Winged Stallion and felt reasonably safe, Darrik turned to Chael.

"Hey!" Darrik said, concern coloring his voice. "Are you alright, down there with that guard, you seemed..." Darrik struggled to find the right word. "Different," he finally managed.

"I'm fine," Chael replied casually. "In fact, I don't really feel anything."

Darrik looked at his friend, still clearly concerned.

"Come on," Chael asserted before Darrik could say anything else. "It's a long journey and we still have to sneak by the gate if we're gonna get out of the city tonight. I want to make it back before sunup."

Chael gave Darrik a look that didn't brook any dissension and the two quickly headed toward the city gate.

Chapter 6

Present Day

The terrain through the Western Forest was even rougher than Chael remembered. Or at least it felt rougher when in the company of, at best, unenthusiastic foresters.

Chael took up the lead and had immediately begun to forge a path through the wilderness. It still amazed him how dark the place could get while almost completely shrouded by the dense canopy of trees. Yet despite the dark and foreboding nature of the wood, the Great Western Forest wasn't without beauty. Most things were covered in a lush, vibrant green interspersed with flecks of purple and yellow. There were giant creepers that snaked up the giant trees and mushrooms large enough to sit on grew from their trunks.

Stupid! Chael cursed himself. He had been reckless worrying about Michik; the wolf was not easy prey, even for a demon this large. or whatever a demon had—was departed, banished back to the Dark where its kind was from.

"It really is beautiful in the right light isn't it."

Chael did his best to conceal the start the speaker gave him and turned his head to look. Sir Andon had managed to come up beside him undetected.

"Yes, I suppose it is," Chael replied, mildly irritated that Sir Andon had apparently guessed at what he was thinking. "How are the others fairing? Sister Aelisa?"

Sir Andon gave a slight chuckle, "oh, the sister is a great deal stronger than she looks. The Baron, however..." Sir Andon trailed off as the two simultaneously looked back down the trail to where they could just barely see the Baron shambling along through the underbrush.

Chael stifled a laugh as he examined the growing shape of Baron Janus. He had eschewed traditional traveler's garb and was wearing a flowing ermine coat over purple silk pants and matching slippers. The coat would probably keep him reasonably warm as the days of autumn marched steadily into winter, but that only mattered if the coat survived the journey. Thus far, the Baron had managed to catch it on every twig, burr, and cobweb that adjoined their makeshift path.

"An impressive sight, the good Baron. Is he not?" Andon asked Chael with a knowing smile.

Chael returned the smile and responded, "Indeed, I had no idea Baron Janus was such an accomplished woodsman."

Andon raised an eyebrow, unsure of Chael's meaning.

"A few more hours collecting sticks and foliage and the Baron will have assembled himself some fairly impressive camouflage."

Andon looked at Chael for a moment and burst out in a fit of laughter; Chael couldn't help but join in. Despite his amusement at the Baron's struggles, Chael was concerned. They'd only be able to put in about a half day's trek through the forest today, but the Baron was already showing signs of deep fatigue. He could already tell Baron's slippers were going to cost him dearly come nightfall. He was already moving slow enough without a patch of blisters covering his feet.

The Baron's guards weren't doing too much better than their liege lord. They all wore studded armor and mail and had to carry not just their own supplies, but those of the Baron as well. The foursome had not taken long to fall behind, and were huffing and tromping around with an unsettling amount of noise.

To Andon's credit, he had ditched the plate armor normally worn by those of his station. He wore sensible trousers and boots and a plain cream-colored shirt under a traveler's cloak. He did opt for a thick leather vest, but it was unobtrusive and probably fairly light.

Chael resumed the task of forging a usable path through the underbrush. This time with Andon by his side, helping to make a slightly wider path for the encumbered noble behind them.

"Say, where has your wolf gotten to? I haven't seen any trace of the beast since we entered the forest." Chael soured slightly at the word beast but let it go, Sir Andon seemed to mean well enough.

"He's patrolling the perimeter of the forest around our passage. If we don't see him all day that's a good sign, it means he hasn't found any demons on our trail." He glanced back at the ponderous baron and his trio of lumbering guardsmen and bitterly added, "yet."

Andon nodded, clearly impressed by the capabilities of the wolf, but still more than a little discomforted by it.

"And where did you come across such a creature?" Andon asked.

Chael sighed, "His name is Michik, and he's currently engaged in keeping you safe from the terrors of this forest."

Sir Andon blushed at the small rebuke and quickly cut in, "My apologies Goodman Chael. He truly is an impressive specimen and clearly means a great deal to you, I meant no offense."

"It's fine, I'm a little too sensitive about him I guess..." Chael paused. "Goodman?"

"It's proper protocol for a knight to address people by appropriate title and well, I'm not sure what that would be in your case."

Chael snorted derisively. "Trust me, 'Goodman' is not an appropriate title. 'Chael' is fine."

Sir Andon nodded curtly.

"As for Michik," Chael continued, "I found him in a place not too dissimilar from this." He gestured all around him as they walked. "I had occasion to be in the Aazeran Forest when I came across a shewolf and a litter of dead pups. The wolf mother attacked me as I unknowingly neared the den."

Chael's eyes took on a distant, sad glow before adding, "I'm not sure why she was so aggressive towards me, perhaps it was grief for her dead children, I can't be sure. But I had to kill her. When I investigated the den, I found one little gray welp still clinging to life." Chael smiled at the memory.

Sir Andon nodded again before adding, "and his face was that... erm..." Andon struggled to find the right words without offending Chael's protective sensibility regarding his dog. "Was that affectation present when you found him?"

Chael smiled at the stumbling knight. "No, his injuries are a more recent concern."

An awkward silence fell between them at that moment. Chael could tell that Sir Andon wanted to ask more about Michik, more about himself and the powers that he possessed. Chael didn't trust his traveling companions enough to share all that he could do or the price it took to accomplish. Sir Andon would be far more familiar with alchemists of the order. Through the manipulation of chemicals and herbs, they could do a number of incredible things. And while alchemists could manifest incredible power, it was simply nothing like what Chael could accomplish.

His companions all had some knowledge of his abilities and his connection to his undead wolf. They suspected his gifts came from the Dark, but none knew the full extent of the awful truth of the matter.

The origin of his abilities was death, or perhaps more accurately, the power released when a soul is severed from living tissue. He hated the cruel necessity of extinguishing life to fuel himself, but what he hated most was the feeling of emptiness when he did it. Every time he drew upon that well, he seemed to care less about the cost and that was what truly frightened him.

Chael turned back to Andon, wanting to break the uneasy tension that had filled the space between them.

"So," he asked the knight. "How did you end up with a Sister of The Order?"

"That," Sir Andon replied brusquely. "I'm not some Order zealot if that's what you were thinking. When this Darrik fellow told the King about a potential war, a series of scouts were sent to confirm if men were massing in the East. None of those men returned to confirm his story. The King became unnerved enough to convene a war council and so he needed to assemble the Barons."

Sir Andon paused his story for a moment before adding, "You know it's only recently that the seat of the western barony is in Ehbing? The reason is you, apparently. Nobody was quite sure why shipments down the Amberwyne stopped being molested so often by demons. But it was important enough that Janus set up shop in Ehbing to more appropriately oversee the increased traffic of shipped goods."

"And collect the substantial new taxes," interjected Chael. They both chuckled a bit at that.

"Anyway," Andon continued, "the King was still worried about missing scouts and despite the improvement these last years, everyone is still hesitant to sail up the river through the Dark Forest. So, King Inarus…"

"Your uncle." Chael cut in. Sir Andon smiled.

"Yes, my uncle. He asked his knights for volunteers to carry the summons of war to the Western Barony. I volunteered." Andon sighed before continuing, "Sister Aelisa caught me just before I departed. She said the living stars bid that she join me on my quest and handed me this."

He reached into his pack and picked out a slightly crumpled piece of parchment and handed it to Chael. On the top was the seal of the King and below it simply read:

Lifeless because of him, Chael mused.Can't let them see you dealing with the town spook, Chael thought as he was quickly conducted by a timid house servant to the third level of the keep and into the lord's apartments.

Damn, Chael thought. The Baron probably had a point there. Chael fought back the retort that had flown to his lips. He was annoyed that the Baron had figured him so well. A carpenter I am not, he thought out loud, looking at his questionable work. He turned to look down the path that led from his home and into the forest towards Ehbing. After a moment, he was also able to hear the approach of at least several people and a horse which had set off the keen senses of his dog.

Chael handed the parchment back to Sir Andon, "Does the order have that power in the capitol these days?" The knight shrugged.

"They've been gathering more influence the last few years. The Prefect of the Fhaerhold chapter, Aelisa's direct superior, has a seat on the Kings council now. They supply Fhaerhold's legion with alchemists and apparently they've now begun assisting interrogations."

Chael immediately thought back to Sister Aelisa's story about the man claiming to be Darrik. When he had fled West, he was certain nobody from his previous life had known where he ended up. But he had hardly managed to keep a low profile like he had planned. Sir Andon broke him out of his momentary reverie as he continued.

"Thus far they haven't really exerted any political power in the capitol but across the Kingdom more and more people are flocking to their chapter halls. Everywhere it seems, Dark tidings are upon us, and the Order of Celestial Light offers succor."

Chael nodded, his own dealings with the Order were few. They were not overly popular in the Republics and Ehbing had no chapter house. Though outwardly benign, Chael didn't trust people who practiced alchemy.

"Alright, I think that's enough travel for today!" the horse voice of Baron Janus called from the rear of the group. Chael turned around, glancing at the struggling noble and then looked up. The light that broke through the dense canopy indeed was beginning to dim. They had maybe an hour of good daylight left, and Chael had to admit that it would be prudent to use it to make camp.

Chapter 7

Present Day

After a quick search Chael and Michik managed to find a suitably open area to make a camp. Janus's guardsmen immediately got to work erecting a tent for their patron and Sir Andon prepared a small tent for Sister Aelisa.

Chael volunteered to acquire firewood for the night's supper. He took a small woodsman's ax out of his pack and slapped his thigh twice indicating that Michik should follow. As he made his way to leave the small clearing and go back into the dark overgrowth, Sister Aelisa called to him.

"You aren't leaving the camp are you Chael? Surely you can find firewood right here within sight of the rest of us?"

"I saw a downed tree around two hundred feet away back toward our trail," Chael lied. "That should make for better firewood." Aelisa immediately frowned at him.

"Odd," She replied coolly, "I don't recall seeing any dead or fallen trees near our trail."

"I guess you must have missed it," Chael answered, beginning to lose his temper. "Afraid for my safety sister?"

"Oh no, I'm sure you can handle yourself out there in the dark just fine. I'm merely concerned for the rest of us if a demon comes out of the trees while you're away." She managed to put on an innocent face and the tone of her voice softened significantly with the last comment. *She is probably used to giving orders and being obeyed,* Chael guessed.

"I won't be gone long and besides," Chael added, forcing a fake smile to his lips. "You have four able bodied protectors to keep you plenty safe while I'm gone."

Before she could say another word, he turned his back and strode briskly into the dark tree line. He continued for about two hundred feet, as he had told the sister, but he didn't find any dead trees. He just needed an excuse to come out and seek privacy to use his abilities.

He found a relatively young tree, its branches and trunk not quite reaching the upper canopy of the forest. Chael concentrated on the tree, breathed in, and reached out with his senses. He could feel its life force pulsating along the branches down the trunk and into the roots. It was far more subtle than animal life, but he could feel its life, its soul if that was even the right word.

Chael reached out with his power and tore the soul asunder. The reaction was immediate. Curled brown leaves began falling from the surrounding branches like snow. The trunk creaked and groaned as it drained of fluid and shrank. After only a few heartbeats, the entire tree was gray, dry, and lifeless.

Chael felt the familiar jolt of strength and energy as he stole the energy of the now dead tree. There wasn't much and it would have taken significantly more if he had to fight another demon like the one from earlier that week.

Chael also felt the emptiness that using the power always left within him. The greater feeling of power he absorbed the greater his sense of detachment became, as if using this gift separated him from the rest of humanity.

The feeling, or lack of feeling, eventually faded after each use of the power, but Chael feared for a day when it wouldn't, so he used it sparingly. He regretted its necessity today, but it would give him the strength to quickly reduce the tree to firewood and hopefully leave enough left over to help keep him awake during his watch tonight. It also conveniently gave him easy access to dry-dead lumber which genuinely was superior firewood.

Chael hacked away at the trunk. Every stroke enhanced by the tree's own life, helping to fell it to the ground. The irony was not lost on Chael.

Suddenly, Michik stood up, tail erect, sniffing at the air. Chael looked at him intensely; even enhanced, his own senses paled in comparison to his dog's.

After a moment, Michik turned to Chael, barked once and took off in the direction of the camp. Chael collected his ax and sprinted after his dog, using the energy he had already taken to fuel his legs and keep up with the wolf.

After a few seconds of running, they burst into the clearing where their party had made camp. Sir Andon gave him a confused look, but all Chael could manage was to point at where Michik was headed as the two of them sprinted past.

Michik darted into the Baron's tent a second in front of Chael. He heard the Baron yelp and Michik growl heartbeats before diving through the opening himself, passing right between two confused spearmen.

Michik had immediately engaged an attacker that went after the Baron. The wolf's powerful jaws were clamped around the head of a giant insect as another one snapped impressive black pincer-like mandibles at his flank. They had long tubular bodies covered in red and yellow chitin about eight feet long and another as wide. Along their sides they had seemingly hundreds of hairy black legs that propelled them along the floor of the tent in a disturbing snake-like weave. Michik had bitten the one that was latched onto one of the Baron's bloody blister strewn feet, preventing it from moving any further up his leg.

Chael used the last of the energy from the tree and infused his leg with all the strength he could muster and kicked the other creature across the tent. He then took up his ax in a strong two-handed grip and brought it down as hard as he could in the middle of the squirming body of the insect. The Chitinous shell of the bug crunched but held under the blow.

Chael brought the ax down again and again, orange ichor splattering the walls of the tent. He hammered the creature with his ax, crushing and splitting it until the thing fell into two squirming halves. The second one had already started snaking along the floor after Chael before he had even finished killing its mate. Chael braced defensively with his ax as it lunged at him with unnatural speed. But before it could reach him, a long sword came crashing down on it, swatting it out of the air and severing one of the arms of its giant mandible.

Sir Andon immediately pressed his attack, laying blow after blow of his fine longsword on the creature till it stopped squirming and lay still.

Chael patted Michik on the back, indicating it was ok to let the creature go. "Good boy," he praised the wolf as he gave his ears a quick scratch.

Michik dropped the head of the giant insect, its jaw still clamped around the Baron's foot. Chael and Sir Andon both heaved at the maw, prying it apart until the dead creature finally surrendered Janus's limb. Baron Janus, for his part, had been remarkably calm up to this point; but upon seeing the mutilated remains of his left foot, he began to wail uncontrollably.

At that moment, Sister Aelisa entered the tent flanked by two sheepish looking guardsmen. She quickly surveyed the scene blanching slightly at the orange slime dripping from the walls and ceiling. When she noticed the Baron's foot, she quickly got to work, ordering the guardsmen to fetch various herbs and strips of sterile cloth from her pack. Chael and Sir Andon took that opportunity to slip out and leave the sister to her work.

"What in Darkness were those things?" Sir Andon burst out after they had extricated themselves from the tent.

"I don't know that they have a name," Chael replied frankly. "I've seen them a few times while out hunting. They seem to enjoy pursuing wounded game. I'm guessing they could track the Baron's bloody feet. The recent increase in demon activity has probably threatened their food source, making them more aggressive. They've never attacked a human before as far as I know."

Sir Andon mulled over Chael's words for a moment before speaking. "Increased demon activity?" He finally asked, a tiny, almost imperceptible tremor in his voice.

"I've killed more demons in the last six months than in the previous three years," Chael replied. "And they're getting bigger." Andon did his best to hide a shudder.

Chael didn't blame him; the knight was brave, but not foolish. Though the varieties that generally haunted the Great Western Forest were called lesser demons, that didn't mean they weren't extraordinarily dangerous. Even the smallest of the specimens were well over seven feet tall and were several times stronger than an average man. They often used small boulders or tree branches as weapons, but on occasion would scavenge real weapons from any unfortunate traveler they happened upon.

The only positive aspect was that until recently they didn't appear in great numbers, and they rarely left the borders of the Dark Forest.

"How do you suppose the Baron will fare?" Sir Andon managed after a long moment.

"Most of his foot seemed intact but it was hard to tell, " Chael replied with a shrug. "I'm guessing the sister is reasonably skilled at healing. I think it's standard training in the Order."

"Aye," responded Sir Andon, nodding. "All initiates receive extensive training in the art of healing as their first lesson in alchemy. That way they can weed out any potential problem students before teaching them anything more dangerous."

"Smart," Chael replied offhandedly. On the other side of the camp, he spied the only spearman not currently being used by Sister Aelisa. "Excuse me a moment, Sir Andon," he said to the knight as he stalked over to the third spearman who was, at the time, doing his best to remain out of sight in the growing darkness of the camp.

"You there!" he called to the lilting guard. "I never bothered asking your name, what is it?" The guardsman was becoming visibly pale even in the waning light of the day.

"Erm… Antos, my um sir," the scared guard managed to stammer.

"No need for sirs dear Antos," Chael replied with false congeniality. "I was just wondering, were you always a craven weakling or was today just special?" A flash of anger appeared across Antos' face but quickly faded as Chael came closer. "Where were you while your lord was being eaten by an insect, hmm?"

Antos stammered and blustered, but was unable to come up with a coherent justification for his absence.

Chael gave him a snarl of disgust before continuing, "You three are going to stand watch in shifts tonight. If I have to wake in the middle of the night to cover for your incompetence, I'm going to feed you to the wolf."

He pointed back at Michik who was sitting on his haunches next to Sir Andon, glowing eyes boring straight into those of the cowardly guard.

"Take heart, Antos," Chael continued after a moment. "You may yet have the chance to redeem yourself this evening." He gave the stricken guardsman a final wink and called Michik with a whistle.

He walked calmly toward the trees and called over his shoulder, "I'm going to fetch the firewood I left behind. Try not to get eaten while I'm gone."

Chael gazed into the flames of the campfire, watching the flickering bursts of light and heat as the fire rose and fell. The camp had died down for the night; Aelisa was still tending to the Baron, attempting to save his foot, Sir Andon had retired to a bedroll and the three guardsmen had worked out night watches.

Chael sat alone save for Michik who was blissfully snoring next to him. Whether the wolf needed breath or if he even had functional lungs was a question to which Chael didn't want to know the answer. Nevertheless, his dog laid contentedly snoring, nuzzled at his feet.

"Are you not tired?"

Chael's head shot up looking at the speaker. It was Aelisa. She had apparently finished her ministrations on Janus and sat next to him by the fire.

"I don't tend to sleep very much," Chael explained, "and the night's excitement has left me with some excess energy I suppose. Speaking of which, how does the Baron fare?"

Aelisa sighed and took a long breath before answering. "He has lost his great toe and small portion of the surrounding tissue. He will certainly live; I've managed to staunch the bleeding and my poultice should stop it from festering. However, I don't know how he will continue through the wilderness on one leg."

Chael had been mulling over that problem as well. The sensible thing to do was to turn around and help Janus shamble out of the Dark Forest and back into his keep to heal. But Chael was as invested as any of them at this point. He had to get to the capitol and find the truth of this person using Darrik's name.

"I suppose we'll have to build him a litter. On two legs the Baron could hardly make it across the forest, I don't think simply giving him a crutch will work. And if I'm being honest, he was moving so slow on his own I think carrying him may actually prove to be quicker." Sister Aelisa let out a small giggle and immediately put her hand to her mouth, covering a smile. Chael thought it may have been the first honest emotion she had displayed on their journey, other than some occasional flashes of genuine disgust. Chael allowed the mutual mirth to hang in the air for a moment while he continued to stare into the flames. At length he interrupted the amiable silence, "tell me Sister Aelisa. Why did you come all the way out here to this cursed place?"

Aelisa exhaled slowly and responded, "I thought it was rather obvious. Sir Andon came here to fetch the Baron so that Janus may report to the King the strength of arms he can levy in case of any actual war. I came here to fetch you, and I am equally as interested in the strength you have available to muster. I suppose you thought that the Dark Forest would hide you away from the world. And indeed it may have, but tales of a mysterious cloaked warrior hunting demons alone in the cursed Western Forest were bound to leak out. And leak they did."

Aelisa smiled at him again, this time displaying none of the genuine emotion of a moment ago. It was a practiced if not unkind but mechanical gesture. "Then there is the matter of the animal," she added flatly, pointing at Michik with an aged finger. "That particular rumor raised many questions and when this stranger appeared he seemed to confirm at least some of the rumor. I was asked to investigate; we feared that there was a plot by Dark worshiping cultists." Aelisa once again displayed authentic disgust at the mention of hypothetical Dark cultists. But the mention of the man claiming to be Darrik grabbed his attention.

"What did this man look like?" Chael asked, doing his best to keep his tone neutral. He didn't want to give anything away to the sister just yet.

"Tall," she began. "Much taller than you, and broad of shoulder. His face was a mask of old scars and all over his body he…" Aelisa stopped herself before describing any more. She looked up at the sky for a moment as if searching for guidance from whatever power she believed resided there and added, "he had a shaved head."

Chael thought for a moment; "big and tall" certainly fit the description of his old friend. The shaved head was new, but not necessarily dispositive. *What did she not want to say?* Chael wondered.

They sat once again in silence. Chael continued to stare into the fire while Aelisa opted to return her gaze to the heavens. For several moments, they both quietly kept to their own thoughts until the stillness was broken by Michik. The wolf snorted loudly, waking himself up as well as jarring Chael and Aelisa out of their quiet contemplation. Michik looked around for a moment. He quickly found Chael and nuzzled his scarred snout under his master's hand.

Chael smiled and scratched his dog's ears. Once again, he mused on the physical connection his skin and ears had to long dead nerves and whether Michik enjoyed the sensation or simply enjoyed the affection. He glanced up and saw Sister Aelisa studying the wolf with icy focused eyes. After a long moment, she cleared her throat and spoke.

"Have you ever heard the name Tenebrian?"

"Tenebrian?" Chael repeated, rolling the unfamiliar name around on his tongue. "I don't believe so." Aelisa nodded, finally raising her eyes from Michik.

"There are few who have. Fewer still who believe he actually existed. I heard the Baron's men call you Darkborn when we first met, it's ironic because that is where the story of Tenebrian begins.

"The legend tells of a war between the forces of the Dark and those who follow the light of the living stars. A battle of gods played out here in our world. At its pinnacle, the two sides delivered champions into the mortal realm. Two men blessed with echoes of the power of the gods themselves. They are referred to in the histories as the Darkborn and the Star born."

Chael suppressed a laugh as he searched Aelisa's face for any hint of jest, but there was none. The sister of the Order was absolutely sincere and, as far as Chael could tell, she was one of the people who believed this story to be true.

"Tenebrian," Aelisa continued, "was said to be this Darkborn. He led his followers on a crusade that engulfed the continent in blood and death. The stories have little to say about his origins except to say that outwardly he appeared as a normal man, and he came not from any noble house of the time. However…" Aelisa's eyes became even more intense as she stared directly into Chael's. "The stories are all of accord on two points as it pertains to Tenebrian. He had striking, some say glowing, azure eyes."

She paused, expecting Chael's stunned reaction before continuing. "And it was written that he could raise the dead to fight his enemies." Chael looked down at Michik and back at the zealous priestess, stunned by her frank implications. Aelisa simply stared back at him, expressionless save for the steel in her eyes.

"Sister," Chael managed after recovering from his shock. "Are you suggesting that I am some Dark demi-god here to destroy the world?" Before she could answer, Michik snorted loudly again, as ever Chael was amazed by the wolf's timing.

"No, of course not," Sister Aelisa responded, once again donning the cold mechanical smile. "These are stories describing events centuries or perhaps even thousands of years old, we aren't really sure. There probably was a man named Tenebrian and he most likely fought a bloody and vicious war. Was he some Dark scion here to end the world? I seriously doubt it, but he may very well have consorted with Dark powers to help his cause. And we do know that demons are quite real, don't we?"

Her face visibly softened, and Chael could sense that she was making an effort to be less severe. "Now imagine my curiosity when the rumors and tales of your exploits come to my ears." This time, her smile almost appeared sincere as she studied Chael's face.

Chael wasn't sure he believed her, and he knew he didn't trust the odd priestess, but the notion that she may genuinely believe he was some Dark champion was preposterous. *I've probably killed more Dark spawn than any other man alive,* he thought bitterly.

"So, what happened?" Chael pressed, curiosity overcoming his previous bewilderment.

"Well," Aelisa continued. "The stories refer to an alliance of the remainder of the human kingdoms and the elves."

"The elves?" Spat Chael incredulously.

"That is what the stories say. It would seem that this Tenebrian was a threat to them as well. Some of the tales even claim that it was the elves who first taught alchemy to our ancestors and that my order was founded by their descendants. But certitude has been lost with the centuries. Many of the stories have conflicting histories in some of their elements."

Aelisa once again turned her head to stare at the stars, a pensive look appearing on her face. It was clear that lack of certainty bothered her deeply, she wanted answers and she had traveled all the way to the Western Forest to find some. Her gaze lingered on the stars for several seconds before returning her eyes to Chael and continuing. "All the stories agree on one final point. The armies of Tenebrian, both living and dead, clashed with the armies of men and elves in the northern reaches, now called the barrowlands. In the moment of greatest despair when all hope seemed lost, the Star born emerged from the human faction and the army of the Dark was vanquished."

Chael joined her stare at the sky, bemused. The Dark was real enough. Even if the demons didn't serve as proof, he could feel its pull in this forest. There was something primordial and hateful that seemed to filter up through the ground, as if whatever layer of reality that separated the mortal realm from theirs was thin in this place. Thin enough for creatures to slip through from the other side. Its presence corrupted the natural creatures of the forest, twisting them into terrifying forms like those he encountered in the Baron's tent. But if a similar force existed—one that acted in an opposing fashion to the Dark—he had never seen it manifest. Hate seemed like a much more natural manifestation in the world than any other force.

At least they untied my feet, he thought bitterly. Damn demons, Chael grumbled to himself.

"So, Sister Aelisa Treadmane, second prefect of the Fhaerhold chapter of the Fraternal Order of Celestial Light," Chael recited, invoking her honorific title. "You have met me, broken bread with me, and seen me fight. Am I the monster of your stories, am I perhaps the heaven-sent help to vanquish all evil, or…"

Chael paused for a moment attempting to emphasize his final statement. He allowed a hard edge to show in his voice, not quite anger but indignation. "… Or perhaps I'm just a peculiar man who lives alone with his dog in a haunted forest and would much rather that the wars and worries of the world pass him by."

Having said his peace, Chael got up and strolled over to his waiting bed roll. Michik, who generally had some sort of parting gesture for people like Aelisa, padded quickly after Chael, his tail unusually still and hanging limply between his legs.

Sister Aelisa's words echoed in Chael's mind as he tried to fall asleep. Between ancient mythological demi-gods and the specters of long dead friends, it seemed the past was determined to make his present more miserable. He could feel the eyes of the Order priestess still upon him as he curled tightly in his bedroll, fighting off the autumn chill.

I hate people, he thought glumly as sleep finally overtook him.

Chapter 8

11 Years Ago

Chael looked around the empty barrack of the school where he had spent most of his childhood. School didn't really seem an appropriate word for what was done here, but that is what the others had always called it.

Over the years of harsh training and harsher circumstances, the pool of youths that called this place home had fallen to a mere two dozen. Two dozen hardened killers. Chael looked down at the torch in his hand and tossed it into the center of the room. The torch caught on the oil-soaked floor and immediately took to flame.

A forge, Chael supposed. For in essence, that's what the school was. Minister Khalim bought forgotten and unwanted children and hauled them out to this small property in secret, not to educate them, as the word "school" implied. They were cast into a furnace and forged through fire into tools that served the cruel minister's needs. And those that couldn't serve were simply burned away by the flame. But now the tools would be brought to bear, and the survivors of Khalim's brutal school would finally emerge into the light. Election season had begun in Kazaam.

Chael rapped his fingers against his knees. He had been sitting in the study of Master Khalim's office for several hours waiting to greet his special guests, the esteemed representatives of the Black Hand, whatever that meant. Darrik and the others from the school had all been given assignments in the city. While he sat here literally twiddling his thumbs, they were out conducting espionage, fighting, and otherwise winning glory.

"Figures," he said aloud to the empty room. "Master Khalim sees that I'm the smallest so he assumes that I'm also the weakest. So now I greet visitors," Chael groaned as he dropped his head into his hands.

He had hoped to hit a late growth as he entered his twentieth year, but it had yet to materialize. As it was, he stood only a little over five feet tall. *I'll just have to prove my worth,* he thought.

The surrounding study was fairly simple for a man as high in station as his master. It was on the top floor of the apartments that Khalim kept inside the city. The walls were stone, as were most of the buildings in the city. A small bookshelf sat beside a fireplace and was ringed by several comfortable chairs. Chael imagined all the different meetings Master Khalim had held here over the years. Across the room was a large wooden door that led to his private office. Chael had never been inside.

Another hour ticked by, leaving Chael musing over how best he could prove his value over the others, when finally the door to the study pushed open. At first, all Chael could see was Master Khalim's servant Garold holding the door, but eventually, three figures strode confidently through the opening. Chael jumped to his feet and plastered on a wide smile that he only hoped wasn't too obviously fake.

"Welcome to the home of Minister Khalim," he said with false joviality. He turned to the servant, "that will be all Garold, thank you." As Garold took his leave, Chael took a moment to size up the mysterious visitors he had been asked to receive.

Striding confidently in the lead was a woman. She was tall and had flowing black hair that cascaded over a similarly black cloak. The hood of her cloak was pulled back and revealed a strikingly beautiful face and piercing green eyes. The other two were men, each around six feet tall, Chael reckoned. In the dim light of the study, he couldn't properly make out their faces under the hoods. However, one was clearly more heavily muscled. The other, thinner man had a series of blue runic tattoos on his hands and arms outlining strange symbols and writing Chael didn't recognize.

"Welcome honored guests to the home of Minister Khalim of House Ourda of the honored high houses of Kazaam." Over the hours of waiting, he had practiced that greeting more than a few times, dealing with people was not Chael's strong suit. The woman continued marching into the room and though they were roughly the same height, she still managed to somehow look down on him as she strode by saying nothing.

The thin man with the tattoos followed her past him as they walked right through the door of Master Khalim's office unannounced. Chael grimaced at the lack of protocol and made to go after them, but the large man barred his way.

"It is alright," the large man said, staying Chael with his hand. Chael flashed with sudden anger at the man, nearly slipping his dagger out of the hidden sheathe up his sleeve. The hooded man immediately sensed the tension and backed away half a step and held his arms up plaintively. "Easy there lad, your minister knows my mistress well enough, there's no offense here."

The man pulled back his hood revealing short brown hair and matching eyes and was otherwise completely unremarkable. "I do appreciate your fire," the man chuckled, revealing a broad white smile. Chael immediately felt ashamed at his rashness.

"I beg your pardon my lord," Chael quickly spat out.

"No lords here, son. Just call me Mason." The large man smiled and extended his hand. Chael accepted it, a smile beginning to creep across his own face.

"My name is Chael," he replied.

"Ah," Mason chimed merrily, "then you must be my guide." Chael gave the large man a confused look. Mason nodded once and added, "I'm staying in Kazaam to coordinate business between your master and mine. I was told that Minister Khalim would leave me a guide to show me around the city." Chael had received no such orders, but Master Khalim rarely deigned to explain himself very thoroughly.

"I must say that I'm a little confused," Chael commented, still blushing from his recent outburst. "Guide to what?"

"Your master has enlisted the services of our organization to provide him certain resources here in the city. I am going to stay here and help coordinate those resources." He gave Chael another broad smile.

He's patronizing me, Chael thought. He didn't like being spoken down to, the man was big and obviously strong, and Chael guessed he was used to intimidating people. But Chael had been exhaustively trained on how to deal with people who were bigger and stronger and felt quite confident about his odds should they come to blows. However, he had been ordered to play host, so he was largely impotent to teach Mason a lesson.

After a moment, Mason continued, "in order to do my duties I need to be better acquainted with Kazaam." He gave Chael a wry look, "acquainted with the social structure." He gave Chael a quick wink. Chael merely rolled his eyes, his irritation mounting.

Chael choked down his frustration long enough to say, "well, I suppose I need to educate you on the intricacies of the city."

Chael led Mason out onto one of the balconies that jutted out from the second floor of his master's apartments. Kazaam had been built on a large, gradually sloping hill at the foot of a mountain. The city was stratified by concentric rings that progressively moved up the hill. The houses occupying the highest places on the hill were also the houses that held the most influence.

It was commonplace for there to be a bit of familial shuffling up or down as a consequence of an election. The disparity in power and wealth could also be viewed as the layers of construction wound their way up the hill. At the bottom there were wooden shanties that served as crude homes or shops.

Chael pointed out the gang territories and other notable political segments of that poorest circle in the city. He looked on to where those rickety buildings quickly thinned out as they moved away from the city proper and gave way to leagues of farmland.

For a moment, his eyes lingered on the small tract of land that had been his home for so much of his childhood, hidden away anonymously amidst the surrounding agriculture.

"The first circle of stone," Chael continued, pointing down from where they stood, "houses the market district and is where we conduct most of our business." His finger drifted along the river and where it converged at the so-called four fingers before flowing outside the city.

He continued pointing out different political alliances and notable houses who controlled various segments of the rings that made up the city. The further he pointed up the hill, the more lavish and ornate the buildings became. His master's apartments here at nearly the highest level, though grand in their way, were positively spartan compared to some of the other buildings erected this far up. The grayish blue stone that was used for most of the lower layers of the city eventually turned into white marble that was quarried from high in the peaks of the nearby mountains.

"At last, we come to our primary opponents here in the city." Chael let out an exacerbated breath before continuing with his visual tour. He pointed to a large manse below the apartments of Minister Khalim. "That is the current residence of House Faasa. Their current patron is actually a woman."

"Is this rare?" Mason asked. It was the first question he had bothered asking since Chael began his impromptu presentation. Chael hesitated, thinking about the difference Mason had paid the woman when they first entered.

"Yes, it's rare," Chael finally replied. "It is generally the custom of the great houses to choose their eldest male to lead. Anitaea Faasa is unique in this regard."

Chael glanced at the large man trying to gauge any reaction, but Mason's face was impassive. "House Faasa has become quite wealthy under her patronage. They control all of the whitestone quarries and a good measure of the craftsmen in the city. The other great houses pay a premium for the work of their smiths and..." Chael suppressed a chuckle before finishing, "and masons." Mason smiled at him but didn't say anything. Chael cleared his throat before continuing.

"Occupying that estate over there," Chael pointed to a palatial residence not too far from that of Minister Khalim, "is the home of Hemlan, the patron of Great House Arda. Great House Arda are the principal benefactors of the High Minister." Chael pointed to the building on top of the hill, where the offices and home of the High Minister resided.

The building was a large, whitestone keep with four towers that overlooked the city below. Just inside the walls were the offices of the various functionaries that ostensibly governed Kazaam. Chael's master Khalim technically had an office here as well. All the high houses helped mark their status by occupying one of the offices of High Minister's Keep.

"Great House Arda run most of the city's criminals and serve as spies for the High Minister." Chael clapped his hands lightly, attempting to signal the end of the tour. "That's probably about all I can show you from up here," he began to say, but he was cut off when suddenly Mason leaped off the balcony. His dark cloak fluttered around him as he plummeted down the two stories and landed softly on the street below.

Chael gaped, utterly stunned. A fall from this height wouldn't be lethal, but the large man hadn't even turned an ankle, and he landed silently with more grace than a house cat. Mason simply smiled up at him, clearly amused at Chael's shock and confusion.

"Come on down boy!" Mason called, "I told ya, you're supposed to be my guide and we have business to attend." Chael quickly recovered from his momentary lapse and peered over the railing of the balcony. Mason was watching him. *Probably curious if I'm as insane as he is,* Chael thought. He briefly considered jumping off the balcony to prove that he was just as capable, but his better senses won out and he turned toward the door to the stairs. *I could have been out on a real mission,* Chael sighed as he made his way out of the building.

Chapter 9

Present Day

Chael was sore when he awoke in the morning. Not from sleeping on the hard ground, he was used to such discomforts, and they rarely bothered him, but his sleep had been restless, and he tossed and turned in his bedroll. He could not escape the feeling that the entire night Aelisa's eyes were upon him, even though she also went to sleep not longer after he did.

It was with great resignation and more than a few creaks in his back that he eventually rose and surveyed the camp. There was a dim light, although he guessed it was still predawn, and all the others seemed to be asleep.

Chael stretched, popping some of the aching bones and sore muscles in his back. He glanced down at the ground and noticed Michik still blissfully asleep, tail wagging in rhythm to some dream. Chael smiled at his dog and started the preparations to break camp.

Chael took a deep breath of the frosty morning air, then froze.

I hate people, he thought, and then glanced down at his dog. I suppose that's sufficient mockery for the moment, he conceded to himself. "Now," he continued more earnestly, "why in Darkness have you come here?"

It hung in the air like a foul stench that only he could smell. There was greater power to it than that of the plants or some animal of the forest. *Human,* he thought.

"Up! everybody up!" Chael yelled at the sleeping members of his party. "Someone has died, everybody gets up and out here now!"

While Chael quickly took stock of the camp, Sir Andon rose immediately and glanced over at Chael. He gave a quick nod, grabbed his sword, and dashed into the tent of Sister Aelisa. Chael began running towards the Baron's tent glancing at the groggy, slowly rising figures of two of Janus's spearmen.

Chael reached the tent and threw the flap aside and rushed into the Baron's tent. The Baron was the only occupant that Chael could sense inside, and he was sleeping deeply and rather noisily. *Probably still affected by whatever curatives Aelisa gave him,* Chael surmised.

As Chael exited the Baron's tent, Sir Andon and a startled-looking Sister Aelisa emerge from hers. Michik had gotten up and could sense the wolf circling the perimeter of the camp.

"Good boy," Chael muttered under his breath.

The two erstwhile slumbering spearmen had finally risen and gained control over their mental faculties. Chael could see that one of them was Antos whom he had yelled at the night before.

"Antos," he called. "Who was left on watch this morning?"

"That would be, erm, Durnik." Antos replied, a look of shame mixed with worry creeping over his face.

"Durnik," Chael simply repeated. *It must be him, then; he's the only one unaccounted for.* Michik barked at exactly that moment, as if he had been waiting for Chael to come to this conclusion independently. Chael's head snapped instantly in the direction of the sound and made his way toward what he knew to be the corpse of this Durnik.

Sir Andon immediately jumped into action organizing the two remaining guards into a defensive posture around the priestess and the still sleeping baron. Sister Aelisa immediately rebuffed the offer of protection and marched in the direction of Chael. Andon sighed and turned to the two spearmen.

"I guess the two of you can stay here and guard the Baron. Keep your eyes open and yell if you hear or see anything out of the ordinary." Andon sighed and jogged to catch up to the surprisingly fleet footed order priestess. Chael winced as he saw the two of them catching up to him.

"Look, I will take care of this. You really shouldn't be leaving the safety of the camp." Aelisa cut him off with a scathing look and Chael knew that there was simply no dissuading her. Sir Andon gave Chael a sympathetic shrug and indicated that he led the way. Chael exhaled one final exacerbated breath and turned away from the others and headed back toward the tree line.

He didn't have to go far. He could sense Michik's presence only a few dozen paces into the trees and soon found his loyal companion pacing around the body of the third spearman sniffing the air. The kill was fresh, less than an hour old judging by the amount of power that still lingered in the area.

Chael threw up his hood attempting to shield his eyes from his companions as he breathed it in. Every living thing had a soul, from the grass and trees to animals and people. When something dies, the soul separates from the body breaking whatever connection that held it there. The shattering of those bonds is what fueled Chael's powers, he had understood that from very early on. That energy would linger in the area for a short time depending on how much there was and if Chael was quick enough could leave a discernible echo of what had killed its host.

Chael felt the familiar rush of power to his limbs and the widening of his senses. He needed to act quickly, when a human died the power was incredibly potent, but it burned through him much faster, and the power leftover from Durnik's death was already fleeing this world. Chael touched the dead man's leg giving himself a point of focus for all the chaotic energy that was swirling within and without him.

The world grew immediately darker, Chael and Durnik were standing at the edge of the camp looking toward the sleeping forms of the others. The fire had almost completely burned out but for embers and the light of predawn had not yet touched the clearing.

Through the dim light provided by the dying fire and stars, Chael could barely make out most of the camp. There was a thin ethereal gray haze that obscured his vision beyond about a dozen paces in front of him. The echo, as Chael called it, of this death was fading.

A noise in the trees made both Durnik's and Chael's heads jerk around at once. The spearmen tightened the grip on his spear and slowly began to inch toward the sound.

"Who, who's there?" The spearman called out softly, clearly trying to avoid waking the others over what was potentially nothing. Durnik continued walking slowly and deliberately in the direction of the noise. His eyes and spear were constantly swaying from left-to-right scanning for threats.

"Stop panicking," Chael murmured to Durnik uselessly.

The spectral image of the dead guard couldn't hear him and certainly couldn't alter his fate. Chael trailed a few paces behind him watching Durnik enter the dark trees. The poor spearman only made it a few steps into the forest proper before he met his fate.

A man in a black cloak seemingly materialized out of thin air directly behind Durnik. He swung his left hand around grasping Durnik by the head and covered his mouth and nose in a vicious grip.

Durnik immediately tried to scream but was muffled by his attacker who held him fast in strong deliberate hands. The black cloaked man produced a dagger in his right hand and with the precision of a surgeon, he expertly plunged the blade into the side of the guard's neck. There was a sick, sloshing sound as the edge of the dagger was forced out through the front of Durnik's throat and blood began to spew from the giant gash in his neck.

The attacker let the guard drop to the forest floor, continuing to spew his life's blood all over the ground. Durnik grabbed at his throat and for a moment attempted to speak but all that came out of his mouth was a few pathetic gurgles and he fell, once again. Unmoving and lifeless. The cloaked man watched his victim for a second, dispassionate eyes surveying the efficiency of his work.

It was then that Chael was able to truly see his hands and arms in the false light of the echo. Blue writing covered his hands and arms and continued as it disappeared up the sleeves of the man's cloak.

Chael stifled a gasp, recognizing the foul Dark cultist. Almost as if he had heard him, the cultist looked up from the body of his victim and smiled eerily in the direction of Chael. *Impossible.* The world went completely dark as Chael hastily shut down the vision. The disturbing smile of the Dark Cultist still lingering in his mind's eye.

He opened his eyes into the living world and was amazed at how bright and clear everything seemed after the wan gray light of the echo. As his vision adjusted to the light of the morning, he immediately noticed Aelisa staring at him. She was crouched down on the other side of the body staring directly into Chael's eyes. His glowing azure eyes.

"So, young hunter, what did you see?" Aelisa was still boring into his soul with her gaze, what she found there he couldn't say.

Curious, Chael thought. But it was no use. This time, he was completely immobilized and wasn't going anywhere. As he came down from the spike of adrenaline and began to breathe normally, the words of the woman flowed back across his conscious mind. She called me precious, he mused silently. And st-starborn? There is no escape, she thought, even if you could free yourself. "You're only going to chafe your wrists doing that," she finally said.

Finally, after exhausting his power and not finding any immediate threats, he turned his eyes to the sister. She gave him a look as if to say, "well, I'm waiting."

"This man was killed by a member of a Dark worshiping cult called the Black Hand that I've had dealings with before, his name is Cooper. He led him off into the woods, slit his throat and dragged his body to this spot."

"Dealings?" Sister Aelisa asked suspiciously, narrowing her eyes at Chael.

"Trust me these people are no friends of mine. But as you can see, they are extremely dangerous." Chael gestured down at the corpse of the unfortunate spearman to emphasize his point.

"How do you know this?" Sir Andon's voice uttered from behind him, scarcely concealing the bewilderment in his voice. Chael sighed; this was a conversation that he had been dreading since they started on the journey. He dreaded it even more so now that the sister had so plainly laid her concerns bare the night before.

"You know my dog isn't," Chael hesitated slightly, "normal. I have certain abilities that go beyond what can be done by alchemists. One of those abilities is to detect a sort of echo of a violent death. I saw his final moments and the man who killed him." Andon was about to comment but Chael held up his hand to silence him.

"Look," Chael continued. "We don't have time for me to explain. The man who did this is still out there somewhere and neither I nor my dog can detect him. That means he has figured out a way to hide from us and I'm guessing he's not alone. We have to move now." Chael glanced over at Aelisa. She was still staring at him, but his words apparently proved effective because she nodded back and rose heading for camp. He gave Sir Andon a weak smile before following the priestess toward the others.

Despite a bevy of objections, particularly from the Baron, Chael was able to convince the party to immediately break camp. Antos and the other remaining spearmen wanted to bury and say words over their fallen comrade, but Sister Aelisa had managed to dissuade them. She at least seemed to understand something of the gravity of their situation.

Once again, it seemed that specters of his past were coming back to haunt him in the present. He had come out to the Dark Forest to escape them, but they had apparently followed him even here.

What could they possibly be doing here? Chael wondered while absentmindedly packing his bedroll. Around him was a flurry of motion as the others hastily packed their belongings, all under the steely gaze of the order priestess.

Chael glanced at Baron Janus hobbling around with a makeshift walking stick, trying to make up for his half-eaten foot. The Baron had been slow enough with two nominally functional feet. He looked on to where Antos was packing up the Baron's tent.

"Stop!" Chael called to Antos. "Baron Janus, I'm sorry but we need to use your tent." Janus looked at Chael suspiciously, but said nothing. Chael simply smiled a slightly sinister grin. "You can barely walk; we'll make your tent into a litter and carry you until your foot has a better chance to heal." Janus looked elated for a moment until Chael added, "which means you will be sleeping out in the elements with the rest of us." Janus scowled but nodded and Chael simply smiled back.

It took another half hour to finish packing as well as converting the Baron's canvas tent into a litter to carry him.

Chael had needed to cut down some stronger branches to reinforce the sides, but all in all, they made good time.

He couldn't guess what the goal of the Dark cultists was. They were utterly mysterious even when he was working with them back in Kazaam. They were always faithful to the dealing they had with his former master, but that didn't mean they were loyal. These people always had their own agenda and reason for doing things, and now he couldn't fathom what that would be here in the shadowy confines of the Western Forest. But they had deliberately targeted their group; that much was clear from the echo. They had lured poor Durnik away from the relative safety of the camp to kill him.

So, they're not sure if they can take us all on at once, Chael surmised. He hadn't seen anyone with Cooper in the vision, but he highly doubted that the enigmatic Dark Alchemist would risk exposure out here alone.

"We have to increase the pace today," Chael commanded the others. "These people are vicious and dangerous and for some reason they have taken an interest in us. Our best hope is to get out of the forest and onto open ground." Sister Aelisa nodded at him and produced a small vial from her robes and tossed it to Sir Andon, who had taken up the back end of the litter.

"Sip this tincture, you won't need much, it is quite potent. It will give you the strength to carry the Baron without fatiguing. However, the effect is not unlimited, eventually the cost will tax your body too far." Andon gave the vial a wary look before downing a fifth of its contents.

"I said sip!" scolded Aelisa, giving the knight an exacerbated and matronly look. Sir Andon chuckled and offered the vial to Chael, who declined.

"I have other ways," Chael said to Andon with a small wink. He could sense the knight going back to the moment in the forest where Chael had openly displayed his abilities, but Sir Andon didn't say anything. "How do you feel?" Chael asked after a moment. Sir Andon looked at him for a moment as if he didn't understand the question, but after a moment, he opened his mouth to reply, but all that came out was a hacking cough.

"You drank too much my foolish knight." Aelisa clucked at the struggling man but did nothing to help. Andon's face flushed, and he started scratching desperately at his arms as if some army of insects were burrowing into his skin. Chael looked at the impossibly calm order priestess for help, but she simply stood impassively, arms crossed. Chael grabbed Andon by the collar and forced the panicked knight to look into his eyes.

"Andon, look at me. I think I know what you're going through. All the sensations that normally pass us by, the smell of the forest, the feeling of a gentle breeze on your arm. These things have been magnified to a blinding, deafening degree." Chael did his best to speak in a low, soothing voice, trying to coax Andon's rational mind out from where it had retreated deep within himself. "Breathe, rise above your senses and take control."

Chael kept taking large demonstrative breaths, and after a few minutes the knight began mimicking him. It took an additional ten minutes, but at length Sir Andon was able to focus himself. He gave Chael a short nod of thanks, which Chael returned.

"Alright we can't waste any more time," Chael called out, grabbing the other end of the litter and took off at a near jog into the trees. He breathed in, both to steady his legs and to absorb more of the available life energy in the wilderness around him. He didn't need to take much, but inevitably he was going to leave an trail of death in his wake, a trail that could easily be followed by Cooper or Mason, if either were around. But that didn't really matter in his estimation, they weren't going to lose Cooper no matter what they did.

Their only hope was to get out of the Dark Forest and into the open plain in front of Fhaerhold. There, the cultists couldn't sneak up on them, and there was a chance they might find some of the King's legion out on patrol. He thought back to the things the dark worshippers had done and what he knew they were capable of. Chael shuddered; they were not capable of winning a fight with them. Not here in this place of Darkness.

Chael continued breathing in the precious life energy of the forest as he quickened his pace even further. Time melted away as he pressed his group further and further into the forest. He could vaguely make out calls of protest from behind him, but he paid them no heed. His only goal was to make it out of the forest.

It's not possible, it couldn't be. But someone knew him and knew to use that name; that was deeply concerning.

Subtly, a presence infiltrated his mind an evil consciousness that he thought he had long since banished to the deepest and darkest recesses of his being. It whispered half truths into his mind and urged on the basest instincts of his flesh. Normally, Chael was on guard for this type of assault, but frustration, exhaustion, and fear had left his defenses open and the worm slithered back in.

I hate people, he thought bitterly once again. Why had it come to his home? That was particularly strange. Creatures of the Dark had a sense about these things, and most knew to avoid the man who had taken residence in the wood.Do demons get cold? he thought absently. He then shook his head, clearing his mind for the fight. Michik snarled and barked, but there were no sounds of the demon retreating from his mighty wolf.

At that thought, Chael laughed maniacally while still dragging the Baron's litter through the forest. *This would be easier if I could just carry the idiot, but I'll need more strength.* He thought back to the hapless spearmen remaining in the company. There was enough strength there to make a mad dash to the edge of the wood. The Dark thoughts swirled around in Chael's mind, and that voice of seeming rationality further influenced his thoughts.

"The spearmen are here to serve the Baron. They protect him with their lives. Allow them to do their duty." The voice was cold, calculating, but it wasn't alien to his own. It was just harsher, as if he had inhaled a puff of smoke or shouted his voice hoarse. But the more he heard it, the clearer and more sensible it sounded. Chael stopped his mad sprint and set down the litter containing the still irate nobleman. He turned to look back at the others when an unseen force smashed into his side.

Take initiative. Chael ground his teeth, trying to come up with a novel strategy to surprise his long-time sparring partner while also ducking bone shattering swings.

Chael drew his sword, preparing to end this threat once and for all, but when he looked down, he didn't see a tattooed man in a black cloak. He saw a wolf, whining where it lay impaled on the broken limb of a tree. An ache materialized in his chest where a moment ago there was simply numb resignation and even a touch of gleefully murderous excitement. He exhaled, banishing the Dark energy that had infused him.

As the power faded, he could feel the ache in his limbs from the heedless flight through the forest. His hands were a tangled mess of bleeding blisters and raw flesh. His human heart, regaining feeling after such a prolonged period of frozen indifference, shattered in anguish at the sight before his eyes.

Michik was crying at his master. A jagged tree branch Chael had surely killed in ignorance was skewered through the wolf's right shoulder. Chael rushed over to his dog's side and ripped out the branch and bound his beloved companion in a tight embrace. Michik nipped at his arm until Chael let go. The wolf's glowing eyes bored into his own and the wolf snarled at Chael.

"I'm sorry, buddy. I haven't drawn so much over such a great time for a while. I was careless." Michik continued staring into Chael's eyes, but stopped growling. After what seemed an eternity to Chael, the wolf lurched forward, tackling him to the ground assaulting Chael's face with his tongue. They were still like that, playfully wrestling on the forest floor, when a red-faced Andon finally caught up to them. Chael glanced up at the knight, noticing an empty vial around his neck.

Sounds about right, Chael thought ruefully as his head slumped back down. A bit on the nose, Chael thought, considering the business alleged to be conducted out of the basement of the alehouse.

Further examination of his surroundings revealed a stark stripe of death and decay leading up to his feet and back from where he came, disappearing in the shadows. It was as if some god or giant being had painted a neat line of extinction about six feet wide to mark his passing. Here and there a fleck of purple, red, or green, poked out of the decayed gray morass, but the amount of damage done was incalculable.

Chael swallowed hard, fighting back the urge to retch on top of the destruction he had already wrought. This place was tainted by the Dark; he had always felt that. The plants and creatures that grew here often evolved in sinister unnatural ways, like the giant malodorous insect that had attacked the Baron. But that was not the entirety of the forest. There were still green things and innocent creatures untouched by the taint that had taken hold here. A distant echo of what existed before it had fallen to shadow. Now Chael had added even more Darkness to this place.

Chael finally looked up at Sir Andon, who was still staring in shock, awaiting some explanation. He hesitated; they were well beyond the point of concealing Chael's abilities now. But he was not eager to share every last one of his secrets with these people.

"Well?" Beckoned the knight still looking for an answer.

"I uh…" Chael began. "I got a little carried away." He didn't know what else to say, would they trust him if he admitted that the power that gave him such incredible strength and endurance was also incredibly addictive? That it brought out and encouraged his most base desires and even tempted him with desires that he didn't have.

Sir Andon was still staring at him expectantly, not satisfied with his short and uninformative answer.

"Look," Chael began, "as you have probably noticed I can take power from my surroundings." Chael intentionally hid the fact that this power could also be harvested from the deaths of people. "This power affects me in largely the same way that I think you felt after drinking that tincture of Sister Aelisa." Chael gestured at the empty vial. "However, prolonged use can narrow my focus if I'm not careful. I clearly let it go too far."

Chael gave Andon his most earnest look, hoping that the sloppy explanation would sate the knight's curiosity for at least the moment. "How far behind are the others?" Chael added hastily, doing his best to change the subject. Sir Andon still looked at him skeptically before answering.

"A few leagues, luckily you left a fairly easy trail for them to follow." Andon looked around at the path of devastation left in Chael's wake, suspicion and contempt flashed across his face several times. "I only caught up to you by steadily drinking Aelisa's potion while I ran."

Damn, Chael cursed himself. He had not let himself get so carried away by the power since he first discovered it.

"Alright, you should go back and help them reach this spot, I'll stay with the Baron and make camp," Chael said. At the mention of the Baron, they both glanced over to the litter where Janus was strangely quiet. Sir Andon walked over to the litter to check on Janus.

"By the living stars!" Andon gasped.

Chael jumped to his feet, ready to investigate whatever horror had befallen the Baron.

Andon looked at Chael smiling. "He's asleep." They both laughed now, the tension of the moment bursting into bouts of unseemly mirth.

Chapter 10

Present Day

It took nearly two hours for the rest of the party to catch up to Chael. When they arrived, Chael learned that even that feat had required a small distribution of Sister Aelisa's alchemical formula. After building a fire, Chael set to converting the litter into a cot for the Baron to sleep on more comfortably. He supposed it was the least he could do. Upon her arrival, the order priestess merely greeted Chael with a hard implacable stare.

"You all should get some rest. I will stand watch tonight," Chael offered in an attempt at mollifying the simmering tempers of his companions. He didn't receive any pushback on the suggestion, so after a hasty meal of dried provisions, the rest of the group retired for the night, leaving Chael alone by the fire with Michik. He stared into the fire, replaying the day's events. He hadn't lost control like that in years.

"What's to become of us, Meeshee?" Chael inclined his head at his dog, gazing into his ethereal azure eyes.

Michik sensing Chael's distress, sidled closer and rested his large lupine head in Chael's lap. This earned the wolf several appreciative head scratches.

"There's something else at work here," Chael continued, speaking to the wolf. "We've killed more demons in the last few months than in the previous year. Khalim is marching on Fhael, Darrik and now those Darkened cultists! What don't we know buddy? What are we missing?"

Michik lifted his head from Chael's lap and met his eyes. The wolf stared at him for several long moments, boring into Chael's soul with his stare. Then he opened his massive jaws, exposing long rows of wicked teeth, and promptly licked Chael across the face.

"Agh!" Chael stammered, recoiling from Michik's rough dry tongue. The wolf returned his master's disgust with a puppy-like grin. Well, as best as Michik could approximate such a thing, given his sinister facial scars.

Chael couldn't help but laugh despite himself and resumed the well-deserved head scratches, staring once again, into the fire.

11 Years Ago

The home of Captain Duntos, head of the Kazaam city watch, was anything but ostentatious. It was a quaint two-story bluestone house in the middle ring of the city. The unassuming structure housed one of the most powerful men in Kazaam and yet its owner eschewed the normal trappings that such a station would generally bring. Officially, the city watch stayed neutral during election season, allowing the high houses to perform their perverse ritual of succession without aid or interference. Unofficially, they largely acted as additional muscle for the High Minister.

Chael glanced at Mason and took a calming breath of the brisk night air before rapping on the simple wooden door of the house. A middle-aged woman answered the door. She was pretty, but not overly remarkable.

"Can I help you, gentlemen?" she asked suspiciously.

"My lady," Chael began, "we are representatives of the city ministry and I'm afraid that we must beg the leave of your husband for an urgent matter that requires his attention."

The captain's wife continued to stare at them suspiciously, but at length invited them inside and called for her husband. The captain of the city watch met them in a small sitting room just inside the front door. He was middle-aged, with flecks of white in otherwise sandy brown hair and wore a tightly groomed beard that pointed down sharply below his chin. His expression was somewhere between exasperation and annoyance.

"Alright, who are you exactly and what urgent matter requires my attention?" Chael opened his mouth to speak but was cut off by Mason.

"My name is Mason. I am a servant of the Black Hand, and it is my mission to bring forth and aid the ancient Dark Lord and overthrow the realms of man. That is exactly who I am." He smiled happily back and forth between Chael and Captain Duntos. Chael and the captain both gave Mason the same look of utter confusion and stunned bewilderment.

"Now," Mason continued, "the more important question is why I have come to your home this evening." Mason continued smiling in an odd manic sort of way that made Chael recoil internally. But if Chael was uncomfortable, Captain Duntos was simply bewildered. Mason brusquely pushed past the confused captain and entered the house.

"I don't know who you think you are!" exclaimed Duntos, finally regaining his composure. "But I am the captain of the city watch and I've taken heads for less offense!"

Mason smiled at him once again and pulled up the sleeves of his black cloak. His bare arm revealed dozens of shallow cuts across his forearm, crisscrossing over each other in a haphazard pattern of scars. With his other arm he produced an obsidian knife from somewhere beneath his dark cloak.

Mason's bizarre maniacal smile widened as he drew the crude blade across his arm, producing a small river of blood that dripped onto the cold stone floor of the captain's home. Chael and Duntos could only watch in paralyzed bewilderment at Mason's shocking behavior.

"The recipe is surprisingly simple," Mason intoned with an eerily calm voice despite the crazed smile that had overtaken his face. "Fire and blood." Mason dropped the blood-stained knife to the floor where it shattered into several pieces, the black obsidian glass intermingling with the shallow pool of blood that had already fallen from his arm. He then reached back into his cloak and pulled out a small glass vial filled with a gray powder about the size of his thumb.

He turned to Chael. "Best to close your eyes for this part lad." Mason suddenly and violently threw the vial onto the blood and glass below him. Chael attempted to cover his eyes, but he was too late, he beheld a flash of blinding white light and then he was thrown backward across the room as if some giant invisible club had walloped him in the torso.

Chael lifted his head groggily from the floor, blinking the specter of the searing light from his bleary eyes. There was heat, he quickly patted himself and assured that his limbs were intact and not on fire.

The next thing to register to his foggy senses was a putrid smell similar to rotting meat. The oppressive nature of the smell was being intensified by the suddenly scorching temperature of the room. All at once he was dizzy, nauseated, and claustrophobic.

Chael continued to blink and rub his eyes and slowly the hazy shapes in the room came into focus. He could make out the outline of Captain Duntos laying similarly supine like himself. And Mason, despite being closest to the blast, had somehow remained on his feet. Chael gawked; a third shape was coming into focus standing right in front of Mason.

As his eyes slowly recovered from the blinding light, the third party in the room became clearer. For a moment Chael wished he had remained blind. It was shaped like a human man, about six feet tall as far as Chael could reckon because its head was almost even with Mason's. Its hide was merely a patchwork of different pieces of human skin, roughly stitched together by a thin black cord.

Chael guessed that it had taken dozens of victims to piece together its grotesque human costume because the hue and tone of the sections of skin varied greatly. Here and there, the heedless stitching had come loose exposing black greasy flesh underneath. Its face was one large sheet of flesh that had been stretched over the front and tied in the back with the same black cord that stitched the rest of it together. Apparently, it didn't speak because there was no section cut from its fleshy mask for a mouth, nor did it make accommodations for a nose or ears. It did, however, have eyes. Striking, lidless red orbs could be seen through two rough-cut circles in its ghoulish face covering, and they were staring directly into Chael's own.

For several moments there was silence, out of the corner of his eye Chael could tell that Duntos was still trying to adjust his eyes and understand what had just happened. Mason was regarding the demon—for that must be what it was, Chael surmised—with a look of mild curiosity. But the demon continued to pour its gaze directly into Chael's azure eyes.

"D… d… demon!" Captain Duntos finally exclaimed in a shrill high-pitched squeak. Still staring at Chael, the demon's face twitched slightly, and though it was difficult to tell without a mouth, Chael could swear that it was somehow smiling beneath the horrid death mask it wore. It immediately turned and walked over to the captain. The demon's strides were stilted and awkward like those of a small child who was only just learning to walk, and yet when it reached Duntos, it easily picked him up off the floor with inhuman strength and held him aloft by the neck.

The demon turned its head to Mason, still holding the terrified guard captain in the air. Mason glanced at Chael with the same curious look he gave the demon, then turned around and spoke to the demon in a tongue Chael couldn't comprehend. The demon suddenly disappeared, but Captain Duntos remained suspended in the air, the outline of an invisible hand squeezing his neck.

At this point, Duntos lost all sense of composure and began screaming hysterically. Mason whispered another command to the demon, and it squeezed harder, cutting off his desperate screams. Mason walked to Captain Duntos and gently pushed on the demon's invisible arm until he was lowered to Mason's eye level.

"Now, Captain," Mason cooed maniacally, "let me explain how your life is about to change."

Chapter 11

Present Day

The morning arrived with a chorus of groans and menacing looks leveled at Chael. *At least you got to sleep all night,* Chael thought, grimacing slightly. Despite his somewhat sardonic attitude, Chael knew their complaints were mostly warranted. He hadn't needed to feed on life energy for that long in years and had forgotten just how corruptive it could become if he wasn't vigilant. He had already paid a high price for that lesson and was a little ashamed that he had so quickly forgotten.

"I made breakfast!" Chael announced, shouting over the continued cacophony of grunts and complaints from his companions. Before daybreak, Chael had sent Michik out into the forest to hunt some fresh game. The wolf may have been dead for several years, but he still had excellent predatory instincts from his earlier life.

After a short hunt, Michik trotted triumphantly out of the trees, proudly displaying a trio of dead rabbits hanging limply from his massive jaws. He dutifully laid them at Chael's feet and looked up expectantly. The fresh blood of his kill dripped down the side of his muzzle where no flesh remained to contain it. It gave the already striking face of his dog an even more sinister aspect.

Chael couldn't stifle a laugh as he compared the seemingly murderous visage with his happily wagging tail and round puppy eyes, eagerly awaiting his reward. Chael reached down and gave Michik a well-deserved head scratch for his efforts.

"Good boy!"

The announcement of a hot meal did little to cool the tempers of his companions, especially the Baron, but they ate it readily enough. Sir Andon even managed to give Chael a curt nod after he had finished. When the meal was over and everyone else broke camp, Sister Aelisa walked over and sat down next to Chael.

"Are you fit to continue?" she asked abruptly, searching his face. "I still agree with your assessment that we need to make our way through this…" She hesitated, looking around with a disgusted look on her face, "…place. But if you are a danger to the others, you will tell me now." She said this last part with a tone of command clearly taken from her years as a high-ranking order member. Chael also noted that she did not include herself in the potentially endangered group. *Interesting,* he thought.

"I'm FINE," he responded, doing his best to emphasize the words. She may have been used to issuing commands in her order, but Chael wasn't beholden to anybody. "Like I said, I've dealt with these people before, and they are not to be taken lightly. Yesterday in my haste I let myself get a little carried away, that is all. But if you think you can lead this group out of the forest without me, please do so. I'll take my dog and return home."

Not enough, Chael grimaced. He took a steadying breath, weighing his ever-decreasing options before the serious-looking men would reach him and he'd fight. He caught sight of the serving woman five paces behind and slightly to the left of the man he had hit with the ale mug. *Forgive me,* he sighed, and threw the blade just past the man's ear as it spun and struck the woman in the arm.

Subtle, Chael huffed as the first contender for the lady's honor emerged from the circling pack. He stretched his neck and prepared for the predictable opening attack. Probably off to fetch the watch. Darkness! Chael had to hurry this along.

"Ugh! Did ya have to do that right in front of me!?" Chael glanced across the camp where Antos and his fellow guardsman were breaking down the Baron's tent and reforming it into the litter. They were both covering their noses and pointing accusatory fingers at the other.

"It wasn't me you daft—" Antos began to retort. He was abruptly cut off, a look of horrified confusion dawning on his face. Michik shot across the camp like a bolt out of a crossbow and launched himself in the air toward the guardsman, but he was too late.

Chael felt it the moment it happened; blood and viscera exploded out from within Antos' chest as if propelled by some unseen force from inside him. Antos was dead before the wolf had even left the ground.

The energy from the death immediately saturated the ground around the camp. Chael breathed it in as he unsheathed his sword and reached out with his senses. Chael watched as Michik flew past Antos toward the demon skulking just behind him. To the naked eye it was invisible, but to Chael's unnatural senses it stood out amongst the life in the forest as an inky black void in the shape of a man. Its cruel fist stuck out of Antos' chest, and between the dark silhouette of its fingers, Chael saw what was unmistakably the heart of the unfortunate spearman.

Michik slammed into the demon and latched his powerful jaws around its neck. The wolf ripped and tore at the abomination's flesh, causing suddenly visible shreds of leathery human skin and black chunks of sticky, rotting demon tissue to fly into the air.

The demon must have lost concentration because as Michik tore into its neck, it became visible to the rest of the camp. Leathery flaps of its sick human costume dangled loosely, exposing the skin of the demon proper. There were wide bands of tight, black muscle fiber, but its flesh oozed a sticky viscous fluid that gave off its distinctive, malodorous scent.

Like any other demon, the easiest way to dispatch it was to remove its head, and Michik was applying all of his lupine strength to tear it off. The demon hammered its fists blindly above its head, trying to dislodge the wolf, but it lacked proper leverage to fully bring its terrible strength to bear on Chael's dog. It still scored several good hits, however, earning whines of pain from Michik.

At length there was a loud snap and its lifeless head rolled free of its body, trailing the same thick sludge that permeated the rest of its flesh.

As the capable wolf dealt with his opponent, Chael scanned the area around them and saw several more black demonic shapes approaching from the trees, as well as the unmistakable aura of humans following in the demon's wake. The power of the poor guardsman's death coursed through him as he tightened the grip on his sword.

Well, shit, Chael muttered to himself, then charged at the nearest demon, just now emerging from the trees.

Chapter 12

Present Day

The muted calm of the morning preparations was suddenly shattered by confused shouts, ringing steel, and guttural demonic cries. Chael met the first demon just inside the ring of trees surrounding the camp. The lesser demon bit at him with an impressive maw of needle-like teeth protruding from its rat's head. Chael, still suffused with the energy from Antos' death, easily ducked the bite and confidently swung his curved falchion sword and decapitated the snarling Darkspawn.

Chael effortlessly dispatched another lesser demon charging out of the forest. The power taken from the death of the guardsman made him faster, stronger, and honed his senses to a deadly razor's edge. He took a moment to quickly survey the camp; none of the Dark cultists had emerged, but demons were pouring in from all sides. Andon and the remaining spearman were each fighting one of the rat-faced lesser demons.

The idiots gave them weapons? Chael mumbled in exacerbation. Indeed, the demons fighting Andon and the guardsman were both wielding a crude sword and shield. Clearly made for the creatures, judging by their enlarged proportions.

"The head!" Chael yelled over the din of battle at the others. "You have to take the head!" If they heard him, they gave no sign, but he had no time to coddle them now. In a few moments, the camp would be completely overrun. Michik was sprinting around the camp in a fury like Chael had never seen. He was harrying any unengaged demons from flanking his companions, leaving small but effective bites and slashes across the legs of the Darkspawn, stymying their efforts to fully encircle the camp.

Chael darted back into the fray, switching between his natural sight and his senses, scanning for any more of Mason's favorite invisible pets. He had affectionately dubbed these specimens skulker demons because of the way they snuck around their prey. Mason was particularly fond of them.

If those things are here, he has to be nearby somewhere, Chael thought warily while beheading another lesser demon, this one carrying an enormous double bitted war ax.

Three similarly armed demons were approaching Sister Aelisa about fifteen paces from where he was. Chael knew that even with his enhanced strength and speed, he would not reach them in time to do the priestess any good. He slipped one of his knives from his boot and hurled it at the demon as hard as he could. He couldn't kill it with such a small weapon, but his aim was true, and it cut cleanly through the tendon of its right leg and the beast toppled just over a foot from Aelisa's toes.

Chael was about to launch a second knife, but he was suddenly catapulted from his feet by an invisible battering ram. He landed in the remains of a demon he had just killed ten paces away. *Stupid!* He cursed himself. He could feel several broken ribs and was coughing up gouts of hot blood. But already the power that he held inside was healing him and with the last of its energy he could feel bones and sinews knitting themselves back together. It wasn't perfect, and he'd be in a lot of pain tomorrow, but it would do.

The demon was standing above him now, oblivious to the fact that Chael could effectively see him and was preparing a strike aimed at Chael's chest. At the last moment, Chael rolled to his left, evading the strike, and grabbed the ax from the dead demon on which he had fallen. With a great deal of effort, now drained of power, he heaved the massive war ax over and through the neck of the vulnerable demon.

With a groan of pain, Chael rose to his feet and searched across the battlefield where Aelisa had been. *They would be on her now.* One of the demons was simply gone. The only evidence of its prior existence was the sickly black viscera of demonic gore painting everything in a twelve-foot circle around the priestess. The demon he had hobbled was crawling along the ground toward Aelisa, its leg nearly severed from Chael's enhanced throw.

The third demon was on fire and sprinting as far away from the elderly woman as it could get; directly toward Chael.

Darkness! Chael cursed and dove over to where he had dropped his sword. He managed to grab it just in time to behead the flaming demon on its mad flight away from the vengeful order priestess.

Aelisa stood calmly in the same spot she had occupied when Chael first saw the demons approaching her. She watched impassively while the crippled demon slowly rose and stood precariously on its good leg within a breath of Aelisa. It roared a defiant demonic curse at her, expelling foul green sputum from its jaws. With a heavy stroke that nearly took its precarious balance, the demon swung its ponderous war ax at her.

Aelisa, still unnervingly calm, took one placid step to the side and watched the ax sink into the blooded ground inches from her feet. The enraged demon swiped at her with its vicious claws, but again she took one small step back and the lesser demon's claws slashed only air, just inches from her impassive face. This time the demon did overextend itself and it fell as it tried to use its nearly severed leg to support its attack. Sister Aelisa produced a small vial of one of her concoctions from within her robes and downed it in a single gulp.

For a moment, she merely stood there looking piteously at the tangled demon still trying to regain its feet. Then she raised her arm and allowed the sleeve of her robes to fall back to her elbow. The skin on the inside of her forearm bubbled and, like hot wax, seemed to slough off her limb and drip to the ground. This further exposed similarly melting muscle until only bone remained for more than a foot of her arm.

From the awful gap in her flesh, a surreal glowing vine seemed to grow and as it lengthened, it became brighter and brighter. It grew thus until the end of it touched the ground and was more luminous than the sun at midday.

For the first time, Aelisa showed a hint of emotion as she flicked her wrist and the glowing whip attached to her arm shot out and wrapped around the struggling demon's neck. The glowing cord burned the flesh of the demon where it coiled around its neck like a glowing celestial snake. Aelisa snarled slightly at her foe and lightly flicked her wrist once more and the creature's head was severed from its body as if its neck was made of something no more substantial than a rain cloud.

Chael moved on from the sister. *Obviously, she could handle herself.* He turned back to Andon and the remaining spearman. Clearly, the knight had heard his warning because two headless demons lay at his feet, and he was currently battling a third. The lone survivor of the Baron's guard was not faring quite as well. He had impressively managed to fend off the demon and was furiously stabbing it uselessly with his spear. Chael could see inky demon blood dripping from more than a dozen holes in its chest, but it kept swinging wildly at the man, heedless of the many wounds in its flesh. Wounds that would have killed any mortal being a dozen times over.

Chael raced over to the embattled spearman, gathering whatever comparatively feeble strength he could from the forest around him. One of the lesser demons with a sword and shield blocked his path. It started swinging its gigantic sword in sweeping arcs, all aimed at his head. But this was a game he had played before; Chael cracked a small smile as he expertly dodged the lumbering swipes of the demon's sword.

After a moment, his opportunity came, and he darted inside on its heavy swings and sliced several important tendons in its arms and legs, causing it to drop its armaments and fall to one knee.

Awfully polite of you, Chael thought as he took its head. Another demon stepped in his path but this one fell after a blindingly bright whip shot out from nowhere and removed its head from its muscled shoulders.

Chael was only about ten paces from the guardsman now, but the fight had taken a turn for the worse. The demon, seemingly tired of having its chest ventilated, had trapped the spear with its torso and wrenched it out of the grip of the spearman. Now defenseless, the guard backed away as the demon charged him; the haft of the spear still protruding from its chest.

Chael watched uselessly as the demon swung its greatsword at him, but just before it made contact, a mass of fur and muscle flew through the air and slammed into the demon. Michik locked his jaws around its sword arm and used his momentum to spin the giant creature to the ground, away from the spearman. Michik kept it pinned until Chael darted over and quickly cut off its head with a powerful stroke of his sword.

"You know, I never actually learned your name." Chael called over to the grateful guardsman.

With relief flooding his face, the man opened his mouth to reply just as his neck snapped. The skulker demon behind him twisted the man's head in nearly a complete circle before dropping his lifeless body to the sodden ground.

Chael and Michik simultaneously howled with rage at the cruel, pitiless creature. Michik dove right at its foremost leg, using his keen nose to guide him, and successfully knocked the demon off balance. Chael, channeling the fresh energy of the dead guardsman, combined his own fury, slashed the foul Darkspawn directly through its bent head, neck, and cleanly through its torso in one powerful swing. The demon became visible just as the severed pieces of its body fell weightily to the ground with a sickening, squelching clatter.

Chael hurled his sword horizontally at the demon still engaged with Sir Andon. The sword chopped the head of the demon cleanly and carried on for another thirty feet, where it embedded itself into a tree.

Andon gave him a quick nod of appreciation, but Chael didn't notice as he scanned the desecrated campsite for more of the foul Darkspawn to kill. To his surprise, there were none. He reached out with his senses to see if any more skulkers were about, but could not detect any in the vicinity. He couldn't detect any of the humans either, yet he was sure he saw them just behind the demons at the beginning of the attack. He looked around. Andon seemed fairly intact despite several scrapes and cuts. Aelisa was completely untouched and had somehow remained almost unblemished by black demon blood despite the ring of exploded Darkspawn flesh around her. Chael also noticed that the strange glowing whip was gone, and her arm looked completely normal. Chael took another look around the small battlefield and couldn't help but feel that something was missing.

"The Baron!" Sir Andon called. "He's gone!" In the heat of the battle, they had all seemingly lost track of the rotund nobleman.

the Great Western Forest wasn't without beauty. Most things were covered in a lush, vibrant green interspersed with flecks of purple and yellow. There were giant creepers that snaked up the giant trees and mushrooms large enough to sit on grew from their trunks. Stupid! Chael cursed himself. He had been reckless worrying about Michik; the wolf was not easy prey, even for a demon this large. or whatever a demon had—was departed, banished back to the Dark where its kind was from.

Chael looked down at his dog. Several fresh cuts appeared in his flesh and dark demon blood stained his ruffled coat.

"Find him," Chael commanded, a little harsher than he intended. Michik immediately started sniffing the area and pointed toward the thick trees beyond the camp. He glanced back at Chael briefly and took off in the direction of the Baron's scent.

Chael took a steadying breath, cursing the Baron for his oafishness and the demons for their hateful might. But mostly he cursed himself as he sprinted after his dog, deeper into the shadowy embrace of the dense Dark Forest.

Chapter 13

Present Day

As Chael followed Michik through the forest, he spotted several signs of Baron Janus. *He's being dragged,* Chael determined. Despite leaving obvious signs of their passage, the captors had chosen their path quite well. The forest was much thicker in this section, and very little of the morning light broke through the dense canopy above him.

So, it's a trap then.

Chael slowed Michik down to a walk and warily checked the growing shadows all around them. He reached down to his belt and cursed; his dependable curved falchion was stuck impaled to a tree back at the camp. He moved even more cautiously now, knowing that his only weapons were the element of surprise, his remaining throwing knives, and Michik's jaws. If utilized correctly, they were powerful weapons indeed, specifically his dog, but springing a trap without his primary weapon was still foolhardy. Chael cursed himself again for his recklessness.

The trail stopped abruptly about one hundred paces from the camp. Chael sent Michik on a wide arc of the area to scout for any surprises, and Chael moved away from the trail and hid among the trees. He gave Michik the strong impression that he was to wait until Chael called him; the timing needed to be perfect, and he couldn't risk his dog's well-natured enthusiasm.

He reached out with his senses and scanned the area in front of him. They were waiting for him about forty feet ahead next to one of the giants, old-growth trees that was left untouched in this Dark place. He could see the aura of four humans; one of them was unmistakably the Baron.

He reached out briefly to one of the others, just like he might have done if he was trying to take the life energy from the massive tree. But, as with all humans, when he tried to take that energy, it was as if it was locked away in a glass vault. Visible, but out of reach. It was the same with some of the more intelligent and sentient creatures of the wild, though the barrier keeping his Dark touch out was less substantial. Chael glanced at where he could sense Michik stalking around the gathering and frowned for a moment.

The fact that he could sense the Baron in this way meant that, for the moment, Janus was alive. He needed to come up with a plan to engage quickly and overwhelm them before they could mount a defense.

"Strange company you're keeping these days lad," called a familiar voice in front of him.

Chael froze.

Mason maintained the same lighthearted tone as when they first met, but there was still a trace of the manic, depraved zealot he knew lurked within. "I wonder if the sweet sister would let you live if she knew what I knew about you." Chael sensed a slight hesitation in his otherwise arrogant voice when he mentioned Aelisa.

They're scared of her, or at least they respect her, Chael thought. After the display he had seen back at camp, he didn't blame them. "Come out from behind that tree, I promise we only want to talk."

Chael sighed. *There goes the element of surprise.* He still had some of the power left from the death of the third spearman inside him. He figured that would give him enough reaction time to dodge if they meant to just shoot a crossbow bolt at him the second his head was in view. Slowly, Chael emerged from his apparently lousy hiding place and walked into the small gathering.

No crossbow bolts as he approached the group, *good start.* He immediately noticed Baron Janus, tied and gagged, laying at the base of the giant tree. Surrounding him were Mason, as Chael had already surmised, as well as the tattooed form of Cooper and the dark-haired woman he had only seen once on that day in his former master's office. It was she who first addressed him.

"Greetings, Chael," she said. Her voice had an ineffable, ethereal quality to it, like the caress of silk or the taste of honey. Soft and sweet and intoxicating, but Chael knew better than to trust it. She smiled at him, rich and deep. "I have been watching you these many months. When you left Kazaam I had feared you were lost, but I should have known this place would call to you. I'm sorry it took me so long to find you but unfortunately we were previously engaged."

Chael studied her. She was no less beautiful than when he had glimpsed her years ago in Khalim's study, but there were a few streaks of gray in her otherwise raven hair.

"No apologies necessary," Chael called with as much nonchalance as he could muster. "I needed a change of scenery and when you get past the hideous demons and corrupt fauna this forest is really quite beautiful." He needed to keep them talking while he formulated a plan. He had no idea what this woman was capable of, but Mason and Cooper were incredibly adept at extreme violence.

The woman smiled at Chael once again. "Would you like to know why I chose this spot?" She looked up at the massive old growth tree and continued without waiting for him to reply. "This tree is one of the few remaining of its kind old enough to have been a sapling when He lived in these woods." She put an emphasis on the word "he", as if that should have sparked some recognition in Chael. It didn't.

"Who?" Chael asked, adding a bit of sarcasm to his tone. In his experience, self-important people rarely responded well to mockery, and keeping her off balance could only help his cause.

"Our Lord of course," she responded, ignoring his weak attempt at a jibe. "We do not speak His true name. He grew up here a millennium ago, in fact I believe you have taken up residence in His former home."

Chael earnestly frowned at that suggestion. His dilapidated little cottage couldn't be more than sixty years old, not a thousand. "I think it is only natural that you would be drawn there," the woman continued, heedless of the skepticism on his face. "His influence still blesses this land, exulting some of the creatures that live here and allowing his servants to rise from their home in the Darkness."

She suddenly moved toward him with much more speed and agility than he would have assumed. He just barely wrested a knife from one of the pockets of his cloak before she was merely a hand span from his face. He put the knife against her throat, but she ignored it and pushed closer to him. The blade cut a shallow line into her neck as she reached his ear and whispered. The words were in a language he didn't recognize. Her voice remained sickly sweet as before, but this time there was genuine power in her words. Some hidden, preternatural part of him responded to them, and he felt his conscious mind slipping.

He dropped the knife at her throat, and the power that he had retained from the earlier battle leached out of him as he relaxed and let go. Somewhere a dear and obedient friend silently whimpered.

As Chael's eyes rolled back in his head, they caught the faintest glimpse of a crimson bead of blood flowing gently down the woman's alabaster neck. The sight held his gaze, and a thought occurred to him, piercing the foggy veil over his mind.

Lifeless because of him, Chael mused.Can't let them see you dealing with the town spook, Chael thought as he was quickly conducted by a timid house servant to the third level of the keep and into the lord's apartments.

He wasn't sure what that meant, or even why that thought came to him, but as he held onto it, a touch of clarity came to his mind and some control returned to his body. Control enough to whistle. Michik bounded from his hiding place in the forest and launched himself at the woman. She managed to just lift her arms in time to protect her neck, preventing Michik from grabbing hold, but his momentum sent them both flying away from Chael, where they slammed into the ground.

Chael immediately regained control of his full faculties. Mason was running to free his mistress of Michik and Cooper was reaching into his black cloak for something. Chael threw his last hidden dagger at Cooper and kicked the one he had dropped into the air and caught it as he rushed to interdict Mason. He launched himself at Mason's side and buried the throwing knife into his back as he bore the large man to the ground.

Chael withdrew the knife and plunged it back down, this time towards Mason's chest, but a clawed, black hand latched onto his wrist and held him fast. It was at this moment that Chael noticed that the blood dripping from the knife had blots of inky black flowing with the red. For the first time since he arrived, Chael got a good look at Mason and was horrified by what he saw.

Mason's arm that was holding his own in an unnaturally strong grip had long black, almost talon-like claws and looked as if it had been taken directly from one of the dead lesser demons back at the camp. It was at least a foot longer than his human right arm and gave his torso a hulking ape-like aspect. Mason's once fairly ordinary face was also horribly disfigured. It was swollen and saggy and a great bulbous black orb had replaced his left eye. It had no pupils, but Chael could sense where it was looking, past him and to his mistress who was being thrashed by his angry dog.

Mason twisted Chael's arm and manipulated his wrist, causing him to drop the knife and with demonic strength, he hurled Chael into a tree. Chael smashed into a smaller oak tree and once again felt the crunching of several ribs as he wearily got to his feet. Mason was almost on top of Michik and the woman now and he lashed out with his long, powerful demonic arm, but the clever wolf let go of the woman at the last second and darted away.

Mason's clawed attack swiped only air and narrowly avoided disemboweling his own mistress. The raven-haired woman was covered in blood and teeth marks from Michik, but Chael couldn't tell if any of the wounds were fatal. Mason clearly didn't want to chance it because he immediately scooped her up and bounded into the trees without looking back.

Chael turned to Cooper. He noted with some satisfaction that there was a deep cut across the left side of his face, but unfortunately, it was mostly superficial. He was standing over the struggling Baron pouring some sort of black liquid down his throat, and then calmly walked around to the other side of the great tree. Chael took two steps in pursuit when Janus looked up at him with a confused look on his face.

Then the world went sideways.

The Baron's bulbous form exploded directly in front of Chael. He and Michik were thrown nearly twenty feet by the blast as chunks of flesh and bone hurled outward from the crater that had once been Baron Janus Al-Fhaelan. Several shards of the unfortunate nobleman's bones pierced Chael's skin as readily as an arrow as he flew backward and crashed into one of the many trees.

Chael instinctually grasped onto the power provided by the death of the Baron, but it was far weaker than it should have been. It provided him a few more precious moments of consciousness as the energy began to slowly mend some of his more life-threatening wounds. He watched as Cooper emerged unscathed from behind the tree and took a step toward him and then stopped.

"She needs you alive," Cooper spat at Chael. He regarded Chael for a moment with a look of pure anger and then turned and fled into the forest after Mason.

Chael had just enough energy left to see the Dark worshiper disappear into the trees before the energy was exhausted and he slipped into unconsciousness.

Chapter 14

11 Years Ago

Chael nervously fidgeted while he sat on the cold whitestone marble bench in the upper gallery of the ministerial audience hall. Below him was a vaulted chamber made entirely of the whitestone, quarried nearby and held in high esteem by the city's governors. Several rows of carved wooden pews flanked a carpeted central aisle that led up to a marble and gold podium where the High Minister would announce his decrees.

As with everything in this city, the seating was arranged by the position and power of the people in attendance. The ones with the most influence reserved spaces nearest the podium and so on. Chael observed an empty spot in the second pew on the right where his master would sit when he arrived.

This room is where all the various low ministers supplicated to the High Minister for whatever boon or aid that ostensibly was to be used for the good of their area of influence within the city. More often than not, whatever scraps the minister did proffer them were simply used to further the political ambitions of the ministers and the houses of power they represented.

Politics, Chael huffed. The art of looking pretty and acting ghastly. Though by the nature of his job, Chael was wrapped up in politics as much as any of the hypocrites arranged below him. He always looked people in the face when he brought about their demise. That is, when he could help it.

"Why are you so glum?" Darrik asked, nudging him slightly in the ribs.

Chael hadn't told Darrik about his trip to the guard captain's home a few nights prior. The seemingly jovial face Mason had put on was as much of a mask as worn by the haunting demon he had summoned.

Chael could still see the crazed grin the Dark cultist wore as he summoned forth the Darkspawn. But the thing that had lingered with him most was the almost smile he had detected from the creature as it momentarily bore down on him, barely visible through the stretched remains of some poor victim's skin. It didn't have a human mouth; Chael wasn't confident it had any kind of mouth. Presumed lack of facial opening aside, he got the unmistakable feeling that it was smirking at him, as if the demon knew some joke of which Chael was the butt. He shook visibly at the memory.

"I'm fine," Chael finally said after a long pause.

Darrik still looked concerned, but let the matter go. While they continued waiting for the meetings to take place below them, Darrik regaled Chael of his adventures with the other survivors of their school. Only a few were apparently left in Kazaam; most had been sent out to the other republics to begin preparations there. *He certainly is ambitious,* Chael thought as Darrik illuminated him on the scope of Khalim's plans for the republics.

"So, you've actually seen some action then?" Chael asked Darrik as he was just finishing a story of a suspiciously heroic battle that he had apparently engaged in solo, despite members of the Black Hand cult nearby.

"Oh, yeah!" Darrik replied, "it wasn't as easy as our scrape back in that tavern last year."

Chael recalled the incident with the four fingers gang and finally cracked a smile. Darrik nudged him in the ribs again and smiled back.

"But anyway, after their hired help were taken care of, the merchants' guild was more amenable to our cause."

"Did the black cloaks do anything odd while you were there?" Chael asked hesitantly, thinking again of his own experience with Mason.

"No?" Darrik replied.

So just me then, Chael thought.

"But they may have been more useful in the fight than I let on," Darrik added with a sheepish grin.

This time, Chael nudged his larger friend in the ribs.

"Hey!" Darrik complained sarcastically, but Chael cut him off with his hand and pointed down at the audience hall. Their master, Khalim, had arrived, which meant that the show was about to start.

Indeed, just minutes after Khalim had taken his seat, a regiment of the city watch burst into the white marble audience chamber and marched down the center aisle toward the podium.

Because of the austerity of the occasion, they were dressed in shining plate and carried decorated halberds as opposed to their usual leathers and arming swords. Bringing up the rear of the column was Captain Duntos. It had only been a few days, but he looked as if he had aged a decade. His eyes were worn and bloodshot, and there was a gauntness to his face that didn't exist before. The captain also repeatedly looked over his shoulder as though he was expecting something to jump from the shadows and attack.

Chael knew precisely what lurked there. Even if the captain wasn't acting suspicious, he could tell what was behind him by the wrinkled noses of the ministers and functionaries that Duntos passed by.

When the soldiers of the city watch reached the podium, they parted and allowed their captain to march up to the front. Duntos attempted to regain the air of authority he had so clearly lost over the past few days and stood up straighter before speaking.

"High Minister, I beg your pardon for the interruption, but urgent matters have recently come to my attention." The minister held a look of stunned outrage, but he quickly regained his composure.

"Of course, Captain," he said through a forced smile. "Please, tell us what is so urgent."

"Well…" Duntos cleared his throat and spared one last glance behind him. "A week past I received this evidence." Duntos pulled out the very letters that Chael and Darrik had extracted from the four fingers gang last year. "After carefully investigating their authenticity, I came to the unfortunate conclusion that Hemlan of Great House Arda has been consorting with several organized elements of the city's criminals."

He pointed an accusatory finger at a shocked man sitting in the first pew just to the left of the podium. On the right side, Khalim displayed a rare smile.

"Furthermore," Duntos continued, developing a certain gusto. "I can directly implicate Hemlan and his House in the murder of several members of the merchants' guild just three days ago!"

Damn, Chael thought. The Baron probably had a point there. Chael fought back the retort that had flown to his lips. He was annoyed that the Baron had figured him so well. A carpenter I am not, he thought out loud, looking at his questionable work. He turned to look down the path that led from his home and into the forest towards Ehbing. After a moment, he was also able to hear the approach of at least several people and a horse which had set off the keen senses of his dog.

The representative of the merchants' guild opened his mouth and began to give testimony when he was cut off by

Hemlan House Arda. Hemlan jumped to his feet and screamed at Captain Duntos.

"Liar!" he shouted. "Who do you work for?!"

With a wave of his hand, Duntos sent two soldiers over to arrest the patriarch of Great House Arda. He continued to yell and shout as the soldiers dragged him from the audience hall. It was only when they had reached the doors that he began to call to his former patron to save him. The High Minister could only watch on in horrified shock as his former supporter was forcibly taken from the audience hall.

Once Hemlan's cries faded from the room, the assembled crowd burst into noise once more. Depending on where they sat, the chatter was a mixture of stunned outrage like the minister, bewildered wonderment, or open ambition. As the murmuring grew, the only constant throughout the audience chamber were the stolen glances at the now unoccupied space at the front of the room.

Chael glanced down at his own patron, who, in contrast to nearly everyone else, sat quietly smiling. The sight was nearly as frightening as the lurking demon.

After escorting Khalim home from the audience hall, Chael had a rare afternoon of free time. After some thought, he decided to head to the Northern gate of the city and slip into the Aazeran forest just beyond the city. If he hurried, there would still be a few hours of daylight left to enjoy the peace of the forest before returning to the city. The events of today's meeting were sure to cause quite a tumult in the city, and he was happy to have the freedom to escape for at least a few hours.

At length, he neared the large stone gate in the outer wall of the lower stone circle of Kazaam. As it was still midafternoon, the two-story portcullis was drawn and free passage was still available in and out of the city. That was normal. What wasn't normal was the complete lack of humanity at what should have been a fairly busy gate. Other than the forest, there was still a large section of the poorer area of the city outside the walls and traffic to and from the inner city was nearly constant during daylight hours.

Chael instinctively reached to his belt for his sword and winced. Outside the city watch, no one was allowed to bring weapons into the residence of the High Minister where the audience hall was located. A policy, Chael thought, that the minister was probably reconsidering at this very moment.

She is probably used to giving orders and being obeyed, Chael guessed.

"So, am I meant to guess where you're hidden or are the lot of you going to come out and fight?" Chael yelled his challenge into the empty space before the gate.

What did she not want to say? Chael wondered. *I've probably killed more Dark spawn than any other man alive,* he thought bitterly.

To his left was one of the city's smaller tributary rivers and to his right was a hastily abandoned cobbler's shop. He chose right and dove into the dubious cover of the small storefront.

The space he had occupied a mere second earlier exploded into a spinning vortex of fire. The windows of the shop shattered inward and sprayed Chael with shards of glass as he ducked below its stone wall. *They have an alchemist,* Chael muttered under his breath and cursed.

He inched his way low into the back of the store, hoping for a rear exit, but found only a wall of the solid blue-gray stone that marked this circle of the city. Chael knew that if the alchemist lobbed another one of those bombs into the small confines of this shop, the heat alone would do him in. *Darkness!* Chael cursed and sprinted towards the door.

As he neared the doorway, he spied the faintest glimpse of an arm hiding just beyond, waiting to surprise him as he escaped. Just before he reached the doorway, Chael dove low and rolled out into the street. He caught sight of a sword stuck into the frame as he finished his roll and bounced back to his feet, still sprinting. He tossed one of his knives over his shoulder, hoping the awkward throw might at least wound his attacker.

As he sprinted, Chael scanned the area for the hidden alchemist but came up empty. He did, however, see two more attackers in addition to the one he had left in the doorway of the cobbler's shop, and to his mild surprise and even greater joy, that one had a throwing knife sticking out of his gut.

The three attackers he was able to identify were all fairly nondescript. They weren't wearing armor and were all armed with the same type of simple long sword that was common throughout the city. However, despite the mundane nature of these three, employing an alchemist meant the person trying to kill him had money, lots of money. Chael reached the edge of the river and dove in just as another fiery tornado erupted behind him. The heat of the alchemical blast reached him nearly a full pace under the water as he swam to the opposite bank.

He emerged from the river panting and out of breath. The dead sprint and swim under water had stolen his air for the moment. *No arrows or crossbow bolts; that's something,* Chael thought.

He knew very little about alchemy, but given the volatile nature of the fiery projectiles, Chael suspected they took a moment to prepare, so he used that moment to search for the bastard. Chael concentrated, looking for any movement or out-of-place shadow.

After a few seconds, the world seemed to grow darker. The stone of the street and cobbler's shop sunk into deep shadow and became barely visible. Chael blinked and glanced back to check on the men he left on the other side of the narrow river.

Each seemed to shine with a yellow-white light except the wounded man near the shop. The light emanating from him was slightly fainter but seemed to burst forth all the brighter from the wound Chael had left in his belly. That man was going to die. Stomach wounds were particularly nasty in his experience. But it was more than an educated guess; Chael somehow knew with absolute certainty that the man was about to expire.

Another sweep of the stone plaza and he spotted another source of light crouched behind a crate near the city gate back on the other side of the river. Chael could see a clear outline of the alchemist as he presumably crouched over another one of his bombs.

The alchemist shifted and peered out over his cover, spotting him and threw a round ceramic pot, about the size of his fist in Chael's direction. Chael dove back into the river and swam as fast as he could toward his attackers on the opposite shore. He just barely got out of the water when one of the uninjured swordsmen swung hard down at him.

All Chael could do was flop down on the ground and roll out of the way. The next swing came down to take his head and Chael parried it with one of his knives and struck out with a foot, tripping him. However, before Chael could take advantage, the other man stabbed down at him. Chael was able to partially knock the blade aside, but it sliced painfully into his shoulder.

Chael yelled out in rage and pain at the man standing above him. He successfully parried the next thrust and stabbed his attacker's knee with a knife he pulled out with his left hand. The man buckled and Chael slashed his throat and dumped him in the river.

Chael quickly leaped to his feet to meet the oncoming attack of the final swordsman. He dodged and parried several blows as he worked his assailant around in a circle, putting him between himself and the alchemist. Chael wasn't positive the alchemist wouldn't just burn his comrade anyway, but he didn't have a lot of options at the moment.

Chael pressed, driving his attacker backward with all the creativity he could muster with his knives. This man wasn't terrible, but Chael had been training most of his life for moments such as these and even with a wounded shoulder, Chael was the far superior fighter. Under the onslaught of Chael's vicious knives, the man slowly backed his way toward the gatehouse.

"Come on you darkened asshole!" Chael grunted through gritted teeth, looking over the swordsman's shoulder. They were merely ten paces away from the alchemist's hiding spot now, and the overwhelmed killer in front of Chael continued to give ground.

At last, fearing for his life and trying to gain a safe distance to throw his bombs, the alchemist bolted from his hiding place.

Chael smiled. He kicked the swordsman in front of him in the chest, just below the sternum. The man doubled over just enough to give Chael a line of sight, and he launched one of his knives at the fleeing alchemist. It sank to the hilt into his neck and the man dropped, blood gushing out in thick crimson spurts over the stones.

Momentarily distracted, Chael almost missed the slice aimed at his thigh and barely managed to dodge enough to avoid a crippling blow. As it was, he still received a large gash across his upper thigh.

Chael howled again, mostly in frustration at himself, and pressed his attack anew. This time, he wasn't simply trying to drive him back, and he easily caught the beleaguered man's next thrust with his remaining knife. He forced the sword out away from their bodies and stepped inside his attacker's guard. Chael stomped down hard on the insole of his foot with his heavy boots. The fighter was knocked off balance and Chael easily shoved him to the ground. The swordsman stared up at Chael for a moment and then tossed his weapon into the river.

"Please!" the man begged. "Let me go!"

Chael stared down at the man coolly. It was only in this moment of relative calm he noticed that his vision was normal. He made a mental note to investigate the strange anomaly later.

"Please, I'll tell you anything!" the attacker continued to plead from the stone street.

"Who do you work for?" Chael asked coldly.

"Great House Arda," the man responded hastily.

Makes sense, Chael thought. Chael walked around to the side of his ambusher.

"I'm not lying, I don't know anything else, I swear!"

"I know," Chael whispered softly and plunged his knife into the man's chest. Chael watched, numb and exhausted, as the blood of the alchemist slowly mingled with the blood of the man at his feet. As his nerves settled and the haze of battle lifted, the wounds in his shoulder and thigh asserted themselves more forcefully. Chael groaned against the sudden throbbing pain.

He heard the snap of the crossbow behind him and instinctually flopped unceremoniously down on his belly. The front of his shirt and cloak were immediately drenched in the pooling blood of the men he had just killed. As he got back to his feet, he glanced back to where the bolt had come from. A dozen men were marching up the street a little over one hundred paces away. Several were wearing the seal of Great House Arda, and one had stopped to wind up a heavy crossbow.

There's the rest of the ambush party, I guess, Chael muttered to himself. Chael supposed he should be flattered. An alchemist and three armsmen were merely a delaying tactic until the rest of the group of assassins could catch up. However, at the moment, the best he could do was mild irritation. Seeing that they only had the one crossbowman in the group and hoping there were no more alchemists hidden in the ranks, Chael dashed as fast as he could toward the gate.

Chapter 15

Present Day

Chael awoke with one of the more unpleasant headaches of his life. The first thing he noticed was the bobbing motion of whatever makeshift bedding he was laying upon. *Am I floating,* he wondered absently.

Slowly, he opened his eyes, and the light seared his already gruesome headache. As his eyes slowly adjusted, his memory of the battle and the morbid demise of Baron Janus returned to his memory.

He bolted upright. "Mason! He's… where…?" He was on what appeared to be the late Baron's litter.

In front of him was Sir Andon, grunting as he hauled the front of the improvised stretcher on his shoulders. A glance behind him confirmed Aelisa was somehow supporting his weight and carried the back half of the load. After what she displayed in the battle against the demons, Chael wouldn't have been shocked if she had simply carried the litter herself.

A few paces away, he spotted Michik scouting ahead and clearly guiding their small troupe. Sensing he was awake, his dog looked back and wagged his tail affectionately before continuing on ahead. Although he still felt genuinely awful, Chael promptly jumped down from the litter, eliciting a relieved sigh from Andon.

"So, you're capable of walking then?" said a cold voice behind him. He turned and saw the cool, appraising eyes of Sister Aelisa. Chael patted himself down; there were several sore spots, but he seemed to be more or less intact.

"I think so," Chael responded, giving his best attempt at a confident smile. He was fairly certain that if he marched more than a league or two, he would almost certainly retch all over himself and promptly pass out, but he kept that to himself. "How far have we come?" Chael asked, trying to shake the sister's implacable gaze.

"You've been asleep for nearly two days," came the voice of Sir Andon. "When we found you, you had bits of teeth and bone embedded so far inside you the sister had to cut you open to fish them out. I've seen battlefield surgery before but this… A normal man would be dead." A dozen feet away, there was a faint canine whimper.

"A normal man would be," repeated Aelisa, still giving him her unnerving, icy stare.

"For a moment you seemed to come to," continued Sir Andon. "But you didn't open your eyes, you just took a deep breath and passed out again."

"And as you took that breath, you managed to somehow steal the life from every blade of grass, every bush, shrub, and tree. And only the Living Stars know what else out there."

Aelisa's normally dispassionate expression shifted to anger for just a moment. The same look of indignation she displayed whenever the creatures of the Dark were mentioned.

Chael looked away in shame. He had no memory of any such event, but it certainly explained why he wasn't bleeding everywhere. Andon gave him a sympathetic shrug, but he couldn't disguise his own look of bewilderment at the previous day's events.

"We waited half the day to make sure you didn't expire and then put you on the Baron's stretcher. We were able to march well into the night because of your wolf. Without the ability to see the sun or stars through the trees we would have been lost but he seemed to know the way and we followed."

As if Michik knew he was about to be praised, he had padded over to Chael and was nuzzling his hand with his snout. Chael obliged with yet another well-earned head scratch. While watching the display even Aelisa's face softened slightly.

It took the rest of that day, but as night fell, they finally emerged at the Eastern edge of the Dark Forest. As they stepped out into the wide plain before them, the moods of his companions immediately improved. It was as if a dark veil had been lifted from their eyes, and even the normally stoic Sister Aelisa managed a smile. Looking back at the Dark Forest, it seemed even more foreboding and dismal than when they had been inside it.

"We will stop at Fhaerstead for the night. You should be able to secure some horses there and journey to the capitol tomorrow," pronounced Aelisa.

"Us?" Chael asked the Order Priestess.

"There's a chapter house of the Fraternal Order of Celestial Light in the city. I will depart your company there." Having issued her commands, she charged eastward. Chael let her gain a small lead ahead of them, holding Andon back.

"Did anything happen while I was out?" Chael asked the knight.

"No, the Dark Forest was actually peaceful," Andon responded, frowning. "Odd that, given what we'd experienced so far." Chael nodded in agreement. Chael thought it was odd that the Black Hand, Mason and his ilk, hadn't attacked them while he was incapacitated, but he kept his thoughts to himself.

The journey to Fhaerstead took another two hours. As they approached the outskirts of the city, a grand wooden palisade rose from the horizon, tipped with cruel metal spikes that seemed to dare the Dark creatures of the forest to come forth. Below the palisade was a wall made of carved stone about ten feet high. Together with the wood, the barrier facing the Western Forest easily reached twenty-five feet into the air.

There was no gate on this side of the city, and there was a clear lack of activity outside for a city of this size. As they made their way around the city, the wooden palisade shrank until it just became a series of spikes on top of the fortified stone wall.

As they neared the Southeastern side of the city, the wall spikes gave way entirely and the first signs of human activity emerged. They had to cross through a large apple orchard in order to reach the road to the city gate. Chael made sure to snatch a couple of the ripest specimens when Sister Aelisa wasn't looking. He offered some to Andon, who smiled but politely refused.

Chael shrugged and tossed the apple into the air behind him; the resounding crunch of apple flesh confirmed that his dog had successfully caught it out of the air. Michik didn't need to eat, and Chael had no idea where the food actually went, but the wolf seemed to appreciate the gesture, nonetheless.

Chael's first observations of Fhaerstead were that it was maybe a fifth the size of Kazaam and quite dingier. Overall, he found the caste social structure of his original home to be repugnant, but at the very least, it provided some decent architecture to look up at.

In fairness, Chael thought, you can't really look up at anything in Fhaerhold either, aside from the keep. The city was built on a wide plane, and it was consequently quite flat. But its lack of verticality didn't excuse the lack of creative vision in Chael's eyes.

Despite the lateness of the hour, there were no lights, even on the main thoroughfare in front of the gate. The streets were a muddy morass of cart tracks and hoofprints, and the entire city was built from what looked like entirely salvaged panes of wood in a ramshackle style.

Dark spawn than any other man alive, he thought bitterly.At least they untied my feet, he thought bitterly. Damn demons, Chael grumbled to himself.

Chael briefly considered asking Sir Andon, but he was interrupted by the unmistakable sound of a bowstring. He instinctively dove into the mud and similarly colored substances, completely ruining his last clean shirt.

The missile having passed, he leaped up, sword drawn, scanning the wooden shacks around him for assailants. He didn't have to search hard; three of them had bows drawn and were creeping towards them yelling incoherently. Or perfectly coherently. At the moment, Chael didn't really care because the more important sound that reached his ears was a distinct wolfish whine.

Chael spun around and spotted the arrow embedded in the rear leg of Michik, who instead of his customary ferocious snarl at the would-be attackers, was merely whining and cowering at his master's feet.

A sudden rage filled Chael's chest, and he burned with the same Dark energy as if he had stolen the life energy of a dozen warriors. Now concentrating, he heard the shouts of the men arrayed in front of him.

"Demon!"

"Darkspawn, begone from the city!"

Another one loosed an arrow aimed at Michik, but Chael was able to slap it out of the air on the flat of his falchion. He sprinted at the group, sodden boots filling with more of the thick detritus of the marshy street. He reached the first archer and easily split the bow in half with his sword and kicked the man into the mud. The second man was disarmed just as easily and joined his fellow in the muck. Chael turned to the last man, but he had already dropped his bow and raised his hands in surrender. Chael, fury unsated, raised his sword to the man, but before he could decide what to do, his falchion was knocked aside by a knight's traditional longsword.

"Chael that's enough!" Andon stood in front of him, sword held high but had a sympathetic, pleading look on his face.

Chael nodded at him and lowered his sword and walked away. He saw Sister Aelisa studying him with the same cold, emotionless look she always gave him. She hadn't interfered like the knight, but she did seem to be watching the matter intently. Chael wondered if the outcome was to her liking or not, with Aelisa it was impossible to tell.

Chael bent down to his dog and Michik hesitantly raised his back leg up to him. He gently removed the arrow from Michik's hip; thankfully, it was a bodkin style point. Good for penetrating things like armor, but it lacked the broad barbed head of a more hunting orienting arrow.

Probably for shooting at demons, Chael supposed. *Utterly useless.* Poking holes in Darkspawn was a vain endeavor. Having removed the arrow, he scooped Michik in his arms and hid his features as best as he could under his soiled green cloak.

As he stomped by, he gave a final glare to the three bowmen and snapped the remaining unbroken bow with his boot for good measure. Andon was speaking to them harshly, gesturing emphatically, but Chael didn't pay attention.

After the incident in the street, Aelisa gave them curt professional goodbyes and disappeared down one of the dirty streets, presumably in the direction of her Order House. Sir Andon led them to an inn and ordered them a bath, and even secured a change of clothes for them both.

Chael kept his dog hidden under his cloak and managed to keep his more distinct features hidden despite Michik's size could rival a small horse.

Chael bathed himself and donned the new pair of trousers and shirt. They weren't ideal, but they fit well enough and would suit him for one more day of travel until he could reach the capitol.

He did his best to clean his cloak and hung it out to dry over the washbasin in his room. After that he looked from the soapy tub and over to the still mud sodden Michik, a wry smile creeping over his face. The wolf bolted for the far corner of the room and growled defiantly.

It was nearly an hour before Chael emerged from his room and made his way downstairs to the common room of the inn. Despite his general distaste for the rest of the city, Chael felt the inn was reasonably well appointed. The room upstairs seemed well kept, and the common room, while small, was warm and inviting.

He spied Andon at the bar, speaking to the keeper in hushed tones. Chael looked at him quizzically and the knight gestured to a nearby table.

It took several more minutes, but eventually Andon came over carrying two bowls of steaming stew and accompanying flagons of ale. Chael was informed that both were made in house. The stew was serviceable, if a bit bland, but the ale was perfection. Subtly sweet with bright earthy notes; he made a mental note to stop by here when the business in the capital was concluded.

"It's a mess," Sir Andon announced after they had eaten their meal. "That giant wooden wall wasn't here the last time I came through the city." Andon pointed back at the barkeep. "He told me that demons began pouring out of the forest a few months ago. Before that many of these people weren't even sure such creatures existed. The King recalled most of the city's men-at-arms to the capitol, so they had to deputize many of the citizens. Those men we ran into were one of the night patrols."

"That's why they shot at Michik," Chael responded, shaking his head.

Andon nodded. As far as he was aware, there weren't any four-legged Darkspawn, but scared people rarely act with a surplus of rationality.

After a moment, Chael's mind latched on to the other comment Sir Andon had said. "The King is gathering soldiers, are the Republics really marching?"

"I don't know," Andon sighed. "But strange things are happening, we need to report to the King."

Chael wasn't overly thrilled with meeting his monarch; the blood of the man's cousin still stained his cloak, and rulers didn't generally let those kinds of things go in his experience. Still, he nodded at Sir Andon and slowly sipped the delicious ale.

Chapter 16

11 years ago

Chael limped through the Northern gate of Kazaam, doing his best to staunch the bleeding in his shoulder and thigh. Despite his best efforts, the hot blood trickled down his leg and left a distinct trail of red markers in his wake. He didn't dare look back, but knew that they would certainly be gaining on him. His best chance was to lose them in the Aazeran forest and maybe take a few of them down individually. However, he had to beat them to the forest first, and the trees were still at least four hundred paces away.

Chael broke out in a full sprint, grunting as the wound in his leg protested. He concentrated on his breathing, steadily inhaling and exhaling with the rhythm of his run to block out the pain.

Three hundred paces. The sound of hoofbeats broke his concentration. He looked back in horror as one of his pursuers galloped out of the gate.

Two hundred paces. Chael let out a scream and increased his speed, willing his body to move faster.

One hundred paces. He could hear the breaths of the horse now, snorting furiously as its rider spurred it onward.

Fifty paces. Chael could feel the approaching rider and knew he couldn't make the forest. He pulled out his last knife and dove to the side, blindly flicking it at the horse as he fell.

The knife sliced across the horse's left flank, but its momentum carried it forward and the rider bore down on him with a wicked, curved blade. Chael threw his arms up, shielding his face. Lightning arced across his chest and arms as the rider's sword sliced a cruel line up his body. The cut wasn't immediately fatal, Chael hoped, but all he could do was lie on the ground immobilized by pain.

Ten paces. Chael pushed himself up weakly to his knees. Blood was pouring from his side and parts of his right leg were going numb. The rider was trying to wheel his horse around for another pass, but the wounded animal was bucking and thrashing frantically.

Chael smiled weakly. That was at least something. He looked back at the gate; the rest of the ambushers had slowed to a leisurely walk. They assumed that the horse rider had done the job and didn't need to overly burden themselves as they came to mop up.

Chael rose to one leg, sheer defiance fueling his failing limbs. He dragged himself over to where his remaining dagger was lying in the dirt, slick with horse blood. He picked it up and aimed his best shot at the rider.

With shaking hands, he launched his best throw at the man's neck. It struck him in the hip. The rider howled in pain, and the panicked horse finally bucked its rider and galloped away giving furious howls of its own.

Chael swore and hobbled over to the struggling rider as fast as he could. He launched himself at him just as he was gaining his feet. The two struggled on the ground for several moments, Chael losing large gobs of blood in the process.

The rider punched Chael repeatedly in his bleeding ribs. Chael yelled furiously and head-butted his opponent in the face several times. His hand slid down the man's body and finally found purchase on the knife still embedded in his hip. Chael cried out in furious victory and, with the last of his strength, drove the knife down repeatedly into the man's chest.

He rolled off the rider and coughed up more blood. He looked down at the other men in pursuit and saw that their lazy chase had turned into a run after what he did to their comrade. Chael laughed, dribbling more blood down his chin. If he had to die today, at least he gave as good as he got. He managed to give the pursuers one final rude gesture and collapsed into the dirt, unconscious.

Chael burst from oblivion like it was a cold stream, gasping for air and shivering. He couldn't be sure how much time had passed since he lost consciousness, however it couldn't have been very long because his pursuers were still about one hundred paces away.

He did, however, know the precise moment he awoke was also the precise moment the rider had died. As he breathed, a cold energy overtook him, suffusing his body and adding renewed strength to his limbs. The long hideous gash left behind by the rider's sword was still there, but the bleeding had stopped, and the once gaping wound was simply a thin, shallow cut from the base of his ribs up to his collarbone and across his arms. Still, fairly serious, but no longer life threatening.

I hate people, he thought glumly as sleep finally overtook him.

Chael wasn't sure how his miraculously healed wounds would hold up and felt they were far too numerous for his one remaining throwing knife. He turned and bolted into the Aazeran forest.

He sprinted past trees and vaulted over a small brush as he plunged deeper into the denser core of the untamed wood. After about two minutes of sprinting full speed, the energy that had somehow sustained his body a moment ago subsided and the many remaining injuries began to painfully protest.

He stopped, bent over panting, and surveyed his trail. It was not subtle. A blind, houndless tracker could find him in the dark. *Good.*

Carefully, he doubled back over his obvious trail, doing his best not to leave any new signs of passing. Chael knew he had gained some ground on the pursuit, but he only risked backtracking about thirty paces before carefully veering off the trail. He hid in the hollow of a withered oak tree; it gave him a good view of the trail and should keep him concealed in shadow while they passed.

Chael breathed carefully, trying to steady his heart. His side ached painfully, and it was difficult to take more than shallow breaths, but he pushed through, willing his body to calm and prepare for the immediate trial ahead.

A forge, Chael supposed. For in essence, that's what the school was. Minister Khalim bought forgotten and unwanted children and hauled them out to this small property in secret, not to educate them, as the word "school" implied. They were cast into a furnace and forged through fire into tools that served the cruel minister's needs. And those that couldn't serve were simply burned away by the flame. But now the tools would be brought to bear, and the survivors of Khalim's brutal school would finally emerge into the light. Election season had begun in Kazaam.I'll just have to prove my worth, he thought.

Chael tossed a small stone, aiming at a tree about fifteen feet from the anxious archer. The nervous man squeezed the lever of his crossbow and released an errant bolt at the sound. Several of his companions chided him but kept marching into the forest.

Grumbling to himself, the crossbowman stopped and began the tedious process of cranking his crossbow back into battery for his next shot. The rest of the party moved ahead.

Carefully moving through shadows, Chael approached the man. He was still looking around the forest nervously, jumping at every shadow. He watched his companions slowly disappear into the trees and furiously increased the pace of his cranking.

He's patronizing me, Chael thought. He didn't like being spoken down to, the man was big and obviously strong, and Chael guessed he was used to intimidating people. But Chael had been exhaustively trained on how to deal with people who were bigger and stronger and felt quite confident about his odds should they come to blows. However, he had been ordered to play host, so he was largely impotent to teach Mason a lesson. Probably curious if I'm as insane as he is, Chael thought. He briefly considered jumping off the balcony to prove that he was just as capable, but his better senses won out and he turned toward the door to the stairs. I could have been out on a real mission, Chael sighed as he made his way out of the building.

Missiles rained down on the hired killers from every angle of the forest. *Nine, eight, seven, six.* Slowly, Chael whittled down their number until he ran out of stolen bolts.

The remaining mercenaries of House Arda now huddled together, back-to-back, staring out into the forest for where death might strike at them next. Chael steeled himself and stepped out of the shadows, allowing the fading evening light to wash over him.

"Welcome, gentlemen!" he called cordially to his would-be assassins. "I don't suppose any of you would like to take this opportunity to just run home. Hmmm?"

Chael inched a little closer to the group with every word, garishly flourishing his empty left hand as he did. "No? More's the pity."

He gave an exaggerated sigh and launched his last throwing knife at one of the men bearing the crest of his house. The knife sunk into his neck with an ugly squelch of blood. The group was momentarily stunned, and Chael burst into action. He stabbed low at the next nearest mercenary and plunged his borrowed sword into the man's thigh.

I could have been out on a real mission, Chael sighed as he made his way out of the building.I hate people, he thought, and then glanced down at his dog. I suppose that's sufficient mockery for the moment, he conceded to himself. "Now," he continued more earnestly, "why in Darkness have you come here?"

The remaining mercenaries quickly came to their senses and spread out, encircling Chael. He spun in a slow circle, meeting each of their eyes, challenging each one in turn to be the first to engage him. They were scared, but apparently more greedy than cowardly. *Oh, how I yearn for a more pragmatic brand of assassin,* Chael chuckled to himself.

After several tense moments, one of them finally got the nerve to attack him directly. A rough melee ensued. Once one of the mercenaries attacked, they all rushed forward in a blind charge. Chael chose the nearest one and met his charge at a run. He easily swept aside the ensuing sword strike and neatly hamstrung his assailant as he ran by.

His partner, however, managed to get in a horizontal slice, reopening Chael's rib. Chael cursed loudly, staggering to the side as he met another sword thrust and turned it away. He didn't have any time to take advantage, however, as another blade swung down on his neck and he ducked aside, skewering the man with a quick riposte.

Two more, Chael thought. Well, technically three, but the third wasn't in any condition to fight with his leg hanging loosely like that.

Chael smirked at the two men who remained on their feet. They looked much less committed to whatever prize awaited them back in the city. But just as Chael was brimming with confidence, the fresh wound across his chest spewed an unseemly amount of blood. Chael staggered, woozy from all the blood loss.

This time, it was the mercenaries' turn to smirk. They attacked him together with unrelenting thrusts and slices that kept Chael on his back foot solely occupied with blocking their attacks while blood continued to pour down his side.

He was losing, and he knew it. What's more is his opponents knew it as well, and they pressed him harder and harder as he backpedaled through the forest. Chael lacked the strength to run, and his numb, tired limbs were only just barely capable of staving off death, let alone launching counters at his opponents.

A low growl interrupted the onslaught. As one, Chael and his two attackers turned their heads to the forest just as a gray blur leaped from amidst the trees. It bypassed Chael and took one of his attackers in the throat, wrestling him to the ground. Chael took advantage of the moment and lunged a pathetic stab at the other one, piercing his chest. Had he not been staring at the wolf food that was formerly his companion, the attack would have been easily parried.

Chael fell to the ground, exhausted, watching a gigantic gray wolf tear the head off of the mercenary. After the body stopped flailing, the wolf slowly turned her blood-soaked snout to face him. She growled again, baring rows of red stained teeth. The blood of the mercenary mingled with her own mucus as it dripped from her wolfish jowls and onto the rough dirt. She lunged.

Chael gave every last spec of energy to his sword arm and stabbed across her path, shutting his eyes and turning away from certain death. He blinked once, surprised to still be alive, and glanced at his lap. There lay the head of the female wolf, skewered through the ear by his stolen sword.

"And zero." Chael coughed out bitterly, more precious blood leaking from his mouth.

With significant effort, he shoved the gigantic shewolf from his lap and slowly rose to his feet. He limped over to the man he had hamstrung a few paces away, half dragging his sword. He ignored the man's cries for mercy and, without saying a word, stabbed him in the throat.

The effort staggered him, and he almost lost consciousness right there. He looked up at the sky. The rays of light filtering through the treetops were becoming more orange and distant. He would sleep in the forest tonight; roaming around the city at night half dead was not a winning survival stratagem.

After a small, and somewhat lightheaded search, Chael found a small burrow carved out of the roots of a tree. It was just large enough for him to fit inside, as well as several furry shapes about the size of his boot.

He prodded one with his sword. It rolled over completely still, blood staining its furry face. *Dead. No wonder the mother was so enraged.* Someone or something had killed her pups.

One by one, he prodded them all and found similar bloody results. Chael sighed. He didn't have the energy to remove them from the small hollow, so he just slumped against the wall and slid down. He felt the still bleeding cuts in his ribs and the reopened wounds on his thigh and shoulder. Slowly, he allowed sleep to take him as he stared into the dark recess of the small cave. In the darkness, a small wolfish set of eyes stared back.

Chapter 17

Present Day

Human, he thought.

Andon assured the man that when he went to the capitol to pick them up, he would be compensated for his trouble. Michik eyed Chael's white mare dubiously; the horse, in turn, stamped nervously whenever the wolf was nearby.

After several curiously tense moments, the two animals seemed to reach a detente, and Chael's mount slowly inclined its head to his dog. Michik, clearly satisfied with the exchange, took a position at the head of their party. He seemed to hold his head a little higher in what Chael supposed was a more dignified manner. Chael laughed, gave a shrug to a confused-looking Andon and spurred his horse forward.

According to the knight, the journey to the capitol would take about a half a day on horseback. The road to the capitol stretched across a wide flat plain and was well maintained. Fields of wheat and other grains stretched for leagues on either side of the road. The product of which would make it to every corner of the continent, including the republics and Ehbing, the "breadbasket of the kingdom" they called it. Before long, Chael and Sir Andon fell into a comfortable canter, with Michik nobly taking the lead.

"How are you still alive?" Andon asked suddenly, breaking the companionable silence of the ride. "I saw the sister pluck a piece of the Baron's spine out of your chest that was larger than a plum." The knight motioned his head to Michik, still proudly leading the little parade. "And I still don't know what to make of him."

Chael sighed; he had truly done an awful job at concealing his Darker attributes, but the presence of the Black Hand was unanticipated. At length, he sighed and turned to Sir Andon.

"I truly don't understand it that well myself," Chael began. He hesitated; Andon had been trustworthy to this point, but in his experience, those who understood his abilities had one of two different reactions. They either wanted to control and use him for their benefit or cut off his head like any other demon. However, given what the knight had already seen, it was possible that no explanation was worse at this point.

"When you look around," Chael continued, gesturing to the fields of grain, "you see this wheat. You know it's alive because you observe it grow, and if mishandled, it dies. When I look at it, I can see the small sparks of life that flow from its roots through the stalk and into the seeds we cultivate. There's an energy there, in a single stalk of wheat. It's weak, unguarded. With effort I can reach in and steal that energy from the plant. I can sense this energy and see the moles and varmints in between the stalks as well and with some of these I can take that energy just as easily."

Chael patted the flank of the mare he rode. "Inside this horse is a much larger well of energy, but I can see it just as easily. The energy is too far away to just take, but if the horse were killed in the normal way, that energy would spill to the ground as assuredly as its blood, free to use."

Andon stared ahead, lost in thought for what seemed an eternity. Chael unconsciously squeezed the haunches of his mount with his knees, nervously anticipating the knight's reaction.

Finally, after several agonizing minutes, Andon turned back to Chael and gave him a short, curt nod. Chael let out an exacerbated breath that he didn't even realize he had been holding.

"Have you always had these, erm… abilities?" Andon asked, more curious now than suspicious.

"They appeared around the time of my twentieth year, but I have no explanation why."

"Your parents?" the knight asked.

"My father could have been any number of men my mother serviced during her time in the Kazaam pleasure houses. Pregnancy was frowned upon because it was generally bad for business, as you might imagine. But my mother was a good earner and convinced the proprietor not to simply kill me in her womb. They allowed me to stay there till I was six and then left me on the streets. If she still lives, I do not know."

Chael blurted out his origin so matter-of-factly that it disturbed even him. The knight looked simply horrified, so Chael gave him a forced smile and tried to change the subject. "You fought very well, you know, the Realm Knights must be a fearsome group."

"Yes, I suppose we are," Andon responded, mirroring Chael's now somewhat more genuine smile.

"Was that the first time you've fought a demon?" Chael asked.

Andon's smile quickly evaporated, and he nodded gravely.

"Then your victory is even more commendable," Chael added with an encouraging smile. Chael continued gently prodding into Sir Andon's background and the knight happily obliged and soon they began swapping battle stories companionably.

"The trick is," Andon said after sharing a delightfully naughty story about his time as a squire and a particularly irksome knight, "to cut the cinch around the neck almost to the point of breaking. It usually snaps right before he raises his lance and, oops!"

The knight made a gesture with his hands of the rider and saddle sliding down the side of the horse and ending up underneath the charging animal. Chael looked down at his mount and gave his own saddle a nervous inspection. Andon winked at him.

It was just after midday when the first traces of Fhaerhold came into view. It had once been built after the motte and bailey style. A large stone keep sat on a small, steep hill overlooking the otherwise flat surrounding area. The keep was built of a dark stone into a large rectangle with four towers at the vertices. In the center was an enormous domed roof that seemed to be made entirely of stained glass, the patterns of which were indecipherable at this distance.

Directly below the keep and down a long set of sinister looking stone steps was a large walled courtyard with various tall buildings of both stone and wood. Surrounding that courtyard was the city proper. Buildings of various styles and construction encircled the motte in a ring and sported a wooden wall at its edges. The city reminded Chael somewhat of Kazaam, but it was less striated. Sir Andon let out a satisfied sigh at the sight.

"Happy to be home?" Chael asked him.

"Yes," Andon answered contentedly. He then hesitated before continuing, "Chael we need to talk before we reach the city."

Chael looked at him frowning, but let Andon continue.

"After what happened back in Fhaerstead, I don't think we should take Michik into the city."

At the mention of his name Michik turned and eyed Sir Andon suspiciously. Much to his chagrin, Chael had actually been thinking along the same lines. He didn't plan on being in the capital very long. Andon insisted he accompany him to an audience with the King and then Chael wanted to clear up this business with the person claiming to be Darrik and be gone. He sighed heavily and then turned to Andon and nodded.

"The knights train at a camp about three leagues outside of the city. My squire will take care of him, I give you my word as a knight." Andon delivered the final few words with a serious solemnity that Chael trusted despite the knight's repeated tales of squirely mischief. Chael indicated Andon lead the way, and they veered from the main road onto a path that would take them to the training grounds.

Andon's squire was a boy of perhaps fourteen years who hadn't quite grown into his body. He was tall and gangly and quite possibly the clumsiest youth Chael had ever laid eyes upon. How he ended up as a royal knight's squire, Chael couldn't begin to guess. But when Sir Andon impressed upon the boy the seriousness of his task, the young squire took on a maturity that defied his clumsy youth.

Michik could sense that something was wrong and began to whine and pace around the floor. Chael calmed him and scratched his head and stared into his dog's faintly glowing eyes.

"You need to stay here until I get back. You can't come looking for me." Michik whined a little more, but Chael pressed a little harder through the ineffable bond they shared and, under protest, Michik relented. He stopped whining and nuzzled his snout into Chael's side. In later years, when recounting this part of the story, Chael left out any mention of his own tears.

King Inarus Al-Fhaelan looked nothing like his cousin Baron Janus Al-Fhaelan. Where the Baron was somewhat short and pleasantly rotund, King Inarus was a mountain of a man. He stood well over six feet tall, a good head and more over Chael, and was broad shouldered. He stood upon a raised white dais, a purple carpet flowing beneath his feet to the entrance.

Above the King was the giant stained glass dome Chael had spied from the road. It depicted a different King, presumably an ancestor of Inarus, slaying a giant horned beast with a lance. It had certain demonic features that Chael could recognize, glowing red eyes and black claws, and it seemed to be at least seven or eight paces tall.

Chael had never seen a demon that looked quite like it. Even in the static glass, the body of the creature seemed to defy conventional shape. It could be said that it was roughly humanoid, but its features were flowing and indistinct. It was as if this ancient creature resented its likeness being captured in the glass and refused to maintain a specific profile and instead clothed itself in swirling shadow. Chael stood transfixed at the depiction until Andon loudly coughed, breaking his trance.

Upon entering, Sir Andon immediately bent to one knee and held the pommel of his sword out toward his King. The King didn't reach for the sword, so Chael suspected it was some sort of symbolic gesture.

Chael hated pomp. For his own part, Chael stayed standing, much to the horror of his companion. He didn't really consider himself a citizen of this realm and besides, the King would either kill him or not based on their accounting of what happened in the forest. Whether he showed deference now hardly seemed to matter. If the King did opt to blame him for the death of the Baron, he certainly wasn't going to pay him the courtesy of genuflection.

King Inarus gave Chael a wry grin and turned to Sir Andon. "Rise, Sir Knight," the King commanded. Andon stood and returned his sword to its scabbard.

After an awkward moment of stoic silence, the King burst with laughter and met Andon in a warm embrace. Chael thought his odds of surviving just seemed to have improved dramatically. After a moment, King Inarus broke the hug and clapped Andon on the shoulder fondly.

"My report, your majesty," Andon intoned seriously, handing his King a letter with a small bow. Chael hadn't seen him write anything on their journey, but hoped that at least Sir Andon was charitable in his descriptions.

He studied the King's face as the King silently read the report. A shocked face told Chael that he had probably just read about the grizzly demise of the Baron. After a few quiet moments, the King looked up and eyed his nephew quizzically. Andon gave him one of his tight nods and the King seemed satisfied. He then turned to Chael.

"My nephew speaks highly of you," King Inarus said. Chael breathed a silent sigh of relief.

"I am grateful for his companionship over this journey," Chael responded, doing his best to sound formal and educated. *Not my strong suit,* he thought. "Without Sir Andon's bravery, none of us would have made it through the Dark Forest alive."

The King shot a fond look at Sir Andon, then turned back to Chael. He moved his hand over one of the many red stains on his green cloak. Chael was wearing the clean clothes that Sir Andon had secured for him at the inn but still wore his customary green cloak, tattered and stained though it was. The King looked forlornly at the bloodstains, clearly deducing that at least some of it came from his cousin, the Baron.

"Janus would not be counted amongst the wisest of my advisors," the King said seriously. "But he was loyal, and above all, he was family. Pity that I don't have a body to bury."

Inarus grew distant for a moment in silent contemplation. After a moment, a look of steely resolve replaced the weary haze on his face. "I'm told that you specialize in killing these…" the King stammered, slightly hesitant to say the word as if uttering it would call one into existence there in his throne room. "Demons," he finished, spitting the word with disgust.

"I'm not sure if I specialize in killing them, but the Baron and I came to an arrangement and I did my best to eradicate them from the forest. I fear my efforts represented little more than raindrops in the ocean."

"I doubt that," Inarus responded warmly. "Still, the beasts began emerging in numbers from that Darkened Forest only a few months ago. The order of Celestial light has been doing their best to dispatch them and affect wards but every month hundreds more pour through and ravage the countryside."

"Hundreds?" Chael asked incredulously. At most, he might have killed a few dozen in a month back near Ehbing, but hundreds? He shuddered at the damage they must have been doing.

The King nodded, some of the weariness breaking through the steel of his countenance. "Andon, we'll discuss this later at council, but you may as well know now, Brekinhold has fallen."

The knight looked at his King incredulously. "Brekinhold is not the nearest city to the Republics," Andon stammered.

"They bypassed the southern cities. Stars know how they managed to sneak an entire army undetected, but when they struck, they struck hard. Brekinhold fell in under a day. That puts them at a conservative six-day march from here."

"How long since Brekinhold fell?" Andon asked. The King smiled weakly as he eased himself onto his seat on the dais.

"Two days," Inarus answered.

"So," said Chael. "An invisible army that sacked a major city in a single day marches at you from the south and an army of demonic Darkspawn pours out from the forest to the west. And there are four days to prepare."

"That would be the gist of it, yes," the King said dryly.

"Hmmm," Chael hummed in thought. "Tell me, what's the castle policy on pets?"

Chapter 18

11 Years Ago

"Michik," Chael announced proudly.

"Michik? Where'd you come up with that?" Darrik asked as they walked one of the many alchemically lit streets of Kazaam. They stuck mostly to the shadows between streetlamps and whispered. It would not do to gather an audience this evening.

"It means 'one possessed of great loyalty' in old Aazeran," Chael replied. Indeed, the small wolf pup had scarcely left his side since discovering him in the small cave with his dead siblings. Leaving him behind so he could undertake this secret mission was especially difficult. The wolf was stronger and smarter than many of the people Chael knew and had a particularly strong talent for breaking out of whatever enclosure Chael left him in to follow his new master.

Tonight, he had to resort to purchasing a concoction from one of the Black Hand cultists. They didn't particularly care for the word 'cultist', but Chael didn't particularly care about their feelings on the matter. Especially since what he saw with Mason and the former guard captain, may the Living Stars guide him home. Still, they practiced unsanctioned alchemy, and the sleeping draught they provided him seemed to be effective, and they had provided him with some other useful things.

Chael and Darrik quieted their speech as they rose to the highest tier of the city. It stood on the pinnacle of the small mountain that dominated most of the city, and beyond its walled exterior was a sheer sixty-pace drop on three sides. In this circle at the top, even the streets were made of the bright whitestone so favored by the rich and powerful of Kazaam. The many streetlamps gleamed off the polished white surface and lit the entire area with a grainy artificial glow. After the city watch coup in the audience hall, the High Minister had purchased an entire army of Fhaelan mercenaries to watch his residence, and under the synthetic light, they crawled about the place like ants.

Probably still affected by whatever curatives Aelisa gave him, Chael surmised. It must be him, then; he's the only one unaccounted for. Michik barked at exactly that moment, as if he had been waiting for Chael to come to this conclusion independently. Chael's head snapped instantly in the direction of the sound and made his way toward what he knew to be the corpse of this Durnik.

About forty paces away from the arboretum, they reached the first hitch in their plans. They had run out of shadow to cling to and there were four Fhaelan mercenaries staring exactly in their direction. For several tense moments, neither one of them could breathe. They were dressed in all black for the occasion, Chael eschewing his traditional green cloak. The tight-fitting black garments he wore now did not leave him the many hiding places for his knives that he liked. He also missed the familiar weight of his falchion, but the hefty sword was too large and clumsy, so he only carried a pair of daggers on his belt, painted black to obscure their sheen.

After an eternity, the mercenaries turned their attention to another area of the plaza and Chael slowly exhaled a sigh of relief. The hired guards hadn't actually moved, however, so they needed to formulate a plan to cross the remaining distance. Their former school had taught them a secret, wordless form of communication for times such as these. A flurry of discreet hand signals ensued.

Impossible. The world went completely dark as Chael hastily shut down the vision. The disturbing smile of the Dark Cultist still lingering in his mind's eye.Curious, Chael thought.

He remained crouched, eyes closed, choosing instead to reach out with his other senses. The demon was close. Its very essence disrupted the natural flow of life around him. He had managed to cut it off before reaching the edge of the forest and the people of Ehbing.even if you could free yourself. "You're only going to chafe your wrists doing that," she finally said.She called me precious, he mused silently. And st-starborn? What could that possibly mean?

"Wonderful idea, then we can fight the fifty or so mercenaries the bastard hired." There wasn't actually a sign for "bastard", but Chael used an improvised name for one of the less popular masters at the former school. Darrik got the general idea.

What could they possibly be doing here? Chael wondered while absentmindedly packing his bedroll. Around him was a flurry of motion as the others hastily packed their belongings, all under the steely gaze of the order priestess.

So, they're not sure if they can take us all on at once, Chael surmised. He hadn't seen anyone with Cooper in the vision, but he highly doubted that the enigmatic Dark Alchemist would risk exposure out here alone. It's not possible, it couldn't be. But someone knew him and knew to use that name; that was deeply concerning.

"Disrobe," Chael ordered Darrik via hand signal. Instead of receiving a signal in response, Darrik merely gave him a look of bewildered amusement. "Remove your clothes," Chael signed more emphatically. Tone was a difficult thing to convey with the signs. They really weren't designed to be a true language, just a silent way to convey strategy in clandestine operations. But Chael strained his fingers like he

was trying to squeeze the juice from an invisible tangerine and stared Darrik down with the most serious face he could muster while laughing hysterically on the inside.

After more than a few moments' hesitation, Darrik stripped down to full nudity. Chael promptly bundled his friends' weapons up in his clothes and tossed them over the wall. He listened but could not detect the soft thud they must have left on the level below. Darrik almost vocalized a protest but slapped his hand over his mouth at the last second. Chael gave him a wink and whispered out loud, "you're drunk." Darrik gave him another confused look just before Chael shoved him out of the shadows and into the alchemically burning luminance of the plaza.

Darrik stood stunned for just a moment before his training took over. He effected a drunken stumble toward the fountain at the heart of the High Ministerial Plaza. The guards were equally stunned and remained gawking at the naked drunkard who had somehow materialized in their midst.

Quickly, though not as quickly as Darrik, they got over their shock and all simultaneously converged on him. Even the guards blocking Chael took a couple curious steps away from their post, even though they were hopelessly far away to actually be useful.

Chael took the momentary distraction and vaulted over the wall and clung to the other side, feet dangling over open air. Slowly, he edged along the smooth stone wall, hand over hand, praying to slip by unnoticed. From the other side of the plaza, shouts sounded from the many mercenaries.

"Hey you! Stop!"

"Where did you come from!"

"How did you get here?!"

Not highly original, but they were paid to kill intruders, not shout at them, Chael supposed. Amongst the symphony of overly mundane threats and commands, Chael overheard one that made him pause.

"By the living stars, what are you doing to the fountain?!"

What ensued was a chorus of unintelligible shouts followed by several loud splashes and ending with cries of disgust. Chael almost chanced a look over the wall, but chided himself and continued sliding along the wall. Forty paces was a fairly simple feat on one's legs, but hanging over a black abyss and gripping polished stone was another matter entirely. At halfway, Chael's hands burned furiously. Several of his nails broke while hopelessly trying to keep a grip on the smooth wall and by ten paces, his hands were trembling with the effort.

More shouts and the sounds of hard boots on stone indicated Darrik was now leading the guards on a chase. For a big man, he was surprisingly fleet footed and unencumbered as he was. He probably fared pretty well in a foot race. Reinvigorated by the thought of Darrik sprinting through the night, naked with a dozen armed mercenaries in tow, Chael steeled his resolve and shimmied the last ten paces. He pushed himself about five paces further for good measure, sent a silent prayer up to the living stars, and vaulted over.

To his relief, the Fhaelans that had been guarding the entrance to the arboretum had inched even closer to view the chaos that Darrik had created, and Chael slipped into the spacious garden undetected.

Present Day

Chael marched down the interminable stone steps leading from the keep down to the small inner cloister of the city. Broad walls of gray stone separated this small section from the rest of the sprawling cities. It housed the main three-story building immediately to his left held the headquarters of Andon's order, next to it appeared to be the offices of tax collectors, and so on. Each of these buildings were built of molded red brick and wood and were functional in design to the point of being ugly. The one exception in the small ring of buildings was his destination.

The Fhaerhold chapter of the Fraternal Order of Celestial Light was built like a miniature of the keep at the top of the motte. But unlike the keep and in direct contrast to the buildings surrounding it, the chapter house was seemingly built with every precious material they could cram into its architecture. The four towers were built of the gleaming marble whitestone that was so treasured back in Kazaam. And between its large slabs, gold was employed instead of mortar.

At the top of each tower were pointed bulbs of polished bronze inset with precious stones of every color and size. The whole thing twinkled in the sunlight like hundreds of colorful stars.

The walls of the chapter house were the same gray stone as the walls of the courtyard in which it stood, but every few feet was a window of stained glass depicting various scenes of order members basking in the light of a star. It had a domed glass roof like the keep as well, but from this angle, Chael couldn't make out whatever garish design it showed. The entire building was a colorful assault on the senses and Chael had to forcibly avert his eyes from the towers as he approached.

The ornate wooden double doors of the house were locked when he tried them, so he knocked on the wood, bruising his knuckles. There was no answer. He knocked again, using his palm to thunder as hard as he naturally could without seeking energy from external sources. He was about to hit the doors with the pommel of his sword when a window on the second story opened and an elderly priest leaned out.

"We aren't accepting any pilgrimages for the time being, thank you," the old priest shouted in a withered, nasally voice.

"I'm not a pilgrim!" Chael shouted up at the man. "I am here under the invitation of Sister Aelisa Treadmane." The old man paused, squinting down at him, and then leaned back into the building, conversing with someone inside. After several minutes, he popped back out and yelled down to Chael.

"The sister isn't here," the old man called. He leaned back inside and talked with whomever was there with him and leaned back out. "She's expected back tomorrow morning. You may return then." He gave Chael one last appraising look and slammed the colorful window shut. *The stargazers have become quite hospitable in recent years,* Chael thought idly as he walked away from the building.

For the first time in over a week, he found himself with nothing to do. While the King had indicated he would be grateful for Chael's assistance in the coming days, he had made it clear Chael was not invited to the war council in which Andon would now be engaged.

Michik was being boarded at training grounds outside of the far boundary of the city and he wouldn't be able to make it there and back until well after nightfall. The King had graciously appointed him a room within the keep and after several hard nights on the road through the forest, he was looking forward to royal hospitality. Besides knowing Michik, he was probably being pampered handsomely by Andon's squire.

Chael turned and walked out of the gate that separated the small administrative cloister from the rest of the city. He pulled up his hood and walked through the cobbled street of Fhaerhold.

For a moment, he almost felt like he was back in Kazaam. He could almost imagine Darrik next to him on their way to some clandestine plot. The thought thrilled and saddened him at the same time. This wasn't Kazaam, and though he would get to the bottom of it tomorrow morning, he was confident that whatever person they housed in the gaudy building behind him, it wasn't Darrik.

An hour or so of wandering eventually led Chael to a tavern. He wasn't normally one for drinking—such things were prohibited to him and his peers under Master Khalim, and he never really developed a taste for it. But the inn back in Fhaerstead had gone a long way to converting him, so as he reached the bar he ordered a house ale. It was inferior to the one he had at the inn, but still pleasant. He sipped it casually as he made his way over to an empty table near the fire.

The tavern was arranged as one might expect, a long bar dominated one wall and in front of it were arranged about half a dozen tables of different make and color. In one corner of the room was a raised platform with several instruments he didn't recognize. He supposed that under normal circumstances, this establishment would be quite lively at this hour.

Tonight, however, there were only a few other patrons, and the entire place had a thick, foreboding air. Chael doubted that the imminent attack on the city was common knowledge, but preparatory activities were hard to disguise and talk of demons coming from Fhaerstead had surely reached the capitol.

"Ain't seen you here a'fore," Chael looked up at one of the few other customers who had crept over to his table. The man was possibly in his fortieth year, but it was hard to tell because his skin was so buried in scars. It looked as if he attempted to fend off a demon using only his face. He smiled at him, revealing fewer teeth than Chael thought wholly adequate, and the breath wafting out between them reeked of liquor.

"I just made my way down from the keep and decided to try the local fare," Chael responded, forcing a smile to his face.

He hoped mentioning the seat of King Inarus would scare the man off, but he had no such luck. The stranger sat down across from him and sipped his own tankard of ale. They eyed each other for one tense moment before the stranger reached into his belt, withdrew a knife, and slammed it into the table.

Chael jumped back, hand flashing to his sword, but the man simply kept smiling. He pointed to the knife hilt sticking out from Chael's boot and jabbed his thumb behind him in the direction of a painted plank of wood set into the wall. Chael returned the man's ugly smile with a wry grin.

Seven pitchers of ale and several hours later, Chael had bested every challenger in this quarter of the city at a local variant of a throwing knife game. In Chael's experience, such games required the loser to drink unhealthy levels of alcohol and often needed to pay for the other patrons as well. Apparently, in this particular tavern, champions were required to imbibe until they could barely stand, or so they claimed.

Chael, of course, had cheated.

Several rats now lay dead in the storeroom at the back of the tavern and Chael just barely felt a tingle from the drink. Knife after knife flew expertly from Chael's hands and landed in the increasingly weathered bullseye of the target. He had drawn quite an audience despite the weighty, dark air of the city.

Finally, no one else stepped up to challenge his manhood or claim glory for their own, and Chael went to the bar to pay his tab. The barman waved him off and pointed in the corner where his original, dentally challenged challenger now sat still drinking.

"He paid your tab," the barman said gruffly. The odd man lifted his ale in salute and Chael gave him an appreciative nod back and left the tavern.

Night had fallen some time ago, Chael groaned as he gazed up at the long row of stone steps that reached up to the keep and his royal accommodations. With leaden legs and a minor headache, he began the journey to the keep.

After about twenty minutes of walking, a sudden movement caught his eye. A young woman was being chased by two men in leather aprons. As she ran, the woman clutched a small leather bag to her chest and cast nervous glances back at her pursuers. Chael wasn't sure if it was the minor buzz from the copious amount of alcohol he had consumed or if the chivalrous Sir Andon had rubbed off on him over the last few days, but he reluctantly decided to intervene.

With every step, the two men were gaining on her and, from the look in their eyes, they planned to extract far more than just her small handbag if they caught her. Chael shadowed their movements, drawing on his extensive experience as an assassin in Kazaam. He didn't need Dark powers for situations like these. This was the sort of thing he was bred to do.

The woman turned down a dark alley and cried out in frustration when she found a solid wall where she hoped her escape might be. She turned to the men that cornered her and let out a low, feral growl. Chael slid through the shadows of the alley unseen, silent as the night, ready to strike if these men attacked the young woman.

The first man reached into his leather apron and drew out a wicked-looking cleaver that was attached to it. He raised it, ready to strike, then Chael darted out from the shadows.

Before Chael had made it more than two steps, a speck of black tar the size of Chael's thumbnail flew from the woman's gloved hand and landed on the fist clutching the cleaver. There was a brief flash of light and the smell of burning hair, and the man began to scream.

The knife clattered to the cobbled street as the man clutched his arm. Both Chael and the other aproned man stopped in their tracks and stared. The viscous substance began multiplying the moment it touched flesh and was already crawling up his forearm. In its trail, the black-stained flesh of the man simply fell off in great bubbling chunks that splattered on the ground. After several horrifying seconds, the ooze had traveled to his shoulder and the remains of his arm were just an oily puddle on the stone.

His screaming continued as the fluid slowly consumed his chest, eating his leather apron before exposing muscle, then bone. Then suddenly, the screaming stopped. The man's mouth moved in twisted agony, but no sound came out. He looked down at the open expanse where his lungs used to be, then collapsed dead, the rest of him slowly succumbing to the expanding bubbly black liquid.

His partner, clearly deciding that whatever their grievance was with the woman wasn't worth his trouble, turned and sprinted out of the alley. The woman's gaze now turned to Chael.

I hate people, he thought bitterly once again. Why had it come to his home? That was particularly strange. Creatures of the Dark had a sense about these things, and most knew to avoid the man who had taken residence in the wood.Do demons get cold? he thought absently. He then shook his head, clearing his mind for the fight. Michik snarled and barked, but there were no sounds of the demon retreating from his mighty wolf.

She eyed Chael suspiciously, one hand clutching the leather pouch, and the other gloved hand held another piece of the deadly black substance, rolling it between her fingers.

"I'm not here to hurt you!" Chael yelled hastily, sheathing his sword and throwing his hands in the air. "I saw those men chasing you and followed thinking you may be in danger."

He gave her his best, most innocent looking smile and edged away from the soupy remains of her attacker and toward the wall of the alley.

Still glaring at him, the woman walked over to the dark, oily puddle and pulled a flask from her robes. She pulled the stopper and poured a silvery liquid over the remains of the disintegrated man. The fluid hissed and acrid smoke billowed up from the ground. When it cleared, the terrible black acid was gone, replaced by light gray dust that crumbled and blew in the breeze.

The woman walked by Chael. He noticed that her hand no longer contained the deadly black substance, so he chanced a question.

"Do you know Sister Ae..." he began. The moment he spoke, she spun around and whipped a different item from her robes. A small yellow pebble no larger than the head of a pin. She snapped her fingers with the pebble between them and a cloud of yellow smoke exploded out in front of Chael.

He stumbled backward, choking. His eyes and throat burned like he had just shoved his face into a fire pit. Desperate, he reached out with his senses, looking for any small living thing in the cold, desolate stone around him. He found little more than worms and one unfortunate houseplant, but their meager life energy was just barely enough to clear his vision. As he suspected, the Order initiate was long gone.

Exhausted, Chael slumped to the ground of the alley, leaning his back against the wall. He covered himself with his cloak and looked skeptically at the gray dust near his boot.

"I hate people," he muttered to the night and closed his eyes, hoping to dream of a soft, royally appointed bed.

Chapter 19

11 Years Ago

The arboretum was a slightly unseemly mishmash of different species of plant, flower, and tree from all across the continent; all nestled in a humid glass dome. Deep brown and green notes from the Aazeran forest were randomly mingled with reds and purples of the Western Forest as well as exotic plants supposedly plucked from the homeland of the elves.

It might have been beautiful in a scattered kind of way but the only impression that it left on Chael was the reflection of a mind that wanted to possess everything regardless of consequence. The smell too was overpowering; what individually may have been a light and pleasant aroma was, by virtue of volume, a dense cloud of hot flowery smog that blasted his senses as he wound his way through the maze of plants. *It's no wonder why this place is less guarded,* Chael thought amusedly, holding his cloak against the oppressive odor.

After a few moments of blindly bumping into trees and several spiky thorns in his cloak, Chael found the door that led from the arboretum into the residence. Carefully, Chael eased the door open checking for sentries on the other side. There were none.

Breathing a sigh of relief, he eased forward, grateful to put the dense earthen collage behind him. He found himself in a dimly lit hallway made of a mixture of both gray and whitestone with a red velvet runner. There were several alchemical lamps held in sconces, but they had been turned down for the night leaving just enough shadow for Chael to do his work.

Chael proceeded forward along the hallway. From the blueprints he had committed to memory, he was just behind the audience chamber where Khalim had made his first strike against the power base of the High Minister. The staircase leading up to the residential floors was just up ahead. Chael peeked around the corner, finding once again a suspicious lack of guards. He was about to climb the steps when he stopped cold, his foot hovering no more than a hair above the lush red carpet.

The carpet was completely unblemished, despite the amount of traffic that it must have seen. But the most suspicious thing was that it unevenly clung to the steps and was obviously loose in several places. It was as if someone had hastily hidden the stairs with this new carpet. Chael didn't know the High Minister well, but suspected that he was oafish enough to die all by himself if he climbed these stairs with such loose carpeting.

Chael took out one of his knives and easily separated the red carpeting from the stone step. There was nothing suspicious save the series of intricate engravings that covered nearly half the step. He examined them closely, but didn't recognize the symbols.

He cut more of the carpet away from the steps that he could reach, but instead of some insidious trap all he could find was more of the same, recently carved, alien writing. There was only one way up and he couldn't see how strange etchings could be a threat, so he apprehensively took the first step. It was normal, as were the second and third. Chiding himself for his superstition, Chael proceeded to the fourth step.

The sensation was like being enveloped in a thin sheet of ice. He could move, but a cold pressure pushed down on him from all sides. He took another step, and the feeling intensified, the icy pressure now pressing against his limbs making it harder to move.

By step nine, he was all but immobilized. The force holding him down was so intense that it was taking all of his strength just to remain standing. With tremendous effort, he looked up and despaired. *Twelve more steps.* They would find his crumpled body at the foot of the steps before he had even reached halfway.

A new feeling slowly replaced the cold of the invisible force holding him in place. This was warm, then searing hot, emerging from wounds all over his body. The cuts across his ribs where he had nearly been killed by servants of House Arda now bled like a fresh wound. Everywhere, injuries from as early as this morning's shave to as old as the beatings from his first day in the school reawakened all at once.

Fiery agony had now completely replaced the icy cold of a moment ago. One electric jolt of pain shot across a wound in his back, and he stumbled forward onto the next step. *The next step.* With sudden revelation, Chael realized that despite the horrible agony, he could move. Abandoning all caution, he raced up the stairs, leaving small drops of blood to mingle with the red carpet.

He collapsed onto the second-floor landing. Most of the pain was gone, and he didn't think he was still bleeding, but his strength was utterly drained. Each one of his limbs felt as though it was made of stone, and his usual lithe and powerful muscles failed him.

"That was unexpected," said a muffled male voice from the darkness. Panic overcame the oppressive fatigue in his limbs and Chael wearily rose to his feet. His eyes, which were generally well adapted to dim light, could barely make out the confines of the dark hall. But the figure who spoke was easy enough to spot. He was wearing solid white robes with gold accents and an eight-pointed star. *Stargazer,* Chael realized bitterly. The order priest was also wearing a solid white mask in the shape of a fingernail with just one narrow slit for his eyes.

"Does the Alchemist guild know that the Order is operating in Kazaam?" Chael managed to eek out through the gasping breaths it took for him to stand. The priest ignored the question, leaning his head slightly to the side as if trying to examine Chael in a different light.

"What are you?" he said at last, still tilting his head as if Chael's mere existence was some anomaly.

"What am I?" Chael mused, pumping sheer obstinance and bravado into his body to replace his lost strength. "I suppose you might call me a sinner, but I've never really cared much for moralizing." Chael slowly inched closer to the priest as he spoke, silently urging his numb limbs to cooperate with his swagger. "I'm a lover of cold steel and hot fire. The gentle caress of—"

The masked priest suddenly slammed a boot into Chael's chest faster than he could blink. The alchemically enhanced blow sent Chael careening off a wall and once again he was lying at the top of the warded stairs gasping with unresponsive limbs.

"Do not think to toy with me!" he practically shouted at Chael. "You are infected with the Dark, I could feel it seeping out of your pores as you ascended the protected staircase. Yet you are no demon. A demon powerful enough to resist the wards would be quite a bit more monstrous than I take you for."

He seemed to stop and consider for a moment, his emotions inscrutable behind his white mask. As he did, Chael slowly reached a hand to his knife belt, carefully feeling the two small vials secured there. One was long and thin, about the size of his pinky. Cooper had told him that if he failed to reach the High Minister's bedchamber, he should smash it against a wall and flee as fast as he could. He wasn't that desperate yet.

His numb fingers finally found the second vial. It was about as tall as the first, but thicker, more the size of his thumb. Chael turned over, making like he was trying to rise to his knees with his back to the priest, and quickly downed the contents of the vial. A swift kick sent him sprawling once again to his chest.

"Look," Chael began, flopping over onto his back to face the masked priest. "I have no idea what you're talking about. I am clearly not a demon. If you would just let me explain why I'm here, I'm sure we'll both soon be laughing at this grave misunderstanding."

"Silence!" the priest yelled at him again, now just feet away. "Whatever you are, you commune with the Dark in ways that shouldn't be possible. You must be destroyed." He nodded his head as if agreeing with himself and didn't say another word. He gingerly tilted his mask back, revealing his mouth, and poured his own vial of alchemical solution down his throat.

"Come on!" Chael muttered to himself, looking anxiously at the priest. He had expected a rush of power to flood his limbs, but he felt nothing. He experimentally flexed his arm; at least some of the weariness was gone, but none of the promised strength and speed of an alchemist's drink.

To his horror, the priest who did display these enhancements was now growing a whip made of light from the bones of his right arm where flesh used to be. Chael stood as an eel-like rope of pure white light slithered to the floor.

As if responding to the priest's power as a challenge, the full effect of the potion Chael had drunk finally began to emerge. His right arm and hand suddenly darkened to a dark gray, then disintegrated into ashy smoke. What was left of his right arm was a nebulous cloud of gray embers that floated at the end of his elbow. Chael couldn't see the priest's face but was sure that it was fixed in shock, because for several seconds the man stood motionless, simply staring at him.

"Abomination," the man finally uttered. With a slight flick, he sent the whip hurtling directly toward Chael's throat. Without a better idea, Chael raised his smokey stump to block his face from the assault. Just before the whip would have hit the flesh of his neck, a buckler shield materialized out of the smoke and blocked it. Both Chael and the priest stared at his arm.

Chael smiled, understanding dawning across his face. With a thought, the buckler dissolved back into the mist and a dark gray facsimile of his arm emerged. Chael smashed his fist into the order priest, shattering the bottom third of the surprisingly thick white mask.

The man stumbled back, rocked by the blow, but quickly recovered. He sent another lash with his whip, this time aimed at Chael's legs. A sword similar to his own falchion grew into his hand and he swiped down, parrying the whip.

The alchemical formula that gave Chael his spectral appendage didn't do much for his strength and speed, so he was at a severe disadvantage to his enhanced opponent. But despite his physical prowess, the man was sloppy, clearly unused to being matched while wielding his whip. Again and again, bright snaking light met a dark shadowy blade.

Chael's confidence grew as his opponent became more and more frustrated with his own failure. He pressed forward, grabbing one of his painted knives from his belt. He didn't want to trust the mundane steel against the celestial whip, but he figured the priest's neck was as soft and fleshy as anyone else's, alchemy or no.

Chael slowly closed the distance, his spectral blade cutting off ribbons of light from the whip that bounced against the walls like a ball of sparks. Yet somehow the whip never lost length. Chael effortlessly whirled the alchemical falchion in front of him, blocking more and more lashes of light until he stood a breath away from the masked man. He feinted once with his sword, drawing the priest's attention low and slammed his knife in the man's exposed neck.

From the light of the still glowing whip Chael could see through the mask slit at the horrified eyes of the man. Slowly they went pale and blank, and as they did, the whip slowly dimmed and the hall was once again cast in darkness.

Chael gawked, first at his arm and then down at the dead priest. For once, he had no words. His reverie was cut short, however. Faintly, he could hear the approaching footsteps of a throng of guards, clearly alerted by the shouts of the priest and the sound of battle. Chael gave the masked man one last look while searching his memory for the best route to the High Minister. His path decided, Chael turned and sprinted down the hallway clinging to the shadows of the lamps.

Chapter 20

Present Day

Chael awoke in the same alley as his botched rescue attempt the night before. He rose to his feet; dirty, stiff, and irritable. He had meant to meet with Sir Andon this morning and he was sure the knight was currently looking for him up in the many rooms of the keep, but his appointment with the Order was more pressing. At last, he would meet this imposter and figure out what he knew and how he had come to know it.

Chael looked down at what remained of the dusty gray remnants of the unfortunate man in the leather apron. He didn't know the nature of his grievance with the young woman. Though given his own brief encounter with her, Chael couldn't be certain that it wasn't somewhat justified. But still, no matter what the man may or may not have been guilty of, it was a horrific way to die. Chael tapped his boots against the wall of the alley, trying to shake off any dusty particulates, and made his way out of the alley.

A glance at the sky told him it was close to midday. *Did I really sleep that long?* Chael wasn't immune to the effects of alcohol, even if he could cheat intoxication with his abilities. He made a mental note not to indulge so heavily again. His head pounded with every step.

The early hustle and bustle of the soon-to-be besieged city only made it worse. Everywhere around him, store fronts were being boarded up and fighting aged men were being led around by groups of soldiers. The general air of anxiety that he had felt in the tavern last night now permeated the city streets of Fhaerhold like a plague. They knew what was coming now. It may have been that there was some proclamation announced while he slept or simply that enough people had gleaned the truth from the myriad of clues around them; but whatever the case, the city was preparing for war.

It didn't take Chael long to reach the small, enclosed courtyard at the city center. After a brief argument with a particularly self-important soldier at the gate, Chael strolled through rubbing sore, red knuckles.

He had been tempted to just punch the obstinate gate guard, but after his journey through the forest with Andon and Aelisa, he decided he was a more evolved man now. So, he merely smashed a section of stone street pavement with an empowered fist and made certain suggestions about the relative strength of a human skull compared to stone. The guard let him in without further hindrance.

His display at the gate also had the side effect of dampening his headache, and as he approached the hideously colorful order house, his spirits had lifted greatly. Skipping the door all together, he simply yelled up to the house that he was here for his meeting with Aelisa. Before he could even get all the words out, the large carved wooden double doors swung outward and revealed Aelisa flanked by two of her subordinates.

"Greetings Chael," Aelisa intoned with something that could have been an actual smile. Given her usual stony disposition, he was immediately suspicious, but perhaps he had genuinely grown on her. Or, more likely, she was happy that she might finally get some answers out of her prisoner.

She led him inside of a grand foyer similarly decorated as the exterior. Precious gems set into the walls reflected light in a way intentionally meant to mimic stars, and the many stained-glass windows bathed the marble floor in a rainbow of colors. Inset into the marble was an eight-pointed star made of gold bands, perhaps as thick as his palm.

Chael suspected that on a certain day and time, the colorful light from the windows would form a ring around the star. He had seen similar constructs in Kazaam among the higher tiered houses. Mathematicians of the alchemists' guild charged usurious rates for such frivolities. For all the high-mindedness of the Order of Celestial Light, he saw the same hallmarks of wealth, power, and greed that he had everywhere else.

Above him was the stained glass dome whose design copied the larger of the King's castles up on the hill nearby. However, instead of the singular shadowy demon, it depicted about a dozen, most of which Chael recognized. They all cowered before a robed figure in white with a staff that radiated light.

Unlike the windows on the walls that allowed colorful light to pass through and decorate the floor, the glass in the dome seemed to capture the light. It made the entire sculpture glow unnaturally and had the effect of tricking his eyes into believing there was movement. Aelisa caught him staring upward and gave him another smile, this one just as genuine but seemingly more sinister.

"Come Chael, the sooner we can interrogate the prisoner the better. Who knows what secrets he can deliver us about his master and his plans. Many lives may be saved by what we do here today."

Chael could tell that Aelisa meant it. Whatever her personal qualms with him, she was adamant that this would save the lives of the people. Chael took her leave and followed her to the rear of the hall. She took a lit torch from a wall sconce, as did her underlings, and together led him through a door and onto a winding set of stairs.

At first the stairs were as garishly decorated as the foyer above, but as they descended deeper and deeper into the structure, the gold and bronze accents turned into dull gray. The stones of the stairs even became rougher and felt more ancient. And while they were worn from thousands of footsteps over probably hundreds of years, this path was clearly seldom traveled, as indicated by the layer of dust on everything. As the four of them slowly descended on a helical left-hand turn, drops of water fell from the ceiling.

At first, Chael didn't think much of it; he cool air of the subterranean levels mixing with warmer air above could cause such things. But the deeper they descended, the more numerous the drops became, until he was practically being rained on from above. His cloak was soaked through. He looked at his torch-bearing companions, who not only looked unbothered, but were also completely dry and their torches unmarred.

Chael opened his mouth to voice his concerns to Aelisa but found he couldn't speak. The gray spiraling stairs grew fainter despite the bright light of the three torches. Panicked, he tried to turn around and run back up to the foyer but found that his legs would only continue to carry him downward into the increasingly black void below him.

Chael reached out with his senses. He could see the life energy in the order monks around him, but it was faint and blurry like looking through foggy glass. Beyond the stone walls of the staircase, he could detect nothing and the further he marched downward, the more his senses retreated until he could feel nothing at all. His mind glazed over, he could sense only the vaguest impulses from his limbs that he was continuing to move but to where and in what direction he could not say.

Minutes passed, or perhaps years; he could not say. The only awareness he had left was his steady marching along a path known only to his saboteurs. He was adrift in a black void without shape or depth. At once he was weightless and yet also could feel the steady striding of his legs on what felt like solid ground. The only objects left in his perception were the perfectly visible shapes of three people in white robes that seemed to float above him. But they too abandoned him to the void, and when they were gone, there was only darkness.

Chapter 21

11 Years Ago

Chael ran as fast as he could do so quietly as he picked his way through corridors of the High Ministerial residence. The sound of footsteps from every side told him the noose was tightening, and he was determined to escape it. He met his first resistance about twenty paces from the body of the felled priest. A group of four Fhaelans blocked a necessary passage to reach the next flight of stairs that would allow him access to the High Minister's private chambers. Unlike the ones outside, these mercenaries were covered, head to toe, in gleaming plate armor. Each one bore the crest of the Fhaelan Kingdom on their breastplate and wielded vicious looking halberds, extended toward Chael, blocking his passage in the tight hallway.

In the confined space of a building, Chael wasn't a fan of polearms, but the effect of four extended spear points above crescent ax heads in the narrow hallway was impressive. Each wicked point stuck out a foot or more along a wooden haft away from the heavily armored Fhaelan mercenaries. Together they marched in practiced unison down the hall, keeping their deadly halberds extended towards Chael.

"Darkness!" Chael exclaimed, staring down the moving wall of spikes and steel. He couldn't retreat, already he could hear the same heavy footsteps of their compatriots behind him. Soon he would be pressed on all sides and likely to be impaled, front and back, by foreign soldiers. He looked down at his right arm; it was still a gray smokey cloud below the elbow.

With a thought, he returned the ashy simulacrum of his falchion to his hand. He twirled the weightless weapon around in his wrist. He threw the alchemical construct at one of the approaching soldiers, but as soon it left his hand, it dematerialized into a small gray cloud and disappeared harmlessly amid the ever-marching wall of iron. He supposed he could try throwing one of his knives at the narrow eye slit in the helmets of his attackers, but even he wasn't that good.

As he wracked his brain for any way out of the current predicament, the footsteps behind him grew louder and louder until another group of armored men emerged around the corner. As soon as they saw him, they lowered their own polearms and advanced toward him in the same practiced cadence of their fellows.

With no other options, Chael walked forward into the original group of four that had stopped him. He moved within arm's reach and experimentally slashed at the head of one of their halberds with his re-formed sword. The ashen blade cut through the cold steel of the halberd as swiftly as through the surrounding air. Fully half the blade of the Fhaelan's polearm fell clattering to the floor and where Chael's sword had cut emitted wispy gray smoke.

The clattering of armored sabatons stopped immediately and all the mercenaries stared in momentary shock at the ruined weapon. They seemed apprehensive for a moment, then their training reasserted itself and they began marching again, this time at a slightly accelerated pace. There was now only a ten-pace gap between lowered weapons, and it was closing fast.

Armed with the new knowledge of his own capability, Chael willed his weapon to grow as long as it could. He ended up with a very thin double-edged blade that extended over two paces long. He had to hold it low and horizontal or risk carving a smoking hole in the ceiling. The notion of which tempted him momentarily as a means of escape, but he didn't think he could reach a hole in the ceiling, nor did he wish to fall blindly through a gap in the floor. Instead, he lashed out with his colossal ashen blade, slicing the deadly weapons arrayed before him.

One by one, they clattered to the stone and, once again, the march of the steel wall stopped before him. Chael extended his sword and cut low to high in a backhanded slash. Starting at the hip of the leftmost man, he carved a neat smoking line through his torso and that of the second, ending with a cut that cleaved the head of the third man in half, from right chin to left temple. Once again, the hardened steel parted effortlessly in the wake of his alchemical blade. But when it hit flesh, instead of cutting, it burned and melted its way through their bodies.

The three men fell to the ground and, where their exposed flesh shown, Chael could only see black melted remains of skin and bone. It was like the shadow blade was wreathed in molten metal instead of gray, ashy dust. The sheer brutality of it all even gave him pause. But seeing as how these men were here to skewer him like a haunch of beef, the feeling soon passed, and he stabbed the last man in front of him just as easily as his fellows. Chael didn't even bother glancing back at the men approaching from the rear as he vaulted the broken, smoking bodies and continued down the hall.

The next obstacle came in the form of whitestone stairs. After his experience with the last set, he was much more cautious in his approach. However, these were bare of any carpeting and didn't seem to have any runic symbols carved into the stone. All in all, they looked absurdly ordinary, which naturally made him even more suspicious. With no small degree of apprehension, he began to climb.

After only a few seconds, he reached the landing and felt no worse for the wear. He exhaled the breath that he had been unconsciously holding and made his way to the High Minister.

The door to the outer chamber of the High Minister was locked, as Chael suspected. But unlike the several doors he had picked in the floors below, he simply swiped with his alchemical blade and removed the lock entirely.

The rooms inside were as one would expect the ruler of a highly superficial society to maintain. The first of which was a sitting room with velvet chairs and a silver tray that still held a nearly full decanter of wine. Every surface that wasn't plastered with fine art or golden treasures was covered with lush purple and red carpeting. Beyond were a personal library and an office before finally reaching the bedroom itself.

This would be easier if I could just carry the idiot, but I'll need more strength. He thought back to the hapless spearmen remaining in the company. There was enough strength there to make a mad dash to the edge of the wood. The Dark thoughts swirled around in Chael's mind, and that voice of seeming rationality further influenced his thoughts.

Upon seeing Chael, he unsheathed a thin sword meant for thrusting and went through an impressive array of performative bladesmanship. Chael supposed he was probably quite a formidable swordsman, but with a lazy swipe of his own ashen blade the man fell to the floor in two discrete pieces.

Asleep, the High Minister of Kazaam didn't look especially impressive. He was a little older, possibly in his fiftieth year, and had developed a small belly that his lifestyle now afforded him. And he snored lightly, causing the hairs on his bushy mustache to bristle slightly.

Despite his current state, it must be said that he was a particularly formidable man. He had survived nearly a half dozen elections, and it was only due to the iron will of Master Khalim that it wouldn't reach seven. Chael respected him, despite himself. He considered doing the deed with the ash blade, but he could already feel the alchemical power fading, and leaving the High Minister's body a ruin didn't feel right. With steadily practiced hands, Chael drew his knife across his throat.

The minister now dead, Chael had to consider his means of escape. There was still a score of armored mercenaries below him as well as the men outside, many of whom had probably filled the residence after the general alarm went up.

Chael checked the window of the bedchamber; it was a sheer drop past the base of the residence and to the city tier below. The smooth stone exterior left very little hope of hand holds and his fingers were still sore from sliding along the wall earlier. The fingers on his left hand, anyway. His right hand was still consumed by the ash gray smoke, but the potion was wearing off and he knew he couldn't rely on it to cut through the men he was sure to face below.

Suddenly resolute, Chael grunted and stepped out the door. He had accomplished his mission; the High Minister was dead. Come what may, he would deal with it.

His first encounter was another pair of leather clad members of the High Minister's house out on patrol. They wielded the same thin, needle-like swords as the man he had dealt with outside the minister's bedchamber, but didn't demonstrate nearly as much skill. With the last wisps of the alchemist's blade, he cut them into smoldering heaps and continued downward. He chose a different path than the one he had chosen before, hoping to avoid another patrol of armored Fhaelans. He descended to the lower level without encountering more resistance.

In the long hallway behind the audience hall, his luck ran out. He was flanked on all sides by more armored units supported by the lighter armed men that had been guarding the perimeter of the residence. In any direction he now chose, there were at least eight or nine imposing mercenaries, and he was all out of alchemical miracle swords.

Chael felt along his belt for his knives and stumbled across the other vial. The emergency vial if all else failed. Looking around him at the grim odds he now faced, now was such a time.

Cooper hadn't explained what exactly it did, but his stern warning now echoed in Chael's mind. "Throw it against a wall and run." If he simply smashed it against a wall and ran, he would just run into another group of angry soldiers. Chael steeled himself, gripping the vial and flung it at the visor of the nearest plate-armored Fhaelan.

Immediately after launching the Dark alchemist's potion, he ducked down and plugged his ears, expecting some horrific and fiery explosion, but there was nothing. He slowly opened his eyes and looked out at the crowd of iron clad mercenaries. They seemed quite normal and quite alive.

For a moment he thought that the Darkened cultist had given him a vial of piss, but then there was a change. It was slight at first. The soldiers of Fhael started giving each other odd glances. Their ranks broke as they wandered about, seemingly confused where they were. And then they became violent.

Mercenary attacked mercenary in a sudden violent uproar. They seemed to care not for pain as men with severed limbs launched themselves at their former comrades, attempting to rip out their throats with naught but their teeth.

As quickly as it started, it also ended. They had managed to so thoroughly cut each other to pieces that only a few wriggling corpses remained, still struggling to attack anything in their reach, including their own severed limbs.

The din of battle rose behind him, and Chael turned to see the Fhaelans at the other end of the hall had also succumbed to the same effects and were now tearing themselves apart limb from limb.

Chael sniffed the air; it carried with it the smell of death and blood, but nothing unnatural. Yet these two groups of men, separated by dozens of paces of hallway, had both succumbed to whatever madness-inducing cocktail Cooper had devised. But he was unaffected; he neither felt especially violent nor enraged. *How strange.* After a few precious moments, Chael decided it was a riddle best solved later and bolted past the mutilated corpses in the hall.

He ran at a full sprint for nearly five minutes. He flew out of the arboretum and onto the grounds, dodging more scenes of insane brutality as he went. The entire High Ministerial Residence had been engulfed in a maddened frenzy and, after only a few minutes, the great whitestone plaza was awash in blood.

Chael watched from down the street as the violence slowly died down as they ran out of bodies to massacre. He wanted to blame Cooper; he wanted to blame Khalim. But in his heart, Chael knew he was solely responsible. He had known that the alchemical would be destructive. He couldn't have known to what extent, but he knew it would be devastating.

In the coming days, the people of Kazaam would describe the carnage as demonic and inhuman. Khalim would vow to execute those responsible if he became High Minister. Chael would simply resign himself to the sad facts of his life. Business in Kazaam was bloody, and he had plenty more to conduct before he was finished.

Chapter 22

Present Day

Take initiative. Chael ground his teeth, trying to come up with a novel strategy to surprise his long-time sparring partner while also ducking bone shattering swings.

He supposed he was in some subterranean dungeon underneath the Order house in Fhaerhold. The walls of his small jail cell were made of a dark stone, roughly shaped and seamlessly fit into place like giant puzzle pieces. The only break in the monotony of stone walls, floor, and ceiling was the iron door through which he had spied the torch. There was no furniture in the room save a solitary wooden chair, in which he had been placed. Great iron spikes secured the chair into the stone below, and iron manacles secured Chael to the chair at both his wrists and ankles.

His momentary observation of his cell was interrupted when a cold, wet drop fell upon his head, wetting his hair. He glanced up and saw the formation of another drop on the ceiling that would surely fall in another minute or so. The strange liquid pooled there unnaturally, as if fed from some invisible source. Then a closer inspection of the walls showed they were not so mundane as he thought. In the stone all around him were familiar runic symbols meant to block and fight the influence of Dark energy.

Without much hope, he reached out with his senses and was immediately stymied. He could feel nothing beyond the warded walls of his cell. And even if he could, his connection to his abilities was weak, like a limb numbed by an alchemical potion used in surgery. As he sat immobilized in his chair, he developed a rhythm. A drop would hit him and his connection to the Dark would falter. But little by little it would grow back, and he would feel it again before another drop fell from the ceiling and his senses deadened. It was extraordinarily frustrating to any would-be escape plans.

Chael's next thoughts turned to Michik. Aelisa knew that by betraying him in this manner that she either had to hold him indefinitely or kill him, which meant she would probably seek to capture or destroy his dog. However, Aelisa wasn't with them when he and Sir Andon had dropped him off with the squire. And unless Andon was also behind this trap, which he doubted, she wouldn't immediately know Michik's whereabouts.

Chael gave a silent prayer to the Living Stars and then stopped himself. Even if there was some benevolent force on high, it was their servants currently holding him. For a brief moment, he even considered a supplication to whatever entity held sway in the Dark for intercession. At least then his imprisonment would be justified. Instead of either plan, he simply resorted to struggling against his bonds until the strain made him pass out with exhaustion. The strategy proved ineffective.

Inside his underground cell, Chael had no reference by which to tell time, but he roughly estimated that about twelve hours had passed since he had first come to. Several cycles of struggling and pulling at his restraints had only succeeded in severely chafing his wrists and ankles. Steady drops of blood fell to the floor from his chair, adding a new cadence to the unending drip from above.

But then a distinct sound broke the silence of the prison. Footsteps coming down the stairs outside the cell. Chael strained to listen. There were at least two pairs of heavy steps and the scraping of another set of feet being dragged. Before long, two larger Order priests entered the dungeon with a young red-haired woman in tow.

Sounds about right, Chael thought ruefully as his head slumped back down. A bit on the nose, Chael thought, considering the business alleged to be conducted out of the basement of the alehouse.

Chael didn't have long to muse over the identity of the woman after she passed his door and out of sight into an adjacent cell. Another set of footsteps were now descending the stairs, much lighter than the ones before. And these stopped right in front of his door. Backlit by the torch beyond his cell, her face was cast in shadow. But Chael had no doubts about who this person was.

"Hello, Chael," Sister Aelisa said plainly. She had almost no emotion in her voice. Not malice or wicked joy at successfully goading him into her trap. Chael thought there may have been the slightest hint of sadness in her tone, but the alchemical water torture dulled both his traditional and special senses. He had surely imagined it.

Chael quickly went through the range of responses and emotional tones at his disposal. He was certainly angry; yelling at her had more than a little appeal. But loathe as he was to admit, diplomacy was probably his best option at the moment. Chael swallowed a bitter retort and a non-insubstantial amount of his pride and responded.

"Greetings, Sister Aelisa," Chael managed with his best attempt at a neutral tone. "To what do I owe the pleasure? I apologize for the sorry state of my abode; my roof seems to have sprung a leak." It turns out he was a lousy diplomat. She smiled slightly, then sighed.

"Defiant as ever I see," Aelisa said sadly. "Please know that I take no personal pleasure in your confinement. I truly believe that you don't intend to do any harm to the realm. But the demonstration of your connection to the Dark in the forest, and your ability to withstand the corporeal explosion of Baron Janus confirmed the truth. You are the Darkborn."

"The Darkborn?!" Chael yelled at her, breaking all semblance of composure. "You're still peddling that rubbish!"

"You can deny it, but the texts and your own actions confirm it." Her voice rose, the sadness replaced by a resolute sense of duty. "Naturally, we cannot let you live."

"Then why didn't you kill me when I was unconscious?"

"Some of us wanted to," she replied honestly. "Many of the other prefects argued that we should have taken your head the moment you were in our grasp."

"Let me guess, you were in that group," Chael spat bitterly.

"Oh no," Aelisa said with mild surprise. "I was quite sure my adjustments to your cell would effectively hold you in place and control the Darkness inside you. And I thought you may still provide us answers, either out of a sense of duty from your human side." She paused, the faint sadness reentering her voice. "Or by aggressive persuasion, if necessary," she finally said. Chael considered her words carefully; he had no more insight into ancient mysticism and prophecy than his dog did. But as long as he was potentially useful, he might remain alive a little longer. After a moment of contemplation, a thought occurred to him.

"How did you know this trap would work?" he asked her.

"Because we didn't originally build that cell for you." She gestured to her left at the cell directly next to his. "We built it for him."

Chapter 23

10 Years Ago

Election day was an impressive title, but like all the other euphemisms Kazaam's ruling class abused, the reality was much less grand. The occasion was held on the now bare, rocky hilltop of Kazaam. The same place where the old High Ministerial Residence once stood. After the horrific melee that had ensued in the wake of the High Minister's assassination, no one was comfortable occupying the building for too long, as if the crazed ghosts of dead mercenaries would come out of the walls and continue their bloody spree.

Shortly after Khalim had asserted himself as the new High Minister, he had the building torn down by slaves. He vowed to build a newer and grander building, an actual palace in its place. Chael had no doubt that he would, and construction was supposed to commence just after his ascension.

The ceremony was surprisingly discreet compared to the usual pomp of the Great Houses. The patron of each house approached him and swore the two-faced loyalty of schemers and killers. *Darkness, they were convincing, though.* In turn, Khalim promised to bless their house as well as the city as a whole. At the end Khalim would officially forsake his own house. Officially, the house of the High Minister was

Kazaam itself and they were supposed to cut attachment to their own. In practice, his ascension simply made his house even more loyal and powerful.

One by one, the Great Houses all sent their representatives, save one. Conspicuously absent was Anitea Faasa, the purveyor of whitestone marble and the richest woman in the city. The procession of false oaths continued apace, but more and more murmuring erupted from the gathered nobility. By the end, Khalim had to silence them by command and still one could hear dozens of conspiratorial whispers.

Once the election was decided, tradition dictated that all the losers pay homage to the winner. The Great Houses were supporters of conspiracy, murder, slavery, and every vice and depravity one could imagine. However, they were adamant about their traditions and protocols. They clung to them like flotsam in a stormy sea.

It was their adherence to tradition that kept the city relatively peaceful between elections. By not swearing to Khalim today, Anitea had broken the most sacred tradition of them all. From his spot at the back, Chael watched the eyes of his terrifying master. Khalim gazed out at his audience, a burning fury raging in his eyes. Eventually those eyes met his own and through them Khalim's will was as clear as if he had written it on a giant sign.

"Find her. Kill them all."

Chael, Mason, Darrik, and Michik all stomped heavily through the packed snow of the Aazeran mountains. By unanimous consent of the under ministers and decree by High Minister Khalim, Great House Faasa was outlawed from the city and their assets seized. A search of Anitea's home revealed that she and her entire family had fled at least several days prior.

Chael knew she wouldn't be there and suspected where she may have fled for safety. So, he took some of Anitea's remaining clothes for scent and organized the expedition into the nearby mountains. Mournfully, he left behind his green cloak and secured heavy white clothes for him and Darrik. Mason had refused to wear anything but the conspicuous black hood that all the members of the Black Hand wore.

"At least somebody is having fun," remarked Darrik while gesturing toward Michik. The wolf was avoiding the rough mountain trail and was jumping in and out of every snow drift he could find. "I haven't been able to feel my bits for hours. Remind me why we couldn't take the main road again?"

"Oh, I don't know," Chael replied, sarcasm dripping from his words. "Perhaps it's because they will definitely have the road watched. And seeing how they have enough mining alchemicals to bring the entire mountain down on top of us, I thought we might take the long way round."

Some is up They were heading to the whitestone marble quarry near the summit of the smaller of the Aazeran peaks. Part of the reason that it was so treasured was the enormous difficulty of mining it so high in the frozen mountains. A road did exist, but it was little more than a cart path before Anitea had taken over. She had nearly bankrupted her family, installing extensive tracks for special carts to haul the marble down in a fraction of the time and in much greater volume. The increased production over the last few years had raised House Faasa from the middle tier in the city to the very top.

What Chael and his party currently walked upon was little more than a hunting track, seldom used in snowier months. By the time they stopped for the night, even Michik had lost some enthusiasm for the cold and the snow. He huddled tightly against Chael's side while the three humans similarly gathered for warmth. They couldn't risk a campfire which might alert any watchers Anitea had left out.

"So, what's the plan for tomorrow then?" Darrik blurted out, breaking the cold silence in his usual boisterous way. Mason slowly turned his black cloaked head to the interruption to the quiet and placed a large dirty finger to his lips. Chael could have sworn that the cold mountain wind blew even more icy in that moment.

"Yeah, Mason," Chael added in as quiet a voice as he could manage. "You've been awfully secretive about our actual mission here." Mason eyed him with much less contempt than he had Darrik, and after a moment, nodded.

"Khalim paid my mistress an extra fee to ensure that this mission goes according to plan. He does not want operations at the quarry to be interrupted and has ordered that we minimize deaths of the Faasa staff."

Damn, Chael cursed himself. He had not let himself get so carried away by the power since he first discovered it. At least you got to sleep all night, Chael thought, grimacing slightly. Despite his somewhat sardonic attitude, Chael knew their complaints were mostly warranted. He hadn't needed to feed on life energy for that long in years and had forgotten just how corruptive it could become if he wasn't vigilant. He had already paid a high price for that lesson and was a little ashamed that he had so quickly forgotten.

"Every member of the Anitea's family is to be beheaded. Her children, her siblings and their children. The entire familial lineage of her house is to be erased." Darrik gawked at Mason in shock while Chael merely looked into the snow. He knew this was the mission, even though he hadn't been officially informed until just now. Ever since the cold glare Khalim had delivered at the election ceremony, he knew that this was the measure of his master's resolve.

"We can't!" Darrik nearly shouted, no longer bothering to control the volume of his voice. He turned to Chael, "We can't Chael. We kill thieves and criminals and scheming politicians, just to put the worst of them all in the High Seat. And that's our lot in life and so be it. But she has kids! Little kids! Is that what we do now?" Chael couldn't look at him. He continued to stare down at the frozen trail, absently scratching Michik's head.

"I suggest you lower your voice, my young friend." Mason said calmly through his perversely maniacal grin.

The chill darkness of the night seemed to gather around Mason's body like a blanket and though he and Darrik were of a similar large build, Mason's presence towered over him, and Darrik shrank back.

"This is your mission. You will obey." Mason said the words like pronouncing Dark judgment upon Darrik's soul. The phrase lingered in the frosty air like a particularly foul smell, and it permeated their senses likewise until the very thought of disobedience was as far away as a spring garden from their frozen peak.

Darrik, effectively chastised, said no more words and eventually they all fell into a dreamless sleep.

Chapter 24

Present Day

Chael's gaze panned from Aelisa and to his right at the stone wall that divided his cell from that of his neighbors. He wasn't even aware that it was occupied. Until now, he had assumed that Darrik had simply been an elaborate ruse to get him to the capitol so they could imprison him.

"So, Darrik...?" Chael asked, still unsure if he trusted Aelisa.

"Is alive and in the cell next to yours." Aelisa said, answering his question before he had even asked. "I have not lied to you, even now. I did bring you here in the hopes that you may be able to get some answers out of this man as well as verify his identity. It was only after we emerged from the Dark Forest that I made up my mind that you were too dangerous to be allowed to live." Her face genuinely softened for the first time in Chael's experience, and she looked at him with the kind of gaze he could vaguely remember his mother making. "I'm sorry," she said after a long pause.

"Damn your apologies." Chael spat back at her. "To the Darkness with all of you!" Aelisa snapped back into her customary cold and calculating glare.

"You may hate me and that's to be expected. But before you curse us all to our doom, consider this. If you are not the monster that we fear, then you cannot allow your hatred for me to cloud your judgment. The tens of thousands of innocent people above you may or may not live based on the intelligence that you can glean from your former associate. We are always listening; the clock is ticking." Having said her piece, Aelisa turned and walked out of the dungeon.

Chael watched her go with seething hatred, vowing every curse he could think of. Generally, this was the kind of endeavor where he had a great deal of confidence and creativity, but the alchemical dripping from the ceiling kept his mind in rhythmic malaise that intensified every time a drop splattered on his head. Chael screamed in hoarse, impotent frustration at the situation; wishing he could steal the life from Aelisa and smash his way out of the cell.

After his momentary tantrum her words floated back to him. Whoever occupied the cell next to his knew about the impending invasion weeks ago and had specifically asked for him. Could he really be so selfish as to condemn those people because of the Order and Aelisa?

"Darkness!" Chael cursed, "I hate people!" A peal of laughter rose from the adjoining cell. First low and quiet, as if the speaker wasn't sure if his throat still worked, but it grew in volume and intensity as the person seemed to warm up to the sound.

"Now where have I heard that before?" the man asked, still chuckling lightly. Chael froze; it had been a decade since he heard Darrik's voice so he couldn't be sure. But Darkness, did it sound like him.

"This is a trick," Chael muttered to the man without any real confidence. "You think if you impersonate my dead friend that I'll give you some confirmation about who and what I am." The laughter increased again, but this time more forced, and the speaker ended it with a couple dry raspy coughs.

"Friend? Tell me, Chael, do you stab all of your friends through the heart? Or was it just me?"

10 Years Ago

They set out before dawn. Cold frostbitten feet and even colder icy silence. Chael couldn't look Darrik in the eye and Mason loomed over them both with the same Dark intimidating presence that he had the night before. Even Michik had abandoned his puppy-like fascination with the snow and was silently padding alongside Chael, occasionally sniffing the air. Their journey took them along the outside edge of the mountain, around and above the quarry.

They marched silently for several hours until Michik stopped and sniffed the air more intently. They were very near a ledge that would look down into the mine below. The wolf slowly lowered his head and gave a low growl.

"Someone is up ahead," Chael whispered lightly, immensely proud of his furry companion. Mason was dubious of bringing him along on this journey, but Chael had insisted upon his worth as a scout. Chael was positively elated that his dog had proved him right. Mason gave one skeptical look at Michik and then nodded. He then looked at Chael and gave him the hand signal to dispatch the Faasa scout.

Where did he learn that? Chael wondered, but he shook his head and steadied himself. He gave Michik a command to stay and proceeded ahead down the snowy trail. He heard a faint whine from behind him, but his dog obeyed and didn't follow.

Chael crept along the path as it wound up and around the mountain. Michik's nose could detect people from miles away in the right conditions. He had seen it, so he couldn't be sure how close this scout was. After about ten minutes of walking, he found himself at the final turn before the long sweeping path that led to the overlook. Slowly, he peeked around the edge.

The sun had not yet peeked out over the mountains and the morning light was dim, but he spotted her. *Her?* The figure was dressed in tight white clothing to hide her outline amongst the ice and snow. But she either had bad orders or had gotten lazy because she was standing conspicuously in the middle of the path, the outline of her feminine body clearly visible through her clothes.

There were at least forty feet of sheer iced over cliff above her and there was very little foliage in the ten or so paces between them. He had no way to conduct a stealthy approach. Throwing knives were out as well. At this distance, he couldn't necessarily guarantee a kill and even if he did, there was still ample opportunity for her to alert her comrades below as she died.

Chael thought about what Mason might do in this situation. He imagined a hole suddenly opening up beneath her feet and swallowing her in an instant, sending her directly to entertain his favorite demons in the Dark. Chael had no idea if that was possible, but it seemed like something Mason might do. Come to think of it, one of his invisible demons could probably do the trick but instead he had sent Chael.

Interesting, he thought.Not enough, Chael grimaced. He took a steadying breath, weighing his ever-decreasing options before the serious-looking men would reach him and he'd fight. He caught sight of the serving woman five paces behind and slightly to the left of the man he had hit with the ale mug. Forgive me, he sighed, and threw the blade just past the man's ear as it spun and struck the woman in the arm.

Chael's head snapped up and surveyed the area above the female watchman. The same wall of rocky ice behind her followed the trail around the bend to where he was crouching. An idea slowly crystalized in his mind, and he produced two of his knives. Chael jammed the point into one of the many frozen crevices and began to climb hand over hand. Using his knives like ice picks was going to ruin their blades but he could buy new ones later, he supposed.

Slowly, he ascended the wall and slumped onto a snowy ledge that sharply angled up toward the mountain summit. Chael carefully climbed up the steep, frosty terrain until he was an additional twenty feet above the ice wall that he had just climbed. Nervously, he edged along the mountainside to get above the woman. His already numb feet slipped and slid along the slope and twice he had to catch himself from tumbling down the mountain with his knives. But eventually, panting from exertion and nerves, he found himself staring down at her sixty feet below.

His target was directly above him. A small shelf of loose rock and ice had formed over what was perhaps decades of successive snowfalls and avalanches, creating a loose shelf of frozen debris. The snow on top of the shelf had accumulated to a staggering height and only the Living Stars know how in the world the thing hadn't collapsed already.

Carefully, like poking a sleeping bear, Chael nudged the shelf with his outstretched hand; knife gripped firmly in his numb fingers. The icy wind howled, and several cracks screamed in protest at the intrusion on the frozen ledge as bits of rock and snow fell down the precipitous slope and landed around the female watchman.

Chael sucked in a terrified breath as she glanced up at the source of the disturbance, but she clearly hadn't noticed him. She turned around, once again surveying the mining operations below.

He exhaled, still nervously wedging his knife into the unstable shelf. *Well, here goes something stupid,* he thought. Chael withdrew the knife from the icy shelf and slammed it back in, point first into one of the many small pillars of ice that held it up. The effect was immediate. The ice and hard packed snow holding up the shelf snapped and gave way in a sudden rush of momentum that threatened to carry Chael down with it. He leaped away to his left, abandoning all caution of the steep and snowy terrain to avoid the coming miniature avalanche. He caught himself after sliding only a few feet and was able to bear witness to the results of his hasty plan.

A column of snow ten feet wide and nearly as tall hurtled down the cliff and fell directly on top of the stunned woman. The resulting crash echoed around the mountainside, but as he was hoping, the laborers and slavers down below ignored it completely. The conditions on the mountain were volatile and such things were almost certainly common.

Chael carefully slid down the slope, braking himself with his knife that he was dragging behind. With somewhat less trepidation than last time, he climbed down the wall and finally approached the snowy tomb of the woman. Her torso was completely engulfed but to Chael's horror her exposed feet were flailing wildly in a desperate attempt to free herself.

Chael had never killed a woman before. He supposed he shouldn't be shocked, after all he had been expressly sent here to do just that. But the reality of it here and now was different. He killed men, and heretofore he had killed men who regarded life as purely transactional and only useful insofar as it could be leveraged for their own gain. The men he killed traded human lives to give themselves power, and it sickened him. He worked for such a man, but he took some comfort in ridding the world of others like him.

He looked down at the struggling legs next to him; she was suffocating under the snow. She was almost certainly as bad or as decent as any of the other nameless servants he had slaughtered. But what bothered him was the only pure thing in his life had been his mother. He didn't love her; he had actually spent years resenting her for letting him go. But he knew she loved him. *Was this woman a mother? Would some unknown offspring of hers curse his name and seek vengeance?* Chael pondered these thoughts as the twitching legs slowly stopped struggling and then lay still.

He exhaled slowly and wiped the single tear that had frozen to his cheek. As he breathed, he felt numb again, but not as a consequence of the bitter cold, something else that resided deeper.

Subtle, Chael huffed as the first contender for the lady's honor emerged from the circling pack. He stretched his neck and prepared for the predictable opening attack. Probably off to fetch the watch. Darkness! Chael had to hurry this along.

With that thought, a silent resoluteness stole his nerves and he jogged down the trail to collect the others.

Chapter 25

10 Years Ago

The whitestone quarry was carved out of the mountain in a great semi-circular dome. It looked like some giant hand had plucked a slice of orange from the base of the mountain's summit. The domed roof covered nearly half of the manmade plateau and cast the entire operation in the morning's shadow. Chael and his companions surveyed from the trail above and to the side of the large, flat working area. The guards were mostly concentrated at the far end, away from the stone canopy, at the base of the road. Behind them, several dozen miners and overseers were hard at work chipping away and shaping the bright white marble that seemed to grow in great veins along the mountainside.

The miners were slaves, of course. Khalim had left orders not to harm them unless necessary, but that, as usual, wasn't out of some humanitarian concern. They were valuable commodities and would serve well, regardless of whatever puppet Khalim installed here after Chael's business was concluded.

The overseers were a different matter. The orders had been nonspecific, only that the mine workers should not be harmed more than absolutely necessary. As he watched one particular overseer beat a miner with a wooden cudgel, Chael decided they weren't included in that category.

Beyond the guards near the road and the overseers with their clubs, there were two problems facing them. The first were two wooden watchtowers built on opposite ends of the plateau. Chael suspected they were built to keep an eye on the miners, but today they served as sentries for any assassin's sent to kill their patron. The second were the Kaazan guild alchemists house Faasa employed to blow apart large sections of the mountain. Any loud assault on the mining operation below would draw them out. Chael momentarily shuddered at the memory of what just one alchemist had been capable of back in the city.

"Well, what's the plan then?" asked Darrik, looking at the other two expectantly. There wasn't a strict hierarchy in the small group, but Darrik usually looked to Chael for planning and Mason had mostly asserted himself as in charge since they had begun so he looked to them for answers.

Chael also looked over to the large Dark worshipper and inclined his head. "Well?" he asked.

"I was thinking we might throw snowballs at them," Mason replied.

When he had discovered how Chael had killed the sentry woman, Mason was infuriated at the sheer absurdity and lack of regard for stealth. Darrik, meanwhile, the moment Mason turned his back, had clapped Chael on the shoulder barely able to contain his laughter. Mason eyed them both daring either to laugh at his joke and stoke his rage again. They mostly managed to keep their heads.

After a moment, he continued, "Your wolf may prove useful here," he said.

Chael bristled at the remark. Michik had already warned them of an enemy scout, so as far as Chael was concerned, the wolf's value was beyond dispute.

Stifling a rude retort, Chael asked, "What do you mean?"

"A giant wolf wandering in their midst is sure to provide a quality distraction," Mason answered, his perverse grin returning to his face.

"You want to use him as bait!" Chael huffed, struggling to keep his voice down.

Mason's smile flickered for a moment and the strange commanding aura from the night before returned. Chael couldn't be sure if it was some strange alchemy or just the powerful presence of a truly devoted servant of chaos, but Mason's spirit seemed to push against them and command obedience.

When he finally uttered the words, they carried the weight of the mountain itself. "Yes, I do."

Chael struggled against it pushing back with his own considerable will and met Mason's eye. For a moment all he could do was stare into the brown rings surrounding a black emptiness as deep and foreboding as the Dark itself. Chael had heard somewhere that the eyes were windows into the soul, if that was true then Mason's was as black and empty as any demon. Chael relented.

"Fine," he muttered bitterly, barely allowing the words to sneak past his lips.

Mason gave him a slight nod, respecting at least his attempt to match his iron will. With the hierarchy officially settled, Mason laid out the plan.

Chael carefully slid down the icy mountainside toward the quarry. He had to step carefully; any falling rocks or snow could cause one of the overseers to look up and blow the entire operation. He glanced up at Michik, who descended behind him as easily on his four legs as Chael could walk on flat ground.

"Showoff," Chael muttered silently.

He inched downward, feet grasping at every frozen ledge he could find while his belly scraped against frost-covered stone. He was entirely reliant on the white camouflage he was wearing to hide his approach. If any of the workers or soldiers scrutinized this section of the mountain for more than a passing glance, he'd be pinned to the rock by a dozen arrows before he could so much as twitch.

Michik was naturally suited for this wintery mountain expedition. His light gray fur was speckled with snow and his lithe movements barely betrayed a sound as he followed Chael to the base of the quarry. After several close calls with loose rocks and at least one overseer with a strange fascination with mountain sides, they reached the wide flat plateau that was the base of the quarry. Once his feet were back on flat ground, Chael raced as quietly as he could to one of the pillars that supported the dome and hid in its shadow.

"Ok buddy, you're up," Chael whispered to Michik. The wolf cocked his head to the side and stared at Chael. "Attack," Chael commanded softly and pointed over to the guards standing by the road.

Michik laid down and stared up at his master and whined lightly. "Meeshee!" Chael growled lightly. "Attack!" But Michik just continued to lay there looking up at him with round innocent eyes.

Chael glanced nervously across the quarry; they might spot Darrik at any moment. Chael got down on his knees and leaned forward until he could see eye to eye with his dog.

"Buddy, I know you don't want to do this." Chael hesitated; the round glassy orbs belied more emotion than should have been possible. He was scared, and he was pleading with his master in the only way he could. Chael choked down the internal revulsion he felt and continued. "If you don't go now, Darrik could be killed."

At the mention of Darrik's name, his head popped up, and he tilted it to the side again, still fixing his woeful gaze on Chael.

"I'm sorry Michik, I..." A sudden commotion interrupted his words. Just as he feared, several of the armsmen guarding the road had spotted Darrik and were moving to investigate. Chael stood up and summoned the same force of will that Mason had used to command obedience. He could see Michik start to cower as he purposely towered over him, both physically and in terms of intent. For the first time in their relationship, he truly was the master, and it tortured him.

With his heart breaking, Chael jabbed his finger in the direction of the suspicious guards and commanded, "Attack!"

Michik spun around and shot out from the shadows. Overseers and miners both gawked at the giant wolf as he tore across the broken stone, heedless of all the eyes now fixed on him.

The second he was gone, Chael similarly sprinted toward the base of the nearest tower. He was about twenty feet away when he started and by the time he reached the base of the tower, the watcher had already loosed an arrow at Michik. The missile bounced harmlessly across the icy stone less than a foot from his dog's tail.

The watchtower loomed over Chael ten paces high as he climbed. Another arrow shot out from the tower, this one embedding itself into a workbench as Michik tore past. One overseer swung one of their heavy wooden clubs at Michik's head as he was about to run by. The savvy wolf leaped into the air just as the cudgel descended and clamped his powerful jaws around it like it was a simple stick in a game of fetch. The shocked overseer was yanked to the ground by the force of it as Michik continued on unabated with the cudgel between his teeth.

Chael redoubled his efforts to climb the cold wooden tower as a third arrow sailed high over Michik's head. Eventually, this person was going to get lucky. As Chael crested the edge of the wooden platform, he lashed out with one of his knives, stabbing the bowman in the back of the thigh before he had even heaved himself over the lip. The bowman reeled backward in pain and kicked at Chael with his injured leg. Chael caught the leg mid kick and fell forward, leveraging it to bring the sentry down with him. The man desperately tried to nock another arrow, but Chael brushed the bow aside with one hand and plunged his knife down with the other.

Chael could hear the familiar gurgling half screams as the blood choked his lungs, but he was already standing with the poor man's bow. Chael aimed out across the expanse of the entire quarry at the other watchtower, some two hundred paces away. They, of course, taught archery at the school and Chael was competent, but he didn't consider himself to be much of a marksman.

And at this distance, any arrow would be subject to a lot of wind drift before reaching its target. He aimed high and launched his first arrow. It sailed through the mountain air in a wide arc and thudded into the railing right next to a very surprised sentry. Chael quickly adjusted his aim and loosed another shaft and found his mark, embedding it deep in the other man's chest. He quickly shot an additional two arrows for good measure and hurried down the tower.

Michik had already reached the group of guardsmen before Chael had even dispatched the bowman. He dropped the stolen cudgel as he reached the group and sunk his great canine teeth into the sword arm of the nearest Faasa guard.

The man roared in agony and dropped his weapon as Michik viciously thrashed his head back and forth. He then kicked the wolf several times in the ribs, but still Michik held on. The other armsmen reacted quickly to the sudden attack by a giant wolf and converged on Michik.

As they raised their various arms to fell Michik, a force of nature in the form of a young blonde man smashed into their group. With a huge two-handed broadsword, Darrik cleaved Faasa soldiers in half from collar to waist. Taken by surprise and with the overwhelming force that Darrik could deliver, they were quickly outmatched and killed. One by one, their corpses fell to the earth and Michik let the first man go, his arm now just a dead appendage clinging to a lifeless remnant of his chest.

Chael watched as Darrik killed the remaining soldiers guarding the road. That only left the overseers as the remaining potential combatants. Chael casually strolled out toward them. The eyes of twenty or so slave drivers nervously darted back and forth between him and Darrik as he approached.

The first one he approached was a woman. She had dark hair that extended down to the middle of her back and fierce brown eyes. Like all the overseers, she was wearing heavy furs to protect against the cold in sharp contrast to the relatively scant dress of the enslaved miners. Beneath her hood, the bottom half of her face was hidden by a light leather covering tied just above her nose.

Chael searched her face for some emotion or a clue as to possible hidden intent, but beyond the simple rage in her eyes. He stopped just within arm's reach of her and pointed his falchion at the ground.

"Kneel," was the only word he uttered. The infuriated overseer continued to stare at him with unbridled hatred in her eyes and Chael answered with an implacable stare of his own and continued pointing his sword at the frozen stones. The cudgel twitched slightly in her hand and Chael raised his sword and pointed it at her chest, the tip hovering a breath away from her flesh.

"Kneel," he repeated gravely, but the woman continued to stare at him defiantly. Chael nodded to her out of respect and took a half step closer to her.

Before she could even let out a scream, his sword whistled through the air and separated her head from her neck. Head and body hit the ground in two successive thuds. It reminded Chael of the sound of his heartbeat. For a moment he stared at her corpse, killing the female sentry had been so difficult but now he felt strangely apathetic.

She isn't worth your remorse, a sharp gravelly version of his own voice called to him inside his head. The voice was definitely some altered version of his, but it also felt alien. Like someone else had been able to reach into his mind and whisper. For a moment, he feared he was going crazy, but he shook it off and turned his bloody sword to the rest of the gathered crowd. He had work to do.

"Would anyone else care to defy me?" Chael called out to the rest. One by one hateful glares turned to resignation, shoulders slumped, and wooden cudgels clattered to the stone. "Good," Chael called menacingly.

At that moment, one of the slaves stood and took up his miner's ax. He charged the nearest overseer with righteous fury and raised his weapon. One of Chael's knives buried itself in his throat. The stunned slave dropped the pickaxe and turned fearfully to the man he thought to be his rescuer. He opened his mouth to speak, but only blood escaped his lips.

For a moment, his chin quivered as if he was desperately trying to push some final word or curse out of his mouth and blow it at Chael. But soon the quivering stopped, and he too fell lifeless to the ground. Darrik ran over to Chael and a sheepish Michik followed.

"What in Darkness are you doing, Chael?" Darrik demanded. He gawked in horror at the body of the slave, still issuing the occasional gout of blood from his neck.

Chael ignored Darrik's outrage and walked over to the slave and retrieved his knife, wiping the blade on the dead man's clothes. Darrik seized him by the shoulder and shook him. "What is wrong with you?!"

Chael shook him off and pointed all around him with his sword. "Khalim wants these slaves, we didn't come here to free them. And if they begin thinking that their salvation has come and stop doing their jobs a lot more of them are going to die."

Chael was practically yelling at Darrik; he didn't know why he was suddenly so angry, but he wanted to take his friend's head off. "I just saved scores of lives by taking just one!" Chael spat.

Darrik just looked at him, stunned; his face was eerily similar to the slave's at the moment Chael's knife slammed into his neck.

"Come on, we need to see if Mason needs help," Chael stated, intentionally calming his voice.

Darrik still looked horrified at what had just happened, but after a long pause, he nodded. Chael walked over to the dead overseer and picked up her severed head by the hair. He dumped it into one of the carts on the side of the main road and kicked it off the mountain. The mechanism that Anitea and her engineers had designed would carry that cart all the way down to the base of the mountain, where a small army of the city watch as well as several of their schoolmates waited to advance up the road. They hadn't arranged a specific signal, but Chael was sure that the head would send the appropriate message.

Without another word to Darrik, Chael marched off toward the area of the quarry under the great mountain dome. As he walked, he patted his hip lightly and Michik dutifully padded up beside him. He glanced down at the wolf and frowned slightly. Michik was walking with his head down low and his tail tucked underneath his body.

Chael had never seen his dog act this way before. He reached down to scratch his head and Michik flinched slightly before accepting the touch. That made Chael frown even deeper. He glanced back at Darrik, who was still looking at him like he was some imposter.

Pay them no heed, the odd simulacrum of his voice told him. As it spoke, it wasn't just the words that affected him but a renewed sense of numb indifference to the world. It was like the voice carried with it an icy touch that suffused his being with a sort of sullen apathy. *Look around you and feel. Feel and breath.* Chael hesitantly looked around him at the many pools of blood staining the snow and stone.

For a moment, he could feel the death all around him and at the insistence of the voice, he breathed it in. At once, the world became sharper and more colorful as if a thin cloth had been pulled from his eyes. All the aches and pains that gnawed at him from two days of mountaineering and fighting were gone. He looked down and flexed his hands and felt sudden immense strength in his fingers, he felt like he could crush the stones of the quarry with just his hands, and he probably could. Michik whined at his side, and he looked down pitilessly at him.

"Quiet!" Chael commanded, and the dutiful wolf stopped his protest.

Underneath the rock dome were several buildings made of wood. On the left was the somewhat ramshackle group of barracks that the slave miners slept in. They were simple rectangular buildings with no windows and a crooked door. Loose fitting boards left many gaps that would certainly allow the frosty mountain air to blow in, chilling any occupants.

On the right was the equally spartan albeit better constructed tenements of the overseers. Between them was a smoothed stone pathway that led to the far wall of the hollowed-out section of the mountain. Whitestone stairs, hewn directly from the mountain, led up to a raised entrance platform. Four gleaming white pillars held up the section of domed roof over the platform which framed two solid oak doors. The doors had the crest of house Faasa carved across them. A kneeling man holding a hammer and a pickaxe above his head. Both were slightly ajar marking Mason's passage.

Carefully, Chael opened the door and was met with a truly unique scene of carnage. Bodies of guild alchemists were strewn about the main hall of House Faasa's sanctum. Chael had to guess that they were guild alchemists by the remnants of the few clothes he could see. It looked to him like a giant rabid bear had come through and declared open war on everyone inside. There were parts and pieces of human bodies strewn out across every surface of the wide entrance. He estimated that there had once been a crystal chandelier hanging from the vaulted ceiling, but all that was left of it was a lazily swinging chain attached to the roof and shards of crystal glass embedding about two-thirds of the mangled remains.

Chael heard Darrik suck in a surprised breath when he entered. They were no strangers to carnage and Darrik's sudden empathy notwithstanding, it truly was a painfully awesome sight. Carefully stepping around the larger pools of blood, Chael traversed the stone hall toward the only other door. With a quick glance at Michik, who was still cowering slightly, he pressed onward.

It turned out this great monument to House Faasa's fortunes was only superficially impressive. The interior after the bloody entrance hall was much more cramped, being only a little taller than Darrik. There were a few small rooms with furnishings for living quarters and a small kitchen. *Not much,* Chael observed. But a mountain fortress was probably a lot more appealing in theory than in reality. Which was almost certainly why Anitea and her family lived in the city. Cold and remote, this place was more a monument than a mansion, and the plainness of the interior bore that out.

As they continued down the central hallway, commotion on the far end made them quicken their pace until they found Mason. He was standing in front of a gargantuan rough-hewn stone door. There were tracks in the sides of the walls where it had obviously slid down from some mechanism in the ceiling. Unlike the oak doors at the main entrance, this stone slab was only roughly shaped and unornamented. Chael suspected that this was some emergency escape route and once shut, this giant boulder of a door wasn't meant to be opened again.

The source of the commotion they had heard was two lesser demons pounding away on the stone with their large black talon-like claws. The two rat-headed demons had to duck low in the cramped hallway just to fit and were beating their clawed hands bloody with black demonic blood as they tore at the wall. They seemed completely unconcerned with their destroyed hands or the awkward angle at which they had to stand.

Beside him, Michik let out a low feral snarl, and Darrik whistled.

"Oh, hello, boys," Mason chimed. He had dropped the imposing attitude and adopted his more usual oddly congenial tone. As if the wanton bloodshed out in the main hall of the building was just the pick-me-up he needed.

"Those are with you?" Darrik asked nervously, pointing at the two demons.

"Oh yes!" Mason exclaimed, beaming like he was bragging about his well-accomplished children. "Very useful sorts, very controllable."

Chael couldn't argue with the word useful. He didn't think they had been going long, but they had already gouged out several sections of rock bigger than his head and it didn't seem like it would take them more than a couple more minutes to break through entirely.

"So," said Mason in a pleasant tone that unnerved Chael more than the stern authoritative one from earlier. "How did it go outside?"

"All the soldiers and sentries have been eliminated and we took steps to pacify the slaves," Chael quickly responded before Darrik had a chance to answer.

"Very good. Ah!" Mason shouted happily as one of the demons broke through the stone. It only had broken gnarled stumps left for hands and so it was using its head to smash its way through. The other demon had fared a little better and clawed at the opening with its mostly intact appendages. In a matter of seconds, the weakened rock crumbled and an opening into the tunnel just large enough for a man was revealed.

"The tunnel looks a bit tight. I don't think our friends will fit, dispatch them for me please." Mason smiled at them and waited.

Chael was a little afraid to ask for any additional advice, so he faced the nearest demon and made an experimental slash across its thigh, then jumped back ready for a counter. He had no idea how to kill one or how powerful they might be so hamstringing it seemed like a good first step.

The demon fell to one knee, clearly hobbled, but did not reach for Chael in retaliation. It just weakly tried to regain its feet and fell once again to its knee. Chael glanced at Mason for advice but only received the man's crazy enigmatic smile in return. He turned to Darrik, but he was watching Chael and waiting for him to figure it out.

After a moment, Chael reached out with the point of his falchion and speared the demon through where he imagined the heart might be. The demon let out what could have been a grunt and did nothing. Chael stabbed it again with even less promising results. The black gelatinous blood that spilled out of the demon was now pooling on the floor and threatened to stain his boots.

With a grunt of effort of his own, Chael slashed horizontally at the thing's neck and took its head in two strokes. The moment the head became detached, it crumbled to the floor as if Dark puppet strings had been cut. Darrik swung his much heavier blade in a powerful arc that took his demon's head in one go. As the demon fell, he flashed Chael a wry smile.

Chael grabbed one of the alchemical lamps from the main hallway and stepped over the ruined stone and into the dark passage beyond. As opposed to the smooth squared halls behind him, this tunnel was just a rough path cut through the center of the mountain. Even in the relatively dim light of the lamp, Chael could make out tool and blast marks that the Faasa's hadn't bothered to smooth over for this escape tunnel.

As they moved forward, the tunnel began to slope down, first at such a slight angle it was barely noticeable, but it gradually became so steep that they had to press against the walls to keep from falling. The walls too began to change; at first, they were the same gray stone with the occasional vein of white as the rest of the mountain. However, as they walked, the texture became glassier and smoother with the occasional jagged edge that sliced Chael's fingers as he gripped the wall for support.

"Obsidian," Mason reported. "The mountain has volcanic activity."

He turned and gave a wink to Chael; they both knew the utility that Mason had demonstrated out of an obsidian blade. Thankfully, as the tunnel grew steeper still, they discovered that a series of glassy black steps had been carved into the floor.

After nearly an hour more of descending into the dark depths of the mountain, a pinprick of light showed ahead of them. As they marched down, strength renewed, the dot of light grew until it was bright enough that the lamp was no longer necessary. At last, they emerged onto a small, flat landing. At the front of the landing was a narrow opening that led to the source of light. As he stepped through, Chael was immediately hit with a wall of dry heat, and he had to squint against the sudden light.

They emerged into a gigantic natural chamber in the mountain. Below them, maybe fifty paces down, was a sea of flames. It was as if the base of the mountain was made out of dry kindling and the Faasa's had lit the match. They stood upon a rocky outcropping above the fiery chasm, and even at this height, the heat could have cooked a side of beef. Chael wondered if this was what the Dark looked like; perhaps he would ask Mason later.

In front of the small platform on which they stood was a bridge made of chains and planks of wood. Unlike most of the things back outside, this bridge looked ancient, like some other race of people had dwelt here in the distant past before the founding of Kazaam. The entire thing made Chael more than a little nauseous, but as his eyes scanned the bridge, he saw the platform on the other side. The entire Faasa family, as well as an honor guard were standing there. Two of their servants were cranking an ancient winch, raising another one of the rough stone portcullis doors at the other end. When they spotted Chael and his companions, they redoubled their efforts and the stone slowly slid upward.

"Come on," Chael called, and he ran over to the bridge. It looked ancient and unsteady, but presumably every one of the Faasas had managed to cross it safely. He stuck out a foot and gingerly placed it on one of the wooden planks. The chains squealed a bit in protest, but the wood felt sturdy and the whole thing held.

Chael let out a breath that he didn't realize he had been holding. Mason and Darrik joined him, and they started crossing. Michik sat on his haunches on the platform and didn't follow. "Michik come!" Chael called, but the wolf refused to budge. He looked back over to the steadily rising stone, cursed, and continued along without him.

The bridge groaned and swayed slightly, but held as the three of them strode carefully across with Chael in the lead. Three soldiers in Faasa colors waited for them on the other side. Each wore a chain mail hauberk that covered their necks down to their waists. Over the hauberk was a simple cloth gambeson in the white and gray of their house. In their hands, each one wielded a mid-length arming sword and they stood blocking the way to the family in defensive poses.

Chael drew his own sword and rolled his shoulders, preparing for the fight. The bridge was only wide enough for one person, so he would have to take them on by himself. However, the bridge also meant that they couldn't effectively use their numbers against him.

He approached the first and immediately slashed at the man's neck with his falchion. The adept Faasa soldier blocked the blow and immediately adjusted his angle and thrust at Chael's belly. Chael dodged backward a half step and brought his falchion down hard and fast and scored a strike on his shoulder. The steel bit into the heavy rings of iron and tore several layers of cloth but he couldn't find flesh.

The counter from the guard came swiftly and Chael just barely parried it in time and swung the man's sword wide. Taking advantage of the moment, Chael slipped one of his knives out of his belt and rammed it into the soldier's chest while his sword was pushed out and to the side. The knife sliced through the layers of protection and sank into his chest. Chael held him close for a moment as he died to make sure he couldn't try another attack and then heaved him over the side of the bridge into the fire.

A crossbow bolt slammed into Chael's shoulder, and he stumbled almost falling over the chains of the bridge himself. He spared a second's glance and saw that one of the men winching the door open had stopped to fire the crossbow. The door was no longer moving upward but now he had a bolt sticking out of his chest. *A wash,* he supposed.

The next man lunged at him, stepping on to the bridge. He thought he could catch Chael wounded and quickly dispatch him, but the lunge overextended him and Chael's falchion split his face in two.

Angrily, Chael tore the bolt out and stepped over the second dead guard. As he breathed, the pain eased away, and again he felt the cold blanket of cruel indifference fall over him. His limbs swelled with the now familiar feeling of strength and power, and he met his next foe.

The last one seemed to be moving slower as if his legs were stuck in mud. And when he attacked, he seemed to swing his blade as if it weighed ten times what it did. He looked slow and clumsy. Chael easily ducked the other man's swing and with a lazy swipe of his sword, he sheared completely through the mail and took his head.

The crossbow, said a familiar raspy voice in his mind.

Chael ducked and the bolt that would have hit his head sailed high. He took his knife and threw it at the crossbowman. The knife buried itself in his chest with such force that he was thrown into the fire below.

Chael left the bridge and walked calmly to the only remaining man with a sword. He faced Chael shaking and before he could even swing, Chael reared up on his back leg and delivered a kick that sent him flying to meet his companions down in the inferno below. The only people left on the rocky platform were Anitea Faasa and her three children, the oldest of whom was only six years of age.

Chael looked down on them, his sword quivering his hand. Anitea was saying something but for some reason he couldn't make out the words. *They're all guilty of the same sins as the overseers above.* The cold false version of his own voice rang in his head and the more it spoke the less alien it became. After the moment's hesitation Chael wasn't even sure it was a different voice, just his own thoughts swirling around his head. He felt powerful and just like any act of violence and cruelty he could commit would be righteous, simply because he willed it so. He struck and the endless pleas from Anitea ceased.

With her death his certitude increased. The politicians and the slavers had to be killed and it would start right here. He raised his sword again and brought it down, aiming for the eldest child, now whimpering over the corpse of his dead mother. Before the blade struck home, an overwhelming force knocked into him, taking him from his feet.

"Are you mad!" yelled Darrik. "They're children, Chael!" He was screaming and swinging his sword wildly as he spoke. "We were trained to kill the tyrants, the politicians and their scum underlings." Chael rose back to his feet, insolence and rage had replaced his indifference and he lowered his Falchion at Darrik.

"Move." Chael commanded in a voice that sounded in tone and timbre like the one that invaded his thoughts. Darrik adopted a combat stance and hefted his heavy sword.

"Chael, don't do this," he pleaded.

"They aren't children," Chael answered coldly. "They're just more slavers and politicians. We kill them today or tomorrow it makes no difference." Chael brought his own sword back up. "Stand aside or join them," Chael said, inclining his head toward the fiery chasm where three Faasa soldiers were now burning.

"Something has changed in you lately and I don't know what it is, but it's Dark. It even looks like your eyes have changed color and if I didn't know any better, I would say they were glowing." Darrik shook his head and sighed. "I don't know who you are, but if you are still intent on slaughtering these children then my friend is dead, and I will kill the demon operating his corpse." He said these last words with venom and anger and as he did, he launched into a vicious attack.

Chael saw the attack coming and stepped aside. He was still somehow inhumanly fast, but Darrik was still a force to be reckoned with. His massive blade swept at Chael in practiced motions that they both knew so well. The dance had begun, their last and greatest performance.

Chael dodged and parried and redirected blow after blow. Even with his curious new strength, he couldn't trust himself to meet one of Darrik's powerful strikes head on. But he was much quicker now and when the opportunity rose, he stepped inside the swing and moved for his killing strike. Darrik anticipated the move and slapped the sword away and brought his own pommel down, hard and heavy onto Chael's head.

"Do you really think I would fall for your normal tricks Chael? How many times have we had this fight?"

Darrik was right; even stronger and faster than he had ever been, Darrik's reach and power were still a nightmare to deal with head on. An old, failed strategy came to Chael's head. It failed because he had been too slow by a hair. But he was quite a bit faster right now.

He dodged more attacks as the rhythm of the fight resumed and he waited for his window. Faster than a diving falcon he shot toward Darrik's legs and drove him to the ground. Darrik's shocked face stared at him from a breath away and as he tried to speak only blood poured out. He looked down and saw Chael's knife buried to the hilt in his chest.

Chael knew the moment his friend died. He felt the last bit of life energy flow out of him. In a moment of clarity, he understood what had been happening, what force strengthened his limbs while weakening his spirit. The essence of life that had once sustained Darrik flowed into him as he breathed. It tasted foul, like rotten meat and he choked. The cruel facsimile of himself that spoke to his mind was now screaming in protest, but Chael didn't care. He stared down at his dead friend and wept, and with his tears the Dark energy seemed to flow out of him until his limbs felt as empty and hollow as his heart.

Chael could never recall what happened next. He knew that the Faasa children were slaughtered by Mason seconds after Darrik's death. Mason had been happily standing by watching the two fight. He didn't remember leaving the burning mountain core or how he made it back down the mountain. The only thing that he could recall was his trembling hands and Darrik's cold lifeless flesh.

Chapter 26

Present Day

Chael strained against the restraints in his cell, reopening the semi scabbed wounds in his skin. He groaned with pain and effort but no matter what he did the sturdy iron held fast and he remained confined.

"Struggling won't help, you know," His neighbor said. Chael still wasn't ready to concede that this man was Darrik. He had watched the life drain away from his friend and felt his clammy dead skin.

"If you were one of them, I would expect you to say just that," Chael called back. Another low peal of laughter emerged from the adjacent cell.

"Darkness, but I have missed you," he said. "Tell me, how is Michik? I'm told that he's looking a little rough these days."

"Aha!" Chael exclaimed victoriously. "The real Darrik died before Michik did, but Aelisa traveled with us." The man on the other side of the wall sighed in resignation.

"What can I say to convince you?" he asked. Chael racked his mind but couldn't come up with anything definitive.

"Where did I stab you?" Chael asked after a moment.

"In the chest," the man responded flatly. Exasperated, Chael grunted and called back in irritation.

"Not where in the body, you idiot," he called. "What location were we in?" *He's certainly thick enough to be Darrik,*

Chael thought. The man laughed again in a rumbling chuckle, somehow too deep and low.

"You stabbed me in the heart inside the molten core of one of the Kaazan peaks," Darrik replied.

His voice was no longer playful as it had been when he first spoke. There was an edge to it now, hateful and menacing. His voice also shifted in a disturbingly inhuman way. It sounded to Chael like his voice split and three different versions were erupting from the man's mouth like an unholy choir.

"You murdered me and then fled with your dog like a coward."

The laughter resumed but there was no mirth in it. It held the same haunted quality as his speaking voice and it chilled Chael to his core.

"How are you still alive?" Chael asked as much to himself as Darrik. The eerie laughter stopped.

"Describe your cell," Darrik demanded in that false harmonic voice. Chael hesitated but couldn't see the harm it would do so he obliged.

"I'm shackled to a wooden chair inside a stone cell. The walls have runic script that I encountered once before in Kazaam. They seem to block dark energy, but I don't know how it works."

"And the drops from the ceiling as well?" Darrik asked before Chael could continue.

"Yes, how did you know?" Chael trailed off as he asked and then remembered Aelisa's words. They had prepared this cell for someone else, someone who presumably with Dark energy coursing through them. Chael balked at the implication.

"I think you're beginning to understand, yes?" Darrik asked, amused.

"Are you like me?" Chael burst out a little quicker than he wanted. The laughter increased again full force before Darrik responded.

"No, I don't think anyone is like you," Darrik responded.

"Then what are you?!" Chael demanded.

"I am the first and the last. I am the champion, sire, and servant." The strange chorus coming from his throat hit a new pitch, and he practically sang his enigmatic riddle.

"He's a half-breed," called a female voice from a cell diagonally across from Chael. He had completely forgotten about the strange woman that had been dragged down here just after him.

"What do you mean half-breed?" Chael shouted to her.

"I mean," she said in a superior sort of tone as if her meaning was patently obvious. "His body has been polluted with demon flesh." Chael instantly recalled his encounter with Mason in the woods. The man seemed to have the clawed arm of a lesser demon attached to him. Her cell was directly across from Darrik's so that she could see through his barred door. Darrik fell strangely silent.

"So, when you say you were the first, does that mean you were the first half-breed, Darrik?" Chael asked. Darrik seemed to growl in anger before answering, even more bestial than Michik.

"After you stabbed me, I was well and truly dead." Darrik's voice seemed more human as he spoke of his death. "I don't know how much time had passed or how I got there, but I woke up in a fortress somewhere in the north. A demon's heart pumping black blood through my veins." There was a faintly sad note to his voice now.

"Darrik I…" Chael began. But a sudden rage from the cell interrupted him.

"I reject your sympathy!" Darrik's demonic voice shouted. From the woman's cell there was a small gasp. Chael chided himself for upsetting him, he needed information.

"What have you been doing for the last decade then?" Chael asked softly, trying not to set him off again. The sudden rage was gone, and Darrik's unsettling laughter returned.

"Preparing Chael, preparing to burn this world."

"Khalim wants to rule the world, not end it," Chael replied skeptically. The laughing increased to hysteria and his voice seemed to split again into the discordant demonic harmony.

"I don't work for Khalim any longer," Darrik cooed. "I spent some time in the republics the last few months but that was just to train the new recruits. Why do you think Khalim hired the Black Hand in the first place? We could have given him the seat easily enough." The question bothered Chael, he hadn't really thought about it but other than Mason, the other members of the Dark sect almost never accompanied them on missions.

"So, you work for the Black Hand, then." Chael stated it, it wasn't a question. "So, what were they there for then?" Chael asked, now genuinely curious.

"Khalim wanted an army, a very specific army," Darrik breathed out, clearly enjoying himself. Chael thought about it for a moment, Darrik had just referred to himself as a sire as well as the first.

"So, Khalim hired them to make him an army of half-breeds and you were the first." Chael said, more to himself than anything. "And to make the army of half-breeds you needed a bunch of demon parts am I right?"

Darrik merely chuckled in response, but Chael felt like that was a yes.

"So that's why they were hanging out in the forest then, it's easier to summon demons there."

Darrik didn't answer, but he was certain that he got it right, but it still left one thing unanswered.

"Why did you have Aelisa fetch me?"

The laughter paused again and after a moment Darrik spoke." That was a little selfish on my part. The Lady of the Black Hand wanted to take you from your little cabin immediately, but it turned out that you were quite the little demon slayer. She summoned more and bigger demons and you happily lopped their heads off, it was a brilliantly effective partnership."

Chael let that sink in, if Darrik was telling the truth, it meant that he had been an unwitting partner with the Black Hand the last few years. It even explained the recent demon uptick.

"But alas, her need for more demon parts ended and She was going to take you while I was busy in Kazaam. As soon as I heard I came here and send the stargazers to fetch you." Darrik had become positively cheerful while explaining the intricacies of his little scheme. He seemed to bounce between emotions as quickly and easily as changing his shirt.

Chael's mind drifted back to Aelisa's admonition and the people in the city above.

"What are Khalim's plans for this city?" Chael demanded.

"The city is already lost; my descendants are inside the walls even now." The implication hit Chael like a club. If they were already inside the city walls, the amount of damage they could do was incalculable. They could open the gates and take the city by surprise. Fhaerhold could fall in a single day.

"It must wound you to be trapped inside your cage while they are out there winning glory." Chael smiled, "I bet this special cell wasn't included in your little scheme, was it? In fact, I'd wager it was your plan to rip those bars out and murder me the second I showed up here."

The cheeriness on the other side of the wall completely died and the palpable rage refilled the space between them. *I've got you there.* The smug air emanating from Darrik that had permeated the conversation blew away. They were both just as trapped, Chael could work with that.

Chapter 27

Present Day

Darrik had fallen silent again after their last spat, Chael took that as a victory. The next thing he needed to do was gather more information about his circumstances. If he was to effectuate a daring escape, he needed to know more about his prison. Luckily there was a great potential source of knowledge right here in this very dungeon.

"Excuse me, Miss?" Chael began as politely as he could. "Lady who threw powdery acid in my face?" He said the last comment without any hint of sarcasm, or at least he hoped he had.

"What do you want?" came her gruff response.

"Ah, yes umm... hello!" Chael called over to her cell. He hadn't actually been expecting her to respond. Besides pointing out Darrik's new deformity she had been sullenly silent since being dragged down here. "My name is Chael, may I have yours?" She paused for a long time as if considering the downsides to revealing that precious commodity to Chael, then huffed.

"Ischarina," she said haughtily as though that should mean anything to him. "But if you call me that I'll throw more blinding powder in your face. I go by Rina."

"A pleasure to meet you Rina," Chael squeezed as much of the honey into his voice as he could stomach. *Don't be stupid, you need her help,* he told himself. He considered his next words carefully but decided that directness was the best way to go. "I've been unjustly imprisoned, and I plan on breaking out. If you can provide me useful information, I will arrange your escape as well." Chael felt that was very diplomatic.

Well, shit, Chael muttered to himself, then charged at the nearest demon, just now emerging from the trees.

"Would you care to elaborate?" Chael asked straining to keep his voice calm even though he wanted to throttle her.

"That liquid dripping on your forehead isn't water, but I suppose even you may have gathered that already." *Even me? you don't even know me,* Chael thought. "It's called the Alchemist's Lament; it was designed to neutralize the effects of ingested alchemicals. A few drops diluted into water and ingested can nullify the effects of even the most potent personal elixirs, as well as put the victim in a dream-like trance. In its concentrated form it can be absorbed through the skin and inhaled. You have been essentially bathing in it for over a day."

The explanation made sense to Chael; a concoction that would dampen the power of a potion would probably not require too many tweaks to deaden his own abilities.

"If you can muster the strength," she continued, "with the lament steadily sapping your strength to break the iron restraints in that chair, you then have to contend with the bars on the cell door which are twice as thick." Her tone had an almost cheerful mocking nature to it as she listed the myriad of reasons why overcoming those obstacles would be all but impossible.

"And finally," she announced dramatically. "Even if you make your way out of that cell without drawing the attention of the entire chapter house, you couldn't make it up the stairs. As I'm sure you saw, there is a cloud of lament that hangs over the bottom half of the stairs. It doesn't if you cover up because you can't help but breathe it in. A half dozen paces up those steps and you will blissfully march yourself back down into your cell. You'd probably relock your own restraints." She finished with a dramatic huff and fell silent, matter settled.

"How do the Order members walk through it," Chael asked. It was an obvious question, and he already suspected the answer.

"They're immune. Members of the Order are given tiny doses over the years to develop complete tolerance to the effects. In fact, one's ability to withstand the cloud of lament is one of the tests for advancement."

"Are you immune?" Chael asked, genuinely curious. If she could make it up the stairs that was something. For the first time in their conversation her confident superiority wavered.

"Mostly," she answered hesitantly.

"Mostly?" Chael asked, annoyed.

"Yes," she said more confidently and refused to elaborate further.

Chael paused in thought, there were certainly plenty of problems. But he had always been something of a problem solver. And seeing as how Aelisa intended to kill him in the next day or two, Chael was highly motivated.

"Darrik," Chael yelled, "I don't suppose you would be amenable to a truce so we can get out of here?" He didn't have much confidence but, desperate times and all.

"When Khalim takes the city, I will be freed by my descendants, and I will tear the traitorous tongue from your mouth."

"Good to know!" Chael called back with forced joviality. He hadn't had much hope for an alliance with Demon-Darrik, but he had to try. Besides, he was practicing his diplomacy. "So, Rina," Chael spoke shifting to the young woman. "How about you?"

A few hours after his tête-à-tête with Darrik, Chael was still miserably stumped as to how he was going to break out. His usually razor-sharp mind was continually being buffeted by the effects of the Alchemists Lament and they had pitilessly left him with scant tools to work with.

The first concern was his own restraints, but he was closer to sawing his wrists off than breaking the iron. Chael strained with his senses pushing past the dulling effects of the steadily dropping potion. Some mole digging through the earth nearby, the roots of a tree; anything alive that he could use to create a momentary surge to shatter the restraints. He searched until he had a pounding headache that cruelly pulsed with the same cadence as the falling poison.

But it was all for naught. They were deep in the ground and the runes on the walls boxed his energy in. Pushing past those barriers was like trying to squeeze an apple through the eye of a needle. Hours of intense effort and all he had to show was the drumbeat of a searing headache.

The idiots gave them weapons? Chael mumbled in exacerbation. Indeed, the demons fighting Andon and the guardsman were both wielding a crude sword and shield. Clearly made for the creatures, judging by their enlarged proportions. If those things are here, he has to be nearby somewhere, Chael thought warily while beheading another lesser demon, this one carrying an enormous double bitted war ax.

The Order jailors locked the iron door behind them and left without so much as a glance. The other cell had no chair like his and he couldn't see or hear any of the telltale drips of the Alchemists Lament. As the footsteps faded up the stairs the hooded man stirred and slowly rose to his feet. As he did the sleeves of his ebony cloak slipped up revealing a series of intricate light blue tattoos. He carefully removed the black hood from his head and neatly set it down next to him in his cell.

"Hello, Chael," Cooper said with a cruel smile forming on his lips.

Chapter 28

Present Day

Cooper smiled broadly from his cell as Chael gawked, mouth hanging open, like a simpleton. In Chael's somewhat limited experience smiles did not come easily to the Dark worshiper so he was obviously taking great pleasure in Chael's obvious shock.

"How nice to see you so..." Cooper paused, looking Chael up and down with sneering, sniveling appraisal. "Intact," he said at last, his voice nasally and his tone superior. The memory of the last time he had seen Cooper replaced Chael's stunned silence with righteous fury.

"Yes, it's a pity the good Baron couldn't meet us here for this little reunion," Chael responded bitterly.

"An unfortunate step along the Dark path, I'm afraid," Cooper said without a hint of care or remorse. He steps forward, closer to the bars of his door and made a show of sniffing the air as if the air in the narrow dungeon hall was fouler than in the cell. "Now that is a familiar scent," he crooned wickedly. "If I am not mistaken young Darrik occupies the cell to your right, correct?"

Chael glanced to his right unconsciously, all he could see was a warded wall, but the gesture confirmed Cooper's suspicion.

"Darrik," he called, his voice dropping the mocking tone and turning to true anger. "You very nearly cost my mistress her prize. Your unreliability in this matter as been noted." Cooper spat out every syllable like some rotten morsel of food he was trying to expel from his mouth. Darrik let out his low alien rumble in response.

"And what of your failure," Chael shot back at him. "You failed to capture me in the forest, my dog used your mistress to sharpen his claws, and you stand here now; a captive of the order." Chael let his smug satisfaction ring through his words and mockingly tsked at Cooper's plight. The Dark cultist suddenly smashed his own head into the iron bars of his cell door and glared at Chael, pure hatred burning in his eyes. A narrow line of blood began to trickle from his forehead as he squeezed his face further into the space between the iron columns of the door.

"You should burn in the furthest depths of the Dark for what you did to her!" Cooper practically screamed, crazed hysteria replacing the cold calculation of before. The blood dripping down his face found its way to his mouth and spewed forth from his cell as he shrieked the words at Chael. But slowly he pulled back from the bars, wiped the blood on his sleeve and inhaled a calming breath. Cooper closed his eyes for several seconds, fighting some internal battle before continuing.

"But," he said with surprising calm after his brief outburst. "She has not ordained your death at this time. Greater work awaits, and your blood must be spent elsewhere." Cooper seemed to say these words more as an assurance to himself than in a direct response to him. It was like he was mentally preparing for some great task that he found particularly distasteful, and Chael's continued existence is what made it so unsavory.

Chael opened his mouth to launch another jibe at him but was interrupted by the sound of another visitor walking swiftly down the stone stairs. Moments later, Aelisa burst into view, she strode purposefully over to Chael's cell ignoring Cooper altogether. She walked right up to the bars of his cell and Chael could see the panicked look on her usually unbreakably placid face.

"They're here," she whispered urgently, though her voice filled the small dungeon. "Fhaelan scouts have just reported the approach of Khalim's army less than a day's march from the city. The scouts that managed to return that is."

Chael locked eyes with her from his chair. He had never seen the woman so desperate. Since they had met, everything she did had a graceful elegance that implied calculated and controlled action. Now she simply looked tired. Her usually impeccable white robes that she managed to keep clean and unwrinkled through leagues of dense forest were disheveled and untidy. Her hair was done up in a loose bun on top of her head with several stray hairs jutting out at odd angles. The only thing that Chael truly recognized about her were her eyes. As they bored into his, Chael could see the same ice-cold determination that she always emanated.

"It's worse," Chael said sadly. Most of the anger at his capture had dissipated as he reflected on the impending doom of the city. "More like him," Chael nodded to his right, "are already inside the city."

Chael paused, unsure how much he should reveal about his past. He didn't need to give her any new information to condemn him with. "I did once know a man named Darrik. Ten years ago, I stabbed him through the heart and watched him die. I do not know what creature you have ensnared, but he must be powerful if you needed these sorts of restraints to contain him."

He pulled weakly at the iron bindings for dramatic effect.

"He claims that man," Chael pointed with his lips at Cooper, "and his cohorts stuck the heart of a demon inside of him and brought him back to life. I have no idea if that's possible, but it doesn't really matter." Chael took a deep breath, *diplomacy,* he repeated in his mind as if the repetition of the word would impart some innate skill.

Chael stared back at her with what he hoped was a reflection of the sincerity he genuinely felt. "If you do not let me out the city will fall," he insisted desperately. "The Fhaelan soldiers will be threshed like wheat before Khalim, he doesn't just bring soldiers he is bringing monsters to this battle. How many of those men out there have fought a demon? How many have yours?"

He let the words echo in the dungeon as she continued to stare into his eyes silently, hopefully seeing reason. He cursed himself internally for being a little too melodramatic, but it seemed appropriate in the moment. After a few seconds she closed her eyes and shook her head, and Chael's hopes were dashed. His heart sank as she opened her eyes and he saw absolute certainty there.

"I am sorry, but no I cannot let you out. Even if it means this city must fall, the danger you represent is greater than any single city." She pronounced his sentence with finality and Chael knew there was no argument she would take. "Is there any more intelligence you can glean from the prisoner?" she asked, the stern edge that he was used to returning to her voice.

Chael balked; he had no further information to give her but if he told her that she had no further reason to keep him alive. Khalim was at the very gates and from her perspective he was now just a liability.

"I personally know Khalim, High Minister of Kazaam." Chael blurted a little too quickly, the anxiety of impending death leaking into his voice. "I was his..." Chael trailed off.

Over Aelisa's shoulder, he could see Cooper doing something peculiar. He had been standing in the middle of his cell with his eyes closed like he was meditating. Then just as Chael began to stall for his life Cooper stuck out the little finger of his right hand. He hadn't noticed it before, but the nail was long and sharpened to a point that gleamed in the low torchlight.

With a ferocity that broke his meditative stance he plunged his sharpened nail into the tattooed skin of his left forearm. As he drew the nail across the painted skin like a scalpel, Chael naturally expected to see a line of blood following the deep cut. But what leaked out of the wound was a viscous blue ink that seemed to drain the color out of the skin until it regained the pale fleshy hue of his skin.

The blue inky mass clung to itself and stretched as it fell from his arm instead dropping to the floor like a liquid. The more it dribbled out the more the rest of it seemed to congeal and compress into a substance that appeared more like dull blue clay. Cooper quickly kneaded the doughy substance until he had a flat circular disc the size of a dinner plate and a small sphere half the size of his palm.

Chael wasn't sure if he should continue talking and distract Aelisa from whatever Cooper was doing. It seemed obvious that this was the path that had the best chance of prolonging his life, which made it highly recommendable. But he trusted Cooper less than Michik with a side of beef while his back was turned.

His hesitation made the decision for him and in under a second Aelisa followed his gaze and snapped around to look at Cooper. The second she did a blue circle of doughy ink slapped into her face. The thing took on a life of its own and grew tentacles of the same clay-like material and wrapped around her head in a tight embrace.

Chael heard muffled screams as Aelisa tore at the amorphous little monster that was clinging to her face. For brief moments her nails dug through the construct and bits of her skin were visible but as quickly as she tore it free, it bled back into itself and resealed the wound.

Chael looked back and forth between Aelisa now struggling on the floor of the dungeon and Cooper, his face smug and satisfied. It was then that Chael remembered the small piece that he hadn't thrown at the Order Priestess. Cooper was now rolling it between his fingers until it became as thin and as sharp as a needle. A half foot long needle.

Chael leaned back in his restraints, suddenly terrified. He was still witnessing what that stuff could do to a powerful alchemist like Aelisa and he couldn't so much as lift his hands to cover his face. He didn't think Cooper aimed to kill him; it seemed like his group still wanted him for some reason, but Chael couldn't think of any use for that needle that was good for him.

"Know this," Cooper snapped at Chael. The smug satisfaction he had gotten from torturing Aelisa was gone. He slipped back into his barely controlled rage like a hand into a glove. His eyes were locked on Chael's, all malice and ill intent. "What I do today is not for you but for the assurances I have received from the true rulers of this world. Hail Tenebrian! May his Dark tide cleanse this land!"

Then Cooper shoved the needle of molded alchemical ink into his own neck.

Chael froze in absolute shock. On the ground Aclisa was still struggling with the mask of alchemical essence that was choking her life away. In the cell across from him Cooper was still staring murderously at Chael and for a moment nothing happened. Blood didn't spill out of the wound and Cooper seemed no worse than before. But then he twitched, his eyes breaking contact for the first time in over a minute.

Slowly, as though his head was being jerked to the side by an invisible string, Cooper's head tilted to the right until his ear met his shoulder. The Dark cultist seemed to strain against the force, the veins in his neck bulging with the effort.

Then, as suddenly as when he stabbed himself, his head straightened with an audible crack that Chael could hear even over Aelisa's muffled moans. Cooper's eyes weren't looking at anything now, they were glazed over and milky white like a blind man. A scream escaped his lips for just a second and then cut off like his airway was plugged. With one last crunchy, grinding jerk of his head, Cooper fell to the ground and lay still.

A drop of Lament fell on Chael's head and for a blink he forgot where he was and what was happening. But then he felt it. The deathly essence left over from Cooper had filled the small, cramped dungeon and flowed through the barred door of his cell. Though only Chael could sense it, it was like a cloud of mist clung to the ground around him. He immediately began to drink it in but quickly stopped himself. A few seconds later another drop of Alchemist's Lament fell on him and his grip on the small amount of power he had gathered failed and dissipated into the ether.

Chael squeezed his eyes closed and concentrated. He knew the approximate time between the drops, for they were quite regular, but he hadn't counted exactly. Now he did.

"Fourteen, fifteen, sixt..." Chael stumbled as a drop of Lament hit him. He immediately began breathing in the power assembled throughout the room while counting. It was extraordinarily difficult to concentrate on both at the same time, but he measured his breathing with the seconds as he ticked them off in his mind. He could feel the immense power and clarity flooding his body. He felt like a man in the desert tasting water after days of wandering in the heat. Clean purifying energy raced through him strengthening his limbs and sharpening his mind. He strained once again at the thick bands of wrought iron holding his limbs.

"Fifteen!" he bellowed as he tore himself out of the chair and practically flew across the cell with the leftover effort. As he landed his enhanced ears caught the unmistakable 'plunk' of a drop of liquid hitting the stone behind him.

The skin around his wrists and ankles was torn and bleeding but Chael paid it no heed as he rose. He didn't understand how but the leftover life energy from Cooper was the strongest he had ever felt. It was as though Cooper had managed to hold enough lifeforce in his thin frame for three or four people in his thin, lanky frame.

Chael channeled the energy voraciously, and the strength built to a powerful crescendo he had never experienced before. He felt like he could tear the continent in half with his bare hands. He settled for the iron bars on the door. With a grunt of exertion, they slowly bent until the brittle iron cracked and snapped off entirely. Chael expertly stepped through the narrow opening with the grace of an acrobat. *I should have killed him years ago,* he thought smiling.

As he left his cell, he looked down at the unfortunate form of Aelisa Treadmane, Second Prefect of the Fhaerhold Chapter of the Fraternal Order of Celestial Light. Her title rolled across his mind like a troubadour playing with a coin between his fingers, passing it back and forth effortlessly.

He hesitated as he glared at her, she was probably just seconds away from killing him were it not for the actions of the late cultist. But even Chael had to admit that her actions, though misguided, had been to serve some greater good. Simply put, she wasn't evil. Chael had carelessly slaughtered hundreds of nameless men and a few women for simply getting in his way. But leaving Kazaam, leaving Khalim, he had tried to put that person away. That familiar voice pleaded with him to run and leave the priestess to her fate. Slowly Aelisa stopped struggling against the construct blocking her airway.

Chael burst into motion, indecision vanishing as he bent down and, with enhanced arms, tore the blue inky clay from her face. He tossed the squirming mass into his cell directly under the well of Alchemist's lament. There was a hissing sound as the first drop fell upon it.

Chael turned back to Aelisa and swore. Her eyes were bulging out of her skull and all the color had drained from her face except her lips. Her lips were a dark blue, almost purple, and even after her mouth was clear she still wasn't breathing. Chael flashed to his special senses and could tell that she was still alive although barely. Panicking, he slapped her across the face hoping to somehow restart her breathing, but she still just lay there. He felt her life slowly ebb away as he impotently watched on his knees beside her.

And then she was gone.

Chapter 29

8 Years Ago

Khalim's office inside the newly constructed High Ministerial Palace was, in stark contrast to the building itself; small, plain, and excruciatingly practical. Behind a simple wooden desk there was an extensive bookshelf with titles ranging from alchemy to histories of mankind's contact with elves. There was even a tome on animal husbandry on the neatly organized shelf.

The room wasn't giant or vaulted like so many of the other spaces inside the new palace, but neither was it cramped. Adorning the walls were different charts and maps of the continent and even a few weapons but Chael doubted Khalim had ever used them. On the desk itself were a perfectly organized stack of papers, several bearing Khalim's signature. But what caught Chael's eye was a domed glass case about the size of a melon. Inside was what Chael thought used to be a human hand.

The reason he couldn't be certain came down to two factors. It had black veins that pushed against the inside of the skin like small worms trying to escape. The other was that despite having been severed from its original host just past the wrist, the hand was moving. To be precise, Chael would have said it was squirming. The somehow living disembodied hand was spasming around in its glass cage violently but weakly, like it didn't know how to properly use its fingers. It gave the impression of a fish flopping around on the deck of a boat. Chael was so entranced by the spectacle that he hadn't heard the office door open and his master's arrival.

"Spectacular, isn't it," Khalim whispered in his velvety smooth voice. Chael nearly smashed the glass enclosure as he whipped around in shock.

"Umm... Yes, it's magnificent," Chael stuttered nervously. Khalim gave him a simple wave to stay seated and walked around the desk to sit in his own comfortable, but simple chair. Khalim simply looked at Chael for a long moment.

As he did, Chael felt naked before the heavy gaze of his master. Physically, Khalim was hardly impressive. Though quite a bit taller than Chael, most people were, he was lean and had never shown any particular prowess for combat. At least not that he had seen. But despite his unassuming figure, Chael was more terrified of this man than any of the Black Hand that he had met or their demons.

What Khalim possessed more than anyone else he had ever seen was an iron will and boundless ambition. Khalim could meet the eyes of any man alive and bend that man to his own design by the mere power of his presence. Not for the first time Chael reasoned that he could reach across with his sword and kill the man with little effort and be free. But the thought died as quickly as it formed. The longer Khalim gazed at him the smaller and more impotent Chael felt.

"I have a new task for you," Khalim stated flatly. Chael straightened slightly in his chair; at some point he had crouched low in the seat like he was cowering. As he lifted himself up to a somewhat more dignified position, Khalim paused but otherwise didn't note the disturbance. "As part of my payment for the services of the Black Hand I agreed to send one of my agents on an assignment of their choosing. That time has come, and they specifically requested you." Khalim gave him a cold joyless smile that made Chael's toes curl. "It seems that you have made an impression," he spoke dryly. "I trust you will represent me well."

Chael groaned as he stretched his back and clapped his hands. The gesture brought a glare from his two companions in the wagon, but he didn't care. They had been riding straight for five days and he hadn't been able to feel his backside for the last two. He regretted leaving Michik behind, the wolf's fluffy fur made for a decent pillow when he didn't have other options. However, the glowering, black-cloaked figures next to him had forbidden it. They didn't trust his dog and Chael didn't much blame them. In the few years since he had found him in that small cave Michik had earned a bloody reputation in the rougher circles of the Sharaad Republics, but Chael still missed his company.

His two companions for this journey were not much better than Michik when it came to conversation. It seemed to Chael that their predominant form of communication was grunting. They had a grunt for when they wanted Chael to be quiet, a grunt for when they wanted to be left alone, and another grunt for when they wanted him to fall off the wagon and die of exposure in a ditch. They were named Tanner and Miller, though Chael had no idea who was who. And Chael strongly suspected that neither knew the faintest thing about tanning nor milling.

He had been expecting Mason or Cooper, or most likely both, but when the Black Hand came to fetch him it was the pudgy vacant faces of Tanner and Miller, or perhaps Miller and Tanner. They wore the same unadorned black cloak as every other member of their secretive sect and beyond grunting they hadn't said a word the entire time he'd traveled with them.

"So," Chael began for the hundredth time. "Are we getting close?"

"Hmmph," grunted Tanner or perhaps Miller. Chael sighed and peaked out of the canvass cover of their small wagon. It was getting dark and given the pattern of the last few days he had expected to stop for the night some time ago, but his mute companions kept driving the horses along at a steady pace.

They were near the coast now, he could smell the salty air and yearned to leap from the wagon and go for a swim. Instead, he leaned back inside and sat beside the unspeaking cultists. They traveled together in silence for another hour before the wagon was pulled to a stop outside of a small town. They had pulled up to the outer edge of a farm, as Chael looked there was a faint light glowing from the window of a barn maybe two hundred paces away. He looked expectantly at Tanner and Miller but neither gave any indication as to what he should do. They just continued to give him the same slightly sullen stares of the intellectually ill-equipped. Chael looked at one of them and for no particular reason, decided he was Tanner.

"Tanner, are we stopping here to rest or is the mission just meant to test the endurance of my ass on bare planks of wood?" Chael asked, confused and annoyed. The cultist grunted again, this time it almost sounded thoughtful and reached into his cloak and pulled out a sealed letter and a small vial of silver liquid. On the back was a simple red wax seal and on the front was written his name in small, neat letters. Chael tore the letter open, relieved to finally be getting some answers. The handwriting of the message was curved and precise and it struck Chael as decidedly feminine.

Stupid! He cursed himself. He could feel several broken ribs and was coughing up gouts of hot blood. But already the power that he held inside was healing him and with the last of its energy he could feel bones and sinews knitting themselves back together. It wasn't perfect, and he'd be in a lot of pain tomorrow, but it would do. They would be on her now. One of the demons was simply gone. The only evidence of its prior existence was the sickly black viscera of demonic gore painting everything in a twelve-foot circle around the priestess. The demon he had hobbled was crawling along the ground toward Aelisa, its leg nearly severed from Chael's enhanced throw.

Darkness! Chael cursed and dove over to where he had dropped his sword. He managed to grab it just in time to behead the flaming demon on its mad flight away from the vengeful order priestess. Obviously, she could handle herself. He turned back to Andon and the remaining spearman. Clearly, the knight had heard his warning because two headless demons lay at his feet, and he was currently battling a third. The lone survivor of the Baron's guard was not faring quite as well. He had impressively managed to fend off the demon and was furiously stabbing it uselessly with his spear. Chael could see inky demon blood dripping from more than a dozen holes in its chest, but it kept swinging wildly at the man, heedless of the many wounds in its flesh. Wounds that would have killed any mortal being a dozen times over.

Awfully polite of you, Chael thought as he took its head. Another demon stepped in his path but this one fell after a blindingly bright whip shot out from nowhere and removed its head from its muscled shoulders. the Great Western Forest wasn't without beauty. Most things were covered in a lush, vibrant green interspersed with flecks of purple and yellow. There were giant creepers that snaked up the giant trees and mushrooms large enough to sit on grew from their trunks. Stupid! Chael cursed himself. He had been reckless worrying about Michik; the wolf was not easy prey, even for a demon this large. or whatever a demon had—was departed, banished back to the Dark where its kind was from.

He's being dragged, Chael determined. Despite leaving obvious signs of their passage, the captors had chosen their path quite well. The forest was much thicker in this section, and very little of the morning light broke through the dense canopy above him.

So, it's a trap then. They're scared of her, or at least they respect her, Chael thought. After the display he had seen back at camp, he didn't blame them. "Come out from behind that tree, I promise we only want to talk."

There goes the element of surprise. He still had some of the power left from the death of the third spearman inside him. He figured that would give him enough reaction time to dodge if they meant to just shoot a crossbow bolt at him the second his head was in view. Slowly, Chael emerged from his apparently lousy hiding place and walked into the small gathering. good start. He immediately noticed Baron Janus, tied and gagged, laying at the base of the giant tree. Surrounding him were Mason, as Chael had already surmised, as well as the tattooed form of Cooper and the dark-haired woman he had only seen once on that day in his former master's office. It was she who first addressed him.

He had concluded that it looked like a woman's writing but while Chael technically knew how to read, he didn't have much time to do so he couldn't be sure. The only woman he had ever seen amongst the cult was the woman with the raven black hair. He looked at the two cultists in the wagon again as if they might have answers for him, but the letter confirmed that they couldn't speak to him even if they wanted to. Cursing to himself, Chael hopped out of the wagon and started walking to the town.

It took him about ten minutes of swift jogging to reach the small settlement. There were only a handful of buildings in the town proper, surrounded by league after league of farmland.

In his years in Kazaam, Chael had learned a few things about finding people. The best place to start was in a tavern, so that's where he headed. Sure enough, despite the quaint and limited nature of the town there was a tavern and even this late into the night, it was alive.

Chael strode into the establishment with his hood up and tried not to draw any undue attention. The tavern itself was cozy if a bit small and packed with more people than Chael would have believed lived in the town at all. The woman had said that he would recognize the target, whatever that meant, but a thorough scan of this room showed no familiar faces. After a moment of searching the faces of strangers for some sense of familiarity, he became frustrated and decided to resort to a tried-and-true method that worked in any city. When in doubt ask the bar matron.

Chael walked over to the bar and ordered an ale, he didn't drink and had no intention of starting now, but tongues were loosened when plied with a bit of money. When the lady of the tavern poured his drink, he slid over enough coins to buy five of them and smiled politely.

"Excuse me, miss?" he began with an intentionally nervous sort of tone. "I just came up from the South with the promise of a job helping here during planting season."

Chael had no idea when that might be, he knew less about farming than he did about ale, but he hoped she didn't either. He trembled his lip slightly in what he hoped was a pitifully sad kind of way before continuing.

"Fool that I am, I lost the particulars of the farmer who had contracted me." Now he started to blubber and even managed to squeeze out a tear or two. Chael wiped his face with the back of his sleeve and looked back at her earnestly. "I'm told that he has a son about my age, do you think you could point me in the right direction?" To cap off his performance he sniffled a bit as he finished the question and gazed sheepishly at the bar lady.

"Planting season, eh?" she questioned skeptically. "And how many farmers do you know that carry a sword?" she asked, pointing to the falchion on his hip. Chael cursed himself for the obvious mistake. He was so accustomed to the weight of his sword that he sometimes forgot it was tied to his belt.

He sighed and pushed a few more coins toward her and smiled. The bar lady smiled back and scooped the coins from the counter into her hands. Chael immediately brightened, perhaps she was going to help him after all. After depositing the money in a small box behind the counter she gave him one last smile and pointed over his shoulder.

Three of the bar patrons were standing behind him. They were all taller than him and while not rippling with muscle they had the kind of solid thickness one develops after working hard labor for most his life. His heart sank a little. *So, it's going to be the hard way then.* Chael took a steadying breath and prepared for the inevitable.

The closest man threw a right-handed haymaker at his head, Chael easily ducked it and deflected the next strike from his companion. He sidestepped gracefully, avoiding two more sloppy punches and ended up on the other side of the men, closer to the door.

"Now, gentlemen," he spoke softly. "Let's not get this out of proportion." Chael unsheathed his sword and performed a complicated but ultimately useless sword scale. Anyone competent in arms wouldn't be all that intimidated but Chael was betting that the closest thing to a falchion these men had ever held was a wheat thresher.

The men paused and looked at the sword with dubious impressions, and Chael smiled. "My lady," he called to the barwoman. "A round for the house if you please," and he tossed a bag of coins over the bar. All eyes in the small tavern followed the small arcing bag of money and Chael slipped noiselessly out of the door.

Having failed marvelously at gathering information in the old-fashioned way, Chael was once again forced to rely on the advice of the nameless woman who ran the Black Hand.

"Special talents," he repeated to himself idly as he walked away from the tavern. *Did they know?* For the last several years he had become increasingly aware of the special gifts that he possessed. Now, with a great deal of effort he could even control them on command.

He closed his eyes and with an exertion of will he reached out with his senses to a nearby field of barley just beyond the main road of the town. He could feel the life flowing through the stalk like a glowing replica of the plant flowing on the inside. He snapped that glowing stalk and the plant died. When he was done an area ten paces across and five wide were withered, dry, and dead. His eyes snapped open and, fueled by this power, he looked around him and was nearly blinded.

Back in the direction of the wagon, in the barn that he had seen lit up from the road, was a beacon of light that stretched toward the sky. It was like a golden pillar of sunlight had been cast down from the stars and pierced the veil of night over one lonely farm. Chael pushed the remaining power to his legs and set off at a run.

With his enhanced legs he made it to the barn in under two minutes. As he approached the large wooden building, he could hear two voices within. A man and a woman were giggling inside like children. Slowly, he crept in through the partially open main door and found the source of the excited laughter.

They were up on the loft that wrapped around the interior of the barn, and they were doing the sort of thing young people do late at night when they believe no one is watching. Chael began lazily climbing the ladder, he could have set off an explosion in the barn and he doubted these two would notice.

Before long he lifted himself over the ledge and walked over to the occupied couple. Thankfully they still had the majority of their clothes on. The man's back was to him as he approached, and when Chael was only about a foot or two away, he finally turned.

Their eyes locked for a frozen eternity as they met. Chael watched in real time as the pale blue seemed to shift to a dark burnt orange in his eyes. Some deep heretofore undisturbed part of his soul recognized those eyes and roared a defiant challenge through Chael's body. It was like two lions facing off for control of the pride.

Wordlessly they lunged at each other. The voice in Chael's head that appeared when he used his 'talents' echoed the fiery chorus of his spirit. In a strained, hissing version of his own voice it whispered, "kill, kill, kill!" in a rising crescendo in his head. The young farmer was stronger and larger than Chael, but as they wrestled in the hay, it became clear that he was unfamiliar with genuine combat. In just a few seconds after the fight began Chael found himself on top and was raining fists down on the man below.

Distantly he could hear a woman screaming, "Alric, no!" but he paid it no heed. Small feminine hands grabbed at him but he casually backhanded her away. The voice was still chanting its death cry in his head, and he continued pounding his fists into his enemy. A sudden stabbing pain in his shoulder broke his trance.

He looked and most of a pitchfork was embedded in his upper arm. The pretty young woman he had hit was holding the shaft. He could see a purple bruise already forming on one of her eyes. Chael gripped the pitchfork and with a cry of agony, wrenched it from his arm.

He tossed the tool to the floor of the barn and finally took stock of his surroundings. His shoulder was siphoning blood onto the straw and his hands were swollen meaty clubs. The man he came here to kidnap was a bloody groaning mess but still alive. *Thank the stars for that,* he thought.

The woman was staring at him terrified, he thought briefly about apologizing but decided against it and turned back to the man. His eyes were open and despite the bloody mess that was all that remained of his face, his eyes were clear and hard. A golden light gathered in his palm, the same color as the pillar he had seen with his special sight but much dimmer.

Panicked, Chael lunged at the arm trying to point it away from his body. He used up every last drop of the energy he had consumed earlier and willed it into his arm to block away the golden light. A dark vortex of swirling energy met the rod of solid light.

For a moment nothing happened as the two forces met and repelled against each other. Then the black cloud of energy shattered like before a hammer. The golden light shot through Chael's chest like an arrow, and he flew backward against the wall of the loft. Physically he felt ok and found no hole where the rod of pure celestial light had struck him. But the voice in his head was screaming.

Chael staggered wearily to his feet. His body felt fine, perhaps even a little better than a moment ago. The wound in his shoulder was no longer bleeding and his hands had completely scabbed over in seconds. But his soul was on fire. It felt like someone had poured acid into his very essence, and some alien force was combating his spirit. Slowly, he walked over to the other man.

Apparently, the effort of the attack had been too much, and he had passed out. Chael took out the vial and unstopped it with numb fingers, carefully he poured the silvery contents down his throat. Better safe than sorry he supposed. Chael heaved the larger man on his shoulder and started climbing down from the hay loft. The woman was sitting stunned, eyes staring off into nothing as he passed her. *That will make things easier*, he thought.

If he was being honest, he couldn't blame her. If he hadn't spent years slowly becoming accustomed to his strange abilities, the night's events may have stunned him into catatonia as well. With a grunt not unlike Miller's or Tanner's he carried his strange prisoner out of the barn and toward the wagon.

Chapter 30

Present Day

Chael watched, helplessly, as the life energy slowly drained out of Aelisa. He had been too late and too useless. His indecision had cost her life, and he was ashamed.

"Why weep for the stargazer?" came the inhuman voice from the next cell. "The Chael I know didn't suffer the plight of those who stood in his way." Darrik made an exaggerated sniffing sound that reminded Chael of a wild boar. "I can smell her death, it tastes sweet." Chael furrowed his brow and frowned furiously. She had drugged him and locked him away in this dank prison. She was mere moments from killing him herself. Ultimately her death was the result of Cooper's actions not his own, and yet he felt guilty. "May her journey to the Dark be slow and painful," Darrik cackled in his unsettling demonic voice.

That settles it, Chael decided. If Demon-Darrik was pleased with her death, then he shouldn't be, not if there was something to do about it. Chael closed his eyes and reached down into his own soul with his senses. He could see the swirling vortex of Dark energy that he had collected from Cooper.

With a thought, he could push that energy out releasing it from his system or force it into a limb. It was like a flowing black liquid and with just a bit of pressure he could manipulate it into whatever shape pleased him. For the moment he pushed past the flow of Darkness and reached down into the very pit of his being. There he found a tiny remnant of power, a golden ball of light no larger than a quail's egg.

Chael fixed on that little golden sphere and pushed the black essence of Darkness into it. Slowly, like pushing a dull knife through a thick hide he forced the swirling energy into the little ball of light. Chael grunted with the effort of will, but gradually the golden light became speckled with streaks of inky black. Chael opened his eyes and bent over Aelisa, placing a trembling hand on her chest.

First, he gathered up the life energy that had now completely drained from her and was spreading throughout the dungeon. Forcefully, he pushed that energy back into her body. It required most of his concentration to perform, it was like trying to pour water back into a broken bottle. But little by little he filled her up until he could no longer contain the energy inside her by himself. Then he pulled the little ball of speckled light from his soul.

As he did, it felt like tearing his own spirit apart, but Chael gritted his teeth against the pain and forced it through his palm and into her chest. Chael held his breath as he released her energy and stepped away. He watched her with his enhanced senses for several agonizing seconds, but the seal held, her life energy flowed once again inside of her, if a bit weakly. Chael let out a breath of relief, he did not know if she would curse him or thank him for it, but it was done. She could go on and besides, Michik seemed pretty happy.

Confident that Aelisa would recover now, Chael turned his attention to the other occupants of the dungeon. He grabbed a torch from the wall sconce and headed over to the other two cells. He turned first to Rina and gave her a wolfish smile.

"I'll be with you in just a moment, madam," he said, winking at her. He then turned his full attention to the opposite cell. Chael held the torch close to the bars and took a good long look at the occupant. The first thing to grab Chael's attention was his skin. He was shirtless and Chael could see webs of black veins pulsing under his skin. They ran like a network of ebony snakes around his chest and wound up to his head, several veins going directly into his eyes. The eyes were inhuman, they glowed slightly red inside a ring of black. The man was tall and broad like his dead friend, but he didn't have Darrik's blond hair, this man didn't have any hair. His bald head was a maze of scars and overlapping wounds, but as Chael lingered, he finally saw it.

With a sigh of pitiful regret, he finally confirmed it was Darrik. Another wave of shame and sadness washed over him as he beheld the fallen state of his former comrade. He was responsible for this, and he vowed to fix it or at the very least kill those responsible.

"I'm sorry," he finally whispered to the demonic half-breed. There was a roar of unintelligible fury from Darrik, but Chael had already turned around. He took a deep breath and forced the smile back to his face and addressed Rina.

"Now, I believe we were talking about some kind of deal." He kept smiling at her and Rina looked conflicted. "Look," he said, "you have no reason to trust me."

Other than trying to save your life in some dark alley, he thought but didn't say out loud.

"But," he continued, "you heard everything that has been said. More of him are already inside the city and they will make their way down here." He paused letting that information sink in a bit. He didn't need her to get out of his cell, obviously, but he still had no idea how he was going to get past the cloud of lament covering the stairs. Rina looked deep in thought for a few moments more before looking back at him.

"What did you do to Second Prefect Aelisa?" She finally asked, looking at him skeptically. Chael exhaled an exaggerated breath and tried to keep smiling at her, it was difficult.

"She was dead, I gave her a new life. Simple." She looked at him flatly and shook her head.

"That's impossible," she responded incredulously. "Thousands of alchemists have tried to return the dead to the living, it just doesn't work." Chael turned his body to the side and waved his torch at Darrik.

"Look," he insisted with mild irritation. "You can still see the scar where I stabbed him in the heart. Surely the order gave you anatomy lessons, look!" This time he spoke with more urgency and reluctantly she squinted her eyes at the other man.

"Yes, I see it!" she snapped at Chael, annoyed before he could ask again. "It's just not possible." Her words trailed off as she spoke and the conviction behind them died. She seemed to fight with herself for another moment then sighed gravely. "Ok," she relented, "I'll trust you."

"Excellent," Chael beamed at her. "Now how do we get up the stairs?" A deep rumbling in the dungeon, like a small earthquake interrupted her response. Chael could feel the vibrations of a dozen more mini quakes and looked up frowning.

"What was that?" Rina asked with an uncharacteristic note of fear in her voice. The discordant three toned laughter erupted behind him, and Chael turned to see a wicked grin plastered on Darrik's scarred face.

"It begins," he taunted through the peals of malicious laughter. Chael turned back to Rina, still frowning.

"I will admit, this complicates things," he confessed.

Chapter 31

Present Day

Chael cursed at the inconvenient timing and hurried over to Rina's cell.

"Stand back!" he grunted through gritted teeth as he pried at the iron bars with his arms. He had used a great deal of energy performing the ritual on Aelisa and for a moment he was worried that he didn't have enough left. But slowly the bars bent past their breaking point and snapped off leaving a narrow gap that Rina could slide through. Chael offered her a hand which she rebuffed as she gingerly snuck through the opening, careful not to cut herself on the broken edges of iron.

For the first time since he had met her, he got a good look at her under the torchlight. She had been thrown into her cell wearing only her underclothes and Chael found that they hugged her body in a very satisfying way. If he hadn't drained all of Cooper's life energy breaking the bars on the door, he probably could have seen the slap coming. He didn't and the force of the strike left a slight ringing in his left ear.

"Eyes!" she scolded harshly, while pointing two fingers at her own eyes then at his. Chael coughed, a redness filling his cheeks that was only partially due to the slap across his face.

"Yeah, I um... How do we get out of here?" he stammered, flustered and embarrassed. Rina stepped over to the still body of Sister Aelisa and bent down to check her pulse.

"I thought you said that you brought her back?" she accused him sharply.

"I did," Chael responded. "It takes a while." Chael had only ever done this once and didn't really know how it worked. That first time was pure instinct like some other force was guiding his hand. This time he just copied that process as best as he could remember. Rina still looked at him skeptically but nodded.

"What about him?" she asked, pointing to Darrik's cell. Chael had been wondering the same thing and didn't have any good answers.

"I used the last of my energy breaking you out," he said resignedly. "Does she have a key?" He asked, looking down at Aelisa. Rina rummaged in Aelisa's pockets for a moment and found nothing, not a key, not even any alchemicals. She had been counting on the Second Prefect to carry something that might help them escape. Evidently, Aelisa thought it was more dangerous to bring such items down here than their potential worth as defense. She was probably right.

"Darkness!" Rina cursed and looked at Chael and shook her head, indicating Aelisa brought nothing useful down. Chael was mildly surprised by the outburst, most of the Order members he had run into were much too pious to swear like that. Maybe this girl wasn't so bad.

"If we can't get in his cell then I guess we just have to leave him here," Chael groaned.

He was leaving nothing but a trail of loose ends, but they had to get out of here before the city fell around them and he couldn't see any way to get to Darrik unless another dead body fell down the stairs. Michik was also out there somewhere and with the commotion going on in the city his loyal companion would probably try to come find him and was liable to get torn apart by Darrik's demon-enhanced brethren.

Drained as he was, there was little hope of contacting Michik's spirit this far away, but Chael tried anyway. He felt the bond tying himself to Michik like a light string that pulled at his chest. As he suspected that string faded as it reached off into the distance in the direction of his dog. What did surprise him was a second spiritual cord that flowed out and connected to the woman lying prostrate on the floor in front of him.

I'm connected to Aelisa, Chael mused, not enjoying the implications that aroused. He probably should have expected something like this, but he was in a rush and hadn't really thought it through. This was the sort of thing he may live to regret.

"Okay," Chael practically shouted over the continued cacophony happening in the world above him. Things were happening fast up there; the general din of battle was starting to make its way down to them in the dungeon. They had even less time than he thought.

"How do we get past the cloud?" Chael asked, turning desperately to Rina. "We needed a solution yesterday!" The young Order initiate looked around the room nervously and finally conceded.

"We don't," she stated flatly, and put up a hand to stall his sudden outrage. "I thought maybe Aelisa would have something I could work with, but she doesn't. Our only hope is for me to go up and disable the mechanism that feeds the cloud."

Chael stared hard at her for most of a minute. She had very little reason to not leave him down here to rot. And even if her intentions were honorable, there was no guarantee she could make it through. The Order was preparing for war and there was no telling how many alchemists were up there, armed to the teeth. She had been caught the first time, hadn't she? What chances did she have now? Rina could read all of his fears clearly displayed on his face.

"Look," she started calmly, some of that former arrogant superiority filtering back into her voice. "You aren't spoiled for choice here; you have to trust me. Besides, you will have a hostage." She nodded down to Sister Aelisa. "If we leave her here, she'll be torn apart by those half-breeds when they come. I can't carry her up the stairs and I won't leave her to be food for one of those things!" She spat out the words with the kind of venom that actually reminded Chael of Aelisa herself whenever she spoke about the Dark.

"But you said you weren't sure if you were immune to the effects," Chael countered. Rina shrugged at him noncommittally.

"I'm not," she admitted casually. "But if it turns out I can't, I'll just dreamily walk right back down here and take a nap, and we're back in the same mess anyway." Chael still wasn't happy with the plan, but he couldn't see a better alternative, so reluctantly he stood aside and reached out his hand, gesturing that Rina go ahead.

"Right," Rina chirped with less confidence than Chael liked. But despite her obvious nerves she placed her foot on the bottom stair and started climbing. She marched steadily upward gaining confidence with every step and soon she disappeared up the spiraling staircase.

Chael turned from the stairs and walked back to the center of the dungeon hall where Aelisa lay. There was nothing he could do for Rina now. She would either betray him or not, and if she didn't, she may not survive long enough to help. Either way it was all out of his hands.

He looked down at Aelisa for a long time, she should have been awake by now. He was not looking forward to dealing with her when she did, so in a way it was a blessing, but he was concerned that it hadn't yet worked. Chael was not an expert at this, he had only done this once and that time he had help. Sighing, he reached down and checked her for a pulse.

"Nothing," Chael muttered to himself, concerned. He lifted his head and saw Cooper's corpse. He had been fairly pale when he had been alive, but now he was alabaster white, save for a red ring around his neck as if he had been choked.

A sudden movement in the cell caught Chael's eye, and he reflexively transitioned into a combat stance. As he peered closer, normal eyes straining against the dim light, Chael saw a tiny tendril of blue rising out of Cooper's right eye; like a worm slithering out of the mud after a rainstorm. Chael shuddered at the image and turned away from the sight.

He felt suddenly tired as the weight of everything fell upon him. *Can I cure Darrik?* he wondered. *And if I can't, would I be able to kill him again?* Then there was the Order who would certainly hunt him now, as well as the Black Hand. Khalim would probably want a crack at him too, for desertion. He had gone to the Dark Forest for peace, he had been perfectly content to live out his days in relative obscurity. Just him and Michik. Now, there was nowhere he couldn't go where they wouldn't follow. Chael slid down the stone wall of the dungeon and sat on the floor, exhausted.

"It's my fault," he told the air wistfully. "I had to show off my skills. I had to be the great demon slayer of the West!" Chael absently swished around his arm as if he was holding his sword. Chael started laughing hysterically until tears rolled down his cheeks. "I must be the Darkborn, because only he could make an enemy of every powerful being on the continent," he exclaimed while wiping his eyes.

That drew a low rumbling growl from Darrik's cell. Chael couldn't tell if it was agreement or if Darrik was just irritated but he smiled again and chuckled, though less heartily than before. Slowly, the mental exhaustion overwhelmed him, and he closed his eyes and fell into a fitful sleep.

The sound of movement above him jerked his body awake. Chael sprang to his feet as he could hear commotion above him. There was a feminine scream, *Rina?* But he couldn't be sure. Sounds of metal and the scraping of stone drifted down into the dungeon. He curled his hands into fists as he helplessly listened. Rina seemed to be fairly capable, but without her alchemicals Chael doubted she would last long in a fight. He turned on his heel and marched over to Darrik's cell and glared at him through the barred door.

"How many of you are there?" Chael demanded angrily. There was fighting going on upstairs, but if it was simply the Order fighting Rina, it would have ended quickly. Instead, it seemed to be intensifying by the moment, which meant the Order had engaged the army of half-breeds.

Darrik glared back at him wordlessly, the only sound he made was a slight growl every time a drop of alchemist's lament fell on his head. Several minutes passed and Darrik continued to stare, a slow smile emerging on his ruined face. The lines of black demon blood flowed and squirmed under his skin and when he finally spoke black ichor flew from his mouth.

"I will watch as they tear your heart out," Darrik hissed. "You will suffer as I have suffered and then you will awaken to shadow and nightmares, and I will be there too." Darrik's face twisted into a wide maniacal grin, eerily reminiscent of the one often plastered on Mason's face. Chael shook his head and set his jaw as he locked eyes with Darrik.

"We will see," he snapped back.

Lifeless because of him, Chael mused.Can't let them see you dealing with the town spook, Chael thought as he was quickly conducted by a timid house servant to the third level of the keep and into the lord's apartments.

Footsteps once again echoed on the spiral stairs and Chael took a deep breath. There was no more life energy in the room to absorb but practiced inhalation calmed his nerves. He gripped the sputtering torch in both hands and lowered it into a guard stance and waited. There was a deep bestial growl from above.

Chael chanced a glance back at Darrik who was still grinning like a madman. The footsteps quickened their pace, and he prepared for combat. Finally, a haggard-looking wolf emerged from the darkness of the spiral stair and sprinted across the room to Chael.

Chael dropped the torch in shock and its light finally gave out and darkness swallowed the dungeon. Michik tackled Chael in a rough puppy-like embrace but with his mass he sent Chael flying into the dungeon wall. Michik lapped at him with a rough dry tongue but for once Chael didn't mind, Michik had found him. They wrestled playfully for a few minutes before another voice entered the dark room.

"What happened to the torch?" Rina asked, slightly out of breath.

Chapter 32

Present Day

Chael fumbled around in the dark and took hold of Aelisa hoisting her onto his shoulders. He wanted to leave her down here but if the other half-breeds came to look for their sire, they might mutilate her body just on principle. It troubled Chael that she had not awoken. Had it not worked? Lacking better options, he resigned to bring her upstairs and locker her in a closet somewhere. Rina led the way back to the stairs, and they began to ascend but before he lost sight of the small dungeon Chael looked over his shoulder at Darrik's cell.

"I will end your torment brother," he promised too softly for Darrik to overhear. Chael didn't want the demon inside him to have another outburst. It wasn't clear to Chael who was really in charge of Darrik's body. There were aspects of his old friend still remaining and he had acted independently to bring him here but when he got upset the human part seemed to recede and the demon emerged. Whatever the case was Chael was certain they would meet again, and he would keep his promise.

"So, he's yours then?" Rina asked, indicating Michik, as they ascended the stairs.

"Yes," Chael replied gruffly, his mind still on Darrik and the past.

"You need to keep better care of him," Rina stated haughtily. "He looks like he's been dead for a month." Michik let out a low rumbling whine at her remark.

"Three years, actually," Chael said absently. Rina stopped him mid step and stared. They were nearing the top and the light from above allowed him to just see her face as she scrutinized him. He shrugged at her and pressed on.

After a much shorter journey than Chael imagined, the four of them emerged from the spiraling stairs and into the narrow hallway beyond the main hall of the chapter house. The sick metallic scent of blood wafted into Chael's nostrils before he even sensed the power of death hanging heavy in the air.

Chael steeled his mind and took in the power that now buffeted him like the tide. Rina pointed out a seldom used pantry and Chael deposited the still seemingly dead Aelisa. He covered her up as best as he could to hide her from casual looters and followed Rina back out into the main hall.

The ornate entrance hall was completely awash in blood, both black and red. The great eight-pointed star at the center was cracked and incomplete and the shining marble floor was crosshatched with scorch and blast marks. There were several dozen bodies, both black-veined half-breeds and white-robed order members.

Rina's eyes were downcast, and she refused to look at the sight. Chael had to give a mental nod to the prowess of the Order. The bodies littering the floor were mostly the half breeds and several of them were missing heads with the flesh on their necks scorched and cauterized from Order whips. Chael looked from Michik's bloody muzzle to the claw and bite marks on several of the bodies.

"Did you see what happened here?" he asked Rina softly, shocking her from her silent prayer.

"The fighting erupted just as I reached the top of the stairs," she whispered, still staring downward.

Chael caught the beginnings of a tear in her eye, but she wiped it away before it could roll down her cheek.

"The half-breeds rushed in here like animals and my brothers and sisters fought them back." Rina shuddered more tears forming that cascaded down her face before she could wipe them away. "But the monsters were strong and fast, and they were quickly overwhelmed." Rina drew herself up as she spoke, righteous anger replacing the despair of the moment before. She clenched a tear-soaked fist as she continued relating the events.

"Without any elixir or weapon, I was useless to help and had to watch as they were all slaughtered one by one." Rina spat out the last words angrily but then softened and looked down at Michik. "I thought I would be killed as well. But then this giant wolf crashed into them, seemingly out of nowhere."

Michik gave her a ghoulish puppy grin, black blood still coating his half-ruined face. He sidled up to Rina and sniffed her hand hesitantly. She scowled slightly and pulled back which made him drop his tail, but she quickly recovered and at Chael's insistence began scratching his head lightly. Michik's tail resumed its usual animated wagging. Chael smiled at his dog and turned to Rina.

"Where are my weapons?" he asked, breaking her rhythmic scratching. This earned him a certain wolfish scowl. Rina was about to answer when another explosion rocked the palatial Order house. Several half-breeds advanced through the ruined double doors. "Go!" Chael shouted to Rina, "get my gear, Michik and I will hold them off." Rina hesitated to look at the carnage all around them, cursed and headed down a different hallway out of sight.

Chael grabbed one of the surprisingly few weapons from the bodies around him. A gold trimmed, half-moon blade from one of the younger looking priests. *Must not have earned his whip yet,* he thought. Six creatures advanced on him, none quite as human as Darrik still remained. The tallest of them stepped in front, the leader Chael supposed, and issued a guttural howling challenge. He couldn't make out the words, but the intent was clear: step up and fight. Chael obliged.

He dashed quicker than lightning to the leftmost half-breed. It had long demonic arms that were out of proportion to its torso. It gave him an almost ape-like aspect when he tried to run with his dangling arms. Chael relieved him of that burden with two precise slashes of the crescent blade. Demon limbs fell from the half-breed at the elbow, and it shrieked at him with disturbingly human pain and lunged headfirst, trying to bite Chael's neck. He easily dodged the clumsy attack and removed the creature's human head as it fell.

Then next one was trying to take his flank with a curved falchion eerily similar to his own, but before he could even swing Michik took his arm. With a few shakes of his powerful head, the wolf tore the limb from where it had been alchemically attached to the half-breed's shoulder. Chael deftly took its head before turning to fell one of its brothers. As he fought Chael noticed that he couldn't sense when they died as he usually did, and they left behind no residual life essence. Despite being half human, they were essentially demons in that respect.

Chael and Michik quickly finished off two more demonic hybrids, one bizarrely bearing several body parts belonging to a skulker. During the fight they flickered randomly between invisibility and not, leaving just a human head and half torso visible for several seconds of the fight. The final half-breed stared at Chael with bulging red eyes. His mouth was a perfect circle of pointed teeth like a leech. Whistling human speech barely struggled through its maw as it tried to speak.

"Yuh-oo," it wheezed, barely able to hold the sounds together. "I nuh-oh you." Each word came out like he had to fight some unseen force just to expel the breath. Its voice was raspy and tortured but it was also distinctly human, Chael shuddered involuntarily at the sound. It reached long tree branch-like limbs at Chael but before he could react it was blown backwards by a furious explosion.

He turned around to find Rina, fully dressed in the uniform of the Order, holding a smoking clay jar. She casually licked a finger and snuffed out the remaining bomb before it could explode in her hand. A bundle of knives and his sword wrapped up in his old green cloak lay at her feet.

Chael's ears were still ringing from the blast as he watched her. She gave him a wink then an apologetic shrug as she noticed his face wrinkled in pain. The voice in his head urged him to kill her for her insolence and his body strained to obey but he beat the impulse down with an effort of will. He settled for a glare of annoyance.

The grinding of stone and a deep demonic yell interrupted Chael and Rina's standoff. The giant leech faced half-breed was slowly rising to shaking feet. The lower half of his face and most of the right side of his torso were a mangle mess of burned flesh and black viscera. Human organs, stained green and black with rot and Dark blood, were visible through the mutilated and scorched skin. It sprang forward suddenly with deceptive quickness that belied its grievous injuries.

Even with Chael's enhanced senses, he only had barely a half seconds warning before it struck out at Rina. He managed to roughly shove her out of the way and took a swipe across his ribs for the effort. His already tattered clothes received three new tears and scarlet blood leaked down his side. Chael began to slowly rise to his feet once again while muttering under his breath about knights and chivalry but had to fall into a defensive roll as the half-breed took another swipe at him with his gangly tree branch-like appendages.

Before it could swing again Michik locked on to one of its knees, the wolf ripped and tore at the joint until the half-breed was forced to abandon his attacks on Chael. Chael gathered all the remaining strength he had from the death around him and lunged with a flying two-handed swing with his stolen blade at the half-breed's arm before it could retaliate against Michik.

With the strength of the many restless dead, Chael severed the demon limb as easily as though it were made of warm butter. The creature screeched in pain again and lashed at Chael with its remaining limb, but Chael was already moving. He easily avoided the clumsy retaliation and aimed his next strike at the half-breed's leg above where Michik held it. Once again, the leg parted before the power of his strike.

Michik immediately let go of the leg and leaped at its chest, causing it to topple backward. The canny wolf clawed and bit at its already ruined neck until the head came free in a squelching snap of tendon and bone.

"Good boy, Meeshee!" Chael called in a playful voice. Michik briefly shook off all the black blood from his coat and trotted happily over to Chael, tail wagging. He obliged the wolf with the customary head scratches. The revelry was short-lived however, as Rina came storming up to Chael. Her new clothes were sodden with marble dust and blood of both human and demon. She glowered at Chael with her hands on her hips and a bit of her own blood trickling from her upturned nose.

"How dare you?!" she finally cried dramatically, emphasizing her injury with a nasally tone like her nose was stuffed. "I am perfectly capable of defending myself, you know."

Michik whined a little and padded over to her and snorted, little bits of blood flying out onto the ruined floor. As she looked down, her expression immediately softened.

"Oh no, not you, Meeshee! You were magnificent!" She exclaimed brightly, beaming at the wolf. She awarded him a few more head scratches before giving Chael a final glare and walking away, Michik in tow.

"Great," Chael mumbled darkly, rubbing the cuts in his side. They were already scabbing over, and the process tickled him strangely. It would greatly reduce the amount of life energy he had to use, but he suspected that as soon as they left there would be plenty outside. He grimaced at the thought. He watched the two of them saunter off without him to the bodies of the Order priests and priestesses.

Rina dropped her pretenses when she reached the first one, even Michik bowed his head and sat on his haunches. Reverently, Rina closed the dead priestess's eyes and said a prayer to the Living Stars. Chael didn't join her, to him it seemed that if there really was someone up there to hear her supplication, having him join in would only foul the celestial being's mood.

After her ritual was completed to her satisfaction, Rina carefully went through the robes of the dead Order woman and took a number of alchemicals from the special pockets sewn into Order robes. Ischarina repeated this process until every member of her sect was prayed over and pilfered. Chael opted to not point out the seemingly contradictory behavior.

Politics, Chael huffed. The art of looking pretty and acting ghastly. Though by the nature of his job, Chael was wrapped up in politics as much as any of the hypocrites arranged below him. He always looked people in the face when he brought about their demise. That is, when he could help it.He certainly is ambitious, Chael thought as Darrik illuminated him on the scope of Khalim's plans for the republics.

"Michik come," Chael called as he walked toward the ruined wooden entrance doors. Michik spared one mournful look at Rina, his head cocked to the side but after a moment trotted back to Chael obediently his tail limp.

As he predicted, the situation outside the Order house was dire. Fhaerhold was soaked in death and as he breathed in the open air of bailey, Chael almost drowned in it. The city outside the small central ring was burning, dozens of plumes of black and gray smoke rose into the air like pillars of cloudy obsidian. The gate of this heavily guarded inner cloister had been torn from massive steel hinges and lay in a crumpled heap.

There were countless bodies of dead administrators, soldiers, and simple townsfolk laying butchered in the street. Rina gave out a gasp at the sight. Chael looked up and saw more half-breeds slowly pushing back royal guards on the long stairs that led to King Inarus' keep. More of the fiends were simply climbing the sides of the steep motte.

"I'm going to the keep," Chael growled roughly, surprising even himself with the ardor in his voice. Rina gave him a grave nod and dashed away in the direction of the main city. She didn't tell him where she was going but there was nothing for him to do for her now. Besides, she was now loaded up with more combat elixirs and weapons than any two barons could afford.

Chael gathered more strength from the dead that cluttered the street. Again, the voice assailed him with visions of power and bloodlust that stirred his soul to action, but he beat them back. Michik lightly bumped his head into Chael's thigh and looked up at him trembling. Chael reached down and scratched his head reassuringly, "I'm okay buddy," he assured his loyal companion. "Come on!"

The voice wanted him to feel enraged. He was, just not in the way It wanted. But Chael allowed that feeling to consume him and give additional power to the Dark energy coursing through his body. In an instant, he took off, kicking up dirt and blood as he sprinted to help the beleaguered soldiers engaging the half-breeds on the stairs. Michik let out a contented bark and tore after him just barely able to keep up.

Chael hit the stairs and climbed them three at a time in tremendous leaps. He felt the familiar leather handle of his falchion and for a moment felt at perfect peace. His arms and legs churned in perfect concert with his heart, he was where he needed to be.

The first half-breed to die didn't even have the opportunity to face the architect of his death before Chael took his head. The second to react was simply bowled over by Michik as the powerful wolf raced up the stairs. It let out a deep thrumming hiss as it tumbled down the hill. Chael did not relent; he parried claws and severed limbs as he methodically danced through the ranks of half demons. The half-breeds were strong and fast, but also clumsy. And in the tight confines of the stone stairs, they usually ended up doing more damage to each other than Chael.

Panicked, the half-breeds near the top pressed the human soldiers even harder until their resolve broke and the panicked guardsmen routed.

Demonic and human cheers rang out from the small battalion of half-breeds as they chased the fleeing soldiers and were able to finally flee from the cruel blade and canine jaws of their own pursuers. Chael cursed and hamstrung a fleeing enemy causing it to fall on its face. He casually stabbed it through the head as he walked over it. An arrow whistled through the air and Chael only barely managed to dodge it while continuing up the narrow steps.

The half-breeds had quickly taken the plateau and had managed to commandeer a few bows from the castle defenders. Michik yelped as one of the now dozens of falling projectiles landed on his shoulder.

Chael was desperately swinging his falchion in the air, using his enhanced reflexes to swat the arrows like flies but there were too many. As the two of them tore up the stairs they both received wounds that would have killed a normal man or living wolf.

Chael screamed in rage as he pulled an arrow from his shoulder and flung one of his knives at the half-breed holding the bow. The throw was off balance and imprecise and so it only hit the creature in the chest with the pommel, but the force of the throw with Chael's enhanced strength pushed the half-breed into one of his companions and they both tumbled over the edge of the motte.

Finally, after several minutes of dodging arrows and with three shafts piercing his arm, leg, and chest respectively, Chael reached the castle plateau. Michik, bearing two of his own raced off after the bowmen, heedless of his injuries.

As the wolf occupied the attention of the remaining archers Chael saw to his own wounds. He removed arrows from his thigh and arm. He screamed in agony as he ripped muscle and skin tearing the arrowhead out. The one in his chest was of greater concern. He was fairly certain it hadn't pierced his heart, even with all the Dark energy inside him desperately healing his broken body a shot straight to the heart would have ended him. Despite that, he was bleeding from more than a dozen wounds and his breath was coming in ragged wheezing gasps. A wolf's yelp steeled his nerves and despite the pain and the arrow remaining in his chest, he set off again.

Michik was occupying three different half-breeds who were cut off from supporting their brethren assaulting the keep. They had abandoned bows and were slashing out as his dog with what appeared to be the half-breed weapon of choice, black demonic claws. As fast and adept as Michik was, the Dark enhanced half-breeds were more than a match and Chael watched with horror as he took several raking slashes to his hide. At this rate Michik was going to be reduced to a pile of scrap.

Chael poured more of his own Dark energy into his speed, slowing down the healing cycle he so desperately needed. As he sprinted, he flung two more knives which buried in half-breed chests but did little more than momentarily stall their attacks. In the space between Chael's charge and meeting the first half-breed head on, Michik suffered three more vicious wounds. All Chael could do was watch as the last vicious attack permanently severed Michik's front left leg.

Chapter 33

Present Day

Ischarina

Rina sprinted away from the Order house as quickly as she could on elixir-enhanced legs; she would pay dearly for it later.

"Elixirs are imperfect imitations of the power of the stars," she said, repeating the words of her former mentor, Brother Zehlus. The power that flowed through you after taking an elixir made you feel like the Starborn, unfortunately you were still running on perfectly mortal bones and muscles and the additional strain added up.

So just me then, Chael thought.Damn, Chael thought. The Baron probably had a point there. Chael fought back the retort that had flown to his lips. He was annoyed that the Baron had figured him so well. A carpenter I am not, he thought out loud, looking at his questionable work. He turned to look down the path that led from his home and into the forest towards Ehbing. After a moment, he was also able to hear the approach of at least several people and a horse which had set off the keen senses of his dog.

The thought now consumed her mind as she raced past the remnants of mutilated corpses and razed tenements. Here and there she could see pockets of resistance, whether city soldiers or city folk with little more than kitchen utensils. It didn't seem to matter, the half-breeds fought with the strength and speed of demons. Rina yearned to unleash her now impressive collection of alchemical constructs, but she simply couldn't spare the time.

Familiar buildings, set to flame by the monstrous invaders, were just red and black blurs in her peripheral vision as she flew through the city. At last, she came to her destination and her heart sank. A small wooden house, more a hovel really if she was being honest, had collapsed. The second story of the neighboring home had been blasted to the side in a tremendous explosion and a chunk of brick as large as the wolf had fallen onto her father's little wooden house and collapsed the roof. Amid the wood and stone rubble was a familiar arm, barely poking out from the wreckage.

Rina drained another elixir and with sudden strength, she shoved the wreckage aside and found him. Her father's face was the same as when she had last seen it. The stubble of several days was evident on his chin and the brown wrap he used to cover his milky white eyes wasn't even askew. He was the image of peace and acceptance.

He must have been asleep, she supposed. Most of his chest down to mid-thigh, was simply gone. Red gore covered everything in a five-foot radius, and the only thing that remained of her father's torso were shreds of pale and tattered skin.

Tears rolled down Rina's face as she stood. She clenched her fist with alchemically enhanced hands and blood ran from her palms where her nails bit in. She glared ruefully at the blood for a moment, anger slowly rising to replace the torment in her heart.

She immediately searched in her uniform for a certain combat elixir, the Stellar Scourge. It was the most advanced elixir the Order of Celestial Light could produce; it was reserved for the most advanced alchemists in the Order.

Even some of the prefects couldn't use it because of its effects on the body. It took years of physical and alchemical training to use it safely and Rina had only been an initiate for two years. It was also forbidden to use it in conjunction with all but a few elixirs as the interactions were potentially lethal, and Rina had no clue which ones those were. She gulped down the silvery liquid without a second thought.

It tasted, as most elixirs did, of pure alcohol and it burned her throat a bit. As it hit her stomach, she became immediately nauseous and almost vomited it right back up but held it down.

Slowly her belly settled, and a mild tingling sensation started moving down her right arm, like an army of a thousand spiders crawling from her elbow to her fingertips. She almost vomited right there. But quickly the sensation painfully intensified like all the spiders had stopped crawling to bite her.

Rina screamed as her arm was wracked as with fire, and then it was gone. She didn't remember closing her eyes but had to open them to view the result. The flesh of her arm from elbow to wrist was gone and a vine of pure golden light laced around her bones and tucked neatly into her outstretched hand.

The whip buzzed with power, and she found that it obeyed her very thoughts as she experimentally lashed it around the ruins of her father's humble home. She bent down, careful to avoid touching her father with the whip and kissed him lightly on the cheek.

"I failed papa, I could not bring you back your sight or protect you from this fate. But on my soul, I will slaughter every half-breed that crosses my path!" Rina stood and gave her father one last sorrowful glance and turned. She would go find Chael again.

The prefect had called him Darkborn, but as ominous as that sounded it had no further meaning to her. Besides, she had joined the Order to learn the secrets of alchemy, not to worship the stars.

Rina knew only one thing for certain, Chael was no friend of the half-breeds, and he could seemingly kill them with as much effort as swatting a fly. And besides, he beggared countless questions, and her scholarly brain simply couldn't pass up the opportunity to ask. She would track him and his odd wolf down. But first, she had accounts to settle in the city. Rina's tearful grimace turned into a twisted maniacal half grin as she gripped the buzzing whip in her hands.

Darrik

Darrik raged against the restraints holding him down in this infernal dungeon. He had, of course, allowed his capture but had underestimated the ingenuity of the stargazers. His demon heart pulsed its own frustration at the circumstance. The longer he sat under this accursed dripping pool above his head, the weaker his symbiotic heart became, and it had been weeks. *And Chael,* he growled in his own head.

That slippery little snake had eluded his grasp, and these humans had even served the bastard up to him. Deep human rage bubbled inside him, and he begged the demon heart to give him more strength to escape. Black blood pumped furiously through his limbs, and he heaved against the steel holding him in place. But all he accomplished was spilling more of the inky black substance on the ground.

Darrik slumped back in the chair, defeated for the hundredth time. Exhaustion broke his concentration, and the demon slithered into his mind again. It was weak inside this prison, but so was he. Most days he was himself, but it took a constant battle of will to control the beast within him. He fought the demon back to its home in their heart and sighed.

It couldn't speak to him in words, but it did give off certain impressions. Right now, it seemed to be asking, "why?"

"Because," Darrik said out loud. "I am in charge of this body." The demon gave him the impression of great strength and freedom, if only it were in control. "Ha!" Darrik yelled to the air, "you wouldn't be any more successful than I have been." The demon seemed to sulk and its attacks on his mind subsided for the moment.

Darrik smiled with genuine pleasure for the first time in months. His own self-satisfaction almost made him miss the tromping of heavy footsteps outside his cell. After a moment, the glowing red eyes of one of the Children stepped into view. When it saw him, it gave Darrik a formal bow.

"Sir," it said clearly without any hint of demonic overlay in his speech. *This one must be asserting quite a bit of control,* Darrik thought. Without any hesitation he replied, allowing the demon to suffuse his voice slightly.

"Get me out!" Darrik snarled.

Brod

The people of Ehbing were growing restless without their baron around. Brod couldn't say what the man did from day to day, but the people here had grown used to having a noble and they supposed that gave them some sort of standing in the realm.

"Foolish," Brod muttered under his breath while walking up the squat hill toward the keep. He had known many nobles back in his day, and the best asset they seemed to deliver to a city was adding to its problems.

Still, the town—well, burgeoning city, really— was currently lacking leadership, and that was causing problems all of its own. Currently the issue bristling his own expertly quaffed mustache was over milk. Or rather the cost of exchange of milk and for some reason the townspeople had come to him as an arbiter. Brod let out a weary sigh as he continued up the slope.

The problem had escalated to violence, and he needed to involve the imbeciles that called themselves the city watch. The lot of them had holed up in the keep, the moment the Baron had left. They were growing fat on their master's stores while the town below ate itself. When he arrived at the palisade, he found a fat clerk on guard duty holding a spear with dubious expertise.

"I need ter get inside." Brod stated firmly to the man. He didn't want to be too harsh; this poor bean counter had clearly been pressed into service by the slothful guards.

"Well, I um…" The man stammered unsure of himself.

Brod was about to insist when he heard the faint ringing of a bell. At first, he thought it must have just been a trick of the wind, but it grew in volume and frequency like someone was frantically ringing it.

Brod peered down at Ehbing and saw the source of the sound and his breath caught in his throat. It was the small brass bell in the town square; it had been built as a warning for demons that rarely ventured into the town. He had not heard it since Chael had come to live in the forest and even before then only once or twice. He and the nervous clerk were now both staring at the source of the sound, but it was Brod who noticed first. There were four demons walking straight through the center of town.

"Darkness!" cried the fat clerk would-be-watchman. Brod grabbed him by the collar and shook the shock from him.

"Go!" Brod shouted angrily. "Go up there and tell those cowards to get down here and defend the city!"

The man trembled, staring at Brod's searing eyes for a moment but then nodded and hurried through the palisade toward the keep. In his haste he dropped his spear which Brod picked up. He looked down at the town grimly clutching the rough haft in his calloused hands and took off at a sprint.

Chapter 34

Present Day

Flesh, both human and otherwise flew through the air under the fury of Chael's sword. An eternity passed in just seconds as Chael annihilated the half-breeds from this realm of existence, piece by piece. Mere death wasn't good enough, Darrik proved the fragility of that state. Chael kept carving his enemies like roasted meat until they were just a pile of individual mouthfuls. Finally, he stopped swinging. He was breathing heavily, though the power of life essence still suffused his limbs, and thick black blood like globs of tar covered him from head to foot.

It took Chael precious moments before he had the courage to look down. Michik lay on his side in a pathetic ruinous state. His flank held almost more scars than fur and there were still arrows protruding from him. With a soft whine, barely above a whisper, he lifted the stub of his severed limb up to his master. Tears stung Chael's eyes as he knelt down to look. The leg was severed just above the joint halfway to the shoulder.

"It's ok, buddy," Chael reassured him as he stroked what little fur remained on his side. "I'm going to fix you, I promise." Michik whined a little more and let out a loud exhale as he lay back down on the ground. Through bleary eyes Chael began searching for the severed limb and gasped.

It was only a few feet away, but it looked like it had aged a decade. The fur had all fallen off, and the skin was leathery and desiccated. As Chael picked it up, the bones beneath felt like they would crumble to dust at the lightest touch.

"Meeshee," Chael began, fighting to keep his voice calm. "I know you're hurting. And I know you're scared, but I need you to get up." Chael's whole body trembled as he struggled to say the words. "Get up buddy please," he half whispered through new tears as they fell down his face. Chael suddenly felt a tugging at his soul, soft and fleeting like a hair being tugged from his scalp. The sensation was not too dissimilar to the feeling of letting go of power when he was done using it. He felt diminished, not greatly, but it was as if some small part of his will was gone.

Michik stood up. He was still a ragged mess, and he had to balance on three legs, but a sense of vitality emanated from the wolf that wasn't there before. He walked, awkwardly on three legs, over to Chael and nuzzled his hand affectionately. Chael scratched his head and wiped the tears from his eyes. Michik's eyes always held a faint azure glow, but now Chael would have said they blazed.

"Are you ready, buddy?" Chael asked hesitantly. The wolf stared back at him with an intensity that Chael had never seen before. Slowly Michik opened his wide and vicious jaws and snapped them closed menacingly as his growl filled the air. He could almost hear the silent intentions of his dog, Michik was out for blood. Chael was ok with that.

Together they dashed toward the broken gates of the keep. The heavy wood and iron framed doors had been, not quite smashed, Chael supposed, but clawed. The broken fragments of the gate had giant foot long gouges in the wood as if it had been assaulted by a bear as large as a house. Together they vaulted the remains and headed into the keep.

Shouts and screams of men and women echoed off the lofty stone walls. Half-breeds darted across like maddened hounds on a thousand different scent trails. And where they ventured, death followed behind. Chael drank it in and waded into the fight.

Three half-breeds greeted him at a grand staircase. His falchion cut down two and Michik tore the third apart with his jaws. The newly revitalized wolf seemed even faster and more agile on three legs than he had just moments before with four. And he exuded a bloodlust that he had never expressed before. Together they cleansed the lower levels of Fhaerhold's keep, neither wanting for power in the sea of death and anguish.

They dismembered, eviscerated, maimed, and generally slaughtered scores demonic half-breeds as they proceeded up through the floors and rooms of the keep. *How many of these things did Khalim create?* The presence that invaded his mind every time he breathed the power of death was screaming in his head for him to stop. It commanded real authority over his body and spirit the more power he consumed and used. But right now, Chael was too enraged to care, he was going to purge Fhaerhold of these creatures and the Darkness leech on his soul could watch.

Eventually, they made it all the way to the King's audience chamber. The room was a ruined mess of its former self. Craters of bombs and scorches marred the pristine polished stone of the chamber. The great stained-glass dome was shattered, and its glass pierced several human corpses. Bodies of a score of Fhaelan knights were on the floor, broken and bleeding.

One in particular caught Chael's eye as he quickly searched the room with his eyes. Sir Andon was lying in a crumpled heap on top of his king. Between Chael and Andon were two members of the Kaazan Alchemists Guild and the largest half-breed Chael had yet seen. It was like a giant twisted spider. It had all four human limbs, but the legs had been cruelly twisted backward to support its arachnid gate.

Four additional demonic limbs had been attached with the same gleaming black claws as the others. The half-breed's head was a terrible mask of pained existence. The entire right side of its face was a bulging demon head complete with jagged, sword-like teeth.

As Chael approached, it drank an elixir tossed to it from one of the alchemists. Black veins pulsed, and it almost seemed to grow. Not in height, but in breadth, like all of its gangly limbs became denser and stronger. Without further preamble it struck out at Chael with astonishing speed. The spider half-breed seemed to blur as it closed the distance between them and even to his own enhanced senses, Chael could barely track the attack. He dodged one clawed demon arm after another but there were always more.

Luckily, the creature ignored Michik entirely, much to Chael's relief, but the alchemists did not. Hissing bombs flew at the wolf and exploded in fiery detonations. Even hobbled as he was, Michik was still much more agile than mere humans and dodged the small exploding clay spheres with ease. He ran to attack one of the alchemists but a chitinous demonic claw backhanded him and he flew into a wall.

Chael snarled at the creature and flicked a knife at its face while dodging. The half-breed easily knocked the weak throw out of the air, but the distraction was enough for Chael to strike a limb with his falchion. Demon blood spurted out of the limb in great black gouts as Chael tore through it with the raw strength of the swirling vortex of life essence inside him.

The half-breed fumbled for a moment on the missing limb but redoubled its attack, ferociously slashing at Chael with mad abandon. Michik slowly recovered from being thrown into the wall and just barely managed to dodge yet another barrage of thrown explosives. Yet still undeterred, the wolf tore after the alchemists once again. Chael watched out of the corner of his eye as Michik descended on the first alchemist and ripped out his throat. The second one changed tactics and quickly downed an elixir of his own and faced the wolf head on. He needn't have bothered. Whatever enhancements the potion gave him were irrelevant to

Michik's fury and his blood joined the puddle of black and red pooling on the floor.

Steel met black talons as Chael continued to clash with the half demon spider. He had scored dozens of hits and its sticky black ichor burst out of the wounds, but none had been lethal or deep enough to disable the remaining arms. It was too fast and too all-consuming for Chael to get the proper leverage to break through the tough demon hide of the limbs, even with his inhuman strength. Something had to change to unbalance the fight and give Chael the opportunity he needed to strike.

Michik happily obliged.

The wolf launched himself from the dais across the room and landed on the back of the half-breed while it still engaged with Chael. Chael could scarcely believe such a feat was possible on four legs let alone three, but Michik soared through the air and when he landed, he latched his powerful jaws on the thing's neck. The half-breed reared back in violent anger and clawed at the wolf ripping into the flesh of its neck.

Chael pushed all the power he could muster into his legs and leaped with a jump of his own and abandoned his falchion to the ground. Instead, he reached for two more knives as he flew and slammed them down into the base of the monster's skull and cleaved, wrenching his arms in the air as hard as he could. Half its skull fell to the floor with Chael and clattered at his feet. Greenish rotten brain tissue spilled out over the floor as the half-breed thrashed around in its death throes. Michik let go and was tossed aside again but this time landing more softly on the ground.

Chael casually lopped off a few of its spasming legs, causing the half-breed to come crashing down to the floor. He removed its head, and the thrashing ceased.

Chapter 35

Present Day

"Disgusting!" Chael spat at the corpse of the spidery half-breed. The depravity of the Black Hand, and that of Khalim, truly knew no bounds.

Chael gave the remains one last contemptuous glare and rushed off to check on Michik. The wolf was lying on his side in a pool of blood, thankfully not his own blood, Michik didn't have any. But the image disturbed Chael, nonetheless. He looked disconcertingly similar to how he had looked outside after his leg had been cut, wasted away and helpless.

Chael knelt down next to him, ignoring the blood seeping through his light pants and stroked Michik's fur. The wolf's head shot up and glared at him, and he let out a soft bark. Chael didn't need any special connection to him to understand what that meant. "I'm just resting you idiot." Chael chuckled softly, and Michik gave his hand a playful nip before laying back down.

Satisfied that Michik had sustained no significant further damage, Chael turned his gaze to the dais where Andon and King Inarus lay. Chael's immediate instinct was to reach down inside his soul for more of the glowing light but knew it was futile. He had used too much on Aelisa and he wasn't even sure if that had worked. There was simply no way he was going to be able to attempt to resurrect either of them.

Even if he could, Chael wasn't sure he understood the implications enough to try. Darrik would know, sometimes it was better to just remain dead.

Chael looked woefully at the King, there was no hope there. His throat had been slashed and he could tell that King Inarus had died well before he had entered the room. Chael's gaze turned to Andon and his heart skipped. Though the knight was battered and bleeding, he wasn't dead. There was life essence still flowing inside of him, weakly, but flowing just the same.

Chael immediately began tearing away sections of armor with his strength until he could see Andon's bare chest and neck. There was long bleeding cut across his chest, but it was reasonably shallow. The greater concerns were burn marks across his right arm, shoulder, and face. Clearly, Andon had taken a blast from the alchemical bombs head on. A twisted shield, half melted and broken was lying in a smoldering heap just a few feet away.

"You tried to shield the King from the blast, didn't you," Chael sighed while ripping bandages out of Inarus' clothes. "Idiot," Chael chided Andon's unconscious form.

After applying the bandages to the claw wound on his chest, Chael got a good look at his right arm. It was broken in several places and his hand was a gnarled, pulpy mess. The fingers that still had skin were bent and twisted into hideous knots and there was more bone visible than healthy pink flesh. Chael grimaced; Andon would likely lose the hand.

"Michik," Chael called. The wolf lifted his head up one ear flopping to the side. "We're leaving."

The wolf gingerly rose to his three remaining paws and slowly padded over in hopping steps to Chael. He sniffed, and for the first time Michik seemed to be aware of Andon's presence. He hobbled over to Andon, whining and nudging his burns with his nose. Michik then looked up to Chael with a look that seemed to ask, "what are you going to do about this?"

"I don't know, buddy," Chael answered the implied question sadly. "But I do know that we have to get out of the city, for both your sakes."

Chael eyed Michik seriously and imparted as much of his intent through their bond as he could. It was inexact and as unique as Michik had become over his exposure to their bond his mind and understanding was still that of a wolf.

"Can you hold on just a little longer?" Chael asked, almost pleading. Michik straightened and though battered and maimed much of his former strength seemed to return. Chael felt that tugging sensation again, like bits of his soul were slipping away.

The wolf returned Chael's serious stare then, azure eyes blazing. Without further comment Chael turned and hoisted Andon on his shoulder and marched out of the chamber.

They only met token resistance on their way out of the keep. Their earlier rampage had apparently cleared out most of the half-breeds inside and Chael only had to kill two more of the Dark hybrids before they could exit. Even encumbered with the weight of Sir Andon, killing them was trivial. Tens of thousands of human lives had been extinguished in the city over the last few hours. Even up on the high hill of the keep, Chael had access to an ocean of power.

He sighed mournfully; it was the terrible paradox of his existence. He had the potential to be the most powerful being in the world, or so he assumed. He simply had to swim through rivers of blood to achieve it. The presence inside him reveled, it had received more nourishment in an hour than it had in its entire existence. It strained with renewed strength against the bonds of will that Chael carefully held, lashing it down.

She is probably used to giving orders and being obeyed, Chael guessed.

Suddenly, visions swam through Chael's mind of power and dominion, he had only to surrender his will to this constant shadow and their combined might would make him powerful beyond reckoning. The very foundations of the world would shake under his authority. It sounded very nice.

"Can you give Michik back his leg?" Chael asked out loud, angrily. He was already gritting his teeth against the psychic onslaught going on inside his head and the words came out even more harsh than he intended. The presence paused its mental assault, Chael could detect confusion in the way it reacted.

His will strengthened on that thought and the balance shifted back in his favor. "You can't," he declared triumphantly. "All the power in the world and you can't even do that."

With an effort of will he beat the beast back down, and it shuddered. Chael smiled, it would not go away forever, but he had won this battle and he found it utterly gratifying. He was so pleased with himself that he only half grimaced as he gazed out over the city.

He knew that it was lost, but he didn't expect it to be quite so ransacked. *Did Khalim intend to rule over a pile of corpses?* That thought bothered him. His former master was cruel and was possessed of boundless ambition, but he wasn't insane. *What was the point of capturing a city just to raze it?*

But he didn't have long to dwell on it, already the main force of Khalim's army was surrounding and purging the city. If he didn't want to face the entirety of Khalim's forces, he had to find a way to escape, fast.

As far as he could tell, they hadn't yet fully concentrated in the Western part of the city. If he was quick, he might be able to miss the bulk of the invading army. *I'll only have to kill a hundred or so,* he thought sardonically.

But there was no time like the present, so reluctantly, he started running down the long stairs. It was so much easier than coming up.

Chapter 36

Present Day

Chael carried Sir Andon all the way to the Western gate of the city. Despite his predictions they actually encountered suspiciously little resistance. Khalim's forces were still concentrated in the southern half of the city. The wanton destruction and assassination team turned out to be the ones that had already been in the city as Darrik had said.

The bulk of Khalim's army came up from the south and were still engaging with the city defenders there. Chael knew that Fhaerhold would officially fall in the night but he, Michik, and Andon were able to slip by after only meeting a dozen or so more of the half-breeds.

Chael did find it suspicious that Khalim hadn't tried to surround the city, or at least block the few main gates. It seemed that he was more than content to let the terrified populace flee out of the other exits. It couldn't be mercy; Chael knew better. His former master did not think in those terms, if he was allowing the people to escape it was for some unknown purpose.

The Western gate, though not nearly as impressive as the gate of the inner bailey, had been tall and built of thick planks of brown oak. It was now broken and scattered in front of the exit, though Chael saw very little signs of half-breeds. The gate had been torn from its house by the feet of the fleeing citizens of Fhaerhold.

As they left the city with the flood of terrified civilians, Chael bucked the tide of people heading West and turned North toward the training grounds where they had previously left Michik.

"If his squire isn't there I can at least see about a horse," Chael told Michik as they walked. Michik looked up at him, stumpy leg curled up to his chest and cocked his head. "How does that sound?" he asked Michik who unceremoniously snorted back at him.

"All right it's decided." Chael responded, and they continued on to the training grounds of the former Realm Knights. *Now, it's just Realm Knight,* Chael thought sadly.

Chael stared into the night sky idly. The stars didn't seem more alive than the grass, but all the talk of ancient evils and Dark portents had him thinking. He didn't feel evil, there was of course the impressions he received when he was using his power but every so-called normal person he had ever met felt the corruptive influence of power when it was obtained.

Is mine different? He didn't know, but if the Living Stars had a problem with his existence, they could come down here and smite him themselves. He looked down at his lap where Michik lay, curled up tight against the chill night air. His mood darkened when he saw the stump where his leg should have been.

In so many ways, he was still just a puppy. He could kill scores of men single-handedly and had, but he was also a playful and loving companion. He had tried to sleep on Chael's lap, and sort of succeeded, but half his giant frame was still resting in the dirt despite being curled up. A groan drew Chael's attention elsewhere.

"You're safe," Chael reassured the knight lying on the ground next to him. Chael didn't have any of his normal supplies since fleeing the capitol but had done his best to wrap Andon up in his cloak.

"Chael?" the knight asked groggily.

"I'm here," he assured him. Andon suddenly sat upright, which brought out a new groan from his mouth.

"The King," he gasped through gritted teeth. "Chael, the King I…"

"He's dead," Chael answered flatly. He didn't want to be so frank but soothing people wasn't among his talents, better to just rip the bandage off quickly. Andon sat silently for several moments with his eyes closed, giving Chael the distinct impression that he was searching for some memory or explanation. At last, he appeared to come to some sort of conclusion because he looked back at Chael with less confusion in his eyes.

"How am I still alive?" he finally asked grimly. Chael quickly related to him how he killed the spider half-breed, Andon shuddered at the memory, and how they left the city.

"I was able to find a horse at your training ground," Chael continued, pointing over to the animal tied up nearby.

"My squire?" Andon asked hesitantly. Chael simply shook his head, and the knight nodded.

"We rode West with the refugees from the city until nightfall. I didn't want to continue onward in the dark, so I took us off the path for a few leagues before stopping for the night."

Sir Andon nodded again, then for the first time he looked down at his ruined arm. He must have felt it or been aware because he didn't gasp or cry out, he only grimaced.

"I tried," Chael began nervously, unsure how he would react. "I tried to set the bones in your arm but I'm no healer and even if I were, I don't know what could be done about your hand."

Andon grimaced again as he strained to move his mutilated fingers but got nothing more than a slight twitch in his knuckle. Then Michik rose from Chael's lap and limped on his three legs over to Andon. Michik had once again lost the odd spike of agility he had received earlier and was now hobbled once again, but Chael felt that he was putting a little extra effort into his limp.

He walked unsteadily up to Andon and sniffed his ruined hand gently, then he promptly fell into Andon's lap. He looked from Michik's missing leg to Chael but before he could ask the obvious question Michik lifted his snout toward Andon's good hand and gave a demanding whining growl. Andon got the hint and started scratching the wolf's head and let the question die.

Chael returned his gaze up to the stars and Andon followed his eyes. They both sat there for several moments just staring up in comfortable silence. Then Michik bolted off into the darkness. It happened so suddenly, even Chael couldn't anticipate it. The wolf began sniffing at the air curiously then sprinted away from their rough camp without so much as a bark.

"Wait here," Chael hurriedly called over his shoulder at Andon as he chased after his dog. The energy he had consumed in Fhaerhold had long since dissipated to nothing in his system and even on three legs Michik was significantly faster than Chael if he needed to be and the wolf was sprinting away like he was trying to outrun an avalanche.

What did she not want to say? Chael wondered. I've probably killed more Dark spawn than any other man alive, he thought bitterly.

Whoever it was, was not going down easily though. The person appeared to be an alchemist or at least had gotten their hands on an alchemist's combat constructs. As Chael neared, he could see that the person was a woman, and she appeared to be keeping the demons at bay with a stick about a foot long. It looked absurdly ordinary to Chael, but the demons clearly feared it. Every time one of them tried to find an angle to approach her she lashed out with it, and they instantly backed away.

Before too long, one of the rats' faces got too close and Chael finally found out why they feared the small shaft of ordinary looking wood. The demon swiped at her with its terrible claws but before they made contact with her throat, she desperately snapped the tip of the stick on its arm.

Blue and white sparks flew out from the end of the construct, and the demon stumbled back, roaring in agony. Chael couldn't see any true physical damage on the Dark creature but as long as she held the painful stick, they were not going to come too close.

Michik reached the group a few seconds before Chael. He leaped at the nearest demon and bit down hard on its arm and began thrashing his head wildly. The stunned demon hesitated for just a moment before striking down at this new enemy but by that time Chael was already there. He beat away the demon's claws with his sword and followed up with another swing at its neck.

He no longer had access to the overwhelming well of power that he had after the bloodbath in Fhaerhold, but he had consumed enough of the life energy on his journey here to push his sword through and sever the beast's head. With the first demon killed, Michik immediately dropped the limp arm and ran between the remaining two demons and the woman. He planted himself there, guarding her, his lips peeled back in a wicked toothy snarl.

Chael turned his attention to the next one and slashed a one-handed blow at its left arm. The demon caught his sword in its steely talon-like claws. He pulled with his enhanced strength, but the Darkspawn was a match and kept his falchion in its vise-like grip. The demon's right arm came crashing down at Chael and he had to let go of his sword and duck to avoid the would-be crushing blow.

With his ever-impeccable timing, Michik clamped his mighty jaws down on its wrist and his sword fell back into Chael's outstretched hand as he completed his dodge. In future retellings of this moment Chael would explain how this was all perfectly choreographed movement and had exhibited flawless execution. In reality Chael was so shocked by the handle of his sword falling neatly into his hand that he hesitated for a half a breath and the demon backhanded him across the stocks of wheat ten feet away.

Chael grunted, pain arcing like lightning through his ribs where the demon had struck him. He didn't have time to sit and complain about pain though. He chided himself as he rose on wobbling legs to his feet. He gathered more power, this time reaching out and snapping the life from everything he could touch for scores of paces.

Most people are blissfully unaware of the life teeming in the world around them from insects and vermin to the smallest plant growth. Chael felt it all and what's more he felt their deaths as he stole their lives for his own need. But he was tired and sore already, and there were demons that needed killing.

Newly revitalized, he shot back into the fight. As he moved, he could feel broken ribs stitching themselves slowly back together in a painful tingly sensation. The added power brought added clarity and grace to his movements, and he easily ducked two more hasty swipes from the demons as he kissed exposed tendons and cut precise gouges out of muscles with his sword.

When he was done, they were both in a crumpled heap before him, but still alive. He brought down his falchion with as much force as he could generate and cleanly decapitated the demon on his left. He was about to do the same with the one on the right, but the woman came up next to him and shoved the rod into its eye with a snarl on her face that rivaled Michik.

The demon twitched violently, his eye showering blue and white sparks and a sick burning odor filled the air. The woman kept pushing the construct into its skull until the body stopped thrashing and the sparks died out. Chael was pretty sure it was dead, but he cut off its head to be sure.

"Thanks," she said, panting her hands at her hips. Chael scanned her with the enhanced vision the power gave him and could easily make out details about her in the dark. He was only mildly surprised when he recognized the woman.

"Rina," Chael stated as if he knew it was her all along. He didn't but she couldn't know that. "What are you doing out here?"

"Looking for you," she replied as though it was obvious. His momentary omniscient pretense shattered, and he gave her a questioning look.

"Why?" he asked, confused. When she left, he was fairly certain that he wouldn't see her again. They only barely knew each other and as far as he was concerned, they were square, no favors owed.

"I..." she began and then stopped. She looked at him puzzled this time and then collapsed where she stood. Chael immediately checked her pulse, it was weak, but it was steady. He could see that her bare feet were bleeding heavily but other than that she looked perfectly healthy, but for a few minor scratches here and there.

"So now I'm stuck with three cripples," Chael groaned. Michik let out one of his growling whines and Chael looked down at him skeptically. "Oh, so you're just fine then huh?" Chael asked. The wolf stared up at him defiantly for a moment but eventually ducked his head and gave him a small reluctant snort.

"That's what I thought," Chael chided. He picked up Rina, thankfully she was quite a bit lighter than Andon, and started walking back to their little camp.

Demons were ranging farther East; that was a bad sign. His intention was to leave Andon in Fhaerstead, but if demons were already out here past the small town, was it even still there? And now he had to care for yet another battle worn and weary soul. His list of responsibilities was inflating rapidly, and he hadn't even figured out how he was going to restore Michik's leg. He sighed softly as he trudged through the wreckage of wheat that he had made on his mad flight out here to rescue Rina.

"I hate…" he cut himself off. He was about to say "people", but it hardly seemed fitting now that he had voluntarily become their nurse. He exhaled roughly, annoyed at himself and finished with, "this. I hate this."

Close enough, he thought glumly.

Chapter 37

Present Day

Chael woke Sir Andon up before dawn, he had only slept an hour or two himself, but in a pinch, he was able to use his abilities to supplement the lack of sleep. He would certainly pay for it down the road, but his mind was far too troubled by recent events to find rest, anyway. Andon had been asleep when they got back last night and had not yet seen Rina, he gave a start when saw the red-haired woman lying next to him.

"Who is that?" he demanded, immediately distancing himself from the woman. Chael raised an eyebrow at his reaction but didn't comment.

"Rina," he answered frankly. "Met her down in the Order's prison." Chael had given Andon a brief explanation of Aelisa's betrayal last night, including the Order initiate who had helped him. Andon looked at her skeptically.

"Can she be trusted?" he asked.

"She could have left me down there to rot I suppose," Chael answered with a shrug. "She said she came out here looking for me and I found her wrestling with three demons."

"Resourceful," Andon commented, and Chael nodded in agreement.

"I suspect she overdid it on elixirs, the Order house in Fhaerstead should know how to help her." Chael added, he looked down at her still unconscious, but breathing steadily.

"Is that where we're going?" Andon asked, and Chael nodded again. "Won't they..." He hesitated before pantomiming a knife across his throat and pointed at Chael. Chael smiled and pointed back at him.

"It's a good thing I brought a knight of the realm along then."

At Chael's insistence they traveled through the countryside, avoiding the main road. With all the turmoil in the region and the river of refugees, he felt it was best to travel as secretly as they could. Andon rode the horse while doing his best to ride while supporting Rina with one arm. He still looked uncomfortable being this close to her, but Chael ignored his initial protests. It only took them a few hours to reach the small town even with their less direct route. They approached it from the Northeast and stopped on a small hill from which they could survey Fhaerstead.

The town itself looked the same as when they had been here a few days ago, but the architecture is where the similarities ended. All around the city were great rectangular iron cages filled to the brim with the former citizens of the capitol. Lesser Demons led by half-breeds patrolled the walled perimeter of Fhaerstead and inside was an army of black cloaked cultists, Andon gasped.

"So that's why they let the people flee Fhaerhold," Chael muttered darkly to no one in particular. "Because the trap had already been laid here." Bile rose up in Chael's throat and he had to spit it out before he could taste the bitterness. "Change of plans," he said more loudly, this time looking directly at the knight. "We'll have to head south."

"No," Andon answered firmly, anger rising in his usually calm demeanor. "The capitol may be lost but we cannot stand idly by while its people are slaughtered or worse." Chael had a good idea what worse meant and agreed with the knight that he would rather choose death than to become one of those things. But still he shook his head at Andon.

"We?" he asked him calmly. "You have one arm and can barely stand, Michik is already crippled and she," Chael waved a frustrated hand in Rina's direction, "may never wake up!" Chael was angry now, not at Andon, but at the world. Why was it always his responsibility? He was perfectly content in the forest and now… He glanced down at Michik and clenched a fist. This was never his battle, and he was only here because he had been manipulated. That fact gnawed at him, and he fumed even more anger before Andon spoke again.

"Chael," the knight said softly, "please." He looked over to him and noticed Michik had left his side and joined the night, pleading softly with his wide puppy eyes. *Stars save me,* he thought, groaning internally.

"You don't understand what it is that you're asking," Chael responded sadly, his voice barely above a whisper. Andon looked at him confused but before he could ask why Chael answered. "There's too many down there," he said, not looking the knight in the eye. He held his hand up to forestall the predictable objections.

They have an alchemist, Chael muttered under his breath and cursed.

How could he explain that to Andon without the knight cringing with revulsion? In the end Chael decided to be direct, if Sir Andon found it too repulsive to keep his company any longer, so be it. He cleared his throat and broke the sudden tension that had filled the air. "I could probably do what you are suggesting, but I would have to kill dozens of the innocent to do it." Somewhere deep inside him, despite having almost no life essence empowering him, his presence smiled at the suggestion.

To Chael's relief Andon didn't look revolted, but he did still seem confused, "can't you use the plants as you have before?" Chael's shoulders slumped; the knight still didn't understand.

"Yes, I can use the surrounding vegetation and even animals but there is a fundamental difference in power between that and a human being. Taking the energy from plants and lesser animals is like drinking watered down wine. And the demons are useless altogether." Chael was exasperated as well as fearful for the knight's reaction. But Andon didn't look put off by Chael's Dark abilities or deterred from the task. He looked contemplative like he was searching for a solution to a complex riddle.

"I see," he said at last. "And these half-breeds," anger pierced his voice as he said the word, "they won't help either?" Chael shook his head, which had been a disconcerting discovery. In the metaphysical sense they were apparently more demon than human and whatever life energy that was left in them was useless to Chael. Andon dismounted and drew his steel with his left hand, Chael moved to stop him, but he stepped back and raised the tip of his sword. "I have trained with my left hand since I was a child." He said firmly and executed a complicated sword scale in his off hand. It might have impressed an amateur, but Chael wasn't one. It was slow and Andon's technique was sloppy, but the point was made. The knight wasn't going to abandon the people down there to the whims of Dark cultists.

"Fine," Chael sighed, and Sir Andon breathed out a sigh of his own in relief. He then turned to Rina and started digging around in her robes. The knight looked horrified at the intrusion which gave Chael a wicked grin. After a minute he pulled out two small vials of liquid and handed them to Andon. "Drink one of these and keep the other on your person. I don't know what they do exactly but I'm guessing they enhance you physically like the one you took before." Andon eyed the small vial of liquid with fearful distrust. "It won't be as bad as last time," Chael added quickly. "Your body will be more used to it now and the effects won't feel as dramatic." Andon still didn't look too pleased with the idea but with a glance down at his right arm he grimaced and drank half the bottle's contents.

For a moment he looked unsteady almost like he was about to pass out like Rina, then a silent resolute strength washed over him. He flexed his left hand and Chael could tell that the knight felt power there. Andon's right hand, however, seemed to shrivel up more, and the straighter and stronger Andon stood the more curled and malignant his right hand became. They both noticed the change and Chael gave him his best sympathetic look and Andon waved him off.

"What's done is done," he said adamantly. Chael hesitated and then nodded once. They discussed strategy and the disposition of Rina and decided on a course of action. They left their small hill overlooking the Fhaerstead and headed north for a few leagues and after only an hour of searching they found what they were after. Nestling in another hillside was a small natural cave no larger than a wolf's den.

Chael gently placed Rina inside and covered the exit with some brush. He then reached out with one of his knives and carved the symbols he could remember from his cell; he had stared at them long enough. He didn't know if they had to be etched in a certain way or if they needed to be in a certain order, but he did the best he could and had to hope that nothing Dark would stray this far North. Then he turned to Michik.

"I need you to stay here buddy," he told his dog mournfully. Chael could instantly see the refusal writ all over Michik's lovably gruesome face. He pointed into the small cave until the wolf slowly turned his head to look. "She's part of our pack now. That's your fault," Chael chided unseriously. "She needs you to protect her, can you do that for me Meeshee?"

Michik stamped his remaining front paw, it was really more of a hop, and then snorted. Azure eyes searched his own, and he knew that his dog understood his duty. Without another word Chael turned and strode South, back to Fhaerstead.

Chapter 38

Present Day

The genius of the plan was in its simplicity, or at least that's what Chael had been telling himself over and over as they got nearer to the town. Chael was supposed to hide near the mostly deserted Northern wall while gathering as much mundane life essence as he could while Andon went to the Eastern entrance and caused as big of a commotion as he could live through. With the defenders distracted all Chael had to do was scale a wall that exceeded ten paces in height and kill a score of the Black Hand and steal the power of their souls. Simple.

Chael devoured the life of everything around him as he waited. There would be a patch of dead earth for the better part of a league North of Fhaerstead for decades. He consumed until his soul was full of the energy, swirling like a wispy black tornado inside his spirit. Chael had to explain to Andon earlier that simply taking a lot of essence from lesser life was not the equivalent of that of a human life. The life energy inside a person was richer and denser than anything he could take from a tree or a hiding mole in the ground. It was more powerful on a fundamental level and no amount of grass or wheat could make up the difference. When he was full, he compressed the energy inside his soul and waited, a dark circle of death surrounding him.

Sir Andon worked quickly. Chael couldn't see what he was doing but from the sounds emanating from Fhaerstead and their plans he knew that he was riding around on their borrowed horse opening cages and urging the people to scatter. Chael hoped that more than a few of the demons and half-breeds had lost their heads but he didn't have time to speculate, his time was up.

With a giant running leap reinforced by the power he had taken from natural life around him, he vaulted into the air and latched on to the wooden palisade that had been built above the stone wall. His hands bled from a score of tiny cuts as he gripped the rough carved wood. Slowly he climbed by just the strength of his fingertips until he reached the sharpened tips of the wooden fortification.

Chael pushed all the power he could contain into his arms and vaulted over the top of the palisade and landed on the roof of a building next to the wall. The sound of tearing cloth made him wince as he fell, and he looked back and saw the edge of his cloak had a new ribbon of torn fabric near the bottom hem. *Great,* he huffed internally, cursing the Dark cultists below.

Chael dropped down, as silent as a cat, in the space between two buildings; even his boots seemed to resist squelching in the thick mud of the street. He couldn't risk open combat, not yet. If they found him, there was no telling how much power they could bring to bear before he could kill enough of them to make a difference. He slid along the wall of the building he had landed on, sticking to the shadows. as he neared the edge of the building facing the main street, the true daftness of his plan became apparent.

There were perhaps fifty black cloaked cultists bustling about, oblivious to his presence. A few barked orders and pointed but most were carting around wheelbarrows or had their hands laden with wooden crates. Distantly he could hear screams coming from a building on the far end of the street, Fhaerstead was not large so he should have heard them more clearly. *Underground, then,* he surmised.

"Let's get this over with," he muttered under his breath. He waited until an unencumbered cultist happened by his hiding place, and he lashed out, covering the man's mouth with his left hand. He squeezed with unnatural strength muffling the surprised screams emanating from his throat.

Chael dragged him back into the depths of the shadows near the wall and cut his throat. He made sure that the blood didn't spill over any of the black garment as he did, he needed it clean. With reluctance he removed his trusty green cloak and rolled up, he tucked it neatly away in the shadows out of sight. Chael did his best to at least cover the body in the mud that Fhaerstead called a street. It wouldn't pass even a cursory inspection of the alley, but he didn't plan on being stealthy for long.

Casually, Chael strolled out into the alley clothed in black. The cloak was a little big on him and it scratched unpleasantly at his neck, but it would do. He picked up a random crate and began walking toward the sound of the screaming. Idly, he remembered the words of one of his former masters at Khalim's school. 'Act like you belong and no one will question your presence.' So, he walked with purpose right past one of the cultists ordering people around.

"Hey you! Where are you going with that?" he yelled at Chael with the air of pompous authority that only comes when the intellectually small are given authority over their peers. Chael paused, not turning, trying to decide his best course of action.

It was a little early to start fighting. He had drained life energy from the cultist he killed a moment ago and that was helpful, but it would burn quickly if he had to defend himself from everyone here. "I said come, worm!"

Apparently, the Black Hand and Khalim hired from the same pool of insulting instructors, he thought wistfully. Then again, maybe they did.

Just as Chael started to turn and face the fury of middle management, the sounds of metal on metal and shouts of freedom rose up from beyond the Eastern gate. Half of the Black Hand that milled about the town, dropped their packages and went running to check on the sound of the disturbance. Even the pompous halfwit harassing him turned to see the cause of the ruckus.

"Good enough!" Chael announced, not bothering to be quiet anymore.

He finished his turn and hurled the wooden crate at the man who had stopped him. The crate flew with the force of a diving falcon, and it smashed into his face with a satisfying crunch of broken bone. Chael followed up the attack by immediately throwing two of his knives at the closest pair of cultists nearby. Each one buried itself to the hilt into his enemies and still carried enough momentum to send them flying through the air.

He shed the black cloak muttering, "useless," under his breath. He strode casually down the street toward the remaining cultists. Several of them had seen him and were now preparing weapons but most who had remained were still looking East.

As he walked by the leader with the broken face Chael unceremoniously stabbed him in the neck with his falchion, he needed these three to die quickly. Four cultists rushed him, producing wavy curved daggers from within their robes. To his relief none of them reached for elixirs or alchemical combat constructs. This was going to be easier than he thought.

One by one they reached him swinging their more theatrical than practical weapons, and each in turn fell to the ground gushing blood and clawing at mortal wounds. The entire exchange took only a few seconds.

There were perhaps a dozen men in black robes remaining in the central street of the town, from what he could hear Andon was leading those outside on a rather glorious chase. Of those who remained, none were oblivious to his presence now. Wicked eyes stared under dark hoods as they slowly advanced. To his dismay, half of them pulled vials of liquid from their robes.

Four were the common silvery alcohol-based elixirs but two were a deep blood red. Those gave Chael an uneasy feeling in his stomach. Miniature crossbows flashed from two black cloaks, and they sent their bolts whistling at Chael's chest. With unnatural speed and grace, he swatted them out of the air with a single swipe of his falchion.

The four who consumed the more average looking elixirs shot out at him as soon as the crossbows were fired. The alchemicals they drank gave them speed and agility that nearly matched his own and he soon found himself pressed by more of the wavy daggers.

They struck out at him like serpents, staying out of the superior reach of his sword but using their enhanced speed to launch strikes when they sensed an opening. Chael was faster and much more skilled than any two of them but against four it was everything he could do just to keep their knives at bay.

Darkness! Chael cursed and sprinted towards the door. No arrows or crossbow bolts; that's something, Chael thought.

The life energy from the dead cultist would burn that away with more ease than sewing up the wound in his side but it would cost him additional power. The three to whom he had just given mortal wounds were also stubbornly clinging to life. Their fate was sealed, no healer no matter how skilled could help them now. But they could delay passing on just long enough to not be useful to him, Chael strongly suspected they were doing just that out of spite.

The fight with the four alchemically enhanced cultists was taking too long. The longer it lasted the more power he lost and the more opportunities they had to encircle and overwhelm him. He had to change the rules of the fight.

Stars above, he thought before doing the only thing that sprang to his mind. It was foolhardy, dangerous and had little chance of success. So about average as far as his plans went. He pretended to slow just slightly from the poison, which wasn't all that difficult to feign, it still felt like bolts of lightning in his veins.

The nearest acolyte of the Black Hand seized the opening and struck in hard and fast with her dagger. Chael deflected the blow high but allowed it to penetrate his shoulder. The same white-hot pain scorched his chest and snaked down his arm, but he bit it back. With the knife still embedded in him he turned sharply and wrenched it out of her grip and advanced on the next closest cultist. He received another slash on his arm as he did so but in exchange, he opened up his target from collar to waist.

"One disarmed and one dead," he muttered grimly through the waves of pain. He found that his right arm wasn't responding to his commands like it should have and for the first time in the fight he became genuinely afraid they might actually kill him. But finally, he felt two more sources of life essence burst forth from their human hosts.

He retreated back from the fight and had to block another crossbow projectile as he prepared to take in the new source of power. He breathed it in greedily and almost immediately strength returned to his right arm. With one motion he pulled the dagger from his shoulder and launched it at its former owner's face. Newly empowered he stormed back into the fight, the once lithe and precise movements of his adversaries now seemed clumsy and slow. With only a few strokes of his sword two heads fell to the muddy street. He didn't want to wait for them to die.

The remaining cultists looked to the two who had drunk the mysterious red liquid and back at Chael. Without a word they fled down the street toward the gate seeking easier prey elsewhere. Perhaps someone locked in a cage, Chael would have to wait and kill them later.

"I know who you are, demon slayer," the cultist on the left hissed. His voice was like a sodden blanket full of crawling insects, the very sound of it made his skin itch. "The Lady would be upset if we killed you." His partner nodded to the statement, but they both began advancing on Chael.

"But," he cackled maliciously, "we are under contract of the High Minister at the moment." He gave Chael a devious grin like he had just solved some profound puzzle. "I think destroying his greatest obstacle is acceptable under the terms of our arrangement." His partner nodded again, an evil grin plastered on his face. As they approached, they spread out until they were several paces apart but mere feet from Chael.

"I suppose this is the part where I say something defiantly clever," Chael proclaimed, feigning a sense of detached calm. Internally he was actually quite nervous about what these two might be capable of. They clearly knew who he was and must have had an idea about what he could do. And yet they seemed to think they were more than a match, and he had no idea what that liquid contained so maybe they were.

His mind flashed briefly to the ash-smoke sword construct that he had used back in Kazaam, if they carried one of those, he was doomed but that potion wasn't blood red so he doubted those were about to appear.

They were close enough that Chael could smell their breath and as the weary seconds ticked by nothing happened. They just stood there staring at him, smiling like madmen. He took a cautious step forward, and they calmly stepped back. He tried it again and received the same results.

Every time he moved, they mirrored his movement staying precisely out of reach with gracefully precise strides, all the while grinning like this was their favorite game. Alarms were going off in Chael's head, they were playing at some sort of game, but he didn't know the rules.

Slowly, like sap running down a tree, blood began dripping from between their teeth. Their grins didn't falter, if anything they grew wider as the trickle of blood became a stream and then a torrent. Red blood began to drip from their chins and their smiles became laughter as it came pouring out of their eyes as well.

They were cackling riotously, all the while blood began to spray from every pore in their body, leaving their faces ghostly pale but for the stains of red. White hair slithered out of their hoods as they seemed to age a century in the space of seconds, and their skin tightened and adhered to their skulls giving them a skeletal cast to their face.

Finally, after what seemed an eternity of laughter and bleeding, they stopped and looked on at Chael seriously. Their eyes glowed a familiar shade of azure green. The blood was gone. They each held crimson steel greatswords. The metal looked as solid and sharp as any natural blade he had ever seen but at the same time it seemed to flow as if occupying two different fundamental aspects of reality at once. Chael unconsciously stepped back, but this time they didn't mirror the movement.

The men who drank those vials were dead, he didn't need to use his senses to know that. Their revenants stood before him, skeletal frames and paper skin but not lacking for strength for it was the Dark that sustained them. As one they attacked, and Chael knew immediately that he was no match for them.

Chapter 39

3 Years Ago

Cooper and Mason stared at him like a particularly appetizing meal, Chael wasn't sure he liked the feeling. He was staring at a fawn, laying in the grass about a dozen paces away. Cooper was furiously scribbling notes on a pad he had brought, and Mason was urging him on with his hands. Chael let his spiritual senses drift over to the small deer and he felt the power of life drifting lazily, like a slow river through its body as it slept.

"Now take it," Cooper commanded in his irritating nasally voice. Chael suppressed the sudden urge to punch him and reached out with his mind. While he did so he also physically reached out with his hand though he was too far away to actually touch the deer. He closed his will around the flowing streams of energy he sensed in the deer and as he did, he tightened his outstretched hand into a fist.

Mason and Cooper had both chided him that such pantomimes were totally unnecessary, but it gave Chael a sense of control and helped him concentrate. He felt his will push against the life of the fawn and watched as the essence slowed to a near standstill in its body. It was on the verge of snapping and when it did, the deer would be dead, and its life force would give him further power.

This creature stands as a dried leaf before the weight of a mountain, break it! The sudden intrusion of thoughts alien to his own made Chael instinctively fight back to reassert his own authority in his mind. As he did the pressure on the fawn slackened to a pathetic breeze and he finally gave up. Chael cursed and threw one of his knives into a nearby tree. Mason whistled at the display, but Cooper took on an even more exasperating tone and clicked his tongue.

"What happened?" he demanded, frustration obvious in his face.

"That…" Chael hesitated. He had told Mason about the presence in his mind whenever he exercised the strange powers he possessed, but he didn't want to discuss such things in front of Cooper. After a moment's pause he continued, "that thing inside me spoke again." Cooper made an irritated clucking sound and Mason gave him a glare.

"It's not a thing, Chael," Mason said gently. Since the experience down in the core of the mountain several years ago Mason had taken an even greater interest in Chael, often accompanying him on missions with no greater purpose than to chat.

After Darrik's death, it was nice to have someone to talk to, even if he was a zealot. He had even confided in Mason about his growing understanding of his abilities and his interactions with the mysterious cultist became even more frequent, and regrettably they started to often involve Cooper. They brought him books to read on arcane knowledge and musings on the nature of life and death. Some of the tomes even had speculation on the scope and limits of his powers. He had repeatedly asked them if there were others like himself and they always said no. *Then who wrote the books?* he often thought, but he never voiced the thought aloud.

"The voice isn't some invading force trying to control your mind," Mason continued. His usual disturbing smile was gone, and he looked down at Chael with what seemed like genuine, father-like affection.

"It is you, as much as your arm is you. The voice is your mind's reaction to your awakening abilities. Your powers want to grow, and it scares you, so your brain has created a construct to fight against. The voice." Mason's words were reassuring and soft, but he spoke firmly and with absolute confidence that he was right. "Stop fighting it and you will see."

Chael wasn't so sure. To a certain degree he was, Chael knew that if he stopped fighting the voice, he would have greater access to power. He had caught fleeting glimpses of how great and terrible that power had the ability to be, and it unnerved him almost as much as the voice did.

Chael was skeptical but curiosity won out and he placed his senses over the fawn. But this time, as he reached out, he also relaxed himself, easing his mind to the influence of his abilities.

He immediately noticed that his sense of the deer was much sharper, and the small veins of flowing energy were clearer and more distinct. Even from this distance, and with the animal still very much alive, he could actually feel the energy and precisely how it would add to his power. Chael found that he liked the feeling.

The power made him the arbiter over life and death and the feeling was intoxicating. Inside him the voice only uttered one word, *break!* Effortlessly, the life of the fawn was extinguished, and this time Chael didn't bother raising his hand.

Chael felt cold, though it had nothing to do with the temperature. Six weeks had passed since that fateful day in the meadow with the fawn. Forcibly he had broken down all the mental barriers barring him from the full use of his power and since that day he had not heard a single word from the voice.

"Perhaps Mason was right," he whispered softly to Michik who sat at his side.

The wolf had been more unruly and less obedient these last weeks, Chael would have to start disciplining it more harshly he supposed.

Obedience had not been a problem until recently and he had never needed to train the animal with pain. Obviously, that had been a mistake, his leniency had produced a wolf that was lazy and entitled. He would have to remedy that when he had time.

They were standing in an overgrown field about two leagues outside of Kamaar, the North most of the Republics of Sharaad. Despite the warm summer temperature he shivered, he needed to kill something. His soul hungered for more power and its absence left him hungry and chill.

Patience, he told himself. That time would come soon enough.

Absently, he reached out and stole the life from a nearby rabbit, it was like a single drop of water on the tongue of a man dying under the desert sun. The impotency and weakness of the power insulted him, and he wished he could kill the animal again just out of spite. He wanted to consume the entire countryside but held himself in check. Not only would that look suspicious, but it also felt uncouth, like lowering himself to a lesser meal when a feast was going to march straight into his mouth. As if on cue that feast announced its approach.

Kamaar was the final city of the republics to resist Khalim's rule. Aside from Kazaam, which Khalim openly ruled, he had installed puppets to sit on the ruling seats in Shara and Ahman. Kamaar was ruled by House Kamaar, but that title was ceremonial.

Since time immemorial, the governing house of Kamaar had adopted the name of the city since coming to power. The current House that adopted that title had enjoyed an impressive run of over a century and were loath to give it up now to some Kaazan upstart. For years the heads of the house had kept themselves locked away inside the depths of the heavily guarded city. They resisted bribes, threats, and had even survived several assassination attempts. Chael himself had even been dispatched once but only managed to kill a decoy.

This time however was different. The house patriarch had died a week prior, and their own house tradition dictated that they march in procession to an ancient burial site outside the city. It was said that the sacred ground was the resting place of the ancient kings who ruled united Sharaad before it broke into the city states.

This was House Kamaar's great test, if they ignored ancient tradition now and hid like cowards behind walls and guards, they would only be seen as weak and ineffectual by their subordinate houses. That lack of a united front would shatter their resistance to Khalim and the city would shortly fall. So, they planned a great procession with scores of guards, an open display of defiance to their would-be ruler. And unto them that ruler had sent only Chael and his wolf.

Trumpets blared as the massive gates of Kamaar opened and a wooden bridge lowered into place. The procession began with a five wide column of knights in resplendent shining armor. Chael snarled, that sort of livery was a Fhaelan tradition, and Chael found it cowardly.

The knights marched in practiced synchronicity; each one held a massive glaive that looked like a scimitar attached to the end of a spear. Flapping regally behind the blade of the glaive was the banner of House Kamaar, which depicted the city, but the outer wall was contorted into the shape of a crown.

Behind the knights marched the more mundane soldiers of the city, clad in leathers with a short practical arming sword and a shield with the same emblem emblazoned across the front. A trio of armored knights on horseback led the way for the family who all rode lazily on horses of their own flanking a decorated wagon that held the body of their deceased patriarch. All totaled, Chael counted twenty knights and about twice as many leather-clad armsmen.

"Come," he commanded Michik who obeyed, tail clinging to his back legs and still. Together they casually walked across the field until they were standing firmly in the road directly in front of the armored procession. A slight breeze pushed the edges of his cloak causing it to flutter slightly to the side.

Aside from the light rustling of armor and whispered confusion, there was silence until the heir to House Kamaar rode forward and sneered down at him from atop a brilliant white stallion. He was dressed in fine flowing silks and carried an expression of haughty superiority, though he sat on his horse only a few paces from Chael. That was his second mistake, his first was simply existing in the first place and finding himself in Chael's path.

"You must be one of Khalim's pet rats!" he called derisively to him, eliciting a ring of hollow laughter from his host. "Come, deliver your message and be gone!"

Chael said nothing and continued to simply watch the foppish noble with ill-concealed contempt. Frustrated, the heir urged his horse closer a few steps.

"Didn't you hear me boy! Deliver your message, surely you don't intend to simply intimidate us!" As he spoke, he waved his hand at the small army behind him, and they laughed obediently.

Once again Chael said nothing, and now the noble was beginning to become unsure of himself. Surely, this lone rogue and his wolf couldn't threaten him with his soldiers nearby, but Chael could tell that he was getting nervous. He was about to turn his steed around, and that simply wouldn't do.

Before the heir could turn his horse simply died. A look of stunned horror stole over the face of the man as he fell from his crumpling mount and onto the road. Casually, Chael strolled over and stabbed him in the neck.

The power washed over him like cooling salves soothing a burn. He savored the feeling, completely ignoring the reaction from the soldiers in front of him. Their time would come.

As quickly as the power flowed into him so too did the hunger return, the life from this one noble was woefully insufficient; he needed more. The presence, now more of an impression than an audible voice agreed.

Smiling, Chael darted out into the midst of the soldiers arrayed against him. He felt fast and powerful, and he slipped around their inept attacks like water breaking around a boulder, and like water he flowed. Soldiers fell dead all around him adding to his power as he danced to his own glorious music warming his former chill on their blood.

Through the ecstasy, the ever present gnaw of hunger demanded more, and he obliged, by the time he stopped and surveyed the battlefield with his natural eyes all he could discern was a sea of corpses and a handful of trembling unarmed nobles. He felt an urge to reach out once again and feel their life essence and he obliged, drunk on power. As usual, though he could sense the power inside the frightened idiots trembling before him, the energy inside them was locked away behind something like transparent glass.

Then Chael paused; this wasn't usual. The power was still out of reach, but the barrier preventing him from simply ripping out of them with his will felt weaker. *Accept your authority,* his own voice whispered to him. Chael felt something begin to slide into place inside his soul, one final link between him and power he so desperately sought.

As he accepted the mantle of power that was his birthright the world around him began to die. Grass and trees withered and snapped, even the stones of the Kamaar's walls seemed to grow grayer and sicklier. He was close now; if he simply crossed one more line, his authority over death would be complete. He could strip the entire world of life and satiate the burning hunger that consumed him.

Distantly, he felt another life apart from the shaking humans rightfully bowing before him. As he approached the final evolution of his ability, godhood he supposed this life pushed against his conscience and disrupted his concentration. Of their own accord the tendrils of his Dark power snaked out and had stolen the life around him and now they were wrapped around Michik's neck.

The will of the wolf was strong, stronger than a non-sentient being had any right to be. As his power stressed his life essence to breaking, Michik simply looked up at him with pleading round eyes. Then his dog, finding no mercy there, slumped his head and gave up.

Michik's life snapped like a dry twig and his life energy joined the hurricane of power that was building in front of Chael. When that happened something in his mind surged. A lost sense of himself, buried below the mantle of power that he had willingly accepted, reasserted itself at the surface.

Chael gaped in horror at Michik's lifeless form, tears welling in his eyes. The presence in his head screamed in anger, demanding to retake control over his body.

NO! Chael yelled at the unwelcome passenger. *Mason was wrong, you aren't part of me. You're a parasite and I won't give you control again.* The building torrent of Dark power burst and dissipated into fine mist and floated away, as it did the terrible hunger began to ebb and Chael expelled more and more of the stolen life essence.

When he was done, he felt hollow but no longer numb. As he knelt down next to his dead companion, he prayed to the Living Stars that the numbness would return. They were cruelly silent. With trembling hands, Chael carefully scooped Michik up into his arms.

The wolf was almost as big as he was and without the aid of his power, he could barely hold him, but he strained until he could drape the dead wolf over his shoulder. Chael gave one passing look at the remaining nobles he had come to kill.

They were all frightened and confused. They had no direct sense of the powers that had gathered here or the struggle that ensued, but secondary effects were not lost on them. They were standing behind an army of corpses that this stranger had killed in seconds, and those bodies were amid a ring of corruption and death that spread as far as the eye could see around the main gate of Kamaar. Shaking every bit as much as they were, Chael turned and fled.

Chapter 40

Present Day

Crimson steel forged from blood and empowered by death sliced through space toward Chael. Reality seemed to warp around it, moving out of the way in shimmering distortions in the air as it passed. Chael dodged, and a second came down upon him with astounding speed and he had to dive out of its path.

He immediately rolled to his feet and faced the two revenants in front of him. They shambled like corpses but somehow possessed speed that rivaled his own, even when bursting with life essence. Their weapons oozed a terrible aura of death and decay, like the rotting corpses of a thousand demons. But it was their eyes that stood out most to him, they were like Michik, like himself. In those eyes he saw a glimpse into a future he had given up everything to avoid.

They came for him again. The first tore across the ground with lightning speed and blood red sword held in front of him like a lance. The other leaped into the air and was coming down in a terrifying arc, both hands clasping the hilt of his weapon like he was attempting to split the very ground.

Chael had a fraction of a second to consume more life essence and move. The second undead cultist crashed into the street and left a crater the size of a small house while the other stole a glancing blow against Chael's arm as he rushed past with his strike.

Pain erupted from the wound like the hand of death squeezing his arm just below the shoulder. He winced for a moment but then the pain abruptly stopped. He was used to his power healing him of fairly grievous wounds, but this was quite a bit faster than he was used to. His enemies seemed content to wait for a moment and he chanced a quick glance at the cut. A line of black with subtle hints of sickly green stretched across his arm and was maybe as deep as a fingernail. Instinctively, he forcibly pushed the life essence into his arm and to his horror there was a void around the wound like the flesh no longer existed.

"Darkness!" he exclaimed, terrified, and caught the hint of an unnatural cadaverous smile.

They struck out again, and he slipped the first by a hair and brought up his falchion to catch the second. As the crimson steel hit his own the metal of the falchion shattered. Shards of steel from Chael's sword exploded outward in all directions, cutting Chael's flesh and embedding themselves in the surrounding buildings. Fortunately for him it was ordinary steel that his powers could heal, but he was still covered in lacerations and blood. Instinct alone saved him from the follow-up as he ducked and leaped away like a frightened rabbit. A few of his shards embedded themselves in his opponents as well but they had no blood left to bleed and if they were affected at all, they gave no sign.

Inside his mind, the presence laughed at his misfortune. He wanted to remind it that they shared a body and if he died it died but he couldn't spare the attention. He was desperately dodging relentless attacks from dead men and their steel hungered to drag him down into the depths of the Dark with them.

There is another way, its ghostly unnatural mockery of his own voice told him. The power that circulated through his body and his own desperation gave his presence bold confidence. It understood the nature of these creatures and the energy that fueled them. It explained to Chael that it was identical to his own, only they empowered themselves with the essence of their own souls mixed with clever alchemicals.

Their sacrifice makes them strong, such is the nature of things, it cooed seductively into his mind. His presence gave him the solution and then explained to him the cost. To continue facing these creatures was certain death, but Chael soon found out that the power to stop them was a death of a different kind.

"No!" Chael responded bitterly to the air while retreating from yet another flurry of blurring red strikes. The voice didn't respond, and Chael got the distinct impression that it was waiting for something. It didn't take long to find out what that was.

Outside of the Eastern gate of Fhaerstead a horse screamed in agony and Chael attuned his hearing. He heard the final cries of pain of Andon's mount and the thud as both rider and horse hit the ground. The battle outside was over, without the horse Andon couldn't stay alive out there, not with dozens of cultists and a lame right arm.

Choose! The voice cried shrilly in his mind, but it really wasn't a choice at all. They were both going to die in seconds.

Time seemed to slow to a crawl as Chael searched deep inside himself again. He unlocked the gates keeping the full weight of his power from overtaking him. For a moment he looked back on his fireside conversation with Aelisa, he had scoffed at the idea of a Darkborn not out of incredulity but out of denial. Now to save himself, to have the power over his enemies he had to accept the mantle. And what was the Darkborn if not a general?

The life essence inside him burst with new strength, if before it was a fire now it resembled a towering inferno inside his soul. His movements became faster and more graceful, and his senses attuned to an impossible precision. But in his mind was a battle of will, he and his presence met in a battlefield of dreams and thought for control. Their battle wasn't fought with steel or fist but with will. The indomitable ancient will of Darkness itself and Chael. Outside, a revenant struck with the force of death, and he raised a palm.

"Stop." Chael barely whispered through gritted teeth as he continued to wrestle with the voice. But to his shock the revenant obeyed. It stood there, less than a foot from slicing him in half frozen. "Go!" Chael breathed barely able to form the words. "Kill everyone in black, and then I shall release you from my service." More than words, Chael poured intention into the command. They were to eliminate the remaining members of the Black Hand and then their souls were to return to the Dark. The two revenants immediately turned and with their unnatural speed, they flew out toward the gate. Chael didn't watch to see what they would do, he couldn't.

The presence was winning the struggle for their body. Chael pulled up images of the last time he gave control over and fixed on the memory of Michik lying dead in his arms. Pure animal fury ignited in his soul, and he pushed back against the voice he shoved it away for a glorious moment and felt freedom again. But in response there was only deep malicious laughter.

A weight like a mountain settled on his shoulders driving him to his knees. The full intention of Darkness bore down on him crushing his anger and flattening him against the recesses of his own mind. Chael was being squeezed and if he didn't do something, the last of his will would be abolished and he truly would rise as the Darkborn.

With his last gasps of control, he let go of everything. The mantle and the life essence inside him, he shed it like a heavy cloak and as he did the pressure eased and eventually died. *You will never be strong enough to defeat your enemies. When you are most desperate, you will come back to me. It is inevitable.* Its last word trailed off and died as the final wisps of power left his system. Chael collapsed to a knee suddenly exhausted, but he smiled anyway.

"Maybe," he said aloud. "But not today."

The revenants did as commanded, and when Chael finally gathered the strength to go check outside, he found Andon standing in a field of corpses wearing black cloaks. He walked over to where two emaciated bodies lay, the revenants were even more frightening now that they were truly dead and where the weapons must have been, now only bloodstains in the grass remained.

"Friends of yours?" Andon said weakly. He was leaning against a tree and but for a few new nicks and bruises had come out of the fight fairly intact. Or at least as intact as he began the fight, Chael thought darkly.

"You could say that," Chael responded. "Can you walk?"

"If I have to," the knight answered a bit more brightly than before.

"Good, then you'll be able to round up any priests that survived. I'm going to go fetch Rina." Sir Andon nodded to him, and Chael began walking, "it would be a lot easier if we still had a horse," he added slyly under his breath.

"Hey! I heard that!" Andon called after him, putting his hand to his chest as if wounded. Chael let a smile pass his lips for just a moment as he turned and jogged away.

After a few hours, Chael, Rina, and Michik all made it back to Fhaerstead, Michik hobbling on one leg a little more lamely than Chael thought truly genuine. Chael suspected it was to compensate for Chael's own slow pace while carrying Rina. After all that had happened before, he felt it best not to rely on his power for a little while, so he was using his plain mortal strength. He supposed that from Michik's perspective, being used to Chael being capable of such impressive physical feats, struggling to carry a skinny girl for a few leagues must have looked especially pathetic.

When they arrived, Sir Andon Knight of the Realm had everything running quite smoothly. The once caged refugees and citizens of Fhaerstead were hard at work preparing their small settlement for the inevitability of attack from Khalim's forces at the capitol. Andon had many digging a wide trench in front of the walls and others were collecting the materials to make arrows and spears. Inside, Andon was drilling about thirty men and women with long sticks on spear tactics.

"As one!" Andon yelled in a commanding voice. The would-be spearmen all stepped forward in unison holding out their spears. They were arrayed in three columns of ten and were arranged in such a way as to make a wall of spears.

Back at the school, they never really focused on learning tactics that relied on teams, but they did learn various strategies that might be employed against them on a battlefield. This formation was among them. Its strength came from a near impenetrable wall of spears that was effective against both cavalry and foot soldiers. Its weakness was that it was difficult to maneuver, and well-trained professional soldiers to pull off. Since they were protecting a fortified town, the former wasn't going to be much of a problem, but these people were hardly professional soldiers. Chael grimaced, if Khalim sent more half-breeds to take the city it was going to be a bloodbath.

When Andon saw him approach, he told his spearmen-in-training to take a short break and walked over to Chael wearing a false smile. He kept that smile securely pinned to his face like a mask as he spoke.

"They're doomed," he admitted sadly, before Chael could even ask. He nodded his head in agreement but didn't trust himself to say the words out loud, even though Andon was freely admitting the truth he still may get upset if Chael genuinely predicted their odds of a successful siege defense.

"Did any of the Order chapter make it?" Chael asked hopefully. Andon's smile flickered into a scowl for an instant before he answered.

"Oh yes," he said darkly through his fake smile. He paused to give encouragement to one of his trainees and waited until he left before continuing. "Most of them fled South the moment they knew it was safe," Andon spat. He seethed for a moment with a rage uncharacteristic of the usually congenial knight, but after only a few seconds his anger subsided, and his face softened. "A few did stay," he added, clearly trying to force a sense of hope into the words. "They're working on whatever combat alchemicals they can scrape together. I told them about Rina, and they said she should be fine but to bring her to them when we could."

"I best be going then," Chael replied and lifted Rina again. Andon nodded to him and marched back to the training area calling his spearmen back to formation. Chael turned off the main street and headed in the direction of the Order house.

Chapter 41

Present Day

The chapter house of the Order in Fhaerstead wasn't nearly so grand as the one in the capitol but it was no less ostentatious. Perhaps even more so given the humble nature of the buildings that surrounded it. Chael had Michik wait outside—he didn't need to be too obvious about his identity—and walked into a wooden main hall with a large brass eight-pointed star set into the planks. There were still gems and other colorful and reflective materials covering the walls, but the stained-glass windows had been smashed, probably out of spite by the Black Hand, Chael surmised.

The tables and chairs that might have held food and drink and dozens more priests and priestesses were now laden with bits of iron and brass as well as powders and liquids of many colors. The few order members that were left, six by Chael's count, were busy constructing what combat capable artifices they could muster in the town's defense.

An old man with a great white beard hanging down past his belly was tittering over a series of copper and glass tubes that boiled and steamed and produced a dripping gray liquid at one end. He was clearly the oldest among the remaining Order members and Chael guessed he was in charge, at least nominally given the flight of the others.

"Priest!" he called gruffly, half hiding his face in the shadow of his cloak. He was hoping to get through this exchange without formally introducing himself, but the old man's eyes scanned his face for a moment and instant recognition dawned over his features.

Chael sighed before continuing, "She is of your Order, and she's been unconscious for a day, can you help her?" He lowered Rina down onto the least cluttered area of the table that he could find and looked at the priest expectantly. The old man gave him one more appraising look before turning down to examine Rina. He poked and prodded her with his fingers and inspected her mouth and lifted her eyelids, muttering to himself all the while. Finally, he deigned to look back at Chael and scowled at him.

"She's fine," the priest said shrilly. "She took too many elixirs in too short a span." He tsked with his tongue while shaking his head as if scolding his least favorite grandchild. "She's too young and has too low of a tolerance for the amount of elixir she surely took."

He crossed the room and spoke to a priestess too quietly for Chael to hear but the woman nodded and rushed off to room deeper in the chapter house and returned with a small dropper filled with clear liquid. The priest smiled at his colleague and thanked her but gave Chael another scowl as he walked by. He then unceremoniously pried open her eyes and squeezed out a few drops of the liquid.

"She will regain consciousness in moments," he said matter-of-factly as if he was announcing tonight's meal, rather than explaining that the young woman would miraculously awaken. But true to his word, within seconds Rina began to stir.

"Thank you," Chael said as graciously as he could. The old priest charged up to him as close as he could get without bumping noses and glared hatefully.

"I voted to kill you," he sneered, so close that Chael could feel the man's breath on his face. Chael took a step forward, forcing the priest onto his back foot and pushing him up against his bubbling contraption. Chael stared seriously into his eyes before leaning close and whispering into the man's ear.

"Then why don't you?" The priest paled as Chael stepped back and gave him a wink. He then collected Rina, who was just starting to come to herself, and ushered her out the door. As they left, he could hear the spiteful priest finally sputtering out some retort to his back before he closed the door behind him.

As soon as they were outside Rina was immediately accosted by Michik. He whined in his concerned tone as he alternated between sniffing her and licking her hands. Chael was forced to physically restrain his dog lest he completely bull over the still slightly dazed woman.

"Oh, it's good to see you too, Meeshee," Rina said in a slightly airy voice. As she reached down to scratch his head, Chael noticed a slight tremble in her hand but dismissed it as she was still fully recovering from her ordeal.

"Are you okay?" he asked, trying to mask his true concern. She gave him a smile and nodded.

"I'm a little out of sorts but I'm still awake enough to take this." She reached beneath her grimy robes and pulled out a book with the same eight-pointed star of the Order emblazoned across the front. "That was the First Prefect!" she exclaimed brightly, holding up the book for him to see. "This is... was," she corrected herself. "His personal scriptorium! It was just sitting on the table, and I nicked it when he went over to threaten you." She beamed at him like she had won some sort of prize instead of stealing an old man's book. "It has all of the alchemical recipes of Order elixirs as well as different constructs and even wardings! All with his personal notes!"

Just then he heard a stream of curses from within the Order house and the old priest came storming out, his skin practically steaming with anger. Rina quickly tucked the book back within her robes.

"Where is it?" he demanded, looking from Chael to Rina. His face contorted as he came to some sort of conclusion and then sneered at Chael again. "I understand now, this is all some Dark plot of your design. You come here feigning to be our savior only to steal the Order's secrets for your own Dark experiments!"

He was practically raving now, and Chael was afraid that he was going to have to physically subdue him before a call came up from the Southern gate. Glad for the excuse to leave, he grabbed Rina's arm and together they walked over to investigate the commotion.

One of the few remaining town watchmen was on the simple parapet overlooking the Southern approach, and he was calling that a stranger was walking up to the gate. *Strange,* Chael thought as he walked. If they were coming from the Capitol, it would most likely have come from the Eastern gate, not the Southern.

Rina tugged at him, and he realized he was still holding her arm, she gave him a withering look and he released it, trying to hide his slight blush. Chael's embarrassment was quickly overshadowed by curiosity as he tried to imagine what could possibly be in those drops to make her recover her faculties so quickly. He might have to steal the scriptorium for himself. Andon joined them as they arrived at the gate, and he was the one to call up to the lookout.

"Ho there!" he called to the man in the parapet. "What do you see?" The watchmen looked down at them nervously.

"I um… it's a man," he yelled hesitantly. "He doesn't look well."

"Open the gate," Chael ordered the two people standing in front of the large, fortified doors to the city. They looked to Andon who nodded then they lifted the giant beam of wood barring the entrance and swung the doors open. It was a man, at least he had been in life. Now a twisted hideous mockery of a human being shambled up the path toward the Southern gate. His right leg was more than three times the size of his left and was overgrown with rotting pustules that oozed black liquid. Much of his face was covered in the same pulsing sores as his leg and Chael had the distinct impression that if he came too close, this man might simply explode from all the painful-looking sores on his body.

"Stop!" Chael ordered as the thing reached the shadow of the wall. It looked up, seeming to notice them for the first time.

"Am I in the presence of the one called Chael?" he asked, every word a scratching hiss barely above a whisper.

"I am Chael," he said. "State your business and begone from these lands!" Chael hoped that sounded official, it was a strain to not look at Andon for his reaction, but the stranger continued.

"I have a message for Chael from the one known as Darrik." The tortured creature sputtered as though the words were painful to say. At the mention of his former friend's name Chael jerked to attention.

"What did Darrik say?" he asked, now much more interested in the message.

"He said," the creature continued, "that he's sorry that he missed you in Fhaerhold. But circumstances required him to return to his masters. He anxiously waits for you to join him."

"Join him where?" Chael asked, dreading the answer. The creature smiled for the first time and the gesture threatened to pop one of the many bleeding sores on his face.

"Ehbing," it said in its strangled voice. Chael darkened as he considered the implications. *Darrik has gone to Ehbing with the Black Hand. So, the entire city is a hostage, then.* Chael heard Andon draw a sword, and he looked back at the creature. It was slowly walking toward them in its broken shambling gate muttering to itself.

"My reward, give me my reward!" It repeated this phrase over and over as it approached.

"I have no reward for you," Chael shouted as pulled one of his knives out. He winced at the reminder of his shattered falchion. "Come any closer and I will kill you," he told the creature darkly.

With those words, it seemed to smile once again and it charged Chael, shrieking wildly. It stopped flat in its path as Chael's knife sunk into its forehead, exploding one of the giant pustules. He had been slowly gathering life essence in anticipation of the throw.

Makes sense, Chael thought. Chael walked around to the side of his ambusher. There's the rest of the ambush party, I guess, Chael muttered to himself. Chael supposed he should be flattered. An alchemist and three armsmen were merely a delaying tactic until the rest of the group of assassins could catch up. However, at the moment, the best he could do was mild irritation. Seeing that they only had the one crossbowman in the group and hoping there were no more alchemists hidden in the ranks, Chael dashed as fast as he could toward the gate.

As he walked back toward the heart of Fhaerstead, he could hear the faint sound of cascading pops, like a series of loud bubbles. He shuddered slightly with disgust. "No, definitely not," he muttered darkly.

Chapter 42

Present Day

"I will ride to Westfhael and take the river," Chael said, stuffing some meager supplies he could scavenge into a borrowed pack. Going back through the forest would be faster but he would be a much easier target for the Black Hand if he chose that route, at least on the open road he would see the threats coming.

He gripped the handle of the sword he had also taken from the village. After the display he and Andon had put on, the people of Fhaerstead were more than happy to help him with supplies. He had refused most of the foodstuffs they had tried to give him, they would need them more in the coming days than he would, and besides he could forage on the road. But he had accepted a short straight double-edged arming sword, though they would desperately need weapons as well. It wouldn't be nearly as well suited to chopping as his falchion and he didn't like the weight, but it would serve. Andon nodded at him and seemed to be lost in thought.

Just that moment Rina burst into the room weighed down with more luggage than Chael could scarcely imagine the entire town could contain. She blew a stray hair out of her face and smiled brightly. "And where are you going so laden?" Chael asked her. Rina tapped a finger on her lips and hummed, staring off to the side as if trying to puzzle something out.

"Do you mean to ask if I am going somewhere, or is it the amount of supplies I'm carrying that draws your keen curiosity?" She smiled again and Chael heard Andon cover a laugh with an obvious cough.

"Both, I suppose," Chael replied irritably.

"Ah," Rina chimed, "Well I shall inform you then." Her eyes twinkled as she condescended to him, she enjoyed toying with him too much. Chael simply found it irritating, but that didn't stop the smirk on Andon's face. "I am obviously coming with you, which should answer the first question. As for the second, these are alchemical supplies that I will need as well as clothes graciously donated by the people of Fhaerstead."

"You're not coming with me," Chael declared. He had meant it and despite his momentary irritation with her the flash of fear that swept Rina's confident face pained him, though he didn't know why. "Look," he continued trying to be a little kinder. "Ehbing is clearly a trap, my dead friend is going to be waiting there with more Darkened cultists and more demons and who knows what else, and they're all there for one purpose. To kill me."

Chael let the words hang in the air for a moment but if he was hoping to frighten them it backfired. Rina looked more determined than ever and began arranging the many supplies she was trying to carry, and Sir Andon seemed to reach a conclusion of his own.

"Do you see what I've had to deal with," he jokingly asked Rina. She flashed him a wicked smile and looked back at Chael.

"Oh, I know," she said. "Poor Michik loses a leg and he isn't half as grumpy as Chael." At the mention of his name Michik lifted his head up from the floor where he was laying and looked around at them expectantly, but when no one bent over to scratch his head, he laid it back down and huffed.

"I can't do what I need to if I'm too busy protecting you," Chael insisted.

"Who here needs protecting?" Rina asked, challenging him with a raised eyebrow. Chael finally lost his temper.

"You do!" he yelled. "Everyone does! I just wanted to be left alone, and now..." He trailed off, anger fading as he looked down at the sad state of his dog. *I couldn't protect you from them, I couldn't even protect you from myself.* Rina was about to speak again but Andon held up his good hand and then placed it on Chael's shoulder.

"You can do things that I would never have dreamed of, but we face enemies that are beyond nightmares. You saved my life; I owe that debt. I may be..." He hesitated, lifting his arm for inspection. "Diminished," he finally said, the words soaked with regret. "But I am not helpless. Until I can repay what is owed, I go where you go."

Steel returned to his words as he spoke, and Chael let the protest die in his throat. For the knight it was a matter of honor and besides this wasn't just his own fight anymore. Not a person in this room, nor even the town was untouched by the wave of Darkness washing over the Kingdom. He nodded at Andon and they both turned to Rina.

"What?" she asked incredulously. "I'm just coming along to kill half-breeds." From below Michik snorted his agreement.

They managed to secure two horses from Fhaerstead, Andon had immediately insisted that Chael ride and he walk but relented when Chael pointed out that with very little effort of his power, he could jog alongside the horse indefinitely.

Rina started the journey in a bit of a huff because both he and Andon had pointed out that her borrowed farm horse could hardly carry the weight of the supplies she wanted to bring. Andon had also insisted that she return the priest's scriptorium lest she angered the Living Stars. She had plenty of retorts for that, but in the end, she relented and unenthusiastically gave it back.

Chael had promptly stolen it again; he was curious about some of the elixirs the Black Hand had employed and wanted to see if the Order had some answers. If they met another pair of smiling revenants like before, he didn't like their chances. He waited until they were more than a dozen leagues outside of Fhaerstead to reveal that he had re-stolen the book. The knight groaned ruefully but Rina's mood improved dramatically.

Soon the light grew dim, and Andon insisted that they stop for the night. Chael wanted to press on, even though he had been jogging all day he still felt fairly fresh, but the knight felt that travel was safer during the day and had pointed out that the horses at least required rest. So not long after sunset they moved off the southern road.

Chael scanned the area around them and couldn't detect any nearby people but that didn't necessarily rule out demons and the so-called half-breeds. Though he could detect them by the lack of life essence they gave off, it was hardly an exact method. Warily, Chael settled down for the night, Michik by his side.

As sleep finally began to take him, he was jerked awake by a rustling near his makeshift bedroll. Chael shot upright, his knife thrust outward toward the noise. Rina didn't so much as flinch as the blade came within an inch of her ear. She was bent down examining Michik's stump, making notes in the priest's scriptorium.

"What are you doing?" Chael demanded groggily. She shot him a slight glare, only barely visible in the dim light of the stars.

"You seem totally unconcerned that poor Meeshee has lost his leg," she scolded him.

"Michik," Chael corrected her, though it was more out of annoyance than anything. He had called his dog by that nickname an untold number of times, still her words bit him hard, and he had to forcibly stifle several more aggressive retorts. "If I knew a way to restore his leg, I would have done it by now," Chael added honestly. He had actually been thinking about it a lot while he jogged but hadn't come up with any ideas beyond attaching a stick to his leg, but Michik would hate that.

As if reading his mind Rina responded, "well I think it would be best if we left the thinking up to me, you might hurt yourself." Again, Chael swallowed the angry insult that had rushed to his lips. She obviously had some sort of idea and for Michik's sake he didn't want to upset her.

"Okay," he said, forcing the tone of his voice down. Her subsequent frown told him that he hadn't done a very good job. He tried harder, "what is your plan then?"

"I'm not entirely sure," she answered, tapping her finger on her lips, completely apathetic to his rising temper. "But those half breeds have me thinking, they take dead demon tissue and manage to reconstitute it for use with living humans. It's fascinating!" As she spoke the last word her voice took on a slight squeal of excitement that made Michik ruffle his sensitive ears.

"You want to give him a demon leg?" Chael responded incredulously. Rina looked at him like he had just suggested the grass was blue.

Shaking her head, she answered, "no, obviously not. But in principle I don't see how we... I mean I," she corrected herself, "couldn't use an ordinary wolf's leg and attach it to him with the same process." She began mumbling to herself while scribbling down more notes in the book and occasionally inspecting Michik's stump. After several more minutes, heedless of Chael's attempts to go back to sleep, she poked him in the shoulder with a slender finger. "Could you go fetch a fresh wolf forelimb for me?"

"What?" Chael half yelled half whispered at her incredulously. "You want me to just go tromp off into the wilderness in the middle of the night and hunt down a wolf?" Rina gave him another look reminiscent of a person peering down at an especially stupid animal and nodded.

Am I floating, he wondered absently. Dark spawn than any other man alive, he thought bitterly.Chael took a deep breath of the autumn air, letting the scent fill his lungs. No, definitely not demons. The Darkborn creatures, as the poor guard in Ehbing had discovered, were a pungent sort. Definitely men, And st-starborn? What could that possibly mean?

"Now?" he finally said to her.

"Yes!" she yelled back at him impatiently. "I have a method I would like to try."

Chael sighed. Normally, telling someone to go on a wolf hunt in the middle of the night with no knowledge of the terrain or of the existence of a nearby pack would be laughable. He wanted to express to Rina just how laughable it was, but he wasn't normal. And sure, enough when he got up and stretched his spiritual sense outward into the wilderness that surrounded them, he managed to pick out a pack disturbingly close to their camp. He almost didn't say anything to Rina, preferring to avoid the smug look on her face but he owed it to Michik to put his own pride aside.

Chael rolled his shoulder and flexed, loosening his body for the coming hunt. He didn't have a bow and even with the inhuman speed of which he was capable, he didn't have much hope of outpacing a wolf if it came to a chase. Stealth would be his most useful tool. Beside him, Michik rose and stretched out on his three legs, mimicking the motions of his master. Chael bent down and met him at eye level scratching his head.

"Not this time buddy," he said sadly. Michik would normally be an asset on a hunt such as this. His perfectly normal canine senses were, at times, even more keen than the unnatural ones Chael possessed and he hated to leave him at camp. But the idea of Michik watching him slaughter one his kin to take and use its leg gave Chael a foul taste in his mouth. Michik didn't need to see the coming butchery. Alone, Chael strode out into the darkness, azure eyes glowing.

The wolves were on the hunt, he didn't know what for, but their movements and the way they seamlessly maneuvered around each other was impressive. Without words or any communication that he could detect they slowly closed an intricate noose around their prey. It wasn't until the last moment before the kill that Chael even realized what they were after, a young spiked male deer, bedded down for the night.

By the time it realized it was in danger, the trap had already sprung. As the pack descended, distracted by their prey, Chael sprang out in a single burst through the concealing underbrush. He had been careful to remain downwind of the pack, and with Dark speed and strength he was able to grab one of the stragglers. His left hand went over its torso holding a knife and his right clamped down hard on the wolf's muzzle, preventing it from calling to its packmates.

"I'm sorry," Chael whispered, torn by the sad necessity and plunged his knife into the animal's throat. When he returned to camp, he carried two pristine forelegs and just enough meat to cook breakfast in the morning. The rest he left to the wilderness.

Rina looked like she was going to give him some sort of quip but one look at Chael's face and she thought better. As he handed her the wolf's legs she merely nodded and got to work. Rina immediately began mixing different powders and foul-smelling liquids from the supplies she had been able to retain from the Order house in Fhaerstead.

To Chael her measurements seemed haphazard and sloppy, he didn't know much about the science of alchemy, but he understood enough to know that precision was key. Unhappily, his mind flicked back to the failed experiment that had stumbled up to the gate of Fhaerstead to deliver Darrik's warning. But when Chael attempted to bring this up to Rina, her scowl was hot enough to melt steel, and she insisted that she was being perfectly precise.

"Aha!" she exclaimed after nearly an hour of mixing, grinding, and chattering to herself. "This is it, you know, we're lucky I had the supplies. Some of the ingredients are… well they're tricky I can tell you that."

She fixed Chael with a triumphant grin and ushered him and Michik over to her. Michik gave him a reluctant look but reluctantly came hopping over to Rina at her continued insistence.

"Now Chael, if you would be so kind as to hold him down," she said clinically to him before turning to Michik. "I'm sorry Meeshee, this may not feel very good," she told the wolf in a much softer and kinder tone.

Carefully she applied the product of her labors to the end of Michik's leg. It was a thick brown paste that smelled vaguely like pine needles if those pine needles had just been sprayed by a particularly malodorous skunk. After applying her mysterious salve, she produced one of the legs Chael had provided and deftly sewed it onto Michik's stump. Through it all the wolf didn't so much as yip, though his head was buried in Chael's lap.

"Alright," Rina proclaimed brightly. "If I'm right, and let's face it I'm always right by daylight the limb should start to see some movement." Chael was skeptical but hopeful as he went back to bed and hoped to catch a few hours of sleep before dawn and maybe Michik would be whole.

It didn't work. When they awoke in the morning, their collective eyes all swirled to Michik's severed leg and what they found was a foreleg the same as it had been ever since a half-breed cut it in half and the dissolving remains of the donated limb bubbling into a soupy mess on the ground.

Rina tried again the next night to similar results. After the failure she insisted that Chael go hunt down more limbs for her experiments, but he was unwilling to go out of his way to kill any more innocent creatures until she was sure her formula could produce results. So, she tried different recipes and permutations all along the Southern Road to Westfhael. It took them a little over a week to make the journey and all Rina had been able to produce was a series of pastes and poultices, each one more smelling worse than the last.

"It's hopeless," she finally admitted the night before they reached the city. "The Fraternal Order of Celestial Light are," she mockingly used their full name, "they're dullards! Cowards even!" she exclaimed while tossing yet another failed batch of Michik's treatment into the fire. "They're not academics," she proclaimed disdainfully. "I came to them hoping to learn how to heal my father."

Chael and Andon both leaned closer at the mention of her family, since joining them Rina had been reluctant to share details of her past.

"I was enrolled at King Inarus' royal academy. They were both so proud, I was going to be a scholar, perhaps an advisor to the King himself one day. But then my mother came down with a mysterious sickness." Rina stared into the fire as she spoke, her words inflected with both anger and sadness. "They couldn't afford a physician and she succumbed. My father caught it too, but it merely left him blind. That's when I joined the Order, they're known as the best healers in the realm. I thought they could teach me."

Rina reached over and picked up the stolen scriptorium and looked at it with longing in her eyes. "But they're frauds," she finally declared and tossed the book aside.

After several minutes of uncomfortable silence Andon finally cleared his throat and asked, "how so? Or I mean to say, how are they frauds?" Andon glanced up at the sky for a second as if expecting a bolt of lightning to come screeching down from above and destroy him for daring to question the Order. Rina gave him a sad half smile before answering.

"They don't learn. Everything they know about alchemy today is what they knew about alchemy a thousand years ago." Rina asserted while idly tossing kindling into their fire. "They only exist to hoard the knowledge for their own power." Andon blanched at the direct accusation directed at what amounted to the state religion in Fhael.

"So, you're not a believer then?" Chael asked while gesturing up with his eyes.

"Do I think the gods reside in the stars and intercede on our behalf if we pray to them in faith?" Rina asked haughtily, "no I don't."

"Then why were you praying over their bodies in Fhaerhold?" Chael asked, genuinely curious.

"Because," she answered quickly, almost shamefully, then added, "it seemed like the right thing to do." Chael nodded; he could respect that he supposed. An awkward silence once again fell over the group and for this time it was Chael who decided to break it.

"A bit strange isn't it," he began looking around at their camp. "We're less than a day from Westfhael and the road has been barren." It was Andon's turn to look mournful now, and regret coated his words as he spoke.

"War," he said quietly, staring intently into the fire. "The Baron of the Southern Province will have called his subjects to Westfhael."

"King now, I suppose," Chael interjected. Andon snapped his head up, realization dawning on his face. "King Inarus had one sibling and no heirs so naturally his brother would be king…" Chael then realized it too and looked back at Andon who had gone ghostly pale.

"We can't go into the city," the knight announced seriously. Chael gave him a puzzled look before Andon continued. "I'm too well known there, if I'm seen I won't be able to leave."

Chael almost pointed out that Andon should probably stay in Westfhael and that he didn't have to accompany him to Ehbing, but he stopped himself. Andon had given his word to see this through and the knight was the sort to take such oaths seriously but more than that, and to Chael's own surprise, he found that he didn't want Andon to leave. The idea frightened him for some reason, but before he could think on it further, Rina interrupted.

"I'm sorry, why can't we go into the city?" she asked, confused.

"My father is Grecious Al-Fhaelan, Baron of the Southern Province and ruler of Westfhael." Andon said with no hint of familial love.

"And as of a fortnight ago, the rightful king of all Fhael," Chael added. Andon nodded without looking at him.

"And though my oath as a knight forbids speaking ill of the King, at least while in mixed company, and I am loath to so insult my grandmother, but I would be remiss if I didn't add that King Grecious Al-Fhaelan is a truly odious son of a bitch."

Chapter 43

Present Day

The following day they left the road and instead cut West across open terrain. Chael had pointed out that avoiding the city entirely meant that they couldn't hire a boat; but Andon was certain that, given the state of war, they couldn't have found a boat even if he could travel the city anonymously, which he insisted that he couldn't.

Chael was dubious but didn't argue. *What had his father done to him?* he wondered without speaking. Chael didn't know who his father was, which, considering the grief of his companions, was seemingly a blessing.

A few hours after turning West they encountered the Northern bank of the Amberwyne River. Its dark golden waves were oddly comforting to see though Chael had rarely visited the river during his time here.

They rode farther, sticking close to the river, Chael jogging beside the horses. Michik had taken to riding on Rina's lap though he was almost half as big as the horse itself. Rina had rigged a sort of swaddling contraption that wrapped Michik up and kept him secured to her chest as she rode. Chael found the whole enterprise mildly undignified, but Michik enjoyed the pampering. Several more hours passed, and they finally encountered a bit of human civilization since avoiding Westfhael.

"Ah," Andon exclaimed excitedly, "Bridge." Chael looked over at the sparse group of shabby buildings and found a distinct lack of anything he could accurately call a bridge. Andon noticed his confusion and explained, smiling. "Bridge is the name of the village. Some time ago, perhaps centuries no one is sure, an attempt was made to bridge the Amberwyne at this spot and it failed. The village is the remnant of that failure and as long as anyone can remember it has been called Bridge."

"The village is what remains, not bits of bridge?" Chael asked, mildly confused. The knight shrugged and prodded his horse onward. The people of bridge lived up to the spirit of their namesake, which is to say that they didn't seem to exist. Doors and windows were left open, fish waiting to be fileted were left to rot in the sun, even meals had been abandoned on tables in the apparent rush to flee.

"They left in a hurry," Rina whispered as though the ghosts of the former residents might hear her.

"Your father?" Chael asked Andon, gesturing to the vacant village with a hand. Andon looked seriously at the abandoned state of Bridge and shook his head.

"The call to arms certainly reached here but it's not as if the soldiers would demand that they evacuate so hastily as to abandon their supper." The knight kept looking around, a puzzled look on his face. "These people were scared." Chael looked ahead to the West beyond the village, just a few leagues away was the Southwestern edge of the Dark Forest. If something scared these people into abandoning their homes, it would have come from there. Andon followed his gaze and the look on his face became graver.

"They want us in Ehbing," Chael reminded them. "Darrik sent that poor retch all the way to Fhaerstead because that's where they want me, that is where they will spring the trap." Both Andon and Rina nodded, but they didn't look any less concerned than a moment ago. Chael sighed; he wasn't sure if he believed the words himself. "See if you can find a boat,"

Chael told them. "Michik and I will go scouting." Rina gave him a look like he had just announced plans to set his hair on fire, but Andon gave him one of his curt professional nods.

"Be back by morning, we'll set out at first light." Rina threw up her arms and mumbled something about idiocy and disappeared into one of the abandoned homes in search of more supplies. Chael gave Andon a nod of his own and patted his hip. Michik immediately rushed to his side, if a bit slower than usual. Chael looked down at him affectionately.

"We're gonna see if there's anything in those trees, and then we're gonna fix your leg."

3 Years Ago

Cold tired and excruciatingly human legs propelled Chael forward. For a time, all he could feel was the ache in his knees and the terrible weight on his back. A dead weight. He was an assassin, from the time he was expelled from his mother's pleasure house he had been trained and conditioned to kill, to strike from the shadows and do the bidding of his master. *Assassin is such an elegant word, it almost sounds noble,* he thought. The reality was much less grand, Chael was a murderer. When Darrik had tried to stop him, he became a kinslayer. As the shame of the past collected in his mind the weight on his back became heavier.

"Now I am nothing," he lamented to the air. He had found himself inside a small, cramped cave, not too dissimilar to the one in which he had found Michik in the first place. He had no recollection of stopping, or of laying Michik down in front of him. Cave was perhaps too strong a word, he thought idly. It was more of a rocky overhang, but it was shelter enough. Chael put a trembling hand on

Michik's fur, and stroked it fondly, his eyes growing foggy and his arm heavy.

"What do we do now buddy?" he asked, holding back tears. But the wolf didn't answer, he couldn't because of him. Chael staggered out of the shelter of the rock, aching legs from his flight protesting every movement. He couldn't stand to be in there with Michik anymore, and as he stared up into the vast night sky, he finally allowed himself to weep.

Present Day

Chael and Michik stalked through the forest, it felt good to be the predators again. Immediately obvious were signs of travel, a dozen or more people passed through here from the village of Bridge. They moved as silently as they could, Chael the perfect hunter, his skills honed through training and practice. Normally even his well-earned stealth paled in comparison to Michik's but today the wolf's hopping gait seemed especially loud. Every crunch of fallen leaf or twig made Chael cringe with guilt over the present circumstance of the once mighty wolf.

Movement in the trees caught Chael's eye, and he signaled for Michik to crouch low and remain unseen. His dutiful wolf complied and for several tense breaths they waited for the creature to appear. At the moment Chael began to feel acutely aware of how weak he felt without the power of life essence aiding his senses and his movements. He had gathered some from the surrounding flora as they passed but nothing compared to the strength from even a single human life. The difference was like a single match in a dark cave as opposed to a roaring bonfire, there simply was no comparison.

3 Years Ago

Chael's tears failed to wash away the bitter feeling deep within his soul, as he glared up at the night sky. He wanted to blame fate or blame the insidious presence that lurked within himself, but it was hollow comfort. He had wanted power and when offered up to him he didn't even think about denying it. Now he was friendless, probably jobless when Khalim found out how badly he had botched the job, and utterly hopeless.

Chael was so enthralled by his own self-pity that he didn't even notice the approach of the giant white beast until it sat on its haunches and growled at him. Looking down he saw that it was an enormous white wolf possibly even bigger than Michik, and Michik's size was prodigious even for a wolf. The white wolf stared at him, eyes glowing a brilliant shade of gold. Broken from his self-flagellation Chael's instincts came back to him in an instant and jumped back, falchion flying from his hip.

But the wolf didn't budge, it had stopped growling at him the moment he made eye contact and now just sat there eyeing him with an intense wolfish curiosity of the sort Michik might have displayed. Warily, Chael continued to hold his sword out in front of him but now that his initial surprise had faded, he felt no malice from the beast. As he looked into its eyes, he felt a peaceful sensation wash over him, cleansing the bitterness from his soul for a moment. And then it turned and bounded off.

Chael felt like a cooling balm had just been torn from his ravaged soul and though he was loath to leave Michik's body, a feeling in his gut told him to run after it. Not the Dark impressions he received from the presence but a natural longing from his own soul, so he ran. He had to draw on the bounty of life around him to keep up, but he suspected that if the wolf so chose, it could have easily outpaced even his enhanced speed. So, on they went at a near all-out sprint for Chael until he lost track of place and time. In order to keep pace all of his concentration was bent on gathering the life essence from around him and keeping his eye on the ever-uncatchable white tail, always swishing just out of reach.

Present Day

The half-breeds had made a small camp a few leagues into the Dark Forest outside of Bridge. Chael and Michik got as close as they dared to observe the foul creatures without giving away their own presence. Hiding in the shadows of the trees, they watched.

Six half-breeds were sitting around a fire, though it was still light out, roasting meat. Most of what they had, skewered and rotating over their fire, looked like the normal fare a hunter might cook after a successful day in the wilderness. But the last item on the large wooden spit immediately drew Chael's attention. A human foot, untrimmed and with the skin remaining was rotating lazily around the skewer. Chael could hear the hissing of the juices inside the appendage as they turned to gas and escaped the butchered flesh.

Knives flashed to Chael's hands unbidden and with no particular plan of attack he charged the nearest half-breed and plunged his knife into its bulging red eye. Surprise alone eased the kill for there was little energy for him in the small camp outside of simple flora. The villagers the half-breeds were eating must have been killed elsewhere, or they had been dead so long that the essence they left behind had long since dissipated.

Whichever the reason, Chael couldn't rely on superior speed and strength to overcome the half-breeds. Without human life powering him he was at best equal if not a little weaker than the Dark hybrids. And unlike true demons, they fought with the wisdom and cunning of men.

Probably for shooting at demons, Chael supposed. Utterly useless. Poking holes in Darkspawn was a vain endeavor. Having removed the arrow, he scooped Michik in his arms and hid his features as best as he could under his soiled green cloak.

Three came at him bearing the signature claws of their kind as well as one rust pitted short sword. Chael wouldn't call them especially coordinated but strength and superior numbers were a great equalizer to skill, and they were advantaged in both respects.

Chael parried a high slash on his new sword, he pivoted the blade pointing it down and stabbed the offending half-breed in the face, but not before the one bearing its own sword caught him on the opposite shoulder. He managed to lean away from the blow and eventually swatted it away with his sword but in that fraction of a second it had managed to scratch the bones of his shoulder, rendering the arm useless. He could already feel the comparatively anemic power inside him healing the gushing wound, but it would take time and energy he didn't have to spare.

Sensing weakness the two remaining half-breeds facing him redoubled their attacks and Chael was forced to slowly retreat as he parried blow after blow with one hand on his sword. He needed to regain his reach advantage so he could end the fight quickly, so he focused on the creature with the sword. They clashed, steel on steel binding their blades against each other. The finer metal on his own sword chipped and bit that of the half-breed as they both pushed against each other for leverage. But before Chael could make use of the bind, its companion attacked with its black claws and forced him to break off and retreat.

Feeling was returning to his left hand again as the power within him partially healed the wound. He experimentally flexed his fingers and found enough strength to fight but healing such a grievous injury had cost him and he was running low on power. When their next attack came, they seemed even faster than before, and he felt weaker.

Giving up on parrying, he dodged the next attack and managed to slice a wound across the sword carrier's arm. It roared in pain and sprayed black blood but was undeterred as it kept advancing, swinging the sword wildly. As he fought Chael desperately sought out more sources of life around him and quickly stole their energy to refuel his limbs. But that required a moment's concentration that he couldn't afford as his attackers bore down on him.

Growing tired of the fight and the myriad of small wounds inflicted upon it, the swordless half-breed came up with a novel strategy. It lunged at Chael, both arms extended with murderous claws gleaming black in the dim light. He dodged the attack and, seeing his opening, plunged his sword down in a two-handed swing at the thing's exposed neck. Just as his blade sank into flesh Chael realized his mistake. The crude sword of the other half-breed was already whistling through the air, tip pointed directly at his unguarded flank and there was nothing he could do about it.

A wolf's jaw snapped around the extended arm of the half-breed no more than hair's breadth from Chael's flesh. The wolf forced its arm wide and drove it into the ground with a powerful twist of its graceful white furred neck. As Chael's attack sliced through the neck of the over-extended half-breed, he caught a glimpse of Michik. Not at his side but at least ten paces away still contending with his own half-breed. Stunned, Chael spun around at the remaining Darkspawn and the giant white wolf that was tearing away its sword arm. Chael effortlessly flicked his knife at the creature's head just as Michik finished off his own attacker.

Chael stared, wide-eyed, at the great white wolf in front of him. It had dropped the now limp appendage from its mouth, its pristine snowy muzzle now stained with demon black. Golden eyes stared calmly at him for several moments and Chael felt the same peaceful feeling as he searched them. Even Michik seemed transfixed as they gazed at the mysterious wolf. Then it attacked.

3 Years Ago

The wolf led him through a tight thicket of trees and slowed to a trot. When Chael finally caught it, he was breathing so hard he nearly tripped over the body that was lying on the ground. The wolf looked from Chael to the dead woman in the dirt and back, lingering on him expectantly.

"What?" Chael asked it through gulping breaths as he tried to recover from the sprint across the countryside. The wolf cocked his head at Chael a moment then laid down. "Ok," he said uncertainly as he approached the body.

She was perhaps a little older than himself and dressed in simple sturdy clothes. She was apparently neither noble nor overly poor, just average he supposed. Her cause of death was not immediately apparent as he examined her further, but for some minor scrapes and scratches on her arms and legs. If she had been carrying any supplies or any coin, they had also been taken.

As Chael instinctively felt with his other senses, he could immediately tell that a good deal of her life essence was still near the body and hadn't dissipated. *Fresh kill,* he thought.

"I don't know what you want me to do," Chael told the wolf. *I'm trying to reason with a wild animal as large as a small horse,* he thought, chiding himself. But the wolf just kept looking up at him with its bright golden eyes.

Chael sighed as he reached down to touch the woman's leg as he gathered her essence inside him. He had accidentally discovered this use of his powers a few years ago. A death echo he had called it because of the way it seemed to reverberate the final moments of a life.

The world around him grew dim and a faint gray cloud obscured everything further than a few paces around him. The woman was running through the forest as fast as she could, ignoring the thickets and small branches that got in her way.

After a moment, she found what she had apparently been chasing. A little girl perhaps in her eighth year was huddled under in the lee of one of the nearby trees, fists clenched and trembling. In contrast to the dead woman whose memories Chael was currently observing, the girl was dressed in fine silks, but they were torn and her face was dirty, like she had been living in the wild for some time.

"There you are, Szimella," the dead woman screeched, slightly out of breath. "Thought you could get away?" The woman smiled ghoulishly as she stalked closer to the frightened child. Sticking two fingers in her mouth, she whistled one long shrill note. Immediately Chael could hear the tromping footsteps of her companions as she answered her call. "They'll take a finger for this, stupid girl."

The woman leaned forward to grab Szimella's hair and as she did, the child opened one of her shaking fists and flicked its contents at the woman. It turned out to be a fine yellow powder, and it coated the face of the woman. Stunned, she staggered backward as she unconsciously breathed in the yellow dust.

"You little bitch!" the woman screamed but voice was already horse and her breathing ragged. The girl, displaying more courage than she ought to possess at such a tender age stood up and stared down the woman who had obviously been her tormentor.

"Sister Ihlsa says you shouldn't curse!" and the girl took off and disappeared into the gray mist of the echo, out of sight. The woman tried to give chase but faltered, her body already beginning to shut down. As she fell to her final resting spot her eyes caught the sight of two pairs of boots as they pursued the girl. They blinked once and then went dark forever.

Present Day

More than two decades of training and experience fighting and surviving was the only thing that kept Chael alive when the wolf struck. The serene peaceful feeling that the wolf seemed to exude was gone now there was only predator and he and Michik were prey. It lashed out with powerful jaws and Chael kicked it away as he brought his sword down. But the wolf leaped away, impossibly fast for a product of the natural realm.

Michik snarled at it and snapped his own jaws in its direction but hobbled as he was the more lithe and agile wolf easily outmaneuvered his dog. The wolf turned to Chael once more, golden eyes blazing like the sun and pounced, crashing through the air like a thunderbolt on top of him.

3 Years Ago

Light returned as Chael dismissed the echo and he had to blink his eyes against its sudden intensity. The woman was lying, still very much dead, where she had fallen in the Dark memory. The white wolf was on the other side of her now, looking back at Chael with its glowing eyes, body pointed in the direction of this Szimella's pursuers. He didn't need to ask any questions this time, the intent was clear.

"Let's go," he grunted to the wolf, and they both took off, following the recent trail. The sound of girlish screams pierced the still night, and they abandoned caution in their haste, direction now clear without needing to scout the trail. They emerged into a small, shaded clearing that obviously served as the base of operations for the group of child napping brigands.

The two pairs of boots Chael saw belonged to two large men. They were wearing furs and bore strange skintight leather caps on their heads. One was watching as the other pinned Szimella down and held a knife to her throat. Without any communication or planning Chael instinctively knew what the white wolf was going to do, as if the wolf was an extension of his own mind.

It leaped at the man holding the girl down, using its impressive mass to bowl the large man over and off of Szimella. Chael immediately threw one of his knives at the other, the blade finding its home in the man's heart. The battle was over in seconds, the two captors laying in pools of blood. Chael rushed over to Szimella's side, but the girl was already on her feet, with a horrified look on her face.

"It's ok," Chael calmly assured the frightened child. "We're not going to hurt you." She still shook with fear, her eyes wide. Then the wolf slowly padded over to her. At first, she recoiled back in terror, frightened that the giant canine was going to eat her but she stood in place. Carefully the white wolf lowered its massive head down to her trembling hands, gave them a playful lick, and a nudge with its nose.

At the wolf's prodding, Szimella hesitantly stroked its smooth white fur, somehow unblemished by the bloody fight the moment before. As she pet the massive wolf, she began to stop trembling and even began to show a tenuous smile.

"I'm Szimella," she told Chael politely, voice strong and not trembling despite her obvious remaining fear.

"Nice to meet you Szimella," Chael intoned as gently as he was able. "I'm Chael. Can we help you get home?" The girl nodded and the wolf, sensing his cue, started trotting forward, the girl desperately clinging to his fur as they went.

The white wolf led their party onward and soon they arrived back where he had started. The rocky outcropping that couldn't properly be called a cave, and Michik's still corpse. Szimella gasped when she saw the dead wolf and it gave her hand another encouraging nibble as they drew nearer.

When the three of them were huddled up next to the little cave just a foot or two from Michik's body the wolf turned his golden eyes back to Chael, Szimella clung to his side gripping his fur like it was the only thing holding her to the world. Perhaps at that moment, it was.

"What do you want?" Chael demanded harshly of the wolf, the intensity of it causing little Szimella to wince. "Why did you bring us here?" he asked a little more softly this time. The wolf only stared, but as the same peaceful feeling washed over him again, he knew. Somehow, Chael knew exactly why he was here, like the battle before in an instant the wolf's intention became manifest in his mind. Chael scarcely believed it was possible, but he got to work. It was time to resurrect his dog.

Present Day

To Chael, it happened as if over several minutes, time slowing to a standstill. In reality the entire interaction occurred in less than a blink. The wolf came down, jaws flashing like shiny white death, right onto the tip of Chael's outstretched sword. In the frozen moment while the wolf flew through the air at Chael, he suddenly understood the wolf's exact intentions. And though its face was snarling, and its fangs bared, Chael managed to whisper, "Thank you," as it descended.

Time sped back up again as it died, and Chael got immediately to work. Taking out a knife he slowly and expertly extracted one of its forelegs. The wolf's intentions translated into his mind, expertly guiding his hand. He then called Michik over and his dog dutifully came and without prodding presented his severed limb. He wondered for a moment if the wolf had imparted the same sense of certitude to Michik as he had to himself.

Chael placed the white foreleg on the end of Michik's stump and wrapped it in a bandage he scavenged from a half-breed's ruined clothes. It wasn't ideal or strictly sanitary, but Chael supposed that Michik was unlikely to die of disease. With the limb tightly bound in place by the makeshift bandage the real work could begin.

Utterly useless. Poking holes in Darkspawn was a vain endeavor. Having removed the arrow, he scooped Michik in his arms and hid his features as best as he could under his soiled green cloak. I hate people, he thought glumly as sleep finally overtook him.

Chael reached beyond the Dark core and felt the small ball of golden light that resided in the depths of his soul. After trying to bring back Aelisa it had shrunk to just barely the size of a pebble and was growing ever dimmer. This would be the last time he could call upon it. He pushed his swirling Dark energy into it expecting resistance but this time the two energies fused together like two sticks of melted butter.

Straining, Chael pushed that little glowing speck of gold and black through the bond he shared with Michik with the effort of rolling a boulder uphill. But slowly, and with no small degree of effort, it was done, and Chael could see with his extra sense that it was circulating through Michik's system.

Chael collapsed onto his back panting with the effort and closed his eyes. He heard Michik hesitantly trot over, testing his new leg until he was right on top of Chael, looking down. Chael opened his eyes, gaze traveling up a bright white foreleg to his face to find a glowing pair of eyes looking down at him. One azure like his own, and one golden like the setting sun.

Chapter 44

Present Day

Chael and Michik emerged from the forest triumphant, if a bit bloody. They marched down to a pier stretching out over the Amberwyne where they found Andon and Rina preparing a small riverboat for departure. Michik ran ahead of Chael, eager to show off his new leg. Rina met him with open arms practically squealing with delight.

"Oh Meeshee, Chael got you a new leg!" Michik desperately rubbed against her, whining with excitement and lapping at her hands with his rough dry tongue. As Rina showered the jubilant wolf with affection Andon walked over to Chael and simply raised one eyebrow.

"It's a long story," Chael breathed happily. "Perhaps best told on the boat, we need to keep moving."

"And the villagers?" Andon asked hopefully, though doubt showed across his face. Chael merely shook his head and Andon nodded seriously. Chael clapped him on the shoulder in what he hoped was a consoling gesture and struggled to find the appropriate words.

"We will find vengeance in Ehbing," he finally said to the knight. Andon gave him a tight smile then returned to packing up the boat, a task made even more difficult with his one good arm.

The boat was a small wooden craft made mainly for fishing up and down this section of the Amberwyne. It had a small cabin underneath the deck and a single sail, but the river's current flowed swiftly West in the direction of Ehbing so Andon didn't think the sail was strictly necessary. This came as a relief to Chael because he hadn't the faintest idea how to sail and he doubted whether Rina or Andon could either. True to Andon's words the small craft sailed quickly on just the river's current and only needed occasional steering from the hand tiller in the back.

"What do you expect when we reach Ehbing?" Andon asked Chael, teeth clenched through pain. His hand had grown steadily worse over their days of travel and now exhibited clear signs of fester. Rina was applying different alchemical curatives and medicine but one look at her face told Chael that it was all hopeless. Sooner or later the hand would have to go, or the knight would risk his whole arm if not his life.

"I'm not sure," Chael answered, grimacing as Rina dabbed a bloody cloth over one of the countless sores on his hand. "Darrik will be there as well as many others of their cult. And I'm guessing more than a few half-breeds and genuine demons as well."

He gave Andon a forced smile, but the knight had already closed his eyes against the newest wave of pain. Rina and Chael both looked at each other, then back to Andon, and when he finally opened his eyes and saw, he knew.

"It has to go," he finally said resignedly, and they both nodded. Andon nodded again and glanced down at Michik who was curled up on the floor of the boat, white leg sticking out proudly. Andon desperately turned back to Chael, "after we remove it could we…" he let the sentence trail while nodding down to Michik's new leg.

Chael sighed, he'd known Andon's hand was a lost cause for a long time and ever since emerging from the forest with Michik's new limb he had dreaded when the knight would ask him that question.

"No," Chael answered softly, avoiding Andon's eyes. "The power I used on Michik, what I tried to use on Aelisa, isn't mine. It was something I took from someone else like me, but it's gone now and so is he." Chael forced himself to look Andon in the eye and added, "if there was anything I could do I would."

Andon looked perhaps the most crestfallen he had ever seen the indefatigably good-natured and upbeat knight. But after a moment that same resolute determination stole Andon's features, and he nodded back.

"Do it now," he demanded of Chael, before adding more softly, "before I lose my nerve." Chael got up and unsheathed his borrowed sword and strode gravely across the deck to Andon.

"Stop it, you idiots!" Rina shouted, stepping in between them. "You don't just go chopping hands off with a sword like a couple of barbaric morons! You," she pointed an accusatory finger at Chael, "I believe it could be that stupid, but Andon…" Rina softened her tone ever so slightly as she addressed the wounded knight. "You ought to know better. You need surgery to remove it." Andon caught Chael's eye and for the first time in hours, cracked a genuine smile.

"Okay," he said, admitting defeat. "What do we do, Rina?" She smiled back at him and put away her righteous indignation and resumed her normal haughty superior look.

"Well," she started, "we can't do this on the boat. I'll need to make some elixirs and we'll need a fire to sterilize the tools." She looked around for a moment, brows furrowed then asked, "speaking of, what are our available tools?" Chael hefted his sword again in his right hand and spun a dagger around his palm on his left.

"Take your pick!" he chimed enthusiastically. Rina grimaced and rolled her eyes but eventually took the knife.

It took them until nearly sunset to finish preparations. Chael had a roaring fire going and had even managed to hunt down a few rabbits for supper with Michik's help. Ever since regaining his limb the wolf had been extra enthusiastic about any activity that involved running around and chasing rabbits more than qualified. Andon laid on the ground, a leather strap ready to put between his teeth.

"Here drink this and then this," Rina ordered, handing him two vials of elixir.

"What do they do?" Andon asked skeptically, eyeing the two alchemical concoctions skeptically. Rina rolled her eyes and gave him a look as if to say, 'just trust me you idiot,' but eventually sighed and answered.

"The first will help numb the pain, the second should hopefully prevent the wound from festering."

"Should?" Chael questioned, mirroring Andon's own sudden look of concern.

"Will," she responded more confidently this time. Andon gave Chael a small shrug and downed both vials in a single gulp of each. Within moments a glazed and dreamy look seemed to wash over the knight. "Chael, if you please," Rina said, gesturing to him.

"Right," Chael responded nervously and moved closer to Andon. Chael directed Andon to put the leather bit in his mouth and gathered in power from the surroundings. He used that power to hold down the naturally stronger knight and keep his arm steady. "Ready," he informed Rina when he felt Andon was secure.

"Alright, let's do this," Rina murmured more for her own benefit than his, Chael thought. With one final exhalation of nervous breath Rina marked a spot just above the wrist and lowered Chael's knife.

Chapter 45

Present Day

The river rocked the small boat gently as it drifted through the night. Andon was down in the small cabin sleeping, as he had been most of the time since the surgery. Rina had promised to keep Chael company as he steered the small vessel, but she too had succumbed to sleep in the end, curling up on the deck and using Michik for a pillow.

In her left hand was the stolen scriptorium which she had been pouring over like it held the keys to eternal life, and in her right hand were two small rods of copper connected to some mechanism that she had been fiddling with all day. Chael sat alone at the stern, gently guiding them along and all the while his gaze once again turned toward the skies.

Good.

Typical. If the Living Stars were sending him help, they were certainly more subtle about it than their demonic counterparts. Chael laid back, resting himself on the lip of the stern and hung his arms over the side to catch the cool air and sighed.

"I don't think there will be any more white wolves to save us in Ehbing." Chael murmured to the night.

"What's this about a white wolf?" Rina asked sleepily, sitting up from the deck of the ship. Her movement woke up

Michik which earned her a scowl from the wolf as he readjusted himself to sleep.

"Oh," Chael answered, caught off guard by the question. "I was just talking to myself about the wolf that we killed to heal Michik's leg." The wolf's ears twitched slightly at the mention of his name, but he didn't rise, instead he huffed in his wolfish sort of way and rolled over so his back was to his master. Chael and Rina both chuckled at the sight.

"Do you often talk to yourself?" Rina asked, Chael gave her his best exasperated face but didn't stop smiling.

"You know I never asked you why the Order put you in that dungeon with the rest of us." Rina's smile immediately soured, and she looked skyward for several seconds before answering. Chael wondered what it was she saw up there. She had expressed, at best, agnosticism when it came to the religious beliefs of her sect but battling demons and half-breeds was liable to make anyone question their preconceptions.

"I joined the order after illness stole my father's sight," she began seriously, still looking up. "I was already on a scholarly track, so they were glad to take me in even though I was older than most initiates." A slight note of anger began to color her words as she continued. "Much to my dismay I found out they were frauds, at least where scholarship is concerned. They practice no alchemy that isn't already written in their dusty old tomes."

She finally looked down at Chael, a small sad smile creeping back over her face. "They didn't have what I needed, or at least they wouldn't let me access all of their knowledge until I advanced," she corrected herself. "So, I sought it out on my own. They called my actions heretical and ordered me to stop, the incident in the alley was the last straw. I thought I found a potential alchemical remedy, but I needed certain supplies. I didn't have any money, so I stole them from those men."

"So, they threw you in a prison full of monsters?" Chael asked incredulously.

"Full?" asked Rina curiously, eyebrows raised.

"Yes," Chael answered firmly. Rina kept her eyebrows slightly raised but didn't press further.

"I was tried by the prefects and pronounced a heretic and murderer. I argued that the man I killed was in self-defense."

"It was," Chael cut in, more emphatically than he intended. Rina gave him an appreciative smile and continued.

"They said that his death was the result of unauthorized research and needless, Prefect Aelisa called it tantamount to murder." Rina looked back up at the stars and whispered, "it was." Her face seemed to age in front of him as the weight of her actions weighed down the confident front she presented to the world.

Chael was bursting with things to say, he knew only too well the pain of needless death and regret. The words raced across his mind, he wished to tell her about what happened with Darrik. She already had an inkling based on what she overheard in the dungeon, but she only saw a monster, not the kind decent man that he had killed. He opened his mouth to tell her, to reassure her if he could, but the words died on his lips. Rina gave him a curious look, expecting him to say something. Chael smiled and shook his head.

"It's nothing," he lied. "You should try to get some more sleep; I suspect we'll arrive in the morning." She gave him one last inquiring look, but when he remained silent, she nodded her head and laid back down next to Michik. The wolf gave a contented sigh as they both drifted off, rocked to sleep by the gentle rolling of the boat.

Their little boat drifted into Ehbing on the morning of the fourth day. He'd been gone less than a month but to Chael it seemed an eternity. The town looked about the same as it always did, neat little stone square filled with shops hawking the latest shipments from across the continent and beyond, or so they claimed; rows of simple wooden tenements squeezed into place between the newer construction of more the opulent stone houses of those who were able to manipulate the sudden trade boom to their benefit. It was all there with just one notable exception, everything seemed to be on fire.

The acrid smell of smoke mixed with burnt flesh wafted down to them on the docks along the Amberwyne Delta. The only buildings that weren't currently ablaze seemed to be the ones already burned to cinders. Chael leaped from the boat onto the shore in one leap followed closely by Michik; he could vaguely hear Rina and Andon shouting protests, but he ignored them. He knew what they would be saying anyway, Andon would be complaining about being left out of the fight and Rina would be scolding him for not coming up with an adequate plan. But fury and stubborn pride got the better of him and he raced toward the heart of the city, and the towering inferno it had become.

Fearing the worst, he reached out with his senses to feel life essence that was sure to be freely blowing about him. There was some, and he quickly drank it in to further enhance his senses, but not nearly as much as he had anticipated. There were at least a thousand people or more in Ehbing at any one time, its population ebbing and flowing with the seaside port. But while there seemed to be a substantial amount of death hanging around the city like a cloud, Chael thought it couldn't be more than a few dozen, one hundred at the very most. Either the majority of the townsfolk had died days ago, and the aura of their lives was washed away by time or most of the people still lived, though he couldn't see how that was likely. Perhaps anger got the better of him, or maybe it was the Dark influence of his power, but he decided to throw prudency to the ash-soaked wind.

"Darrik!" Chael screamed into the hazy clouds of smoke. "I've accepted your invitation, come out and greet me brother!"

There came no answer but the sound of the walls of a house collapsing under their own weight, strength reduced by the flames. He paused for several seconds, waiting for an answer that wouldn't come. Preoccupied as he was, Chael didn't catch the quiet crunching of soil or the smell of rotting meat that came up from behind him, thankfully he was not alone. Michik caught the scent of the skulker in his nose and its arm in his jaws as it invisibly swiped at Chael's back. Reflexes took over as Chael unsheathed his sword and spun slashing blindly at the air behind him.

The demon apparently ducked because air was all he caught in the swing. He recovered quickly, making his next swing by judging where Michik was still holding on to its arm and aimed his sword at where its head should be. His new sword was shorter and lighter than his old falchion making it less suited to the task of severing limbs and breaking bones, but as it struck, demon skull parted and brains splattered over the ashy ground. The skulker demon suddenly materialized out of thin air, thrashing around wildly with blind eyes. With one two-handed strike of his sword Chael banished it to Darkness.

Now more wary, Chael searched around with his senses for any more skulkers in the vicinity. It was an imprecise exercise, looking for the absence of life, but enough essence was floating around that the next skulker stood out like a boulder parting a stream. Chael allowed it to come closer, keeping Michik at bay with a hand, as it approached for its silent strrike, he released Michik who threw it off balance with his claws and made quick work of it with his sword.

Another noise behind him made him spin with his sword extended again but this time he came face to face with Rina as he spun. He quickly pulled in his sword arm at the last second narrowly avoiding her throat. Chael gave her a startled glare to which Rina merely arched an eyebrow.

"We need to find shelter, it's not safe out here," he muttered. Rina looked down at the two dead demons, lip curling in a feral snarl and nodded. Despite the indignant cast to her face her eyes were wide, and Chael read an unmistakable tinge of fear in them.

"I should say so," she half whispered, still staring down at the creatures. It occurred to Chael then that this may be the first time Rina had ever seen a skulker demon before. The ones that caught her out in the plains before Fhaerstead were all the rat-faced variety of lesser demons. "I didn't know they came in different types," she murmured, almost sounding awed.

Michik suddenly growled, teeth bared at an invisible point about a pace to Rina's left. The wolf lunged, taking the invisible creature to the ground as Chael moved to block Rina. But the shock and wonder had melted from Rina's eyes, replaced by steel and vengeance. She pushed past Chael, unstopping a vial with her teeth.

Instead of drinking it as he assumed, she poured greasy gray fluid all over her right hand. It had the consistency of sap and clung easily to her hand. As she strode over to where Michik was wrestling with the creature, she took a small U-shaped piece of metal from her opposite hand. She placed the bit of metal between two fingers and snapped. Her hand erupted in searing white flame. It hurt Chael's eyes just to look at it, it was so bright. And though Chael could feel the heat coming off of it, her flesh remained perfectly intact.

When she reached the invisible demon she reached down, careful to avoid Michik, and gripped the Dark creature with her blazing fist. An otherworldly howl of pain erupted from it, and it flashed into existence in front of their eyes. Rina had the Darkspawn by the throat, her eyes reflecting the scorching fire at her fingertips.

The demon thrashed and screamed and even caught Rina with a random glancing swipe, but she held on, determination written across her face. After only a few seconds her fist closed and the demon's black flesh collapsed under her righteous fire. Chael whistled at the charred remains of its neck, and Rina gave him a sly wink.

"Impressive as that was, we really need to get out of here," Chael asserted quickly, breaking Rina's triumphant smirk. "Oh," he said while looking around, "where's Andon?"

Chapter 46

Present Day

Rina led him away from the burning town square and the corpses of the felled demons. As they walked their destination became clear to Chael as they began to ascend the small hill that led up to the deceased baron's keep.

"We were going to chase after you," Rina was saying as they mounted the hill. "Then Sir Andon noticed people were still alive in the little castle up here." Chael couldn't help but smile at the moniker 'little castle,' the keep was plenty big, perhaps much larger than a small burgeoning city like Ehbing demanded. But it obviously paled in comparison to the impressive seat of King Inarus, that Rina had grown up around.

"He wanted to go see about the survivors, but I insisted that we needed to come rescue you," Rina continued. "So, I came after you while he went up here, and it's a good thing I did too." Chael wasn't so sure that he and Michik needed rescuing, but he let Rina have her moment; he had been foolish to go seeking out Darrik on his own. If he, and the rest of the people of Ehbing, were going to survive whatever this was he needed to keep his mind sharp.

When they reached the top of the squat hill that housed the keep, he noticed that the wooden palisade had been burned away. The wood was already reduced to ash and much of it was scattered by the wind. Rina marched up to the main gate and rapped it as hard as her slender hands would allow. The gate itself was charred from the flames but miraculously still standing even though it was made out of the same sturdy wood as the palisade. Something was odd here.

"Who is it?" came a call from a raspy voice inside.

"Hello? Ah yes," Rina fumbled momentarily. "I am Sister Ischarina of the Fraternal Order of Celestial Light, I come with aid in this dark hour."

"Did ya bring an army?" the man inside asked.

"No…" Rina said uncertainly, a frown emerging on her face. "But we can help if you let us inside." There was a quiet discussion between the man behind the gate and someone else with a strong male voice that Chael instantly recognized. In moments, the large wooden doors began to swing outward laboriously. At first, he could only see one figure behind the gate, and he recognized them, but it wasn't who he thought.

"Mustache?" Chael asked curiously as the short and portly man emerged wagging a furious finger in his direction.

"You!" he shrieked in accusation, pointing his finger as though it were a crossbow aimed at his chest. "I should'a known who commanded the spawn of Darkness," the mustachioed guardsman bellowed. At that moment the second person who had spoken stepped into view. Brod was still a mountain of a man but, for some reason he looked weighted down and diminished. Nevertheless, when he raised his fist and brought it down heavily across mustache's face, it came with the power of a hammer striking hot steel.

"He's come to kill us all," The guard screamed. "He's…" His voice cut off as the punch drove him into the wall and out of the realm of consciousness. Brod looked Chael up and down and nodded. Michik then padded over and pushed his head into Brod's thigh, at first the weathered blacksmith was taken aback and almost attacked, but his reaction passed and with the wolf's gentle touch he relaxed and even managed to give him a few head scratches. At that moment a new figure emerged from within the greater depths of the keep.

"Oh good, you found him before he could kill himself," quipped Andon with a smile. It changed to a slight frown when he noticed the unconscious gate guard and gave Chael an exasperated look.

"Demon," Chael claimed, trying and failing to keep a straight face. "As big as a house, we were lucky to survive." The knight turned his attention to Rina who flushed slightly under the scrutiny.

"It's as Chael said," she lied poorly. "Big as a horse, erm house."

Andon raised an eyebrow, "uh huh," he muttered skeptically. "Well close the gate, we can't have any more demons coming in, can we?"

As the four of them emerged from the shadows of the shrouded gatehouse, Chael couldn't help but suck in a surprised breath at the state of the courtyard that was the heart of the keep. There were tents and cots strewn across the previously well-manicured space. To Chael it seemed that more than half the town was now milling about nervously in the area. He caught many faces he recognized, some sneered or gasped as they saw him walk by. But, to his surprise, a select few gave him respectful nods or pleading looks as if they looked to him for salvation.

"I don't think you're very popular," Rina commented, below them Michik snorted.

"Ya could say that," Brod commented seriously. "Always pickin' fights, this one," he added wearily. Chael clutched his chest feigning great offense but stopped himself when the blacksmith's face remained stone serious.

"Brod," Chael began, starting to suspect something awful. "Where's Maelon and the twins?" Brod stopped and turned to face Chael, tears welling in his eyes. The large man seemed to shrink and whither as the source of the tremendous weight he bore became apparent, his family was dead.

Even now, the powerful essence of their souls was probably flowing through Chael's veins; the thought sickened him. Chael didn't have words, not for something like this, so he did the one thing that was least expected from him. He stepped forward and embraced the blacksmith tightly. Compared to his hulking frame Chael almost felt like a child, eyes barely coming up to his chin, but he squeezed him all the harder. Brod hesitated for a moment, as he had done with Michik, but he too eventually wrapped his arms around Chael, tears falling freely from his cheeks. "I'm sorry my friend," he said at last.

The words caught Chael off guard even as he spoke them. Since his time in Kazaam he hadn't really considered himself worthy of friendship, other than Michik. He had come to the Dark Forest specifically to limit his interactions with people. But the truth of the matter couldn't be denied, Brod was his friend, and because of him, his friend's family had been slaughtered by monsters. Brod roughly broke the hug and wiped the tears from his face.

"Come on," he directed gruffly, moving for the stairs to the higher sections of the keep. "They're waitin' for us."

Together, they moved to the higher sections of the keep and before long found themselves in the Baron's vacant study. Gone were the precious silks and colorful tapestries, the only reminder of the overly opulent baron was a large wooden desk. They opted to leave Michik outside when they entered; as they did, they joined two other citizens of Ehbing around the desk.

The first was a woman named Ascha. Chael didn't recognize her, but soon found out had run one of the more successful import businesses that had recently moved to the town. The other Chael did recognize, though only vaguely.

His name was Aeryl, and he had been an administrator under the Baron as long as Chael had known him, and though he wasn't very well acquainted with the man, Aeryl gave him the same sort of impression that one might have to an especially monstrous slug. He was overdressed, overweight and carried an air of sniveling superiority to the people he considered mere country folk.

"Excuse me," Aeryl cried in a burbling falsetto that contradicted his round features. "We are conducting a private meeting."

"Aye," responded Brod impatiently. "And yer weren't supposed ter do that until I came." Aeryl sniveled and ground his teeth but eventually nodded.

"Very well, as the representative chosen by the people," He put a certain disdainful note on people, "you may stay but the rest of these…" He trailed off wrinkling his nose in their direction. Chael unceremoniously sniffed himself drawing another look of disgust from the former clerk. Even Chael had to admit, he didn't smell like daisies. Hard weeks on the road killing demons and the like would do that to you.

"No," Brod answered firmly. "If anyone stands ter get us out of this mess it's them." Chael absently wondered where his confidence in Rina might have come from considering they never met but the Order robes stained with black blood were an impressive resume given the circumstances. Aeryl resumed grinding his teeth but didn't respond.

"It's fine they can stay, I daresay the famous demonslayer of the Dark Forest will come in handy," Ascha cut in, speaking for the first time. Chael winced at the word famous, his fame is part of what brought this mess upon them all. But he did appreciate the vote of support. That triviality decided, Brod cut in again, speaking mostly for Chael and the others' benefit.

"This is the situation," he said, giving Aeryl one last glare. "About a week past four'a the Darkened beasts raided the square. They caused a ruckus, but we were able ter drive em back." Brod's face darkened as he continued the account. "They came back with fire," he said mournfully.

"How many?" Chael asked.

"Hard ter figure," Brod answered, staring at the floor.

"Perhaps a dozen, maybe more," Ascha cut in after Brod's pause. "They came first for the docks and burned any ship still moored here. Then they attacked the keep and burned the outer wall."

"But they didn't get inside," Aeryl interrupted proudly as if he had personally built the fortification. "This thick stone was too much for them." He added patting the wall. Chael merely shook his head.

"They didn't leave the keep because they couldn't get in," he insisted, the full picture coming to him. "They left it alone because they wanted you in here. You aren't safe, you're hostages. Let me guess, the next day is when they started burning homes, pushing all of the citizens here?"

Aeryl and Ascha eyed each other silently confirming his words and then turned back nodding. "Perhaps we can make it more difficult than they suppose, Rina?" he asked, turning to her. "Does that scriptorium have descriptions of warding runes?"

Rina nodded instantly.

"I think so," she said, already reaching for it in her small pack.

"I'd start with the gate," Andon suggested, earning a nod from Rina.

"I doubt they are as few as twelve," Chael opined. "I'm guessing that was just a small raiding party. Andon, I think it would be best if you saw to the defenses." The knight nodded and strode from the room, Rina following close behind already pouring over the book. "Now..." Chael began, but he was immediately interrupted by Aeryl.

"Now see here!" the fat man imposed, jowls wagging. "As the executive assistant of Baron Janus, I am in charge until he returns." *I don't have time for this,* Chael thought. He whistled and clicked his tongue twice and everyone but him turned as a lumbering weight stomped in from the hall. Michik padded in teeth bared and walked right up to Aeryl, the wolf only stopped when his muzzle was a foot from the pompous man's chest.

"Baron Janus is dead." Chael said calmly, eliciting at least one shocked gasp. "If you wish to join him, you have my leave, but I will not suffer the whims of a useless fop or condemn the people of Ehbing to die under your care." Chael clicked his tongue one more time and Michik returned to his side.

Aeryl didn't protest or respond in any specific way to Chael's words, Chael decided to take that as his assent. With the hierarchy now firmly set, Chael swept from the room and ascended more stairs until he reached the top of what little the keep boasted for battlements.

In reality, it was little more than wooden scaffolding that rounded the top of the square keep interspersed with occasional raised platforms to view the surrounding countryside. Chael trained his eyes over the still smoldering town, everything that could burn had been cruelly set to light. Even if the people survived the coming storm, Chael doubted if Ehbing could ever recover.

Movement along the tree line along the edge of the Dark Forest caught his eye. From all around the town shadows seemed to squirm and writhe inside the black expanse under the dense forest canopy. Movement behind him made Chael turn as Brod emerged onto the roof of Ehbing's keep and joined him on the viewing platform. He gave Chael a questioning look, but he simply put a finger to his lips and pointed out at the trees.

After a moment came the deep rumbling blast of some giant horn, it was immediately followed by the peels of sound from several more horns, though from the sound it was obvious they were smaller.

Brod stood frozen, eyes transfixed on the dark trees. Chael's shoulders slumped and his heart sank, he didn't even need to look up to know what was coming next. Like rolling thunder, demons began to march in time out of the forest. The coordination they exhibited was far beyond what Chael would have said such creatures were capable. Lesser demons were flanked on the side by skulkers not deigning at this moment to hide themselves.

Behind them were contingents of half-breeds, many of them holding leads restraining terrifying four-legged beasts. They somewhat resembled dogs in shape but were larger, about Michik's size. Along their backs were spiked red quills, as thick as his arm and serrated like saw teeth. Figures in black cloaks stood behind their army of demons and demon hybrids, shouting commands and directing their army. Chael couldn't estimate the full number but dozens, not even scores did them justice. Hundreds of Dark creatures now descended upon Ehbing, their human masters not far behind.

"Darkness!" Brod cursed as he watched the horrifying spectacle.

"Yes," Chael replied, himself also awed. Darkness itself had fallen upon Ehbing.

Chapter 47

6 Days Ago

Darrik

The demon blood pulsing in his veins made Darrik stronger and faster than any mortal man. He could run without tiring for days on end if it was required, and it had been required. By the time the children had broken him out of the stargazers' prison, Chael was already gone.

He didn't know if the bastard had left the city or not, but it didn't matter. The paltry examples of the new race they had given to Khalim would be no match for Chael, he knew. His death would lay elsewhere, so Darrik had run.

By the time he arrived deep within the heart of the Western Forest, the human parts of him were weary and starving. As he smashed his fist against the gate of the wooden fort, he was nearly some mindless Darkspawn, the demon in him exerting more control as the human faded.

A man in a black hood peaked over the top of the spiked walls of the fort, "Darrik?" he questioned. Darrik struggled to concentrate his mind against the influence of the demon inside of him enough to respond intelligently.

"Inside," he finally managed to choke out, his mind clouded. Instantly, the heavy door swung inward, and he lumbered inside. A slave, steel collar gleaming around her neck, was carrying a tray of raw meat over to a pen of barking fellhounds.

Darrik snatched the tray, shoving the slave girl to the ground and tore into the food. It would take a while for the nourishment to strengthen him enough to fully reassert control, but the warmth of a full belly steeled his will, at least for the moment. He grabbed the nearest black robed acolyte by the arm, dragging him closer until they were face to face.

"Where is the Lady?" Darrik demanded, his voice coming out mixed with human and demonic tones, the sounds weaving themselves together in a chilling dissonant chord. It was a sign of how close the demon was to the surface, but at the moment, it helped carry the urgency of his tone across to the terrified acolyte.

"They've gone," the hooded man squeaked. "She and Master Mason went North to the House of Glass." Darrik found that curious, they wouldn't abandon their mission here. Chael was much too important to their plans, much too important to kill, at least not yet.

"Why?" Darrik hissed, allowing more of the demon to come through in his voice.

"The Lady she..." the man stumbled over his tongue as Darrik squeezed harder. "She was injured by the Darkborn and his beast." Darrik smiled at his own dumb luck.

"We need to make preparations," Darrik announced to all the Black Hand acolytes that surrounded him. "We're going to war." The man still held in his hand quivered but at length opened his mouth to object.

"We are to wait for..." the acolyte never finished his objection. Allowing the demon to fully control their body for just a moment, Darrik slammed his fist into the man's torso, crushing his chest. His last words were an unintelligible burble as blood filled his mouth and choked him. Not wanting to deny the fellhounds their meal, Darrik heaved the acolyte's corpse into their pen, smiling as he heard the dog-like demons tear apart their supper.

Present Day

Chael

"It isn't nearly enough," Andon commented as they counted up the food and water supplies for the entire town. "The townsfolk didn't have time to prepare, they just fled here when the demon's started burning houses."

"That is..." Chael clenched his teeth, "most unfortunate," he finished resignedly.

"I don't suspect we can hold out for more than a few days, if that," the knight admitted sadly, adding to their growing list of problems. Andon moved to scratch at his chin with his right hand, an unconscious gesture that Chael was sure he had performed innumerable times. This time however, nothing but the stump of a wrist touched his face, the knight hesitated, startled by himself then sighed, lowering his hand.

"I'm sorry Andon," Chael offered honestly.

"Bah," he replied, waving his left hand this time. "I would have died in service to King Inarus," he continued, and Chael had no doubts about the sincerity of that claim. "Merely losing a hand in the effort? I call that mercy." Chael nodded though in his mind mercy was definitely not the word he would have chosen.

A forge, Chael supposed. For in essence, that's what the school was. Minister Khalim bought forgotten and unwanted children and hauled them out to this small property in secret, not to educate them, as the word "school" implied. They were cast into a furnace and forged through fire into tools that served the cruel minister's needs. And those that couldn't serve were simply burned away by the flame. But now the tools would be brought to bear, and the survivors of

Khalim's brutal school would finally emerge into the light. Election season had begun in Kazaam.I'll just have to prove my worth, he thought.

An audacious plan began to form in his mind, it was likely to get a lot of people killed but so was anything else they tried, including just waiting behind their walls. "Darkness," Chael cursed, drawing a raised eyebrow from Sir Andon. "We have to go to another meeting."

Once again Chael found himself in Janus's study, facing off with the prodigious jowly might of Aeryl.

"Out of the question!" the former administrator wheezed. "The beasts haven't breached these walls and I see no reason to go courting death." Chael shot a look at Andon thumbing one of his knives anxiously. The knight gave him a placating gesture with his hand and cleared his throat.

"Master Aeryl," he began politely. "I don't believe we have been properly introduced; I am Sir Andon Al-Fhaelan, son of Baron Grecious Al-Fhaelan and sworn Knight of the Realm." The stodgy clerk lifted his eyebrows a bit but seemed unmoved by his title. "The matter is simple, there isn't enough food for the amount of people being housed here." Andon eyed everyone in the room, striking the syllables like a hammer. "Even with extreme rationing we will run out of basic supplies in days."

"So, you want less mouths to feed!" Aeryl raged. "Kill them now good Sir Knight, if you must. But don't go asking me to volunteer my neck!" Chael found that particular prospect quite appealing but decided to permit Andon to continue negotiations.

"How would this work?" Ascha cut in, cooling some of the steam coming out of Aeryl's ears.

"Three teams," The knight responded. "Chael and I will lead a group of volunteers to stage a block." Aeryl huffed looking at Andon's missing hand but didn't comment. "Group two will go and raid the homes on the south side near the river for any food left unspoiled. Group three will go down to the river." Andon paused and looked to Brod suggesting he continue.

"There's a culvert that feeds the well down the courtyard," Brod began. "It's filled with… well Stars know what, but it's jammed."

"Unblock the river culvert and the well fills up," Chael finished for Brod. "With fresh water we can hold out for a few weeks rather than days."

"How long will you need to prepare?" Ascha inquired, pinching her brows as she tried to imagine the needed logistics.

"We can't spare more than a day or two," Andon replied, frowning. "I wish we could have more time to train some volunteers and gather what resources we can, but the water situation is that dire."

"Two days then," Ascha declared, still looking like she was furiously trying to think her way out of the predicament. "Can you get the volunteers up to speed in so little time?" The knight gave her his best attempt at an encouraging smile, which was something coming from Andon, but even he couldn't instill much confidence.

"I think I can help," Rina cut in, splitting the uneasy silence like a knife. "I've been working on a new type of alchemical construct that I think we can use to cover those working down by the river."

"Which brings us to the other part of the plan," Andon continued, nodding to Rina. "A crew of three will split off once the culvert is clear and board the river craft we took to get here. With more water we should have enough time for them to reach Westfhael and beg their aid."

"You mean the aid of your father." Aeryl snidely hissed. "And I suppose you will be going on that mission hmm?" Andon fixed him with the gaze of a man who had seen the light die in another's eyes and found the belligerent clerk wanting.

"No," the knight replied fiercely, the very air seeming to freeze in the space between them. "I will be at Chael's side fighting whatever the powers of Darkness can conjure up." Before Sir Andon the little man quaked and but for the trembling of his lip, he didn't move his mouth again. Chael couldn't help but gaze at him with absolute, unremitting pride.

Chapter 48

Present Day

He's patronizing me, Chael thought. He didn't like being spoken down to, the man was big and obviously strong, and Chael guessed he was used to intimidating people. But Chael had been exhaustively trained on how to deal with people who were bigger and stronger and felt quite confident about his odds should they come to blows. However, he had been ordered to play host, so he was largely impotent to teach Mason a lesson. Probably curious if I'm as insane as he is, Chael thought. He briefly considered jumping off the balcony to prove that he was just as capable, but his better senses won out and he turned toward the door to the stairs. I could have been out on a real mission, Chael sighed as he made his way out of the building.

"Shouldn't we be trying to stay quiet?" the knight asked him with an arched eyebrow.

Chael shrugged and looked back at the thoroughly unstealthy mob that awkwardly marched behind him. In the dim and misty dawn light he could see many people clearly holding weapons for the first time in their lives.

Andon had done his best to drill them in spear formations as he had in Fhaerstead, but the kind of spears they were able to cobble together within the Baron's keep were long and ungainly, Chael didn't have high expectations for them. But he had been honest about that in his recruiting pitch, much to Rina's chagrin and Andon's approval.

Rina for her part had tried to come but both Chael and Andon had forbidden it. As useful as she had proved herself on the battlefield, she was the only qualified alchemist amongst their little rabble and couldn't spare the time away from making elixirs and constructs. He only wished that they could have given his tiny volunteer army some elixirs, but they simply didn't have enough to go around.

As they neared the bottom of the hill, Chael began scanning the surrounding area with his senses, "nothing yet," he told Andon.

The knight quickly began organizing the ranks of his volunteer spearmen and in impressively little time a column of spear-wielding villagers three rows deep began marching in slightly fractured formation away from the hill and toward the city center. Sir Andon eyed his people with beaming pride.

As the armed wall moved steadily towards the town, the people behind began to break off into their various assignments. About half of the remaining people walked timidly behind the spear wall, ducking their heads as if hoping to hide in the shadow of those marching.

The other half, led by Brod, turned away and proceeded down to the docks on the Southern face of the keep. A few of them bore swords though Chael was more than dubious as to their personal proficiency with the weapons. Brod simply held one of his medium smithing hammers, worn leather grip clasped comfortably in his rough hand. Other than Brod and the few inexperienced sword wielders, their primary protection would come from the wooden ramparts at the top of the keep. A score of bowmen as well as others with tubular explosive constructs provided by Rina, stood poised ready to rain fire down on any cultist or demon that got near the mission down by the river.

"You know you didn't answer me," Chael prodded Andon as they continued their march at the head of the little column, more than once receiving an accidental poke from a wayward spear.

"Hmm?" Andon answered confusedly, though he suspected that the Knight was just playing coy.

"How good are you with your left?" Chael asked him impatiently.

"Knights of the Realm are trained to fight with both hands since childhood," Andon replied without much conviction.

"That was not my question," Chael pointed out. Andon sighed heavily before looking him in the eye.

"Shite," the knight replied honestly, taking Chael aback. "Better than most brigands or highwaymen, mind you," he added quickly. "But I've seen firsthand what we're up against," Andon didn't even try to conceal the shudder that shook the leather pauldrons of his shoulders. "With both hands and a full set of armor, I'm afraid I'm no match."

Chael respected the other man's brutally honest self-assessment, even though he didn't necessarily share his pessimism. He had seen Andon fell several lesser demons after only having seen them for the first time in that encounter. Still, that seemed an eternity ago, and it had been with both his hands.

Lacking comfort in the silence that followed Andon's remarks, Chael roughly clubbed him on the shoulder and gave him his best reassuring smile. To his disappointment Andon looked less than reassured, Michik gave a snorting little huff beside him. Still the knight gave a nod of appreciation and reached for the vial hung around his neck.

"Nasty stuff," he remarked before downing it.

Rina had assured him that he could drink it all at once without overwhelming his system like the batch Aelisa had given him. Chael watched curiously as the effects took hold, at once the already rigid knight seemed to stand straighter and his muscles began to tighten and twitch like taut leather. Chael smiled at him again, but this time more genuine as he could see the confidence build in his companion.

"Hold them," Chael said as he stepped forward with Michik.

Andon raised his only fist, high into the air and with less bumping and stumbling than he had predicted, the spear wall stopped. Michik meanwhile had begun sniffing intently at the air and was now baring his wicked teeth in his half-lipped snarl.

"It's time," he whispered to Andon, drawing the short arming sword he had taken from Fhaerstead. While the small sword was practical and well made, he desperately missed the weight of his familiar falchion. It had become the perfect tool for the dispatching of demons.

Nine, eight, seven, six. Slowly, Chael whittled down their number until he ran out of stolen bolts. I could have been out on a real mission, Chael sighed as he made his way out of the building.I hate people, he thought, and then glanced down at his dog. I suppose that's sufficient mockery for the moment, he conceded to himself. "Now," he continued more earnestly, "why in Darkness have you come here?"

He beat that thought down with a mental hammer.

He wasn't sure if it was from the presence or if it was his old instincts reasserting themselves in the face of danger, but he wouldn't allow himself to think that way. The people behind him were relying on him to bring them back to safety, not to allow them to be cut down so he could benefit from their deaths. Still the paradox of his abilities nagged at him like one of those spears accidentally poking him in the spine.

He reached the edge of the town, about twenty paces ahead of the spear column where the ruins of several homes now littered the cobbled street. A lone figure materialized in the morning mist and strode out between the broken homes and rubble. He wore a black robe with a similar dark hood that shrouded his face, though as he approached Chael, he stuck out his chin confidently and it alone emerged from the shadow.

"Greetings," he hissed in a whispering snake-like voice, which was entirely too jubilant for Chael's liking. "I take it that I now stand in the presence of the assassin Chael?" Chael's already poor mood was further soured by the word, 'assassin,' but he chose to ignore it.

"I am," he simply responded in a cold low voice.

Michik continued growling beside him, though if the cultist noticed, he made no sign. "I take it you're here to discuss terms?" Chael asked hopefully.

He suspected that the Black Hand may be interested in a trade for his own life in exchange for that of the town's. He wasn't entirely certain how willing he was to make that trade, but it was best to find out if such things were even on the table.

The hooded man threw his head back and laughed at Chael's question, revealing a little more of his face. This one seemed to be fully human as he could see none of the black veins under his skin. *That should make this considerably easier,* Chael thought.

"There will be no terms," the cultists cooed, laughter still tugging at his voice. "I was bidden to convey this message to you, from your dear friend."

The word friend immediately focused Chael's attention, which almost certainly meant that Darrik was here and if not commanding outright, at least held some authority over the cultist army. There truly would be no negotiations here, not while Darrik lived.

The hooded cultist smiled at Chael's visceral reaction and continued relaying his message. "Ehbing shall burn, and you will witness every death knowing their doom rests upon your shoulders alone. Then you will die."

Chael began advancing with his sword, but Michik beat him to it, the wolf flew across the space separating them from the cultist and leaped. The hooded man only had time to change his expression from a confident grin to pure shock as Michik ripped his throat out. Chael's exhilaration at the kill was short-lived. Almost immediately as the blood began to pour from the dead cultists throat, lesser demons began charging toward their pitiful little band, crooked teeth gleaming and mouths frothing.

"Spears!" Andon called as several dozen long shafts lowered toward the charging Darkspawn.

"Meeshee," Chael commanded softly, looking down at his loyal companion. "Protect Andon and the others. Don't let anything get past them." The wolf looked up at his master ruefully, understanding his role but unwilling to leave his side. "Go," he told his dog more forcefully, and the wolf turned and ran back to the column, placing himself on the other side opposite the knight.

Chael drew one of his knives and placed it in his non-dominant hand, a fighting style usually precluded by his tendency to wield his falchion with two hands for added strength. Sadly, the short sword didn't have a handle long enough for such things so having the small weapon in his off hand at least gave him an extra blade with which to parry. As the rat-faces drew near, he squared his shoulders and sucked up the power gifted to him by the arrogant cultist. The wave would break here, and the Dark would run out of demons before it broke him.

The first one came lumbering at him mindlessly, black claws reaching out for his neck. They met only the cool steel of his knife as he parried the attack and retaliated with a backhanded swipe of his sword. Hobbled, the demon fell to its knees and Chael banished it with another swing.

The next two fell just as swiftly and for a moment he dared to hope that he could keep them at bay by himself. But those first few demons were just the ones too stupid or unruly to march in formation. In their wake came a solid line of demons walking in coordinated steps across the ruined street. Chael could do nothing but back away until he joined Michik at the flank of their spear wall.

What was he thinking bringing these people out here? They weren't soldiers. Even if they were, there was no hope. He had marched all these people out here to die, the thought sickened him even as he watched the coming catastrophe.

"Brace!" called a booming voice from the other side, and the spearmen in the front placed the butts of their weapons in the ground as the row behind pushed theirs further outward toward the lesser demons. "Loose!" Andon called again, and several smoking clay pots were hurled from the back row into the line of approaching demons just as they were mere feet away from the extended spears.

Detonations rocked the demon line as black blood and torn flesh flew in all directions. "Forward!" the knight commanded and to Chael's astonishment the spear wall moved in near perfect synchronicity, and demons began to cry out with new pain as the weapons struck out and found Dark flesh.

Chael was so astonished by their effectiveness that he almost let himself be beheaded by a demon on the far edge of their line as they tried to encircle the spear column. Luckily for him, Michik wasn't so easily distracted and intercepted the demon as it groped for Chael's head.

Reinvigorated, Chael cut the demon down and began doing his best to secure his little army's flank. He had to act quickly he knew, for while the spears were doing surprisingly good work, they weren't killing the demons. Only taking their heads would do that, but the spears were keeping them at bay and wounding the demons enough for Chael and Andon to clean up. Or that was the plan at the very least.

At the moment, all Chael could do was engage the demons trying to encircle their group. If any got around him, or Andon on the other side, their seemingly impenetrable wall of spears would shatter. He didn't want to even imagine the bloodbath that would ensue, so he kept hacking at demons with his sword while Michik tore at them with his jaws.

Slowly, and only after rivers of black gore sloshed between his feet, the onslaught of demons dwindled, and Chael began to push toward the center. Broken demons filled with more holes than a certain variety of cheese stumbled and teetered on unsteady legs.

The cultists, who were certainly driving them from behind, were nowhere to be seen and Chael began the gleeful task of cleanup. Shortly after he began, Andon appeared from the other flank, haggard but unharmed. He beamed brightly at Chael as he too began chopping off every flailing demon head in sight. In only minutes they banished perhaps fifty of the foul creatures.

When the twitching subsided and all the Dark creatures lay still, a lone cry of triumph erupted from the spearmen. Soon it was joined by others until every man and woman who volunteered to accompany the mission was cheering at the top of their lungs. Michik added to the cacophony, leaning his head back and baying to the sky after the nature of wolves. Even Chael couldn't help but crack a smile, though he knew that the danger hadn't necessarily passed.

His fears were proven true. Just moments after the cheering began, two black hoods emerged from behind one of the few standing buildings left in Ehbing. The most significant thing about them wasn't the hoods, however, it was their right hands. Or lack of right hands to be specific, where each one should have had a fleshy appendage emerging from their right sleeves, there was instead a gray cloud of swirling ash.

Chapter 49

Present Day

"Run!" Chael screamed hoarsely as he had barely enough time to fill his lungs with air, as he ran back to the column. Andon was staring at him with a look of bewilderment, but he must have seen something in Chael's eyes because he began issuing new marching orders for a defending retreat. *Not fast enough.* "Drop your weapons and run!" he yelled, more clearly this time. The front line of spears looked from him to Andon uncertainly, so Chael turned and faced the knight head on. "By the Living Stars order them to drop their weapons and run!"

Andon gave him only half a moment more of uncertainty before turning to his little troop and shouting, "Back to the keep! The mission is over, drop your spears and run!" Relief flooded Chael as the volunteers dropped their heavy spears and one by one began sprinting away from what was coming. The two hooded cultists watched them go with disinterest; their attention focused solely on Chael as they calmly walked forward. Slender blades appeared in their hands as they silently creeped forward, and the stomach dropped out of Chael's chest. "What are they?" Andon asked as he stepped beside Chael.

"They are beyond either of us," he answered seriously, turning to face Andon. "You need to go with them," he said, indicating the fleeing spearmen.

"I will not…" Andon began but Chael stopped him with a hard stare.

"You have to lead them; I will do what I can here. Please go." The knight hesitated and then gave Chael one of his customary nods before jogging off in the direction of the keep.

Chael stepped forward and dropped his sword onto the ground, it would not serve in this fight. Instead, he drew another knife out and wielded one of the trusty weapons in each hand. As he walked closer to his opponents, he rolled his shoulders in what he hoped seemed like a casual gesture. The only weapon that their ashen blades couldn't shatter was his confidence, blunt though that particular blade was in this moment.

"I thought I wasn't supposed to die until the end?" he jeered at them, trying to match the smirks painted across their own faces.

Their response was a lance of solid gray ash that shot out at his face like a diving falcon. Chael barely had enough time to dive out of the way as the shaft of death swept the air where his head had just been.

Michik sped off in a wide circling arc dodging lances of his own. Chael rolled to his feet and ducked another slash as it whistled over his head. Gray ash swirled and reshaped a dozen times each, every attack finding a new angle and a new shape to lash out at him with. One of the hooded figures turned from him, satisfied that his partner could deal with Chael on his own and fully switched his attention to the wolf that was preparing an attack on his side. This, Chael could not allow.

He bit down on the side of his cheek hard enough to draw blood and propelled himself with all the remaining life essence upon which he could draw. A great warhammer the size of a tree stump came crashing down on him and in one motion Chael slipped the heavy blow and shot out his left wrist like an exploding alchemical construct.

The knife flew from his hand in a blistering line that seemed to carve the very air in front of it until it slammed home in the spine of the cultist readying to kill his dog. The sword of forged essence disappeared into a mist of gray ash as the stunned killer fell to his knees. Never one to miss an opportunity, Michik pounced, and Chael could hear the satisfying sound of tearing flesh as his mighty wolf made quick work of the disabled Black Hand acolyte.

The gamble paid off, but Chael still paid a heavy price. Unbalanced by his dodge to support the throw he couldn't evade the follow-up from the cultist in front of him. The hammer, after putting a crater in the stone that Michik could comfortably lay in, warped into a curved scimitar sliced upward at Chael as he tried to dive out of the way. A line of black death traced up his back, all the way from his hip to his far shoulder. Pain. His mind was consumed with it in a way he had never felt before. In the space between his failed dive and hitting the ground, a thousand years seemed to pass, racked with the agony and torment of a damned soul.

His chest slammed into the street ,barely registering on his consciousness. Futilely, he reached out in desperation for any source of life energy around him to heal the crater of affliction that twisted his soul. Little by little the scattered remnants of the energy that sustained all that grows, answered his call. It didn't diminish the pain, but it gave him just enough mental clarity to see the strike that was about to end torment for good. At the moment he welcomed it and embraced the coming Darkness.

With a self-satisfied grin, the hooded cultist forged a headsman's ax out of ash and lifted it over his head. Michik had already leaped but the wolf would hit the cultist long after Chael had been split like a cord of firewood.

The ax fell, but before it landed, the cultist was shot backward with the force of a thunderbolt. Likewise, it seemed to Chael that a thunderclap had detonated only paces from his ears, though the sudden pressure in his head was a welcome distraction from the agony on his back.

Fighting back tears, Chael managed to look up and twenty paces away was Sir Andon, holding one of the mysterious blasting tubes that Rina had constructed. Smoke was trailing out the end of it and the front was badly singed. The knight was looking at it in awe, but when he noticed Chael, he dropped the spent construct and rushed to his side. Chael tried to speak, but the words choked in his throat, so he merely pointed to where the hooded figure lay.

"He's not getting up," the knight assured.

Michik had already gone over to the body to inspect it and was pawing the man's head curiously. One check with his senses confirmed the truth for Chael and he immediately tried to consume the life essence trailing from the two corpses. It was like trying to take a deep breath with broken ribs and scarred lungs, but he forced himself to keep going.

Eventually, the pain subsided to a marginally tolerable level, and he was even able to sit up. Experimentally, he wiggled his fingers and toes, and to his relief, they obeyed his command, though the effort felt like trudging through mud that was also somehow acid. Andon whistled as he noticed his back and Michik came over whining his own concerns and licking his face with his dry tongue.

"How bad is it?" he asked Andon, breathlessly. He could feel the tissues slowly fusing themselves back together, but compared to his normal rate of healing with the power of two human deaths, it was being downright sluggish.

Andon hesitated but then answered grimacing, "I think I could reach my hand in and pull out what you had for breakfast." Andon was pale, though he must have seen his share of battle wounds, it must be truly unpleasant then. "And the flesh its, black and decayed like rotted meat."

Chael didn't necessarily appreciate the added color, but the knight had saved his life so he could forgive the indulgence. "We have to get out of here," Chael pointed out, gritting his teeth.

"Can you even walk?"

"I guess we'll find out," Chael replied with a forced grin and shakily rose to his feet. He took one step, screamed in pain and fell directly on his face. Pain and frustration wracked his body anew, and he cycled the life energy even more urgently through his system. He had completely drained all the energy left from the two dead men, but their energy would take time to heal him if it even could. He had seen what that weapon did to living tissue firsthand and the fact that he was alive at all was no small victory.

"Here," Andon offered, reaching out his hand. Chael took it and the knight lifted him up and placed Chael's arm over his shoulders. He was unsteady, but every passing moment gave him more time to heal, and he grew stronger by the step. By the time they reached the hill he could walk on his own, and there was a wave of new energy to aid the now dwindling power of the two cultists. Chael's sigh of relief turned to dread as the realization hit him. There was a lot of life energy in the area, too much.

"How bad was it?" he asked, spinning on Andon. The knight shook his head grimly.

"About half made it back," he mumbled before adding, "your friend Brod among them." That relieved Chael to hear even more than he had anticipated.

"And the mission," he asked hesitantly. Once again, the knight merely shook his head.

"Apparently a squad of half-breeds was waiting by the docks. They were in a fighting retreat from the moment we separated. They never had time to even try to open the water culvert, let alone send a boat to Westfhael."

Chael nodded at the news, even as he greedily drank in all the life essence he could capture from the ill-fated mission on the other side of the hill. He felt guilty for the necessity, and that unlike the townspeople he could once again escape death, but his guilt wouldn't bring them back or defeat their enemies.

Oh, how I yearn for a more pragmatic brand of assassin, Chael chuckled to himself.

Chapter 50

Present Day

The mood in the now less crowded courtyard was somber. As Chael, Andon, and Michik walked through, many faces turned to them, but none was willing to rise and meet their eyes, or at least his.

They blamed him, Chael thought. He supposed that was fair, he planned the operation and led it to failure. He even got to avoid the would-be crippling blow to his back off the lives these people were now left to grieve. It was a good thing then that they couldn't meet his gaze, he couldn't meet theirs either.

"What are we to do?" cried a woman being partially restrained by a man Chael assumed to be her husband. She was speaking to Andon, or at least trying to. "We needed that water. What are we going to do?"

She didn't seem angry to Chael, though she fought in the arms of the man trying desperately to reach the knight. She seemed desperate, like someone for whom all hope of rescue had been taken away.

In another time, Chael might have pointed out that they were in precisely the same situation as they were before they showed up, and at least they tried, but even he didn't have the stomach for the words. She was right after all, to be hopeless, there really wasn't anything to do. These people were condemned to die for the simple crime of living adjacent to Chael's place of refuge the last few years. They didn't even like him and they were still going to pay the price for his sins.

Andon walked over to her, hand raised in a gesture that was probably meant to placate the woman. Knowing him, it would probably work, he was good at that sort of thing. Sir Andon was the kind of person that people wanted to believe in, Chael meanwhile was the sort that people wanted to throw stones at.

Soon his melancholic wandering led him out of the courtyard and away from the people he had so thoroughly failed. A ringing like a dull bell drew his attention into an area of the keep he hadn't visited before. It was a small fenced in courtyard on the other side of the keep from the main central one. It was used to house livestock for the kitchens, though currently it was only occupied by one blacksmith.

Brod was furiously hammering a glowing bar of steel with his hammer, every stroke showering the small uninhabited pen with sparks. Michik sniffed around curiously, probably smelling what remained from when there were live animals in the little pen, but after a moment he walked over and gave Brod a small bump with his head. A small bump from Michik was enough to nearly topple a grown man, and even the sturdy blacksmith had to stagger a step, but Michik got what he was after and Brod favored him with a few grumbling head scratches before the wolf went to lay down in the corner, satisfied that he had been given the proper deference from the humans in the room.

"Are ya gonna stare at me or help boy?" the blacksmith asked.

Chael hadn't really expected Brod to notice him at all with how fiercely he was pounding the steel with his smithing hammer, and truthfully, he had wanted to remain unnoticed though Michik spoiled any chance of that.

"What do you need," he answered meekly. In truth he wanted to be alone, he was only here because of curiosity and definitely wasn't in the mood for manual labor. Absently he scratched the black line that still scarred his back. Brod pointed to a small bellows that supplied air to an open top coal forge.

"I'll need ter heat this soon," he said gruffly, still hammering at the steel like it insulted his ancestors.

Taking the hint, Chael got to work at the small hand bellows and soon the coals flared back to life with deep orange and red light. The heat coming off of it threatened to singe the wisps of beard Chael had allowed to grow since his escape from the Order dungeon.

After a few minutes of pumping air, Brod strode over holding the steel between tongs. The glow had disappeared leaving the metal looking charred and black until the blacksmith roughly shoved it into the hot coals.

"So," Chael began awkwardly, unsure of what to say. "What are you making?"

"Don't know," Brod responded without looking at him.

He was working the bellows with his foot, driving the heat higher and higher until Chael had to back away a step though the seasoned smith hardly seemed to notice.

"The steel hasn't decided wha' it wants ter be yet." Now the blacksmith looked at him, eyes as black as the burnt steel. "It can be like tha' sometimes."

Chael got the uncomfortable impression that the blacksmith was no longer talking about metal.

"A speartip, maybe," Chael suggested, hoping to distract the iron gaze of Brod. "We're going to need more of those, I'm sure."

"Aye," Brod agreed, nodding and turning back to his heated bar of steel. Feeling the metal was sufficiently heated the smith plucked it out of the forge with his tongs and returned it to his anvil and resumed hammering. This time, his strokes were slower and more precise and like some sort of metallic snake the metal seemed to slither out and extend over the edge of the forge. "Spear's a good weapon. Especially for those who ain't used ter fightin'."

"Exactly," Chael answered though he still wasn't exactly clear if they were talking about the same thing.

"But," Brod continued, still pounding the steel with his hammer. "Sometimes somethin' special is needed, if the steel wants ter be special. Otherwise, it may as well jus' be a spear."

"Brod what are we really talking about here?" Chael demanded, tired of the ill-concealed subterfuge.

The blacksmith dropped the hammer on the forge and stared at him again. To Chael it seemed his eyes were searching for something but for what, he couldn't say.

"Listen lad I..." Brod began but cut off. Screaming had erupted from down the hall. Michik was already bounding toward the door before Chael and Brod could even turn, but they did manage to share a final foreboding look with each other before chasing after the wolf. The screaming was definitely coming from inside the keep, the walls had been breached.

Chael and Brod raced through the short corridor that led back from the side of the keep to the main courtyard where Ehbing's refugees had settled. As they ran, just barely keeping pace with Michik, Chael could already feel the weight of death begin to settle over the last bastion of humanity left in the city, it fueled him even as it filled his gut with dread.

The three of them burst out into the courtyard to a sight that was uniquely grisly even for Chael's hardened eyes. A dozen giant dog-like creatures were tearing through the defenseless civilians like a scythe threshing wheat.

"Dog" was perhaps a misnomer, because while they ran on four legs and moved with feral canine grace and tenacity, that was where the similarities stopped. Instead of fur, their backs and flanks were lined with thick black and red chitinous spikes that seemed to move independently of their owner, lashing out anyone who got too close. Their muzzles were long and scaley. Almost crocodilian, Chael thought, though his knowledge of such creatures was limited to tall tales not practical experience.

Michik launched himself at one that was bearing down on a cowering child, her mother was already laying in pieces at her feet. The creature seemed to exhibit a level of sentience that belied its animalistic features. It mocked the little girl, crocodile jaws snapping shut and spraying her with a gout of her own mother's blood.

Michik latched his own powerful jaws on the snout of the creature and thrashed his head violently. Several of the spikes shot out and found his flesh but the wolf held on, continuing to shake the creature at the point of its muzzle.

When Chael finally arrived, a decisive essence fueled chop ended the demon's attack for good. Michik, wasting no time, bounded off for the next one as soon as the demon's head was severed.

Chael moved to go after him but was cut off by another one and immediately began fending off its snapping maw and darting spikes. The creature, though lumbering in size and shape, was impressively agile and quick and Chael had to pour more power into his attacks to advance. The fellhound, or Chael assumed that was what it was having never actually seen one before, lashed out at him with all of its spikes raised like a dog's hackles.

Empowered by all the death around him Chael was quicker and dodged the attack while simultaneously bringing his sword down and taking its head. Michik meanwhile had joined Andon who was being driven back into the stone wall by two advancing fellhounds. Chael couldn't help but stare in admiration as the two seamlessly blended their attacks together. Demonic limbs and spikes began falling to the ground as man and wolf made their own advance on the demonic interlopers.

Chael wasn't so distracted that he didn't notice the fellhound sneaking up from behind him. His enhanced senses picked it up immediately as it made its way nearer and he waited for the last moment to turn the tables on the would-be ambush. But just as he turned to deliver his surprise blow a white corded light scorched the very air as it shot out into the space between them.

The light whip of the Order of Celestial Light, their signature weapon, wrapped around the demonic hound's neck and where it touched flesh it seared. The fellhound screamed in fury at the white-hot pain but was quickly cut off as Rina pulled the cord taut and took its head. Chael gave Rina a quick nod of thanks which she returned with a ferocious smile and a precocious wink. Chael grimaced slightly at the spectacle of her fleshless arm whence the whip had grown but his discomfort at her use of Order alchemy didn't last long.

The demon hounds had identified the threats in the room and divided themselves accordingly. Apparently, Chael merited four which hardly seemed fair to him considering that only left two each for the others, but he supposed he'd have to lodge his complaint with Darrik later.

As one the fellhounds attacked. Chael wielding only his short sword and knife, began parrying scores of razor-sharp bladed spikes and vise-like jaws. He drank more and more of the precious life essence that now pooled around him like a valley during a rainstorm.

Somewhere deep inside him, a voice cackled with the thrill of the bloodshed, utterly unconcerned that what were ostensibly its own allies were also dying. The revulsion at its joy almost made Chael miss a step; almost. But with reflexes honed by years of brutal training and power granted by the very depths of Darkness, Chael turned his gleaming azure eyes to his four opponents.

The ferocity of their attacks was only matched by the velocity of his steel. Every time a spike or a set of teeth came close, he batted it out of the way with a blade edge and a shower of black blood. They came at him from too many angles to effectively go on the attack, but little by little he reduced their appendages to bleeding stumps and as he did, they slowed.

When it was over, four broken husks lay before him, laid low by a thousand cuts and now awaited final execution, Chael swiftly ended their suffering.

A quick scan of the surroundings told him that only one of the beasts was still moving and that one was being pounded into oblivion by Brod's hammer like he was back at the forge working an especially onerous piece of steel. The smith had already crushed its skull and was violently smashing black and green demon brain matter all over Rina.

Chael allowed himself a slight smirk at her obvious discomfort, but it quickly fell away as he surveyed the carnage in the rest of the room. They had engaged the fellhounds quickly and had done very well at mitigating their damage. But the demons were as efficient as they were cruel. Tortured bodies littered the courtyard, black blood mixing with red, and the only thing that held back the screams was the shock of the brutal exchange. Furious, Chael stole across the room to Andon.

"Where did they come from?" he demanded, more harshly than he intended. His anger was at Darrik and himself, the knight was only doing his best. Andon was either too tired to argue or simply decided to let Chael's tone pass by him, probably the latter Living Stars bless the man.

"From above, I think they scaled the walls," Chael had already seen to the gate and found it intact so that made sense.

"Alright," he breathed, willing himself to be calm. "We better go check." Andon nodded, then looked around at the shocked and battered townspeople who were only just now coming to terms with the carnage in their midst.

"Perhaps you and Rina should go," he said, frowning. "I think I'll stay here in case any other trouble comes up and to…" The knight trailed off as they both looked around at the ruined courtyard. Chael nodded to him and clapped him on the shoulder.

"You and Michik fought well together," he added, hoping it would make up for his earlier roughness. Andon smiled and looked down at the wolf who upon hearing his name had obediently come to the knight's side and leaned his massive head against his hip. Black demon blood was still dripping from his exposed jaw, but Andon didn't seem to notice and gave Michik his customary reward.

"Yes, we did," Andon added, straining to keep the smile on his face. Chael gave him one more nod and patted his hip for Michik to follow him as they walked over to the hall that would take them to the stairwell. As he did, he motioned Rina with his head and the young alchemist understood his intention and jogged over to him.

Chael could tell that she was anxious to leave the blooded courtyard behind and was still brushing fellhound brain off her skirt with her left hand. That reminded Chael of Brod and he looked back over to the smith. The fellhound was at his feet, head a pulpy mush of black with flecks of green and red. But even though it was thoroughly disabled, its spines continued to lazily drift out and seek Brod's flesh. The blacksmith happily smashed them with his hammer every time they came close. Chael decided to leave the smith be, given all that had happened he probably needed the victim and Chael wasn't gonna try to take that away.

"Be ready," he told Rina. "I can't sense anything above us, but I can't be certain."

Rina nodded seriously and gripped her whip a little tighter in her hand as they turned a corner and ascended the stairs. They had barely made it halfway to the second level when the cries of mourning erupted behind them.

Chapter 51

Present Day

As it turned out, the upper levels of the keep had fared much better than the lower courtyard. As he, Rina, and Michik ascended to the roof, they only passed a few victims of the creatures. It was true that the bulk of the people were down in the courtyard but there were still plenty of people on the second and third levels that the demons had apparently passed by on their way down to the people below.

Unfortunately, this left one too many sniveling self-important clerks around to berate him. Aeryl caught up to them on the third floor outside the Baron's office which he had commandeered.

"How could this happen?" he wheezed, pointing an accusatory finger at Chael. The man was practically trembling with impotent rage complete with wagging jowls. "I let you go on that fool's errand out there," he continued, rising up on his toes so he could look down on Chael.

Chael scoffed at the insinuation that this trumped-up bureaucrat could 'allow' him to do anything, but the man continued his rant. "And what did you return with? Hmmm? Nothing, nothing but dead townsfolk." That one bit deep and Chael prepared a retort, but once again Rina's whip beat him to the punch. She snapped the length of braided light over the sniveling weasel's left ear. It came so close to his head that Chael could smell the acrid scent of burnt hair after it passed. Aeryl still trembled though now out of fear and his mouth snapped shut, Chael even thought he heard a whimper but that may have just been wishful thinking.

"Listen here you oaf," Rina spat, her voice ringing with disgust. "We don't have the time to suffer fools too base to realize that their little empire has died before its first sunset. You have my leave to march out and parlay with the Darkspawn, otherwise stand aside and allow those that matter to go about their business."

Michik accented her last syllable with a growl and a snap of his black-stained jaws. Without another look or word, Rina turned on her heel and strode off toward the roof access, Michik trotting proudly beside her. Chael let them walk a little ahead of him, feeling like Rina and Michik had earned their dramatic exit and before he also turned to follow them, he gave the fat little clerk a shrug and jogged to catch up.

Contrary to the lack of attention the fellhounds seemed to pay the lower two levels, the roof was a disaster. The wooden ramparts that lined the space, allowing line of sight over the key areas below, were shredded to splinters. The watchmen up here were all dead, body parts strewn about with the broken wood.

One of them, however, had at least gotten a shot off with one of Rina's explosive tubes. A fellhound was quivering amidst the wreckage, a massive hole larger than Chael's fist blown through its chest. When it saw them, it tried to rise and attack but whatever structure that supported its front legs was destroyed and it only managed to flop on its face, its forelegs failing. Rina banished it back to the Dark with a flick and a tug of her wrist. Chael picked up the charred tube that the fallen watchmen had used.

"These are impressive," Chael commented to Rina, indicating the construct. "I've never seen the Order use these, although I don't have a lot of experience with their combat prowess."

Two experiences, he thought idly, going back to the Order assassin in Kazaam and Aelisa. On both occasions that glowing whip had been their primary weapon.

"Oh, they don't," Rina answered peevishly. "These are of my design. I tried to pitch the idea to a prefect, but the Order doesn't really care for innovative thinking." Rina soured slightly but then returned a proud smile to Chael as he continued to examine the device.

"It's really quite simple," she added, taking the tube from him. "We already know how to make explosive constructs and even the prefects don't turn their noses up at such power. But they're crude and overly destructive. I merely harnessed that power and used the force to propel a projectile, in theory it's not that dissimilar to a crossbow."

Rina continued to give him her proud and superior look, Chael wasn't sure if she wanted him to compliment her or bend his knee and declare her his god. He chose to walk over to the edge of the keep and peer down over the wall. He couldn't see but he could almost hear the frown form on Rina's lips as her genius went unacknowledged.

Stepping over the debris of the ruined wooden platform, Chael carefully bent over the edge of the stone and peered down at the wall. The stone was not the first thing he noticed but as he expected, there were deep gouges and scratches all along the stone coming up from the main gatehouse down below. Rina's wards protecting the wooden gate had seemingly held, but the fellhounds found an alternate route to get inside.

What did immediately catch his attention and caused him to involuntarily take a step back was the small army now assembled on their doorstep. Ranks of demons assembled in neat rows along the base of the hill backed by either a half-breed or a figure in a black hood. Apparently, the Black Hand had found a way to effectively control Darkspawn because the chaotic creatures would never assemble in such an orderly fashion naturally.

At the front of the force, in a suit of black armor that seemed to consume the light like a hungry plague, was Darrik. He noticed Chael leaning over the destroyed battlements and stretched his lips in a wicked satisfied grin.

"Greetings old friend," Darrik boomed in that same strange discordant voice he displayed back in the Order's dungeon. Chael hadn't heard Michik pad up beside him but when the wolf barked a hostile retort to Darrik's greeting, he reached down and gave him a few scratches. "Michik, you're still alive?" Darrik questioned, his voice suddenly far more human. "He doesn't look so good, Chael," the half-breed sire commented in mock concern.

Rina joined them next, but not empty handed. Secured discreetly behind her back as she joined him at the edge of the rampart was a familiar cylinder of brass and wood.

"How many of those do you have left?" he whispered to her.

"Last one," she winked and whipped the construct around and aimed it down at Darrik.

With a hard twist, the two halves of the cylinder slid until two copper leads connected on the outside of the tube, there was a small spark like metal striking stone and then it detonated. Fragments of wood and stone blew outward from the broken parapet as a molten fist of glowing metal shot down at Darrik, still mocking them below.

For a moment, Chael dared to hope that it would end right there, but this sort of Darkness wasn't so easily dispelled. With speed that defied the very nature of reality as he understood it, Darrik easily sidestepped the screaming missile as it thundered past him and blasted a smoking hole through the ranks of the demons behind him.

"Impressive," he called back in his demonic voice once again, while surveying the damage.

Two lesser demons behind him now sported massive melon sized holes in their chest and stomach, respectively. Another one behind them was now missing a leg where Rina's missile had cratered into the ground. With one guttural demonic grunt, Darrik shouted an order to his minions in the ranks surrounding the three injured ones. The creatures of the Dark pounced on their comrades and tore them apart until their stilted movement ceased. One more grunted command from Darrik and the line reformed, demons filling the space by simply standing on the shredded bodies of their kin.

"So, you've taken an Order pet from Fhaerhold, then?" he added, gesturing to Rina with his ebony gauntlet. "Your wards worked well, young sister," he congratulated her, maintaining his wicked grin. "But unfortunately, time is not our ally and plans, though carefully laid, must be accelerated."

Without another obvious signal, two Black Hand cultists stepped forward from the rear of the demonic column. Between them they carried a large wooden crate up to the warded gatehouse of the Baron's keep. After placing it directly in front of the gate the two Dark cultists hurriedly sprinted away, and Chael braced himself for what he knew would follow.

The explosion shook the very foundations of the keep. Even three stories up, shockwaves would have sent both him and Rina over the side if he wasn't still empowered by the massacre that had occurred down below. When the dust settled and the acrid smoke cleared, the gate, the house, and the entire front of the keep were simply gone; in their place was a gaping hole that led directly into the courtyard where nearly the entirety of Ehbing's remaining citizens were housed.

"Citizens of Ehbing," Darrik cackled, once again allowing the demon to bleed into his voice in its screeching disharmony. "You have fought bravely for your lives, but as you can see the battle is over. But fear not, for I am only here for the treacherous snake that has burrowed into your nest." He emphasized the words treacherous and snake so loudly that the sound shook some of the remaining gatestones from their housing. "For your bravery, I will allow any who wish to leave safe passage to Westfhael. You need not die for him."

Though they couldn't see him still staring down from the broken rampart, when Darrik pointed his gauntleted hand up at Chael the townspeople knew who he was indicating. The cause of their indignation for three years and the source of their current disaster.

"We have to get down there," Chael blurted in hushed tones. "He isn't letting anyone go." Together they raced down through the levels of the keep, passing only a handful of confused people as they ran. To his dismay, the one person he hoped to see on the upper levels was not there, but he could hear his nasally indignant voice echoing from below.

"This entire calamity is his fault," Aeryl sneered at his captive audience as they approached. The survivors of the fellhound attack were caught between listening to the reproachful clerk and casting fearful glances outside where the Dark army waited. "He brought this Darkness down upon us," he screeched, the target of his ire now in full view.

The eyes of the people now turned to him, some were disdainful mirroring Aeryl's mood, but most were just weary. Over the space of a few hours, they had hope stripped away from them one layer at a time. Starting with the failure to secure water and send out for help, and now the attack inside the stronghold that they thought was safe. And in each instance more of their family and neighbors had been killed, yet another monument to Chael's failure.

"You can't go," Chael insisted, shelving his guilt for the sake of the townspeople. "It's a trick, no one is going to be allowed to escape."

"Liar!" Aeryl hissed, pointing a pudgy finger at Chael. "If they were going to kill us, why not just come in now? What is stopping them?" The pudgy clerk gave a satisfied grin to Chael, "They came here for him, let them have him. We will go East and plead the aid of the King."

"The King is dead," Chael insisted desperately, feeling the emotions of the crowd shift.

"More lies," Aeryl sneered arrogantly. The fat man seemed to feel his momentum build and became bolder. He strode right up to Chael and shoved that bulbous finger into his chest. "Before he showed up in the Dark Forest how many demons accosted the town? Hmm?"

Chael opened his mouth to protest, pointing out that the uptick in demon activity was not his fault but Aeryl just kept going. "And now after everything we have suffered, he would deny us our only escape just to drag us down with him."

"They can't cross the threshold!" Rina shouted, cutting off the speech. She paced over to the edge of the courtyard where her line of warding runes remained intact. "I made sure that the wards protecting the keep were layered, the demons cannot cross it. But if you go out there, they will slaughter you like sheep."

Aeryl scoffed at her proclamation but finding himself slightly outside the warded boundary, he slyly took a step back inside though Chael doubted that anyone else noticed.

"He is a liar," came another voice, this time from outside. Darrik had dropped the demonic overtone to his words and now sounded frustratingly human. "And a murderer," Darrik continued. "He murdered his best friend because he tried to prevent him from slaughtering children. Deny it, Chael."

The collective eyes turned back to him and though the truth was far more complicated than Darrik had outlined, Chael hesitated just a moment before his refutation. That moment was all Aeryl needed to seize control.

"You see!" he screamed in unrighteous delight. "Even he cannot deny it! Come, let us take this opportunity of mercy before Chael's Darkness infects us further."

Several people began moving toward the ruined gate and Chael sprinted ahead of them, cutting them off from the entrance.

"Please," he pleaded desperately. "Don't do it, you will die."

"You have my oath of safe passage," Darrik declared loudly from behind him. "What are you going to do Chael? Kill them if they try to escape?"

And there it was, he had been defeated. The first person, a young man perhaps two or three years his junior, hesitantly edged around Chael and walked out into the light. Darrik waved a hand and the lines of demons parted, making a path that led to the river.

As he walked between the columns of demons, he shrank back and the crowd gasped, but none made a move to block his passage. Dozens more of the people began filing out, growing more and more confident until slightly more than half of what remained of the population now marched out to supposed safety.

Among the last was Aeryl, who gave Chael one last self-satisfied sneer before joining the people he had so brazenly led to their doom. All the while, all Chael could do was impotently hold his arms out and silently beg the terrified people not to go. Chael couldn't bear to watch when the hammer fell, but the sudden rush of life essence and the screams, both inside the keep and out, signaled Darrik's betrayal. Chael simply collapsed, finally too numb to cope with the toll that death had left at his feet.

Chapter 52

Present Day

After the massacre, Darrik led his army back to the edges of Ehbing near the forest. He had already had his fun for the day and was now satisfied letting those few that were left stew in their fear.

Despite the new sources of power now readily available, Chael couldn't muster the strength to stand up, his failure was complete. The wards were not a real obstacle, any human cultist could march right in and destroy them, or Darrik could blast them to rubble with more explosive alchemical constructs. The only way they would last the night is if Darrik preferred to make their deaths slow and miserable.

Michik, who would normally come lay on his lap, was still at the destroyed entrance to the keep. He stood sentinel at the boundary of the wards, vigilant for any trouble. It should have brought a smile to his face, he almost willed one to show up regardless, but the weight of utter defeat dragged his lips into a tired scowl, and he turned his eyes to the floor.

Sleep had come fitfully to him these past few weeks yet when Chael blinked, he was somehow doing so under the light of the stars and not the afternoon sun he was expecting. Michik was still at his watch and the remnants of the people of Ehbing were now gathered in a large clump at the far end of the courtyard away from the gaping hole in the defenses, and away from him. His head hurt too much to try to count them, but he could comfortably say that the population of the town had dwindled to no more than eighty.

Noticing him stir, a woman emerged from the huddled mass of townsfolk, Chael vaguely recognized her as one of the voluntary spearmen of his failed mission. His estimation of her immediately rose, she had shown bravery superior to that of most of the men, who, rather than volunteer to defend their loved ones had elected to cower in the keep.

Chael didn't feel worthy to meet her eyes. Though when he looked up, it was an entirely different pair that captured him. Her daughter stood all of two feet tall but stood proudly if a bit reliant on her mother for support, and with him slumped against the wall their eyes were at the same height. They were a fierce ocean blue, and they displayed none of the panic and terror that rightly should have been displayed across them like reflections of a wildfire. Instead, she looked... Chael would have called it curious.

"Excuse me," her mother said, breaking his trance.

Chael cleared his throat to hide the grunt of effort it took to look her in the eye. She gave him a nervous smile and continued.

"Sorry, it just seemed like you had woken up and I just wanted to say thank you. Thank you for both of us. I don't believe what that man said about this all being your fault. In fact, I think you have been fighting for this town, thanklessly," she spoke that last word loud enough for her neighbors across the courtyard to hear. "Ever since you came here, so thank you. I don't know what is going to happen in the next few hours, but I know whatever happens you will fight for our home."

Chael was speechless, emotions were difficult for him to convey so he gave an awkward smile and nodded his head, though the motion must have gotten dust in his eyes because his vision became momentarily foggy and unfocused. When he wiped his eyes, the woman was leading her daughter back to the rest of the townspeople and another figure now stood over him, smiling like an idiot.

"Shut up," Chael snapped at Andon before the knight could say anything.

Andon made a gesture sealing his lips, ostensibly promising to not speak about his embarrassing display of emotion. But he didn't buy it, the second he could, the Darkened knight would go blabbing to Rina about him crying.

"Come on," Andon beckoned, hauling Chael to his feet with his remaining hand. "I need to show you something."

He led Chael out of the courtyard and back into the cramped pen by the kitchens that Brod had turned into his forge. The blacksmith was there as well as Rina and though Brod was as inscrutable as ever, Rina displayed one of her telltale smirks that spoke of some great new erudite achievement.

She opened her mouth to begin what was probably some sort of treatise on both the inevitability of her greatness and his profound lack of appreciation. Brod cut her off when he marched over to him and thrust a wrapped sword at his stomach, grunting. Rina's face turned into a pout but when Chael caught her eye, he could see the smile hidden there.

"Oh, go on," she insisted exasperatedly, "just tear it open and pay no attention to the work that I put in."

Chael did tear it open. It was a falchion, in size a perfect copy to the one he had lost, but in weight and balance the curved sword was in a league all its own. It wasn't light per se, his weapon needed a certain weight to carry out its function, though it certainly wasn't heavy. What it was, was balanced, the gleaming steel seemed to sing as he sliced the air in easy arcs testing it.

"I have never seen its equal," Chael whispered to Brod in awe, bowing slightly to the smith. Brod grunted and gave him a nod of appreciation. Chael made a move to attach the sword to his belt but was forbidden by Rina with a cough.

"Seriously?" she groaned, snatching the steel from his hand and holding the flat of the blade up to the light.

"Rina, what are you…" the words evaporated on his tongue when he finally saw the contribution of which the young alchemist was so proud.

Meticulously etched into the side of the falchion were a series of runes many of which he now recognized from both here and his cell back in the capitol, but there were far more that were still alien to him. As she twisted the blade back and forth the wards shimmered and danced in the light, giving the whole thing an ethereal almost liquid cast.

"This one won't break when it encounters their foul magick," she pronounced proudly, though with an almost feral tone as she referenced the Dark alchemist's abilities.

Chael was surprised to hear her use the word magick, it was an old word and described alchemy in much more supernatural terms than most were comfortable, especially amongst the generally stodgy Order. Chael smiled at them all, overwhelmed by the generosity but mostly by the implied faith that the gift represented.

"It's time, lad," Brod intoned softly, taking the sword from Rina and placing it back into his hands, much more reverently than he had before. "Let the steel out."

"Brod, you don't know what it is that you're asking," Chael protested, looking to the others for support.

"I know there is another level to your abilities, you demonstrated that much back in Fhaerstead," Sir Andon added. "I also know that it cost you, but we've reached the end of the rope."

The knight clapped Chael on the shoulder with his remaining hand, a grim reminder of what he had been willing to sacrifice for his duty. He lingered for several moments, with what Chael was sure was meant to be an encouraging smile.

After Andon retreated, Chael looked expectantly at Rina, assuming she also had some sort of encouraging speech. She raised an eyebrow at his silent inquiry and then sighed.

"Look," she started, visibly straining with the effort of actual sincerity. "I joined up with you because I thought you could help me kill half-breeds, and you did." She struggled to find the right words for a moment before attacking him with the most aggressive hug Chael had ever experienced. She gave him a light squeeze before backing away, cheeks the color of sunset, then she slapped him.

The blow seemed to surprise everyone but Brod who merely grunted; Andon actually gasped. Her eyes bored into his from only a breath away as his expression shifted from shock, to anger, and finally to grim and reluctant understanding. Satisfied, she gave him a wink and edged away.

Chael and Michik stepped out into the cool night air of the destroyed town. The fires were all burnt out, and compared to the cramped spaces inside, the keep filled with the odors of sweat and fear, this was heaven. He breathed it in, clearing the fog from his head and hoping vainly to wipe some of the guilt from his heart.

He half expected one of the skulker demons to materialize out of the shadows and take his head, but the night remained still and he resigned himself to his task. Now, even hours later, death crowded around him like a cold blanket. He supposed that it was for the best that this should occur during the middle of the night, for better or worse, it simply wouldn't do for the citizens of Ehbing to see what happened next.

Chael breathed in the sickly cold haze of death that surrounded him, allowing it to flood every limb, hair, and facet of his body. Even after he felt positively engorged on it, he kept forcing more and more inside himself until even his soul felt bloated and abused. Only then did his presence stir, curious as to the deluge of power now available to them.

Good, you're awake, he thought.

And so I am, came its familiar yet icy response.

A pressure, like someone pushing down on his temples, began to press in on Chael and the fight for control began in earnest. Staggered by the sudden pain in his head, Chael fell to one knee, it was like trying to stand underneath an invisible waterfall. Chael ground his teeth and slowly began to pick himself up, even as the pressure in his head redoubled.

For a moment, he thought he might collapse again, but a steady reassuring presence came to his side. Michik let out a bark that Chael would have sworn was a grunt as he heaved himself back to his feet, using Michik's sturdy frame to support his rise.

Two more, Chael thought. Well, technically three, but the third wasn't in any condition to fight with his leg hanging loosely like that.Dead. No wonder the mother was so enraged. Someone or something had killed her pups.

The world around him seemed to dissolve, like paint running down a canvas, until he was left in a black void without depth or description. The outside world was gone, time and space lost all relevance. The pressure crushed him from all sides this time, and without ground to support him, he couldn't brace himself or even fall to a knee.

Human, he thought.

A visual array of all his failures passed over him in the void like an art exhibition made up entirely of his worst memories. His failure to protect the Faasa children from Mason, murdering Darrik in a Dark energy fueled rage, the fall of Fhaerhold, the death and failed resurrection of Aelisa, Baron Janus, King Inarus, and all the deaths in Ehbing that hung solely on his shoulders.

The weight of defeat smashed into him like a falling star and all the force pressing in on his body from the Presence was like a gentle stream in comparison. Guilt, it had been eating at him for more than the last few days, it had dominated his existence for years. The solution was simple of course, he needed to just let go. Accept the things in his past that he had no power to change and strive to do better in the future, it was all wonderfully straightforward.

Another wave of force brought on by his internal adversary crushed him like an insect under a rock. The air blasted out of his lungs, and he choked on blood while the forces around him increased. He wasn't sure if a concept like air even mattered in this immaterial spiritual realm but nevertheless his lungs burned as he gasped for breath even as the pressure crushed his rib cage. The Presence was winning, and it cackled in his ear with delight.

Yield control and I will release you, for a fraction of a second the assault ceased, and his lungs sucked in as much air as they could before it brought the pressure back like a hammer.

I don't need air to breathe in here, Chael managed to sputter uncertainly.

It was mostly a bluff, he didn't even know exactly where 'here' was, let alone be able to dictate the realities of a spiritual realm to a creature that, as far as he knew, only existed in spirit. But speaking it into existence condensed some measure of his will and though the pressure didn't relent, he managed to capture a few gasps of precious air.

I am not a failure, he screamed into the void.

The Presence cackled anew and the boulder of searing agony that would have brought him to his belly if possible in this place, stomped him until he was gasping for air again.

Fair enough, he managed to eke out after a moment. That had truly been a stretch, he at least partially believed it when he had said that he didn't need air in this space.

Not my strong suit, he thought. "Without Sir Andon's bravery, none of us would have made it through the Dark

Forest alive." Probably still affected by whatever curatives Aelisa gave him, Chael surmised. *It must be him, then; he's the only one unaccounted for.* Michik barked at exactly that moment, as if he had been waiting for Chael to come to this conclusion independently. Chael's head snapped instantly in the direction of the sound and made his way toward what he knew to be the corpse of this Durnik.

Fighting back was a more recent development in the grand scheme of things but the self-affirming statement made a dent in the pressure that was slowly tearing at his mind and soul. Not a large dent, it was little more than raindrops in the ocean, but Chael didn't have the luxury of being picky about progress.

The Presence focused on his failures since arriving in Ehbing, a menagerie of corpses passed across his vision, each one more grotesque than the last. It showed him the hatred, anger, and fear in the townspeople's eyes when they looked at him and that is when it made its critical mistake.

Among the eyes burning with malice was a pair of crystal oceanic blue. There was fear there, but not of him. It was fear of losing her home and her mother, the primal sort of terror that every person ever born to human mothers knows. But there was also hope and a child's curiosity and suddenly her mother's words came back to him.

"Whatever happens I know you will fight for our home." 'Our home,' the words blazed across his mind like a fiery sword, searing the pressure that threatened to pulverize him. At the moment he hadn't really noticed the inflection she put on the words.

Our home, my home, he roared into the abyss.

He didn't precisely get up because heretofore up was a concept that didn't apply to the space in which he seemed to float; but as his will solidified around the concept, his feet seemed to suddenly stand on something solid like ground.

Impossible. The world went completely dark as Chael hastily shut down the vision. The disturbing smile of the

Dark Cultist still lingering in his mind's eye.Curious, Chael thought. Chael's entire world shifted sideways. What could that possibly mean?

A faint light like a string became visible to him now, though it was the only source of light in the darkness of the void it didn't dispel the shadows. In fact, the shadows seemed to actively attack it and it flickered in and out of existence, but he knew where that light led.

"Wonderful idea, then we can fight the fifty or so mercenaries the bastard hired." There wasn't actually a sign for "bastard", but Chael used an improvised name for one of the less popular masters at the former school. Darrik got the general idea.

The spiritual world shattered like a box made of glass and once again Chael found himself amongst the ruins of Ehbing under the light of the stars. Power surged within him in a way he had never experienced before, when he consumed life essence before he felt strong, stronger than any man alive. But now he felt like he contained the power to move mountains.

A quick check within himself revealed that the Presence was not gone, unfortunately that creature was going to remain with him. But normally with the amount of life essence that he had taken, especially when it was human, would cause it to swell with power and influence inside him. Now it felt shriveled and weak like a starved animal, barely clinging to life.

Michik nudged him with his head and Chael looked down, the wolf's muzzle was stained black once again and the cause was a beheaded skulker no more than a pace away.

"Looks like you were busy while I was out," he cooed to his dog while scratching his head. "Good boy." Michik snorted his agreement, tail wagging. "I guess it's my turn," he mumbled, closing his eyes and reaching out instead with his senses.

Despite the ocean of power that he already had, the many deaths in such a short period of time left plenty of life essence available for what he had to do next. That was good, he was going to need all of it. Soon enough his senses found the bodies of the people Darrik had massacred after promising their safety. Wielding the power of life and death like a wand with his fingertip he pushed it like a cloud of swirling black life, back into each of them. This process was not like the one he had used on Michik, or even Aelisa, as poorly as that had turned out.

Though he had temporarily conquered the evil that accompanied his power, the power itself was still a product of the Dark. It wasn't meant to create, only destroy. That power had been borrowed from someone else. Guilt hit him again at the cruel necessity of what he had to do but he silently promised them a proper burial when this was all finished.

"I'm sorry," he whispered, though the dead couldn't hear him.

But at his words and with a new concerted effort of will, they rose. Slowly men and women, revivified by Darkness, marched out of the gloom of night and arrayed themselves behind him. A sea of azure eyes lit the night and together they moved forward toward the far tree line where Darrik had gathered his forces, an army of ninety-six animated corpses. Chael and Michik marched to war for their home, and the dead marched with them.

Chapter 53

Present Day

The first order of business was arming his new battalion. He could feel the strength that the life essence-enhanced undead could wield but they weren't going to be able to pummel demons to death. They needed something sharp; he thought briefly about turning them around and raiding the already depleted armory of the keep but for what little there was to be had back at the Baron's small castle, he didn't feel like he could spare the time.

The amount of power flowing through him and out to the revenants was extraordinary. It was like an army of marionettes was attached to his back, each one pulling a delicate string of power from the core of his being. He could almost picture the twisted black vortex of energy slowly siphoned through his skin to feed the power of his temporary soldiers. In order for this to work, they had to be quick about it.

Passing through the heart of Ehbing was a necessity to get to Darrik's forces the fastest, so they extracted what resources they could from the ruins. Kitchen knives, wood axes, even shards of broken glass. Anything sharp enough to cut flesh was scavenged for their use.

Now armed, or at least armed after a fashion, he directed his army of revenants to fan out in a line in front of him.

They must have made more noise scavenging for weapons than he thought because as they approached the tree line near the edge of the town Darrik's army of demons marched out, once again arrayed in perfect battle lines as they walked.

"Show yourself, brother!" Chael shouted to the wall of demons sixty paces away. "Let's end this now, just you and I."

There was no response, nor did Darrik emerge from behind his troops. Instead, emerging from between the ranks of Darkspawn, were more fellhounds. They could smell the blood still coating the majority of Chael's revenants and licked at the air with serpentine tongues in greedy anticipation.

Chael heard no command or saw a visible signal, but as one the fellhounds charged his thin line of undead. But before they had even covered half the distance, Michik shot off from Chael's side barking his indignation at the cheap wolf-like imitations that bore down on him. He clashed into a group of three, fangs and claws thrashing the demon hounds.

The fellhounds were quicker and lashed out with more weapons than Michik could bring to bear, but the wolf overwhelmed them with sheer strength. Every swipe of paw and bite of black stained teeth tore demons asunder and before their kin had even reached Chael's line, three fellhounds were reduced to quivering red and black lumps.

When the four-legged demons did crash into his revenants, they were driven back several feet by the force of the charge. For a moment, Chael was worried that his plan would be torn apart right there. But after withstanding the charge, his revenants fell upon the hounds with reckless abandon. Their makeshift weapons rose and fell, each time exposing more black and green viscera until the fellhounds were exterminated.

Twenty fellhounds were banished back to the Dark and only four of Chael's were too maimed to continue fighting.

He severed his connection to those and exhaled some of his anxiety. The first exchange had gone in their favor.

"Your dogs are dead!" Chael taunted Darrik, if a challenge didn't draw him out perhaps mockery would. "Come coward, face me like you once did."

Still there was no response, Chael was going to have to be more direct. With a thought, he reorganized his forces into lines and aimed his attack at the center column of demons. It would risk encirclement from the broader line of Darrik's forces, but Chael had to be direct. He was burning through power at an unsustainable rate, and he had to punch through to Darrik. Besides it wasn't as if his army of revenants would rout or lose their nerve if they were surrounded. Without further preamble or spoken command the undead charged the front ranks of lesser demons at a shambling sprint.

Chael's mistake became almost immediately apparent. His army ran into an invisible wall like a wave breaking on rocks. Darrik had sent out a blocking formation of invisible skulker demons right under his nose, and they stood guard only a few paces from the line.

Revenants being unthinking creatures, instead of attacking the new obstacle, kept running in place trying to follow Chael's command. It took him all of a second to understand the tactic and change his orders accordingly, but the damage was already done. Half of his front line was already cut down to quivering pieces and the lesser demons behind the skulkers began their own charge. If Chael didn't act quickly, he was going to lose his entire army right here.

"Meeshee, go!" Chael commanded his dog, who sprinted off toward the west away from the fighting.

He was loath to see the wolf go, at least so soon, but they were going to have to speed up their timetable and he had a mission elsewhere. Chael drew his new falchion and gathered some of the remaining ambient life essence for himself and charged into the fray.

His revenants silently opened a path for him in the middle of their formation and he crashed into the first skulker. Having already been pummeled by his own army the demon could barely hold up its shroud of invisibility and without that advantage they were far weaker than their rat-faced cousins and Chael quickly reduced it to parts with his sword. The falchion rang like a tiny silver bell as it struck, singing its own music as it cheerfully parted demon hide. And where its blade met Dark flesh it consumed like a starving animal, parting muscle and bone like water.

Chael waded into the midst of the lesser demon line, cutting clawed limbs and severing heads as they presented themselves. The symbols Rina etched into the flat seemed to glow as he fought. Chael couldn't tell if it was a trick of the moonlight or if in the presence of such an overwhelming amount of Dark energy the runes sketched into the blade actually smoldered with disdain.

Chael's charge worked shockingly well. Gripping his new sword in both hands he chopped through the ranks of demons like lumber, and the only way to stop his onslaught was to devote more attention to him. He was surrounded by enemies but his enhanced senses and superhuman reflexes allowed him to meet every attack before it could reach his own flesh and where his falchion struck, demons lost body parts.

Behind him, the pressure eased on his soldiers, and he was able to reform them into two solid lines again. As they pressed in on the demons, Chael fell back into a fighting retreat until he was swallowed up by his own lines again. He allowed them to pass him as they continued pushing the demons back and ground down the ranks of Darrik's Dark army.

Now out of the fight once again, Chael had a moment to catch his breath and gather more power. He surveyed the battlefield with both his mundane and Dark-enhanced sight. His little army was doing an impressive amount of damage to the middle section of Darrik's forces, but his former comrade had yet to commit the remainder of his troops to the fight.

Chael wasn't sure what Darrik might be holding in reserve but as far as he could see and sense, there was nothing hidden back in the forest. At least nothing close enough to be useful to Darrik in the near term. But still even as his revenants pushed through, he didn't send any of his reserve to aid them. His plan was largely reliant on Darrik committing all of his forces to one fight.

Something wasn't right, some piece of the puzzle was eluding him and whatever it was, Darrik clearly felt that it was his trump card. With only a moment's indecision he sent out a mental command of retreat even though his army was only minutes away from breaking completely through. The order came through with only seconds to spare.

In the middle of Darrik's central formation, right where Chael's army of revenants had just been fighting, the earth began to tear itself apart. Fissures spurting streams of lava tore across the ground devouring demons and a few of his own fleeing soldiers, too embattled to retreat quickly with the others.

An enormous red hand with black claws reached out from beneath the broken ground, like the demon was literally dragging itself out of the Dark through the earth. A shoulder emerged and then its giant head came into view, eerily lit by the fires below the ground whence it had climbed. Its head was red and humanoid but for ridges of black stone-like skin that wrapped around its brow like a crown and two horns, each the size of one of Chael's arms. But like the stained-glass representation of its likeness back in Fhaerhold, its entire body defied description. It was like a swirling black and red cloud of energy that was at once solid but also flowing like water.

From amidst the ethereal torso two massive legs emerged that also seemed to flow and solidify at the same time right down to cloven hooves. Standing at his full height it was easily ten paces high or more and it loomed over Chael and his army like a sentient storm cloud.

"Behold, Ugallual, Lord of the Pit," boomed Darrik from somewhere behind the massive demon lord.

As if waiting for his cue, Ugallual at just that moment, seized one of the lesser demons milling around him and raised it to his mouth. He casually bit off the demon's head and swallowed it whole. The demon lord then raised his fist holding out the decapitated demon like a trophy. From its stumpy neck, fire erupted into the sky like a lance of pure flame four paces high and solidified in the same reality defying half state of its body.

So, the demon lord gets his own sword, great, Chael muttered to himself.

Ugallual roared and brought his blade of living flame down on Chael. Where it passed through space, the air detonated showering the lines of demons with sparks.

Chael gave another order to his army to retreat and leaped in a rolling dive out of the way of the falling cataclysm that was the demon's sword. It crashed into the earth like a meteor and though he was several feet away, the heat coming from the blade set the hem of his cloak alight even as the force of its impact with the ground to flung him several paces beyond where he had dived to. Somewhere beyond the line of demons Chael could hear Darrik cackling with amusement.

The one upside of facing down a lord of demons tall enough to rival some castles, was that it didn't care much about collateral damage. Every time it swung its sword or stepped toward Chael it invariably smashed a dozen or more of its own kin. If Chael could simply survive for another ten minutes, Ugallual might just win the battle for him. If he could survive, and if he could then somehow manage to kill the thing afterward, both open questions he didn't currently have the answer to.

An ear-shattering scream of an explosion split the night, a detonation like a crack of thunder had just struck right next to his face, and for a moment the entire sky turned orange. Then, like a fist from the Living Stars, a molten ball of brass smashed into the demon lord's face from the side, toppling him over onto an entire column of demons.

Chapter 54

4 Hours Earlier

"You won't have a lot of time," Chael insisted, still rubbing the spot on his cheek where Rina had unexpectedly slapped him. "We have to do this tonight while the..." he hesitated, trying to think of a more palatable way of explaining how they needed to seize the opportunity the deaths of innocents had caused. "... power is still fresh."

Andon nodded, though he looked a bit grim, "Rina, how many of those constructs can you make?" The young alchemist pressed a finger to her lips in thought for a minute or two.

"We have the materials but in the limited time that we have, I don't think we could make more than a handful. Ten if we're lucky." The knight considered that and then shook his head.

"No," he exclaimed, "not ten, one." He was smiling now, a strategy clearly forming in his mind. "One giant one, can you do that?"

"Hmm," Rina answered, considering the idea. "How big are we talking?"

"As big as you can make it," Andon responded.

"We won't have more than one shot," she added. "We'll have to use reinforced wood if we're going to construct it in a few hours. It will be as likely to just explode itself as launching a projectile, but I think I can make it work."

Brod stepped over to her holding up his hammer. "You tell me wha' you need lass, I'll see it done."

Rina smiled brightly at him, and they both started speaking excitedly about dimensions and materials.

"Good," Andon commented, turning back to Chael. "This Darrik is after you specifically, how do you feel about being bait?"

"That's fine," Chael answered automatically. It was his mess, and he was more than happy to be the worm on the hook if it meant he could clean it up. "But it can't be just me, if I come alone Darrik won't commit. He'll think I have some traps set up."

"I don't think we can ask much more of the people," Andon pointed out.

"Not the ones in here," Chael responded and leaned in to whisper his idea into the knight's ear.

He couldn't be sure how Rina would respond to raising the dead. While she wasn't devout like others of her Order, she did pay the proper religious respects to their dead and what he had in mind was Darkness of the highest order. Even Andon blanched when Chael told him what he planned to do.

"You can do that?" the knight whispered, scandalized.

"I think I can, but it will take a lot out of me, and if I fail you might have to kill me." The knight blinked his surprise and stared back at him in shock. "If I fail, I won't be dead, but I won't be coming back either. Something else will." The knight paled again but nodded.

"I will do what I must," Andon promised seriously, and a silent understanding passed between them.

If Chael failed to control the full Mantle of the Darkborn, his friend would put him down. Brod and Rina came back from their dizzying conversation of maths and alchemical formulae, and Chael and Andon did their best to hide their own conversation from their faces.

"We can do it!" Rina exclaimed proudly, clapping Brod on the shoulder.

"Good!" beamed Andon, forcing a smile back to his face. "Chael will draw out as many demons as he can and when they're the most gathered we'll strike with your device. If he can get Darrik himself to come out, even better."

"Michik and I will leave without you," Chael continued for Andon. "Once his attention is on me, he won't notice you guys hauling that construct. You will have to do it in the dark with no torches, but once Darrik is focused on me, I'll send Michik away to guide you."

"Why not just leave him with us in the first place?" Rina asked.

"Other than the fact that I might need him," Chael answered, "If Darrik sees that I left him behind he'll think it's a trick. In order for this to work he has to think I am fully committed."

"Alright," said Andon, clapping Chael excitedly. The knight was now shining through and he was eager for battle. "Let's get to work."

Present Time

Chael sent the mental order for his revenants to attack even as he pushed himself back to his feet, having been blown backward by the force of Ugallual's fall. He gave them the image of a wedge-like formation to block off any counterattack from Darrik's remaining forces while he dealt with the demon lord.

He forced all the energy he could spare into his legs as he ran, dodging the enormous monster's flailing limbs as it tried to stand up, even though half of its face was missing. It turned out that under its ethereal ever shifting skin it was made of the same mundane green, red, and black meat as any other demon. And if it bled like a demon, Chael could kill it like one.

Laying on his side, one blazing red and black eye, Ugallual spotted him. The demon lord roared a hateful scream at him and slashed across the ground with his flaming sword. With its edge traveling parallel to the ground, Chael had no chance to dodge out of the way, so he dove onto his back sinking as low as he could to the ground and held his warded falchion, blade up, over his chest. He wasn't sure if the etched sigils could withstand the power of the flaming sword let alone the sheer force of the blow, but he was completely out of options.

The sword passed over him setting his clothes aflame and burning his skin. It connected with his falchion and though the demon's sword seemed to be entirely made of fire, it skidded along his sword with the screeching cry of metal on metal. Chael's new blade held fast, and the flaming sword skidded up into the air and over his head. His life was spared, but the entire front half of his body was burned, and his right arm was shattered. Crippling pain obliterated any other thought from his mind, and he couldn't move.

The presence inside him mocked him from its perch on his soul. It was still too weak and fragile to contest for control of their body, but it delighted in Chael's pain at the hands of the demon lord. *Ugallual, Ugallual, Ugallual,* it repeated rhythmically in some sort of primitive chant. Chael's pain blinded himself to all external stimuli, but the Presence could speak directly into his mind where he could not ignore it.

What could they possibly be doing here? Chael wondered while absentmindedly packing his bedroll. Around him was a flurry of motion as the others hastily packed their belongings, all under the steely gaze of the order priestess.

Shut your mouth, worm! Chael managed to think at the Presence.

The dark energy inside him was already causing the pain to ebb and his injuries were slowly healing, but he needed to concentrate to make it go faster. He was still paralyzed, though whether by shock or injury he couldn't say, but whichever was the case, Ugallual was sure to launch a follow-up attack and he couldn't just lay here staring up at the sky.

Slowly, feeling began to return to his legs and he could even wiggle his toes. If he had just another few seconds, he could have even managed to climb to his feet, but it was too late. The Lord of the Pit knew a vulnerable enemy when he saw one and his sword of fire was already blistering through the air down at him.

Two corded whips of pure light shot out like glowing vipers in the night, they wrapped themselves around the demon lord's arm and pulled. Ugallual cried in pain as the light burned his flesh and when they pulled taut, it sawed through his arm like a tree. The light whips didn't cut completely through his limb, but they did manage to divert it enough for Chael to lift his legs slightly and avoid the blow. The sword shattered the ground below him, flinging his numb body another dozen feet.

Andon is using one of those light whips? Chael mused, oddly inquisitive for someone flying through the air with crippling pain. All further thought momentarily abandoned him as soon as he smashed back into the ground.

Michik attacked next and shoved his muzzle into the demon lord's gaping arm wound, tearing at the exposed tissues with abandon. Dazed, but no more broken than before, Chael pushed himself off the ground and staggered to shaking feet. Rina, Andon, and Michik were holding down one arm, but Ugallual still had another and Chael had to do a pathetic flopping roll with one arm dangling uselessly to avoid the demon's claws.

"Come on, lad," called another voice.

The gruff blacksmith picked him up and together, Brod half dragging him, they reached Ugallual's massive head. The right side of his face was crushed and melted all the way to its giant flat nose.

Chael diverted all the energy currently healing his body and put it into one swing with his left arm. His falchion, etched with the runes for rending demon flesh, and powered by all the strength the Darkborn himself could muster; slammed down into Ugallual's neck like a collapsing mountainside. The sword sliced readily through muscle and tendon until it hit the vertebrae of its neck and stuck.

The demon lord roared in protest and seemed to speak words in an ancient language too old and foul for human ears. He stopped fighting to fend them off and dedicated both limbs to helping him rise. Panicked, Chael immediately tried to wrench his falchion free for another swing, but it was stuck fast, clamped down by its massive neck bones.

"Maelon!" Brod screamed in fury, calling out his wife's name and brought his hammer down on the back of his sword, slamming in further through Ugallual's neck. "Ynnette!" his daughter's name, and the hammer fell. "Yosif!" his son and again the smith's hammer drove Chael's steel further through the thing's neck. "Me," he practically whispered, Ugallual's neck hanging by no more than a shred of red skin, and Brod stomped on the sword, severing it completely and banishing the demon lord back to the Dark. Chael clapped Brod on the shoulder with his good hand and nodded. "Stars boy! But you look like death!"

Chael couldn't help but laugh but quickly sobered himself, "come on," he said to Brod, "we're not done yet."

All in all, the battle was going fairly well, he thought. His army of revenants though starting with nearly one hundred, had been reduced to less than twenty but they had successfully held off interference from Darrik's forces while they took care of the demon lord. Now they could focus on obliterating Darrik's army and for the first time this night he didn't feel like they were at a disadvantage.

Rina engaged the fight, taking special pleasure whenever she ran across a half-breed, her whip expertly cutting through row after row of enemies. Andon looked a bit clumsier with his whip, having only now used it for the first time. Chael could only imagine what it must be like for your flesh to melt away, but it was on his arm that was missing a hand so maybe it wasn't so bad. However, despite lacking a hand and being a novice with the weapon, decades of training in soldiery couldn't be denied and where his whip cracked, black blood flowed.

Brod also had a few surprises it seemed, apparently Rina had etched some of her warding runes on his hammer because the ends glowed with a faint golden light as he swung and the devastation to demons that it wrought was far more catastrophic than any normal hammer should have been. If Chael wasn't broken limping and exhausted, he probably would have been proud.

Chael limped awkwardly past the battle towards the trees. His intuition told him where he could confront Darrik, and he knew his friends could clean up here without too much trouble. Michik trotted up beside him, none of his puppy-like features were on display today. His dog showed a grim but determined look that he himself felt, they were both on the hunt to kill one of their oldest friends, even the wolf knew what was coming.

Before stepping into the Dark Forest Chael took one last look behind him at the waning battle. They, especially Rina, would be angry with him for taking on Darrik by himself but it felt right, and besides he wasn't alone, was he? As if he could hear Chael's thoughts, Michik looked up at him and for a brief second gave him one of his puppy smiles before the sad determination stole his wolfish countenance once again.

Good luck, he half whispered to his friends. Then he slipped into the forest.

Darkness immediately swallowed him as they walked down the old overgrown forest path to their cabin. But even though the trees now blocked the stars, Chael and Michik were unaffected. They were both creatures of the night now and with his dog's natural senses and Chael's supernatural ones they stalked through the forest as easily as they might have at midday, which was why the ambush failed.

Two women and one man, all clothed in black with matching black hoods, jumped out of the trees in what was supposed to be a surprise attack. Chael sidestepped the first and used her own momentum to drive his falchion through her gut.

Michik had taken a more direct approach and before his attacker had even sprung his part of the trap, the wolf leaped at him and took him by surprise in midair. By the time the two of them had wrestled to the ground Michik already had his jaws around his throat. That left one woman who, instead of leaping at them with weapons drawn, had instead moved to cut off the path ahead. And instead of steel she displayed two arms that ended in swirling clouds of gray ash.

Heedless of the death of her companions, the woman smiled broadly at Chael under her dark hood. With a swirl of ash, both her arms turned into hatchets, and she finally joined the ambush. Chael barely dodged the first two swings, the second of which nearly shaved his ear off. Normally, he would have had an advantage in speed, but his power was still healing his body from the hit of Ugallual's sword, and the woman was fast.

She backed away a step, licking her lips in anticipation. He was slow and weak, and her smile only broadened. Chael only had one option to survive the fight, and he just had to hope Rina's sigils covered Dark alchemy. A gray hatchet came at his head and instead of dodging, Chael met it with his falchion.

The hatchet rang off Chael's sword like a bell and shattered to gray dust, leaving her with just a stump of an arm and anemically swirling ash.

Her smile vanished, turning to panic, and she turned to run away but Michik had finished with his prey and caught her before she made it a full step in the other direction. Chael threw his falchion, end over end, at her remaining ash-bladed arm before she could reach behind and stab his dog with it, but the canny wolf wasted no time in snapping her neck.

The remaining journey wasn't nearly so eventful, and when they reached their destination, Darrik was standing alone right where Chael had predicted, inside his cabin.

"I didn't want it to be this way," Chael called to him from outside.

Darrik was idly shuffling through some of Chael's scant possessions and didn't look up at him for several seconds. "How else could it be?" he questioned, finally deigning to look at Chael through the window.

Red inhuman eyes, lined with veins of black that seemed to cross Darrik's face like cobwebs, stared at him. He walked to the door and joined Chael outside, making a show of having to duck under the short door in his thick dark plate. Darrik had always been tall, but he wasn't quite that tall. But it also reminded Chael of his old friend's playfulness, maybe the demon inside wasn't fully in control.

"This isn't a fight you can win, surely you know that?" Chael half questioned, half pleaded with him. "Together, we can find a way to fix you."

The demon inside Darrik exploded to life and the half-breed came at him like a black blur. But despite his enhanced speed, Chael hadn't been idle on the journey here. He had gathered more strength from the surrounding wilderness, it was quite a bit weaker than human life essence, but it supplemented his power and allowed him to heal his body.

Darrik passed by, swinging his massive broadsword in a wild arc, but Chael dodged it at the last second and kicked out with an enhanced boot and shattered Darrik's armored knee. Momentum carried the half-breed a dozen paces after he slammed into the dirt, screaming in demonic rage and agony at his ruined joint.

"Traitorous snake!" he screeched, the demon voice splitting into several different grating notes. "You shall never know peace or succor; I will hunt you until your last day!" Darrik so oathed as he lifted himself up, using his sword as a makeshift crutch.

He lunged at Chael, sword tip out trying to stab him from afar but even a normal man could have avoided the attack. Chael didn't even move his feet, instead he twisted his torso slightly allowing the blade to pass by him and then slapped it out of Darrik's grip with his own sword. Once again, he fell into the dirt and skidded to a stop right at Chael's feet.

"So be it," he said sadly, and plunged his falchion through the black plate and into Darrik's demon heart. For just a moment, human eyes seemed to look up at him, mournful and longing.

"Be at peace, my brother."

Then Chael took Darrik's head.

Chapter 55

Present Day

As he had promised, they buried every one of the townspeople whose bodies he had used to create his army. For many of them it was an arduous task, trying to put together only pieces and hope they belonged to the same person. But whenever they got it wrong, Michik seemed to know and would whine in protest.

The former revenants weren't the only graves that had to be dug, Rina led the effort to clean out the bodies from inside the keep and they were added to the growing cemetery on the outskirts of the town ruins. Of the thousand or so people who called Ehbing home less than three hundred now survived.

Ascha, the wealthy merchant who had appointed herself as governess alongside the deceased Aeryl, proved her worth. As soon as the town was liberated, she sent messengers in every direction where they could find her many contacts.

Fhael was still very much at war, but somehow and within two weeks, ships began showing up laden with supplies to start rebuilding the town. He wasn't positive but intuition told him that she was angling to become the next governor of Ehbing, and maybe that was a good thing. Someone with a mind for trade and business was probably the exact thing they needed at this point.

"The people don't know about how you…" Andon made a rising gesture with his arms and Chael hit him in the ribs, and the knight smirked.

"That's for the best," Chael commented, truly meaning it.

To his surprise, Rina hadn't had much of an issue with him raising the dead. She understood the dire necessity at the time, it was Brod who seemed most affected by it. After he had returned from his fight with Darrik, Brod cornered him and berated him about the unholiness of it all for a good ten minutes.

Chael suspected that the smith just had to get some emotion out and found a convenient excuse and didn't comment. A few hours later the blacksmith told him that he wasn't so awful at swinging a sword and Chael took that as an apology.

"The war isn't over Chael, not for me at least," Andon looked at him more seriously now. "I've made oaths that I intend to keep and Fhael needs her knights."

"I know," Chael responded, "and I will help however I can." He had already made that decision days ago. Ehbing really did feel like home now, and every one of her citizens treated him like family and it pained him more than he expected to leave but no one would be safe until he dealt with Khalim and his army of half-breeds. Andon gave him an appreciative nod and smiled at Rina as she walked over.

"What are you two talking about?" she asked, conspiratorially as she approached.

"How to take back the Kingdom," Chael responded casually, as if talking about something as trivial as the weather.

"Oh, is that all?" she asked with mock sincerity. "You know the real battle is with the Black Hand, right?" she questioned more seriously. "As long as they're around they can keep providing Kazaam with demons and whatever else they can summon from the Dark."

"Right," Chael agreed. "So, we need to destroy a death cult of Dark alchemists and stop an evil emperor from conquering the continent with his army of half demons, anything else?"

"Aye," came Brod's rough voice. "You need ter clean tha' sword I made ya."

3 Years ago

Chael and Michik entered a small clearing in the so-called Dark Forest. Chael didn't really understand what the big deal was, but the superstition kept people out, or so he thought, for there was a small, dilapidated cabin here on the Southwestern edge of the forest near the small port town of Ehbing.

"Perfect!" Chael exclaimed triumphantly, though Michik gave it a wary sniff. "Oh, come off it Meeshee, this is just what we want. No one is going to come out here and bother us and we can get supplies from the town. We can live here anonymously and never have to worry about hurting people."

Michik took a break from side eyeing their new home to nudge Chael with his head. He gave the old wolf a few scratches of appreciation.

"It's ok, buddy, it's better this way. We'll be alone and no one will find us way out here."

Michik whined in a slightly mournful kind of way, but after a moment he wagged his tail as he and Chael stepped forward to greet their new home.

Present Day

Chael had one last grave to dig, and it was the one he dreaded most. He carefully removed Darrik's black plate armor and tossed it into the woods. *Let the forest claim it,* he thought.

He gathered water from his well and did his best to clean the rough, dry, and blood-stained skin of his fallen brother. Chael chose a spot of bare earth on the Eastern side of his cabin that had a tendency to catch the morning light as it filtered through the dark trees. He laid Darrik's body there, in a hole about five feet below the surface.

He paused then, considering the terrible weight in his hands that still awaited its own internment and remarked on the crystalline blue eyes that were now closed forever. He remembered that brief moment at the end when the man looked out from inside their pearlescent depths and the demon was torn away, if only for a moment.

He set it down, cradled in the folded arms of Darrik's pale and still body, as tears fell freely from his own eyes. Above the grave he carved a slab of stone he salvaged from the debris around the keep.

Be at Peace my Brother, Darrik.

May the Living Stars Embrace you.

"I'm sorry," he said for the thousandth time, looking down at his grave.

A soft hand reached over and grasped his and held it tight. It was Rina's, he hadn't even heard her approach, but when he looked around, he noticed that she wasn't alone. Andon and Brod were both standing respectfully behind them, arms crossed behind their backs and heads bowed.

Even Michik understood the special solemnity of the occasion and sat next to them, head inclined. Chael hadn't told them about burying Darrik because he assumed they wouldn't understand; after all, Darrik was responsible for hundreds of deaths including Brod's family. But they were here, all of them.

"Thank you, for being here," he barely choked out, his emotions cutting off his words.

"'Til the end, lad," Brod swore. "'Til the bloody end."

Epilogue

Thaylin hauled in the nets for the third time today. For some reason the catch had been scarce for nigh on a week and if he didn't come back with a full load of fish, he was going to be in danger of losing his boat.

Things in Kamaar had been strange lately, for one thing the taxes had increased tenfold and the pittance he was able to keep from selling his catch barely covered the loan on his vessel. But there was also talk of strange men and even stranger creatures visiting the city and abducting fighting men. Thaylin had been a sailor long before he owned his own boat and was accustomed to tall tales and usually shrugged them off but even he had to admit, things on shore were growing strange of late.

He finished pulling in his net and to his dismay but not necessarily his surprise, there were only a few fish to speak of, and none were of the variety that would fetch the greatest price at market.

Sighing to himself, he cast his eyes out to the horizon and nearly dropped the net back into the sea. A tri-masted warship had somehow slipped over the horizon while he was struggling with the net. The sleek curved lines of the bow, and the vaguely alien construction made it seem as if the ship weren't built but grown; and billowing in the stiff afternoon wind were three sets of blood-red sails.

Air desperately filled Aelisa's lungs, and with the strength of a panicked she-bear, she tore herself free of the makeshift shroud covering her body and clawed madly for the light. She emerged from a small pantry inside a hallway that she knew quite well, though for some reason it was unlit but for the sun streaming in suspiciously well from outside.

"How did I get here?" she asked herself aloud. Slowly, pieces of memory like islands emerging from the mist in front of a boat, began to materialize. War was coming, she had to inform the other prefects about what she had discovered.

Just then a smell caught her attention, pulling her away from the well of memories she was so urgently dredging. It was sick and sweet, like rotting meat, and it was coming from nearby. Her natural inquisitive nature won over the battle for lost memory, and she decided to follow the smell directly back to its source.

The entrance hall of the grandest Order house in all of Fhael was a bloodbath. Her brothers and sisters lay in pitiful ruins next to creatures best ascribed to nightmares than reality. At that moment another memory hit her, she had such a creature down in the dungeon.

Aelisa raced down the spiraling stairs and emerged into the deepest dungeon that they held. Most of the bars were bent and broken and there was another body down here that she didn't immediately recognize, but something else caught her attention. A spot on the floor in the middle of the cells, there wasn't anything particularly strange about it, but it held her attention like it was the only thing that mattered in the world. Her hands started shaking and her lip trembled as the terrifying truth snapped into place inside her mind. This is where she died.

"What sort of Dark abomination am I?" she gasped. She turned to one of the broken cells, one she had prepared for a very specific prisoner. As she thought about the man, a connection to him blossomed in her consciousness, an awareness of this man despite not being near or knowing precisely where he was.

"The Darkborn," she seethed, pale hands balling into fists.

Tenebrian struggled against the icy magick of the elven bonds in his prison. He had received no new visitors, no new offerings of blood, but something had changed.

Death.

The continent was saturated in it. He could almost taste it in the air, even in the desolate North. Cracks formed on the surface of His prisoner's throne, and though his lips had deteriorated to desiccated papery vestiges, He smiled from within the ice.

End

Book 1 of The Darkborn Saga

Thank You for Reading

I hope you enjoyed *Dark Tidings*, Book One of The Darkborn Saga. If you did, I'd love to hear your thoughts!

Leaving a quick review on Amazon helps other readers discover the story and supports indie authors like me; your feedback makes a huge difference.

Thank you for joining me on this adventure. Your support means the world!

Want to know what happens next? Sign up for updates on the next book and exclusive content:

www.RyanOneillBooks.com

ABOUT THE AUTHOR

Ryan O'Neill grew up in Superior, Wisconsin, the fourth of five children. From an early age, he fell in love with the many worlds of fantasy after his father first introduced him to the Lord of the Rings. His first book, however, came much later as the result of a challenge from a friend.

The subsequent novel was *Dark Tidings*, the first book of the forthcoming Darkborn Saga. In addition to writing, he enjoys scuba diving and, of course, remains an avid consumer of speculative fiction. He currently resides in Orem, Utah.